WHAT'S A [illegible] YOU DOING IN A COFFIN LIKE THIS?

The corpse's left eye squinted at me from mere centimeters away. Decomposition lent her face an increasingly inscrutable expression; the first time I'd regained consciousness, when I found myself tied to her, she looked like she had died in terror. After a while, she started leering at me, as if she had reached the place where I was going and took perverse pleasure from the thought that I would join her there soon.

For a while, when I'd been hallucinating, the corpse had talked to me. She'd whispered that they would come back and throw me out an airlock, into the hard vacuum of deep space; that my vile mother was stalking me; that I could never run hard enough or far enough to find freedom—that death would be my only freedom. But my mind was clear now. No hallucinations. No talking corpses. Just me and horrible pain. Fire stabbed through my right side, a fire that burned hotter and more horribly with every breath I took. Whoever did this to me had fractured most of the bones in my right ribcage. My right hand throbbed, and when I tried to move it, the fingers didn't respond. My broken right leg twisted backward at an angle.

I wondered if Badger would ever find me. I didn't think he would find me alive. Not anymore. But I didn't want him never to know what had happened to me.

I hadn't wanted to die, and I really hadn't wanted to die at twenty-eight, beaten, shoved into a locker with a snide corpse, and deprived of the chance to make twenty million ducats.

That money would have let me pay off the loan on my ship, and all I'd had to do for the money was find a missing yacht, named *Corrigan's Blood*. . . .

BAEN BOOKS BY HOLLY LISLE

ARHEL NOVELS

Fire in the Mist
Bones of the Past
Mind of the Magic

INDEPENDENT NOVELS

Hunting the Corrigan's Blood
Minerva Wakes
Sympathy for the Devil
The Devil & Dan Cooley (with Walter Spence)
Glenraven (with Marion Zimmer Bradley)
Mall Mayhem & Magic (with Chris Guin)
The Rose Sea (with S.M. Stirling)
When the Bough Breaks (with Mercedes Lackey)
Thunder of the Captains (with Aaron Allston)
Wrath of the Princes (with Aaron Allston)

HUNTING THE CORRIGAN'S BLOOD

HOLLY LISLE

HUNTING THE *CORRIGAN'S BLOOD*

This is a work of fiction. All the characters and events portrayed in this book are fictional, and any resemblance to real people or incidents is purely coincidental.

A Baen Books Original

Baen Publishing Enterprises
P.O. Box 1403
Riverdale, NY 10471

ISBN: 0-671-87768-2

Cover art by Stephen Hickman

First printing, February 1997

Distributed by Simon & Schuster
1230 Avenue of the Americas
New York, NY 10020

Printed in the United States of America

To Jeannie Dees
Thanks for being there
when being there mattered.

Chapter One

The corpse's left eye squinted at me from mere centimeters away. Decomposition lent her face an increasingly inscrutable expression; the first time I'd regained consciousness, when I found myself tied to her, she looked like she had died in terror. After a while, she started leering at me, as if she had reached the place where I was going and took perverse pleasure from the thought that I would join her there soon. Now, having had her moment of amusement at my expense, she meditated; beneath thousands of dainty auburn braids, her face hung slack, bloated and discolored, the skin loosening. Threads of drool hung spiderwebbish from her gaping mouth. Her eyes, dry and sunken and filmed over beneath swollen lids, still stared directly at me.

For a while, when I'd been hallucinating, the corpse had talked to me. She'd whispered that they would come back and throw me out an airlock, into the hard vacuum of deep space; that my vile mother was stalking me; that I could never run hard enough or far enough to find freedom—that death would be my only freedom. But my mind was clear now. No hallucinations. No talking corpses. Just me and horrible pain and aching, tantalizing thirst and a stench that even several days of acclimatization couldn't minimize; the stink of decomposition, of piss and shit, of the gangrene that I suspected was starting in on my right leg. Me . . . and all of that . . . and the body of the young woman who had waited on me during my business dinner with Peter Crane in the members-only club Ferlingetta.

I think it's important not to overlook her. She and I, after all, were sisters of a sort. Kindred spirits. She was dead, and I was almost. We were bound together by our plight, and by flexible moleibond-braid wrist restraints that had been spot-grafted to our skin. And I figured we were where we were because we had something more than that in common. I didn't know what, but something.

I guessed that I had been without water for almost three days. I could see the shifting of the station's light cycles through the slats in the narrow metal door against which my rotting companion and I leaned. I recalled two separate spans of darkness and two of light. Two days that I knew of, plus whatever time I'd spent unconscious, and that felt like a lot. The gag in my mouth—permeable to air moving in but not to air moving out, so that I wouldn't suffocate as long as I could exhale through my nose—didn't prevent my tongue from turning into an enormous ball of hot sand. The worst thing was that my thirst didn't distract me at all from my pain.

I hurt—but such plain words cannot convey the depth of my agony. Fire stabbed through my right side, a fire that burned hotter and more horribly with every breath I took. I'd had broken ribs before, and I had them again. Whoever did this to me had fractured most of the bones in my right ribcage. My right hand throbbed, and when I tried to move it, the fingers didn't respond. Perhaps my attackers jumped on it until they felt the bones give way and grind themselves into pulp. If that wasn't what they did, it was what it felt like they had done. A million needles buried themselves deep in my thighs; my lower legs throbbed as if they had swollen beyond the capacity of the flesh to stay together and as if they would now burst. My left leg was bent so that my knee jammed into the metal wall behind the corpse, while my broken right leg twisted backward at an angle so acute the shards of my lower femur poked forward from above where my kneecap should have been like fingers trying to claw their way out my swollen, tattered flesh.

I wondered if Badger would ever find me. I didn't think he would find me alive. Not anymore. But I didn't want him never to know what had happened to me.

I beat my head against the metal door jammed up against my right side, and listened to the booming echoes thundering away into a cavernous, uncaring silence beyond. The first time I came around, I'd pounded myself into a stupor trying to get free or to get someone's attention. But whoever had grabbed me had made sure I wasn't getting out on my own . . . and equally sure that no one would wander along and rescue me.

My attempts at screams for help came out as throaty little whimpers, my thunderous head-banging left nothing but unbroken silence in its wake, and finally, with my head throbbing and flashing lights whirling behind my eyelids, I gave in and let darkness descend.

Giggling woke me.

The corpse was staring at me, but now she was awake, too. The warmth of our tiny cell hadn't done her any good.

"You're dead," she told me. "Just like me. Now that we're both dead, they're going to come back and break your bones and suck out your marrow. They're going to eat your body, and drink your blood, and beat drums with your bones."

Delightful. It was so nice to have company.

"Nobody's going to rescue you," she told me, and her grin grew wider. "It's too late for that. You and I will never tell our secrets."

I knew all about my secrets; I hadn't planned on telling them anyway. But I did wonder what hers were. I tried to ask her—subvocalized around the gag, but she just laughed at me.

"That's why we're here. We had such juicy secrets."

I hated being dead. I hadn't wanted to die, and I really hadn't wanted to die at twenty-eight, beaten, shoved into a locker with a snide corpse, and deprived of the chance to make twenty million rucets.

That money would have let me pay off the loan on my ship, a refitted single-crew fantail corsair with a full-sized cargo hold and berths for twelve, a ship I'd named *Hope's Reward*.

And all I'd had to do for the money was find a missing yacht, *Corrigan's Blood*, that had belonged to Peter Crane, the owner of Monoceros Starcraft, Ltd., and bring it back.

The corpse flashed a wide smile; it kept growing wider as her face started to rip. The bones bulged out, and her jaws came at me, teeth gnashing. I heard them whirring and clicking and thumping . . . clicking . . . thumping . . . whirring . . .

I beat my head against the door again. Pounded it hard, trying with all my strength to break free from the hungry, grinning corpse, fighting with everything in me . . .

Whirring . . . clicking . . . thumping . . . whirring . . .

Outside of our cell! Those sounds came from outside of our cell. They were the first I'd heard in days. A bot. That wasn't her teeth, it was a bot. I pounded my head harder, and was rewarded with the sound of metal tapping on metal. The bot's sensors had picked up the noise, and now it was investigating. I could hear its arms working the latch that held the door closed.

It beeped and whirred and tapped and scraped, and nothing happened.

Too late anyway, of course—I was already dead. But at least Badger would know what had become of me.

I kept making as much noise as I could. Moments passed, while the bot sat outside the locker, grumbling to itself and tapping and twisting at the latch. And then I heard the sound of running feet. Human feet. Someone had looked up when the auto-bot reported a problem with one of the lockers, had heard the sounds my struggles through its sensors, and had come to help. I hoped.

"Oh, my God! What a *stink*!" a male voice said.

I beat my head against the metal and made such noises as the gag allowed. From the other side, I heard tools working on the door. "Shit. Hold on," he said. I stopped beating my head on the door, and was surprised how much better that felt. Tiny lights flashed behind my eyelids and a red haze of pain throbbed inside of my skull. The man added, "I'll get you out. Someone has . . . spot-sealed the metal . . . but I can break the seals." I could hear him straining in between words, fighting the door.

Then something clanged, and the door flew open, and bright light and cool clean air blew across my face - and my friend and I flopped sideways onto the floor. Hard floor. Why didn't anyone ever make floors soft and spongy? The pain in my arm and leg and ribs and head got a lot worse when I hit.

When I twisted left, I could see my rescuer standing over me. Metallic bronze Melatint skin, wave-cut Chromagloss silver hair, gold-flashed teeth, coppersheen eyes. Very stylish. Badger would approve, I thought. My rescuer held the collar of his worksuit over his nose and mouth with one hand, and worked at the flash-grafted gag in my mouth with a laserclip he held in the other.

When he pulled the gag free, he lunged back and leaned against the lockers some distance from us, and puked on the floor. The bot clicked and chuckled its annoyance at him and cleaned up the mess as he made it. It had been shoveling out the floor of the locker until his accident; when he finished, it went back to its previous work.

"Who are you?" he asked. He kept his face tucked behind his collar, and his cloth-muffled voice sounded weak and thready.

"We're dead," I told him, but even without the gag, the words didn't really come out. "We're dead," I said to my pal the cadaver, and she stared right through me, her bones once again inside her skin and her grin gone. She was pretending she couldn't hear me, and I was annoyed enough with her that if I could have kicked her, I would have.

The dockworker watched my lips move for a moment, then shook his head. "Never mind. Reju on the way." His eyes were watering; the tears that rolled down his cheeks were normal-looking. I was disappointed. I'd almost expected him to cry gemstones.

I heard the approach of a reju, and the voices of men who would undoubtedly be space port controllers: sporcs. And I heard Badger's voice raised over theirs. Good old Badger. He'd been searching for me. Hadn't given up. Probably had links up to all the official coms, doing a little unofficial listening. When the report of bodies in a locker flashed across his compac, he came fast.

While the sporcs took care of my friend, the reju attendants loaded me into the long, sleek gray portable cellular rejuvenation unit: the medichamber. I kept telling them not to bother, that I was dead already. They weren't listening. Nobody listens to a corpse.

I saw Badger leaning over me, asking me things I couldn't answer; heard him tell the officers that this was his captain, Cadence Drake; saw them nod and point from me to the other corpse . . . and then the reju lid came down over my head and I felt the needles and tubes snake into place.

Can't reju a corpse, I thought. Can't.

Can't.

Liquids flowed through my veins. Sprayers washed my skin, and replaced the unspeakable stink with a sweet scent that I recognized from too many previous reju stays as Meadow #2. I preferred designer washes like Talisman or Savage Lust, but at least the stocker hadn't filled the spray tank with Lilac. I don't know what a Lilac is or was, but anything that stickily, sappily sweet ought to have been consigned to deep space, along with whoever made it.

My head cleared. The hallucinations went away. I wasn't dead after all; I'd hung on long enough; I had beaten my abductors and I was going to live.

Since I was going to live, I thought it might be nice not to feel like the inside of an afterburner. I kept hoping for a shot of zorphin, which would have made me groggy and happy and would have chased away the pain, but the sporcs would want to talk with me . . . and zorphin would make that process difficult.

Badger leaned over the reju and smiled through the faceplate at me. "I'm glad you made it, Cady. Really glad. I thought I'd lost you." His voice crackled through the speakers, but even with the distortion, I could feel his emotions. Fear, relief . . . maybe love.

"You aren't going to lose me," I told him.

Badger worried the inside of his lower lip with his teeth for a moment, then nodded. "What happened?"

I gave him as much of a grin as my cracked lips and battered face would allow, and said, "We got the job."

Chapter Two

Three whole days I spent in that reju unit; healing the first two and law-sealed the third. Three days while my quarry ran further and further from me and the trail grew colder. I spent most of those three days lying to the sporcs.

I was lying to protect my client, but I couldn't tell them that, of course. What I did tell them was that I didn't have any idea why I had been attacked, though I suspected it was because I was carrying a fair stack of rucets—originally, rucets were Regulated Universal Currency Exchange Tokens, but now that everyone knows there's no such thing as a universally acceptable currency, they're just rucets; that I didn't recognize the body in the locker with me, though she did seem a little familiar; that I was docked at Cassamir Station to replenish my personal biologicals stocks and to have the origami unit on my ship updated. This last was true, but certainly not the whole truth.

I wasn't entirely honest when I described the people who attacked me, but what I did tell the sporcs was true enough. My usually-sharp memory got very fuzzy when I tried to bring my three assailants to mind. I said I could only remember that they were of indeterminate color, of average height and weight, and of ordinary appearance . . . except for their eyes. I described their eyes; pale and burning with a feverish, hungry intensity, eyes that had spent a good deal of time contemplating death and liking the images such thoughts conjured. Those eyes haunted my dreams and in my waking moments sent little chills across my shoulders and down my spine. I told the sporcs the truth about those eyes, but they weren't impressed. I didn't tell them that one of my three assailants was gene-damaged; that he'd been a giant. That single tiny bit of information I kept to myself. I wasn't sure what I intended to do with it, but knowledge is power, and I wasn't in favor of giving away mine.

I think the sporcs would have kept the lock on my reju until I eventually broke and told them everything, except that my client came to my rescue and through a third party bought them off. Space stations are like that. They are the fiefdoms of the men and women who put up the capital to construct them and who run their businesses in them. Most stations are the result of private enterprise, and none that I know of answer to any planetary government. They have too much independent power to kowtow. As such, they can be benevolent havens or regimented hells.

Cassamir was neither, but somewhere in the middle. It was the communal property of Disney Starward Entertainment, Whithampton-Trobisher Ore Processing, Cassamir Biologicals, Kayne Fantasy Sensos, McDonald's, Monoceros Starcraft, Ltd., Huddle House Intergalactic, and The Ëburgi Group. Because of its corporate ownership, it had a corporate personality, which I don't like, but which does mean that the sporcs know where their paychecks come from and remember that fact when pressure is applied. Even when murder is involved.

If you want justice, don't get killed on a space station. This was an old rule of mine, and one that I'd come too close to breaking.

Badger showed up late on the third day, bringing a few of my belongings for me. I first knew he'd finally come for me when his ugly face filled the reju faceplate, and at last that face was grinning. When I'd seen him the day before, he'd looked fairly normal—at least for him. Now, though, his skin was the most hideous shade of metallic green, and he'd had his irises done in iridescent purple and his hair staticked, copperflashed, and illuminated, so that it glowed even in bright light and every hair stood away from every other and all of them crackled with sparks when he walked. I wish to hell I could keep Badger away from the bodyart shops. He has dreadful taste.

"You ready to go home?"

"Days ago," I told him.

He waited while the sporcs removed the law-seals and helped me out of the reju. He'd brought a mini-holo for me and some clothes. I pulled on the jumpsuit, then flashed myself with the holo. The image took a second to build in front of me.

I felt the eyes of the sporcs on me while I stood there. I'm used to stares; after all, I am a Maryschild. My mother was the founder of the Marys, that short-lived movement that she ostensibly started to eliminate racial tension by creating raceless children. When she started the movement, she purchased three fathers for me from a memorial sperm bank, all as physically different from her type as she could find. Then she insisted that the geneticist who cut and spliced her genes with those of the three dead donors double the recessives and remove the dominants so that my features would clearly reflect the "pure" influences of each of my parents.

They do. From my mother I have my coffee-with-a-touch-of-cream skin and full lips and straight teeth. From one of my fathers I have high, sharp cheekbones and slanting almond-shaped eyes with a pronounced epicanthic fold, though the eyes themselves are a vivid and startling blue, the gift of another father. My hair is straight and the color of amber, my nose is long and thin. My body is long and angular. I look like what I am—an outdated fashion statement.

I am a living flag who was born to be waved in my

mother's little war; her purpose in creating me was anything but benign. She wasn't looking for peace or harmony or even a kid she could love; she was looking for power, trying to create a sweeping army of angry women who would bear their children and sit them at her feet so she could indoctrinate them into bitterness and plans for revenge against a universe she despised. And everything she taught was a lie.

Race doesn't exist.

Skin color exists. Hair and eye color are real. Body type varies from individual to individual, as does tooth shape and color, the form of fingernails, and the amount and texture of body hair. But "race" is a phantom conjured up by people no different from each other than purebred cocker spaniels are. Race is a lie, and the people who conjure by it, no matter their color or their politics, are liars.

The image finished building and I saw that the reju had reshaped my face again, making the jaw slightly rounder. It had also skinned out the little fat I had and stripped off a lot of muscle. Reju is supposed to return you to your genetic peak, but I don't know of a single place that hasn't set its units with local body fashion in mind. On Cassamir, skinny with big tits was the look, and I was going to have to spend additional time in my private unit to get back the muscular, small-breasted body I preferred.

"Looking sweet," Badger told me.

"Go dock a bot, you pervert."

He laughed; I grinned. Alive felt wonderful. Free felt even better.

We took a gravdrop back to our ship, and the entire trip, I tried to remember when I had been attacked and where . . . and how. But it was all gone.

When we were inside and the privacy fields were up, Badg turned to me. "Do you still have everything?"

I grinned. "They didn't have any idea where to look."

"Perfect. Let's have it."

I reached into the right front pocket of my jumpsuit, undid the pressure-seal closure at the bottom, and stretched my hand through to the inside of my thigh. I pressed against my fleshtab. The fleshtab was the result of a black market breakthrough in reju technology on an ugly little private planet that circles the F-class star Tegosshu. The living skin separated and I pulled out two infochips. The first was a standard chip that Peter Crane had given me to help me get started on his job. The second was a dopplerchip I had taken of our meeting.

I handed Badger the dopplerchip and he dropped it into the holoplayer.

There was a soft hum; then the rec room became a gray-on-gray replica of Ferlingetta. Peter Crane and I took shape: solid-looking charcoal-colored three-dimensional forms seated at a gracefully filigreed gray table surrounded by gray plants and the increasingly less solid shapes of decor, staff, and other diners. Badger and I watched my double's hand move away from the pressure point on my abdominal wall that had started the doppler recording.

"—to be so cautious, you must have made some ferocious enemies." Peter Crane templed his fingers in front of his chin and smiled at the recorded me. The corners of his eyes crinkled.

Badger made a face. "My, oh, my. I wonder how he figured that out."

"Shut up and watch."

Peter Crane was one of the five most powerful people on Cassamir Station; the sole owner of Monoceros Starcraft, Ltd., and according to rumor, the biggest stakeholder in Cassamir Station itself. Sitting across from him, I had felt neither the weight of his wealth nor the subtle demands of his power. Easygoing and friendly, he wore his straight black hair in a casual cut and his skin natural. His clothes were tasteful, hearkening back to Old Earth styles without slavishly imitating them. He was a fifth-generation stationer, a direct descendent of Athabascan Eskimos who invested their tribal earnings in space technology and made a fortune doing it. "If you're as good as Lize says you are, I'll make you twenty million rucets richer," Peter Crane said.

Badger paused the recording. "Which Lize?"

"Anelize Daredwyn," I told him. She was a former client—a good one. She had given Crane my contact information, and given me her recommendation of him.

The funny thing was, if Peter Crane had found me without having someone to vouch for him, I might have taken him on anyway. I rarely like my clients . . . but I liked him.

I restarted the recording and my imaged self smiled at Crane. "I'm that good," the image assured him.

"You're that cocky," Badger said, grinning at me.

I damped down the hum of conversations in the rest of Ferlingetta and refined the sound of my conversation with Peter. I didn't bother to answer Badger. He knew I was good at my job.

I call myself an "Independent Reclamations Specialist;" I find things—expensive things—things stolen from their rightful owners. I return these things for fifteen percent of their retail value. I deal primarily with corporations because corporations are where the money is. I occasionally accept employment from a private customer, if the missing item or the manner in which it disappeared interests me; the money is never as good as corporate money, though.

"Good," Crane said. "I admire skill above all things."

A woman sauntered down the manicured grass path to our table; she was small and lithe. My memory supplied the absent details of red hair, ivory skin and freckles.

I hit the pause button and turned to Badger. "That's her."

He squinted and looked uncertain. "The corpse?"

"Yeah."

"You want to go back and track her now?"

I thought about it, then shook my head. "Not yet. Let's finish this first, then focus on her and see if anything interesting comes up."

Badger resumed the holo, and the waiter flipped her

hair back, and the thousands of tiny braids swung over her shoulders. "Mado Crane?" Her gaze passed over me as if I were invisible; she focused entirely on Crane. "How may I be of service?" She ducked her head in his direction when she said it. She didn't acknowledge me.

"A bottle of my private stock, please. The Gorland Harvest '46." Crane turned to me, pointedly forcing the waiter to acknowledge my presence. "And would you like anything else, Mada Drake?"

"Please . . . it's just Cadence . . . and no, I'm fine."

"The desserts are all excellent."

My doppelgänger shook her head. "Really. Old Earth cuisine is much richer than anything I'm used to. I couldn't eat another bite."

"Holy hell," Badger said. "You passed up Old Earth dessert at a place like that? I wouldn't have. They probably bring in the stuff from planet-side. I'll bet they don't use any reconsta at all."

The little things got to Badger.

Crane waved the waiter off.

"What do you want me to find for twenty million rucets?"

He stopped smiling. "A man named John Alder, acting as a purchasing agent for a financial concern called the Winterleigh Corporation, acquired from me a ship—the best private yacht Monoceros builds, our newest model. He said Winterleigh wanted it to permit its officers to travel quickly and in comfort when on business. I'd say fifty percent of my top-of-the-line ships are used for that purpose."

He paused, and my double nodded.

"That true?" Badger asked me.

"Mostly. Monoceros' corporate customers make up sixty-four percent of their business, but I think he was just rounding."

My imaged self was busy trying to look worthy of a twenty million rucet fee. "Your most expensive private yachts sell for right at a hundred million rucets," the other me said, leaning forward and resting my elbows on my knees. This posture change is supposed to tell my client that I'm earnest, eager, and attentive. Probably it doesn't say much more than that I have a hard time sitting in a chair for more than an hour. But I try to give a good impression. "My fee is fifteen percent of the retail value of whatever I can collect. Fifteen percent of the retail price of the most expensive ship you sell is fifteen million rucets. You could do a lot of things with the extra five million, Mado Crane." The other me smiled, trying to look relaxed. I recalled distinctly that I hadn't been relaxed. "Or I could."

"Trying to lighten the situation with humor?" Badger asked.

"Trying to figure out why he wanted to overpay us so heavily."

Crane looked past my shoulder and up; he was watching the cold expanse of space showcased by the enormous window that made up most of Ferlingetta's far wall. I saw my image turn to look at the window; in the doppler holo it was a flat, shiny gray expanse.

"What's he looking at?" Badger wanted to know.

I had to think for an instant. "A convoy of freighters was docking."

"The station's private club could give its patrons a clear view of the origami point, and they chose the docks?"

"It's about money," I told Badger. "The rich don't want to see beauty. They want to watch their money coming in."

Crane's image turned away from the window. "The fifteen is your fee. The extra five million is a bonus for you, because this is personal."

"You were a friend of . . ." My double paused for a second. ". . .John Alder?"

"No."

"You've dealt with Winterleigh before?"

"No."

The doppelgänger pursed her lips, and I felt my own follow suit as I watched the conversation replay. "Five million rucets is a lot of personal."

"Yes. It is. But the *Corrigan's Blood* is a lot of ship."

My other self waited.

Crane sighed, leaned forward, rested his arms on his knees. Sincere, intent . . . or else his butt was getting tired, too. "Like most of our best ships, the *Blood* has trans-fold navigational capability. The *Blood* has a new model of TFN unit, however, that permits on-the-fly course changes while in hyperspace, and the detection of origami points from within hyperspace."

The doppelgänger's mouth dropped open. So did Badger's. "Midcourse changes?" I heard myself ask, sounding stupidly breathless. I was going to have to work on that.

"Almost instantaneous."

"And point recalculation."

"Absolutely. It will even predict new points. I've found several in my trial runs."

"My God," my image and Badger said in unison.

Badger stopped the holo and backed the conversation up. He replayed the last portion of it, then paused it and sat staring forward, as if he could see through the ship's walls to our own TFN.

If you've never run a ship through hyperspace, you cannot imagine what Crane's innovations mean. Hyperspace is convenient but damnably unfriendly. The math makes sense but the place itself doesn't. As far as I know, no one has ever understood enough about it to do more than figure out a way in and a way out. And those lines from origami point to origami point—the fold-points in our three-dimensional universe—were rigid. A drone watching a ship's speed and trajectory as it entered a point could calculate the ship's exact destination. Traffic control has always made use of that capability; interstellar surveillance drones called Spybees were stationed at the periphery of every point to keep records of ship ID, speed, trajectory, declared destination point, and calculated actual destination. The drones send that information to central intelligence-gathering stations, which analyze the ships going through and look for correlations to crimes committed within the relevant time frames. Space travelers had less privacy than the planet-bound; but governments insisted there was a payoff. The Spybees were responsible for catching a number of serial killers, and were supposed to be a preventative to piracy.

With the new Monoceros ships, the Spybees would become worthless.

Badger turned to me and said, "I want one of those ships. Even if we have to steal it, I want one."

"That's evidently what Mado Alder thought, too. Which is why we have a job."

Badger looked at me and sighed, and slowly reached out and started the holo again.

"This was a prototype unit, then?" my image asked Crane's.

"No. It was one of our early production units."

I watched myself tip my head to one side; my puzzlement was obvious. "I can understand your desire to get your property back, but I'm afraid I don't understand why you're paying a bonus when you've obviously registered the technology and secured your rights against other manufacturers."

Crane's image looked into my image's eyes, and for a moment his face looked like it had never worn a smile. "I trusted John Alder. I've built much of my business on my ability to judge the characters of the people who come to me. I misjudged him badly . . . and if word gets out, I'll find more like him waiting in my showrooms every day. This one mistake on my part could cost me everything I've worked for."

He stared out into space again. Unmoving, his gray holo image seemed to transform into a statue for one long moment.

Badger and I watched me say, "Then both speed and discretion are essential."

Crane looked back at me and nodded slowly. "You can't tell anyone who you're looking for or why. They cannot know you work for me. Not under any circumstances. I'm paying you well for your discretion. I demand that I get it."

"I understand. Do you know why Alder or the people who hired him to steal the *Corrigan's Blood* might have wanted the ship?"

Crane raised his eyebrows and smiled. "I can think of a hundred reasons, but I can't suggest one which might be more valid than any other." The other me looked disappointed. Crane shrugged and smiled ruefully. "I'm sorry."

"It doesn't matter. Knowing a motive might save me a few days . . . and then again, it might not. It won't change the outcome."

His image looked at mine—just a single penetrating glance, but even watching it secondhand that glance felt like being dissected alive. Sitting in the safety of my own ship, I could still recall it. With his stare fixed on me, I had felt his wealth and his power as a physical presence; a weight in the air I breathed. For that instant, I had not liked Peter Crane . . . because he frightened me. But then he turned away, and when he looked back, he was just my newest client again.

The intensity of that glance reached Badger even at second hand—Badger, who could be dense as a dwarf star where subtle human interaction was concerned. "I would hate to have him as an enemy," he whispered.

"Me too."

Crane smiled gently. "So you'll take the job," he said at last. Not a question. A statement.

I watched myself nod and sit back in my chair. It was time to talk money; for this, I leaned back to demonstrate confidence in my own power. Plus it was another excuse to move. I decided that I looked pretty good—pretty convincing. "I require twenty-five percent of my fee in advance. For operating expenses."

Crane didn't even blink. "I know. I will have deposited three million seven-hundred fifty-thousand rucets in your Interworld account by the time you get back to your ship.

Twenty-five percent of your actual fee. I'll add the five million in bonus money at the end, when you return the *Corrigan's Blood* and complete this job with the discretion I desire." He smiled slightly. "Additional incentive, you know."

Usually my clients feel the need to quibble about the up-front portion of the fee. I found the fact that Crane didn't a pleasant change.

Crane said, "This will help you get started." He handed me a small, thin crystalline square: a high-density infochip. "This contains the background checks I did on Alder and Winterleigh, plus everything I found out about them after the *Blood* disappeared. You'll also find details of the transaction, and the people involved in that. And in the 'Ship' file, I've included specs and telltale codes to allow you to identify the *Blood*, as well as the ship's last known heading." He laughed bitterly. "As if that were worth anything anymore."

The other me took the chip and slid it into my pocket; at least, that was what Crane saw. The tiny movement that opened the pressure-sensitive pocket and slid the disk into my fleshtab was undetectable. I told Crane, "It doesn't matter. I'll bring back your ship." We shook hands, and Peter Crane smiled again.

I reached out and stopped the holo.

Badger said, "Don't you want to see what he does when you leave?"

I wanted to see what the waiter did first, but Badger was right. I needed to finish watching Crane first. Always do only one thing at a time. This is another of my rules, and the only reason I had to make it a rule was because I broke it so often.

Badger pressed the resume button, and set the focus to stay on Crane as I walked away. We watched Crane sip his wine and watch me leave. His image got a little less distinct as I moved around the corner of the private dining room, out of sight. The braid-mopped waiter returned.

"Follow her," Crane said. "If she goes anyplace at all but back to her ship, notify me." He handed the waiter something small.

Badger and I both hit the freeze button at the same time, with the result that the image kept moving. He held his hands away from the control panel on his holo-chair and I backed up the image, froze it at the moment when the object was most clearly visible, and said, "Shipcom—enlarge and identify the holo target."

The rest of the holo disappeared, and the flat oval and a fragment of the hand that held it expanded until the oval was the size of a door. It hung in the air in front of us. The shipcom factored out the hand, which had begun to take on godlike proportions; then it began peeling away dopplered layers of the image, studying the areas of lesser density that remained. "Outer skin, five layers of moleibond."

The holo image had changed. Now it was a mesh of tiny threads; even at its enormously enlarged size, those threads were only slightly thicker than silk strands. The shipcom rotated the image, and areas of it lit up as the computer followed the threads and discerned their purpose. "The image is at maximum usable enlargement," the shipcom said at last. "The object is a credit chit for fifty rucets."

"Store the image," I said, and the shipcom's enlargement vanished. The frozen holo reappeared.

So he'd paid her to follow me. I wondered why. If it was just that he wasn't sure he could trust me, well, I could live with that. If he had another agenda, though . . .

And whoever had beaten me had killed her. Again, why?

Badger sighed. "We ought to go a little more in-depth on Peter Crane. Fifty rucets to have the waiter follow you seems a little steep if she was a waiter. If she wasn't a waiter, then why was she waiting tables and why would he pay her?"

"His actions don't seem to make sense."

"No." Badger studied the frozen images of the waiter

and Peter Crane. "They don't. Let's see what we can find out about both of them."

The shipcom said, "Your image is stored and cross-referenced."

And Badger glared up in the direction of the shipcom's voice. "Why don't you get a personality for that damned thing? It never jokes, it never says, 'You look terrific,' when I get dressed up, it never offers any opinions on anything. A real personality wouldn't be all that expensive, and we could afford it now." He gave me his best "I'm adorable; humor me," grin and added, "The place next to where I got Melatinted had some terrific shipcom personalities. Jenjer. Dorite. Hank, if you wanted to go male." His eyes dared me to go with a male personality.

I gave him a fixed stare and said, "The *Hope's Reward* already has as much personality onboard as I can stand. If I bought a personality for the ship, I'd have to get rid of you."

He laughed.

I resumed the holo, and the waiter walked away from Crane and toward the front door of Ferlingetta. The image vanished.

Badger stared at me, disbelief clear in his eyes. "You stopped recording?"

I stared back, defensive. "Well . . . yes. I stopped recording as soon as I stepped out of the club. I only wanted a record of the interview."

"Brilliant move," he said.

Not particularly.

Chapter Three

Strebban Bede, born Dante Beddekkar, had been Badger to me since I was eight and he was twelve; he was the only friend I had in the world. The only family, even though the two of us shared no genetic ties. He represented the only stability I ever knew, and I would have done anything for him. Nonetheless, he was the most annoying human being who ever lived. I came to this conclusion not only from my own unbiased observation, but from taking into account the comments of the majority of the clients for whom we worked, and the majority of people who had the pleasure of Badger's undivided attention for more than five minutes.

"Okay, my favorite genius. Let's watch Braids now," Badger said, and started backing up the holo.

"We already know what she's doing," I said, feeling like an idiot for having thought the information I could glean from the interview had ended when I left. Now I wished I'd started recording the moment I walked into the club. The internal doppler recorder was new to me, however, and I still wasn't used to the idea that I could capture the conversations of all the people in an area at the same time, before I even started doing what I'd come to do. In my own defense, I also wasn't sure how completely I could saturate a chip before it stopped accepting data.

"Let's watch her anyway," Badger said.

When he backed up the dopplerchip to the point where the waiter first appeared at Crane's and my table, Badger marked her. With the holo focused on her, he finished backing it to the beginning.

Now we watched the waiter carrying a tray to a table, asking if the people seated there needed anything, walking around the edge of a stand of plants and heading toward our table.

"That was enlightening," I said, intentionally digging at Badger.

He shrugged. "It might be pointless."

I just smiled.

She had her conversation with Crane again, where she pointedly ignored me, then walked away, moved to the very edge of my recording device's range, and slipped beyond it. We sat staring at gray haze for five minutes, while I watched Badger, sardonic smile firmly in place, and he stared at the mist as if life-and-death secrets resided therein.

When she returned, she was carrying the bottle of wine. She brought it directly to the table. I didn't even bother to rib Badger this time. She walked to another table, cleared off the plates that were there, carried them back to the place where she'd vanished before.

Gray mist, this time only for a minute or two.

She reappeared, carrying a tray full of food.

I drummed my fingers on the armrest of my chair and rolled my eyes. I yawned loudly.

She wound her way through the tables, carrying the enormous tray, settled it on a stand next to three diners and began unloading food.

I leaned back in my chair and stared up at the ceiling of the holo-room, noticing for the first time the elaborate designs that had been carved into Ferlingetta's ceiling. I was impressed that the doppler got them.

"She's with him now."

"Thank you," one of the diners said, and at the same time Badger said, "What was that?"

I sat up and watched her walk back the way she'd come, carrying an empty tray.

Badger backed up the holo.

The waiter put dishes of steaming food on the table. I found myself fascinated by the fact that even the steam appeared as a gray mist.

The waiter said, "She's with him now."

The diners looked at her, smiled, looked at their meals . . . and as one said "Thank you," another slipped a packet into her hand. Without acknowledging the packet, she turned and walked away.

Badger backed the holo up again, to the point where the holo showed. Then he rolled his eyes and yawned. "I'm sure you don't want to see this. It's undoubtedly a waste of time."

"Always gracious in victory," I said, inclining my head in his direction. I know the smile I gave him was strained. "Rub it in, Badg."

"Thank you. I think I will."

We watched the shipcom peel the cover off the packet and enlarge the contents.

"Another credit chit," Badger said, beating the computer to the identification by a tenth of a second.

"How much?"

The shipcom traced the circuitry, then said, "The value of this credit chit is ten thousand rucets."

"Ten thousand rucets," Badger said. He gave a contented little sigh and leaned back in his seat.

I paused the holo. "You aren't surprised by this, are you?"

"No. Not a chance."

"Why not?"

"Because she's dead. If she'd done what she was supposed to do, whatever that was, she would still be alive." He bared his teeth at me, skinned his lips back in a poor and gloating imitation of a smile, and said, "Now all we need to do is watch the people who gave her the money."

I hadn't really looked at them. Seated, in the same flat gray as everything else in the holo, they had failed to catch my attention. I guess they were trying to avoid being attention-worthy, anyway. But when I really looked at them, I realized I'd seen them before.

I gasped, and Badger's smile grew even more condescending. "Let me guess," he said. "Those are the three people who attacked you."

"I can't be certain about two of them . . . but him . . ." I rose and walked to the side of the man who had been seated in a booth with his back to me. His hand was frozen in midair. I held mine up beside it, and my own large hand was dwarfed. It looked like a child's hand next to his.

Badger's smugness vanished. "Is the scale on this holo right?"

I stood beside the waiter; she'd seemed taller in the locker but only because we had both been crammed in face-to-face. In fact, though, she was as petite as she'd seemed when she stood by our table. "Scale's right. The only solid detail I've been able to recall about the three of them is that one was a giant."

We watched the holo through several more times: studying the waiter; following the three men at the table as they rose without eating their meals and stalked out into the corridor beyond the club aimed for the docks; looking for signs that anyone else might be involved. We didn't get any other immediate information.

"Here's the way it's going to go," I said. "I'll get as much information on the girl as I can, and then I'll see what I can get out of Crane regarding why he was paying to have me followed. And then I'll drop the little bombshell on him about his helper's other friends and see what that gives me." I stood for a moment, considering. "Meanwhile, you find out everything you can about the three men. Everything. We'll keep that information to ourselves."

"Deciding you don't trust Crane?"

"No." That was the funny thing. I did trust Crane. "I

just want to have a few extra cards to play later in this game."

Badger grinned at me, then instructed the shipcom to give him complete vital statistics on the three men whose images we had captured. When he had them, he settled in with the worm to see what he could fish out of the station records on Cassamir Station.

I followed the same procedure with the waiter. I had to assume that everyone else knew more about what was going on than I did. I had to assume that all of them had reasons for doing things that I didn't know anything about . . . including Peter Crane, whom I was loath to include in my list of people with hidden agendas; I so rarely like anyone, and I did like him.

Badger and I didn't have a lot of advantages, but I intended to get the most out of every one we had. The doppler holos were my first advantage. The waiter's murder; my near-death experience; Crane's wish to have me followed: all of these were related to the stolen *Corrigan's Blood*, and before we left Cassamir Station, I intended to figure out how.

Chapter Four

The waiter's name had been Sarah Idalto, and she hadn't been a waiter. She'd been Crane's niece by marriage, the troubled rich-kid daughter of Crane's wife's brother, McTavish Idalto. From her extensive rap sheet, I could see that she'd spent more than a little time in what Cassamir Station sporcs euphemistically called the "entertainment-for-pay" sector, and that she had occasionally augmented her income by "reallocating client funds." That, again, from the sporcs' reports. Had she been someone other than the niece of Peter Crane, her sheet probably would have referred to her as a whore and a thief, but perhaps I was only being cynical in thinking such things.

So Crane had hired her to follow me and report on my movements. But why? And the three men who later beat the living crap out of me had hired her to . . . what?

And somebody had killed her, but who had that somebody been?

I spent the next few hours digging through the data on Crane's infochip. I read the information he had uncovered on Winterleigh, and I watched the holo interview with their front man, "John Alder." Alder was superb. He walked rich, he talked rich, he dressed perfectly, and he dropped names in casual conversation that made Crane relax. I saw it happen. If I'd been doing the interview, I would have believed Alder was who and what he said he was.

I watched the recording of that interview three times. I was left with the sense that I was dealing with a master. Either this man was as rich and confident as the character he portrayed, or he was one of the finest actors I'd ever seen. Considering what was at stake, I was willing to consider either hypothesis.

I copied his voice print into the shipcom and linked that file to the microphone in the compac on my wrist; I set the shipcom's voice recognition feature to alert me if it ever heard Alder. What were the odds? I wasn't going to hold my breath; if I ran into him again, though, I wanted to know it.

I went over the specs for *Corrigan's Blood*, and spent some time with my desk holo, trying to figure out ways that I would hide her if I'd stolen her. I've been blessed with a criminal mind. I thought of half a dozen things I could do when the soft chime of my comlink pulled me away from my work.

As I reached for the comlink, a voiceover said, "For your security, this call has been scrambled by Gen-ID, the leading provider of security calls in the Verzing Community. Please offer your cell sample now."

I hate Gen-ID calls because they hurt, but at least my new unit uses very small laser samplers. I stuck my finger into the ID unit on the comlink, and felt the sting of the laser. My vital signs read out across the screen, and after the genotype matching of DNA from skin cells, it verified my ID information. The screen flashed from gray to green, then cleared to project Peter Crane's holo into the space above it.

"I'm glad to find you looking so well," he said.

"Me too."

He laughed. "Yes. I suppose you are. I assume the money reached your account?" A slight upward inflection on the end of that question, but his face said he knew perfectly well it was in there.

"It's all there."

He paused, looking worried. "I was expecting you to leave port soon in pursuit of the *Blood*. Have you experienced setbacks?"

"Aside from running into the people who tried to kill me?" I arched an eyebrow and tried to look coolly amused, but I suppose the squeak in my voice ruined the effect.

"I understand your concern with them—"

I thought "concern" didn't quite describe my feelings toward the experience of almost dying, but I didn't say anything.

"—however, I don't feel that the attempt on your life is related to the work you're doing for me. Some of my people are investigating this with the port controllers, and I'm told they have excellent leads. The people who hurt you will be brought to justice, for your sake and the sake of the girl they killed."

It was time to fish for a reaction. "Yes. Your niece. You must be very upset."

His lips thinned and he nodded. "Her parents and I have always feared this would be the way she ended up." He studied me, emotions hidden. "I was careful to keep Sarah's relation to me secret. I'm surprised you discovered it." He didn't look surprised.

"Finding out secrets is my job," I said. "And I'm good at it. Speaking of secrets . . ." Time to try my bigger bait. "Why did you pay her to follow me?"

"How the—?" He paled. I saw his eyes go blank and hard for an instant—only an instant, and then he was charming Peter Crane again. "Your people were very good. I never saw them."

"If they weren't very good, I wouldn't work with them." I smiled. Let him think I got my information from an informant. "Why did you have her following me?"

"Why did you have someone watching me?"

Touché, I thought. "I don't trust anyone."

He shrugged and smiled slowly. He didn't have to say a word; his gesture told me that my answer was also his. "Perhaps you will understand that I am finding it much more difficult to think well of people I don't know, since this incident with John Alder. I had to know I could trust you."

"And can you?"

He chuckled. "You didn't sell the information I gave you to one of my competitors. I'll take my chances with you."

"Fine. Then there's something else you need to know. Sarah was also working for the three men who tried to kill me."

He was silent for perhaps thirty seconds. In thirty seconds, I can take my ship through an origami point from one side of the universe to the other. Thirty seconds can be a long, cold time. "You're certain of this?" he asked at last. His voice was icy cold.

"Yes. She pointed me out to them when you and I were having lunch. They paid her."

"This is very specific information. How can you be sure?"

"I have a voice recording of the conversation and a picture of her taking the payoff."

"You have holographs of them?"

"No," I lied. "Rather poor-quality digital micro two-D's." These were the industry standard for surveillance work, though certainly nothing at the cutting edge of technology. "They're fuzzy and monotone. I'm afraid they wouldn't be useful for a legal ID. They were only useful to me because I knew what I was looking for."

"You've enhanced them."

"As much as I could."

"Send me copies, please. Even if they are of poor quality, they will be better than nothing at all."

"I'll send them over. Gen-ID?"

"Naturally. I do hope you'll be able to begin looking for my ship soon."

"I have an angle on it already," I said.

I didn't mention that my angle was so bad it would make a billiards champion weep. I nodded and signed off.

And then I went back to thinking about the *Corrigan's*

Blood. Unlike other ships, the *Blood* could go anywhere while leaving only false trails behind it. And I had to weed through those false trails, uncover the real trail, find the ship, and bring it home. New technology screws up as much as it fixes; I've long believed this, and have never been proven wrong.

Under normal circumstances, someone with a stolen ship who couldn't reconfigure the ID would stay in-system until the search cooled off, because if that ship went into hyperspace, the Spybees would tag it and give a neatly packaged map to the first authority who asked. If I were Alder, though, I'd take the ship and run like hell with it, going through every origami point I could find. I would change course in hyperspace, come out at some "impossible" destination, go back in, change course, come out again. I would render any records my pursuers got useless; even if they could get data on every point I'd passed through, they wouldn't have anything. They could try piecing my trail together by sequencing times, but the clocks on those Spybees are always a little off. We can't synchronize them once they're in position, because communication through hyperspace is, so far, beyond our technology. Sometimes they're as much as a couple of minutes off. Compared to the infinity of space, a couple of minutes on a clock doesn't seem like much. But it would be enough for Alder.

I stood staring at my comlink and considered what I could do in that time, if I wasn't going to pay attention to the legalities of logging myself in-system, filing my flight plan, and waiting for clearance.

In two minutes, I could take my ship through four origami points, including turnarounds to jump back in. If I did that for ten minutes, always coming out at a place other than the destination the Spybees predicted, I would log twenty entrances and twenty totally unrelated exits. With all of the clocks recording slightly different times, the resultant snarl would have me arriving at a place before I'd left the previous one, and could show me in several locations simultaneously. When I finished, I could stop anywhere. My trail would be the same as no trail at all.

I smiled. There were, however, better and worse places to stop, and I knew exactly the sort of place I'd try to find.

I keyed in the link to the navigation deck, and Badger's face floated in front of me. "Any luck?" he asked.

"A fair amount. I have an idea on where we can start looking for our client's ship. We need to get ready to run. Meanwhile, have you gotten any information on the holos?"

"The strangest information of all," he said. He looked weary and frustrated. "Whoever the three men were who came after you, they had the best security I've ever seen."

"Why do you say that?"

"Because according to all official records, none of the three of them have ever been here."

"What?!"

"Never. I've run the worm through every databank on Cassamir Station, and pulled the data stream from every security monitor. Hell, I located the security cam that shows the view of you and Peter Crane having lunch. It also shows the table where the three of them sat while you ate."

"So use that."

"You don't understand. They aren't at the table."

I felt my mouth drop open; I knew I looked like an idiot. Still, no one underrated the magical art of making yourself disappear more than I do. "You mean someone has completely cleared them out of every record in the station?"

"Yes."

"My God. That's impressive."

So the three men who had killed Sarah and who had nearly killed me had someone on Cassamir Station covering up for them. Someone well-placed enough to gain access to every security file on the station that included the men, and talented enough to erase the men from every record without leaving signs of tampering. "Could you do that?" I asked Badger.

"Not a chance."

I nodded. I couldn't have done it either. "Connect into the VeCRA system and see if you can find any records on any of the three of them there. If they don't show up in VeCRA databases, we can spread out further."

VeCRA is the Verzing Community Regulatory Agency, the bureaucracy that keeps tabs on the loose coalition of settled planets in this sector of space. The other sectors have their own agencies that work with VeCRA; and the nonallied planets usually have *their* agencies (and those may or may not cooperate); and the fanatical confederacy, Öoslong Legion, has its slew of agencies. Even if we searched through all of those databases, we still might not find our people, because settled space is too damned big for bureaucracy to keep under its thumb. There are scores of settled planets that opt for anarchy—they don't keep records; they don't pay dues; and they don't answer anybody's questions unless they want to. If our thugs were from one of those places, we would probably never run them down. Still, we had to look.

"Before you start the VeCRA search, though, I need you to make me some fuzzy, ugly, digital two-D's from the doppler images, and I need them fast." I told him the shots I wanted, then added, "Mess them up some when you print them. Make them look like we got them from a . . . oh, a Clarion MicroSure-Shot digicam, and make them look like we've enhanced the hell out of them." I paused for a second, thinking. "Be consistent with the angle. Something that someone could have obtained from long-range, or at least from outside the dining area, if that's the best we can do. I have an idea; find someone in Ferlingetta who could have taken them, and create the series from that person's viewpoint."

Badger grinned. "Invent an insider, huh?"

"Yes."

"I'll do it."

"Send them via Gen-ID to Peter Crane as soon as they're done . . . and time is important, here. I told him they already existed. While you're doing that, I'll file our flight plan."

"Right."

I went back to Crane's infochip, and spent a few unhappy minutes searching it for one single tidbit of information that I desperately needed—information which wasn't there. I thought about having Badger try to worm it out of Crane's records without having anyone the wiser, but decided in this instance forthrightness wouldn't hurt. I called Crane.

Crane appeared, looking happier than he had when we'd last talked. "Thank you for sending your two-D's so quickly. I'm sure they'll be useful."

I nodded.

"How can I help you?" he asked.

"How many of the new ships have you sold so far?"

He didn't even have to think. "The Stardancers? Twenty-seven."

"Have you ever used the new hull configuration on other ships in your line?"

"No. The enhanced TFN required a leaner shape and more area in the dispersal fins. Those twenty-seven are the only ones out there."

I'd wondered about that. The *Blood* could never have been mistaken for any ship I'd ever seen. An in-system ship without TFN capability can look like anything, and usually looks like stacks of metal boxes loaded on to each other. TFN ships have always looked like pregnant guppies sculpted by the Art Deco god. *Hope's Reward* was a perfect example of that look. Crane's *Blood*, though, was as lean and sleek as new-minted sin, and just looking at holos of it had made my fingers itch for a chance to take it for a run. I was pleased to know that gorgeous body only came with the real thing inside; I think I would have been broken-hearted had I known everyday ships were masquerading in beautiful skins they hadn't earned. "Can you send me registration information on every one you've sold?"

"I can," he told me, "but it won't be as helpful as you might hope. Quite a number of the ships have already traded hands."

This was an odd bit of news. "Really? Have the original owners experienced problems with them?"

"Quite the opposite. The ships are so popular that my earlier buyers have been able to resell them at a considerable profit. I've raised my own prices and my orders are still far outstripping my supply."

"Send me what you have," I said.

He smiled. "You'll have it as quickly as I can send it."

"That's good. If I'm lucky, I'll have my flight plan filed an hour after you send me the registrations."

Now Crane positively beamed. "That's tremendous. Well, in that case, let me go and collect everything for you. And good luck in your travels. Or perhaps I should say, happy hunting."

His image vanished, leaving me staring into empty space.

Happy hunting. Hunting *Corrigan's Blood*.

I had the shipcom look for current and historical references to anyone named Corrigan, cross-referenced with any mention of blood. I gave the search an "all databanks" field and a moderate-level priority; with that priority rating I would probably wait a Standard week or two before I'd get any useful answers. I didn't want to tie the shipcom up with a full-priority search, though, when I might get nothing back for the trouble. After all, the name could be purely fanciful.

But every ship I knew bore its name for a reason. Alder had named the ship, and the name was unconventional enough that I couldn't believe he'd chosen it at random or named it after his wife. And if Alder had a reason for the name, I wanted to know what it had to do with me.

With that done, I sat and thought about the three men, their hidden ally, the dead Sarah Idalto, and me.

Sarah Idalto could be dead for two reasons. One, they intended to kill her. Two, she happened along at the wrong time and they killed her on the spur of the moment. I had no way at the moment to prove what they wanted or didn't want with Sarah. I moved on.

What about me? I was still alive for only one of two

reasons. One, they thought they successfully killed me, but were wrong. Two, they didn't want me dead.

That was a little easier to figure. With all the damage they did to me, they hadn't done any of the things they did to Sarah. They hadn't ripped out my throat, or torn open the arteries at my wrists. They hadn't broken my neck or stabbed me through the heart. They hadn't compromised my vital organs in any way. As effectively as they had killed Sarah, I had to assume they weren't incompetent.

If they wanted me alive, there was only one reason for that. I was doing something they wanted me to do. And the only thing I was doing was looking for the *Corrigan's Blood*.

Assume, then, that these three men and their secret assistant wanted me to find the *Corrigan's Blood*. They weren't working with Crane, and were almost certainly working against him. Sarah's death seemed to demonstrate that. And they weren't working with Alder; I could think of no reason why Alder, having stolen the ship, would want someone to find it.

So they were a third party or that third party's representatives.

What did this third party want?

They attacked me after I talked with Crane. They took my clothes, my shoes, my compac, my underwear, my toolbelt, and my ID pouch. It stood to reason that they didn't do that just for their own amusement. I was unconscious when they undressed me; it is damned difficult to undress an unconscious person. I wasn't a threat to them; I was just lying there. So they weren't looking for weapons. That left the information chip that Peter Crane had given me. And they couldn't find that because it was hidden in the fleshtab in my right thigh.

So now I was alive, I still had the information chip, and I was going after Crane's ship.

I had to do several things to make sure I stayed alive a little longer. I had to eliminate all of Crane's sensitive data from the shipcom. I had to hide his infochip someplace secure.

And then, while I was searching for the *Corrigan's Blood*, I needed to watch everyone I met, looking for the person who had a reason to want Crane's ship and Crane's information, and who was, perhaps, Crane's enemy. I was willing to bet that sooner or later, just such a person would come looking for me.

Chapter Five

Badger wasn't smiling when I stepped out of the corridor into navigation. A worried little rat began to gnaw at the inside of my gut.

"I have the course set and I filed our flight plan," I told him.

"That's terrific," he said, but his eyes didn't match the enthusiasm the words implied, and his voice sounded strained.

I would have asked if anything was wrong, but over the years, I've developed a sort of second sense about when to ask Badger what's bothering him and when to keep quiet. Now that second sense kicked in and I said, "Have you done the pre-check?"

He said, "Yes. Everything checked out," and shook his head "no" emphatically at the same time.

What the hell did he mean by that? "Okay? Great. Are you ready for the full pre-detach?"

"Let's go," he said, looking relieved. We rarely did a full pre-detach, since we and only we lived aboard our ship and we therefore kept up daily with the ancillary systems. He acted like he thought someone was listening. I have superb security systems installed on the *Reward*, but I am the first to acknowledge that security can be breached. Badger was acting like he thought ours had been.

"Cargo bay," I said, tapping the monitor that showed us the cargo bay onscreen. It was fairly empty at the moment.

"Masses balance, all secure."

"Deep Deck: lights and wires."

"Check."

"Masses."

"Check."

"Stowage."

"Check."

"Cabin sweep, port to starboard." My monitors flicked from my cabin, first to port, around the arc of the deep, or number four, deck, to Badger's cabin to far starboard.

"Gear stowed, masses balance, all secure."

"Your room matches your face," I blurted, getting my first look at a new decorating scheme I didn't realize he'd installed.

He laughed, genuinely pleased. "Isn't it wild?"

It was worse than wild. It was nightmarish. "I couldn't sleep there."

"When we're in port, I don't," he told me, and his grin was suggestive.

I laughed in spite of myself and moved on to the next item of the pre-detach. We went through the power core and the redundant navigation room on Three Deck, skipped the redundant weapons and shields since private ownership of such weapons was illegal in this sector of the Verzing Community and if anyone was listening, I didn't want to advertise my noncompliance. I kept waiting for Badger to tip me off about what he'd found that had him spooked, but he did the checklist without indicating any problems. We moved to Two Deck and the air plants, the recreation areas and gym and library and galley/dining room and holo room, moved again to Top Deck and the medical room and the navigation room that we sat in. Badger and I overlooked the main shields-and-weapons room, too.

We're heavily armed. A lot of private ships carry battle

armament. Space is, after all, enormous beyond measure; it is the ally of people who want to hide and the enemy of people who want to find them. And the governments can talk all they want about the effectiveness of the Spybees in preventing piracy, but I've seen the little asteroid belts of dead passengers left hanging around empty planets after someone voided them out the airlocks. Dozens, hundreds . . . in one terrible case thousands of people hanging in slow, horrible orbit; crew, passengers, parents and children. They're out there, and so are things even worse. The Spybees do a good job of eliminating the privacy of law-abiding people, but when pirates change their ship registration and telltales before they ever leave a system, the Spybees have no way to tell that they aren't more of those fine, law-abiding citizens; they let them go. I've slipped through the hard white veil of stars feeling the secretive eyes watching me. I've felt the clammy hand of fear grab the back of my neck, and known I was facing my own death. And I've lived to walk away.

If you want to survive, you do what survivors do.

Badger was waiting for me, vertical frown lines furrowed between his eyebrows. With the index finger and thumb of his right hand he pinched up a flap of skin on his left arm and held it there.

"Skin?" I said, and realized suddenly that this was the part of the extended checklist he'd been waiting for. The ship's hull is extruded of layered compressed moleibond, each layer a single molecule formed of atoms artificially bonded and compressed to take up one one-hundredth of their uncompressed space. Moleibond is incredibly dense, almost indestructible . . . our hull had a "Family Warranty," which stated that if the owner or any offspring of the owner ever had a problem with it, the hull would be replaced free by the company. If I had children and they had children and so on, any generation of my offspring until the end of time could collect on that warranty if the company was still around to make good on it. The hull would still be around.

"Skin," Badger said, and flipped on the outside scanner.

We never did a skin check. No one in a TFN ship did skin checks. So why had Badger, and what had he found when he looked?

I waited while he transferred his image to my monitor. The holographic edge of the *Reward*'s bulbous nose slid beneath me, and then stopped moving. On Badger's screen, the scan kept moving as if nothing of interest had occurred, but in front of me, numbers ticked off to indicate enlargement of the image I was seeing . . . though because it was a moleibond hull, enlargement offered no detail.

Then suddenly it did. A tiny edge outlined a bit of a curve, though a huge one. The image was immensely magnified.

Badger superimposed a doppiered image over what I was looking at, expanded both further, then did a doppler peel on both so that I could see inside the ovals.

Spiderweb circuits hung in front of me. The . . . thing . . . was incredibly complex. It had no visible source of power, though. So it was something passive, not active. A tracking device? A listening device? An explosive?

I mouthed, *What does it do?*

He shrugged, pointed to the shipcom unit, and shrugged again. I read his lips. He said, *We don't know.*

The clearance chime rang on the deck—notification that our flight plan had been approved and that we were now requested to undock. I wondered if I ought to cancel my flight plan until I could have the device removed. . . .

Then I thought, Better the enemy I know. This was most likely a gift from the third party, the one who was working against both Crane and Alder. Whoever this was, I would bet if I had it removed he would find a way to hide another one somewhere, or else he would take other steps to accomplish whatever surveillance he felt he had to have. If I knew about this device, perhaps I could find a way to control it, or even use it to my advantage.

I tapped the comlink and said, "*Hope's Reward*, Carolmas registry, ready for departure. Standing by for coordinate feed to origami point." The shipcom lit up and hummed for an instant as somewhere inside the station, someone fed me my outbound coordinates.

Badger brought the engines on line and we detached from our dock, and the *Reward* headed out toward space. As always, I felt the tiny delicious *frisson* of freedom trilling beneath my ribs. The air smelled fresher, the ship sounds sang to me, everything became suddenly more alive, cleaner, clearer, better.

Even Badger's green face and dreadful hair seemed improved.

The *Reward* slipped into her place in line, swimming through space like a fish freed from its aquarium. The traffic ahead of us was heavy—heavier than I remembered from our trip in. Badger noticed it, too. "Wonder what the hold-up at the point is."

I thought the first thing that everyone thinks when there's a problem at an origami point—that this time, the impossible had happened and a ship going into hyperspace had collided with a ship coming out. We waited while the line of outgoing ships crawled forward, and then our shipcom lit up with a boarding demand from a Cassamir Station long-range pursuit cruiser. We signaled our agreement and felt the jolt of the cruiser's ship-to-ship mating with ours; the sporcs made a less-than-graceful docking, but I wasn't going to complain.

Badger and I went aft and watched as two big, armed officers with drawn weapons floated down the gravdrop into view. We waited, and they slowed and kicked to the door. When they stepped through into our artificial gravity, they winced. We keep the gravity at two G's, which would make them more than twice as heavy as they were accustomed to being while on Cassamir Station. We were waiting, hands up to show that we didn't intend to shoot and wanted to cooperate.

The men looked from one of us to the other, then said, "We need quick Gen-ID's, and we're going to have to search your ship to verify that you two are the only people aboard."

I said, "An unwarranted search is outside of VeCRA law."

"It's warranted," one of the sporcs said, looking when he said it like he hoped I'd try to give him trouble, just so he could prove how much of a warrant he had.

His partner was pulling out one of the little Gen-ID Portable Veri-Stat kits that law enforcement of every stripe seems to love so much.

I took a deep breath. "May I *see* the warrant?"

The sporcs gave each other annoyed looks, said, "We're in a hurry and we have a lot of ships to go through," and then, when they saw me tap the compac on my wrist, one growled and pulled out an infochip and slapped it into the wall unit that existed by the gravdrop in every ship built in the Verzing Community in the last twenty-five years, for just this sort of occasion.

"These officers are warranted and decreed to carry with them the full powers of authority of Cassamir Station, and may use such means as are necessary to bring to justice the killer of Sterline Eamonds of Cassamir Station. They will identify this killer by Gen-ID comparison of the killer's genetic material as found on the body of Sterline Eamonds with the genetic material of all persons on all ships leaving Cassamir Station, and that person whose genetic material matches will immediately and without fight submit to custody or be killed outright."

They don't screw around with polite ways of saying things on Cassamir Station.

Badger and I held out our hands and gave our tissue samples for the good of Cassamir Station, and breathed sighs of relief when the green "all-clear" flashed. And when the sporcs returned after a long search to report that we weren't harboring any dangerous fugitives, which we already knew, we were feeling good enough to ask what had happened.

And they were feeling good enough to tell us. "A dregger killed one of the big men on Cassamir today in full view of three witnesses, then got away. The victim was third in line at Huddle House Corporation. Not on Cassamir Station, but universe-wide. They're tearing the station apart trying to find the guy, and we're going to search every ship that leaves, and sooner or later, we'll get him."

"Then what will happen?" I asked.

"We'll try him, we'll sentence him, and we'll send him out an airlock."

Ah, justice. I was suitably impressed.

When they left, Badger leaned against the wall, and suddenly I noticed that he was pale.

"You sick?"

He nodded. "Sort of. Sterline Eamonds . . . I just remembered where I heard that name."

I waited.

"You remember you said to invent an insider? To use somebody who was in Ferlingetta when you were there and who was in a position to have taken the pictures?"

I nodded.

"I did that. And I was just kind of curious. After I did the angles and everything, there was only one person who could have taken the pictures. He was in the right position to see both you and Crane and the three men. So I did the pictures from his point of view and sent them over to Crane. And after I sent them, I got his vital statistics and ran an ID on him."

"Sterline Eamonds?"

"Yes. Coincidence?"

"Probably not."

Chapter Six

We got our turn, and our clearance. I approached hyperspace with the same dread I always do, wondering what I would find out about myself this time that I didn't want to know. The trip through is instantaneous; no time passes on shipboard instruments and from every test we've been able to devise, no time passes in our universe . . . but perceived time in hyperspace is long and can be hellish.

"I'll take the helm," I told Badger, and he nodded and left the bridge. He would fight his fight with the dark realm alone. So would I.

I spoke our destination to the shipcom, then waited until it brought up our insertion path; I double-checked its coordinates against the ones I'd worked out earlier. We were heading for Galatia Fairing, the world that sold the Spybees and was the central repository for all records from them. It was a routine destination, and the insertion paths for it were as clear and time-tested as any have ever been, but I still checked. No one has ever, to my knowledge, become trapped in hyperspace, but I'd rather die than be the first.

The coordinates checked out. I filed the information with the Spybee, received my final clearance from Cassamir Station, and blanked my viewports.

Over the shipcom, I said, "Origami insertion in thirty

seconds." I switched the TFN to automatic, settled into my seat, and braced myself. My hands clenched and unclenched on the padded armrests. The ship's voice continued the countdown I had begun. "Twenty-five . . . twenty-four . . . twenty-three . . ."

I took deep breaths, focused my attention inward, closed my eyes. Calm. Soft and blue and green, the murmuring of waves rolling up onto warm white sand.

"Eighteen . . . seventeen . . ."

Space, still and silent and serene, filled with stars that promise everything. Everything. Think of the perfection of space, the glorious swirl of a nebula splashed against the velvet dark—

"Six . . . five . . . four . . . three . . ."

I am Cadence Drake, captain and owner of the *Hope's Reward*.

"Two."

I am strong. I know who I am.

"One."

I know what I believe.

"Insertion."

I was no longer alone. In my chair, in my head, I could feel the rest of myself, the multidimensional self that takes its mundane shapes as an infinite number of Cadence Drakes in an infinite number of universes connected by the fact that we are one. Infinite. Of a magnitude with the heavens. And we are more than infinite mirrored and fragmented parts; we are also a single whole. An Entity. We touch, we mirror, we remain Me through that portion of our self, or perhaps I should say Self, that has its home in hyperspace. A part of me can look infinity in the eye and not flinch. A part of me is enormous and magnificent and beyond the pain and the suffering and the despair of my infinite mirrored fragmented mortal three-dimensional lives; is so beyond my limitations and weaknesses and frailties that it regards the infinite parts of me with some tenderness but also with mild, superior amusement.

I am small, puny, insignificant. Mortal. Human. A creature of limited flesh and limited intellect, for a burning expanse of non-time forced to see myself not only as I am, but as I could be in all my infinite capacity, knowing that when the moment ends my sudden wisdom, my godhood, will be stripped from me and I will be thrown naked and shivering and frightened and mortal back into the domain of death.

And the infinite frightened fragments of my greater Self clamor in my head. I am a doctor, on my way to a new world, armed with hope and knowledge, but now with fear, too, for I have never taken this shortcut through the stars. I am a dancer; and I am a thief; and a renegade and a lover and a mother and I am old and young and I have a thousand faces and a thousand names a million names a billion names and I know them all all all all and every detail of every life that goes with them and they are nothing nothing nothing because these fragments of my true self are nothing these tiny mortal scraps are meaningless are nothing but I am Cadence Drake I am Cadence Drake I am Cadence Drake—

"—I am Cadence Drake—" My voice, ragged with the strain, broke. I was alone inside my skull again. Hot tears wet my cheeks. "Oh, God," I whispered, and rested my face in my hands. I was mortal again, a shivering ape-woman crouched by her fire, staring up with terror at the stars. But I was still myself. I had not given up my mind or my will to the aching beauty of infinity. This body, this fragment of me, would not die drooling and gibbering in an institution because I had lost myself inside hyperspace. Not this time.

Aching with the loss of all that I had been and could never truly be, weighted with a lingering sense of profound desire, and still shaken from my over-self's bombardment of my identity, I rose and signaled my route to the Spybee. Then I set my course for Galatia Fairing. We had a two-day trip through standard space to reach the traffic information clearinghouse. Due to the nature of the origami points, which occur at the universe's natural folds and which therefore are never near massive objects but always located at central points between them, planets are far less convenient than stations.

I sent my hail to Galatia Fairing and with it my request for records clearance; by the time I got there, everything would probably be waiting for me. Galatia Fairing sent me an inbound route and docking assignment. Once I set my course, I dropped into my seat and stared up at the stars through the now-clear ports. And I tried to shake off hyperspace. I went down to the holo room and got an infochip out of my private entertainment collection . . . one so old that the material on it wasn't even in full-density holo, but instead looked gauzy and sounded thin.

I slipped the chip into the reader and settled back.

Isas Yamamoto appeared before me, sitting in a soft chair in a brightly lit room. A pale-skinned, dark-haired child sat on his lap, kicking her legs rhythmically. She looked up at him from time to time, her expression worshipful. She was his daughter, about four years old at the time the holo was taken.

"This is my daughter, Akiko," he said, smiling at the person recording him. "And I am Isas Yamamoto, the inventor of the first successful hyperdrive engine, which other scientists are now installing into spaceships so that you and your children and your children's children will be able to travel to the farthest star."

I looked at his face. It was so kind. So caring. When he glanced down at his daughter I could see his love for her. I'd first watched this holo when I was seven; when I knew the truth about my fathers, when I was beginning to understand what I was, and when I first suspected that my mother would never love me. I saw this holo, and I made Isas Yamamoto my secret father.

Because of him, I longed for the stars even though I had never seen the stars, or even the sky. I dreamed of flying, soaring, escaping. I dreamed of freedom; because when Isas Yamamoto spoke of space, he believed it was a place of magic and wonder, and so it became that to me. A place of freedom.

"I figured out the key to breaching hyperspace while I was making Akiko a paper crane—like this one." He held up an origami crane. I sat in my holo-chair, an adult woman with tears welling in my eyes, listening to his voice and having him tell me once again the child's version of the story of the beginning of humankind's eruption out of the tiny system that had bound it in from the instant of its birth. I was like a child holding on to the blanket it long ago outgrew but could not leave behind. I knew my behavior was childish, even ludicrous. I didn't care. Without Isas Yamamoto, humanity would not have reached the stars. Without him, I would never have been free.

"Akiko wanted a crane," Yamamoto said, smiling down at his little girl. "And I was folding it for her—like so." He handed the finished crane to his daughter and took a sheet of paper from the little carved table beside him. He lifted it up and made a crease in the paper, and then another. While he folded it, he talked. "It occurred to me that the nature of origami, that is, the art of folding paper, was very much like the problem humanity faced in reaching the stars. Origami is folding two-dimensional paper into three-dimensional objects. Space travel through hyperspace is the folding of a three-dimensional universe into four spatial dimensions to shorten the distances between points."

He held up the partially finished crane. It didn't look like much yet. "You see—I am taking something that was in essence two-dimensional, and I am changing it into something three-dimensional." He told a quick story about the Flatlanders, the fictional two-dimensional people who were bound to their dimension, but who could be lifted free by a three-dimensional hand. He said he considered the argument that, just as no machine the Flatlanders could build in two dimensions could lift them free of their dimension, because it suffered the same constraints as they did, so too no three-dimensional machine could lift three-dimensional humanity into hyperspace.

"I do not believe people are creatures of three dimensions," Isas Yamamoto said. His voice remained soft, but now it gathered intensity. "People are more than their height and their width and their depth. They are more than the machines they build. Life is not a thing of three dimensions. It is not limited by *up* and *across* and *back*. Life encompasses space, and time, and it goes beyond that. It touches infinity. You sit watching me right now, and in another probability, another child who is also you sits watching another me. In another probability, another child who is also you sits where you are sitting, but that child isn't listening the way you are. In an infinite number of probabilities, an infinite number of children who are also you do an infinite number of things, and none of them can see or hear each other. So how can all of these yous do similar things? You are linked together through hyperspace. The infinite number of three-dimensional yous are all part of a single meta-you, whose home is hyperspace."

He smiled. "We believed hyperspace existed for a very long time. But people were certain that the only way to reach hyperspace was to blast into it with enormous amounts of energy, and no one thought humans could harness that much energy."

He held up the unfinished crane by the fingers of two hands. "We were trying to move beyond our dimension by blowing a hole in it and hoping the hole took us where we wanted to go." He poked at the folded paper with a single finger. Then he shook his head and smiled sadly. "There is no control in this method. The entire approach is wrong. Humanity doesn't want to make a hole in space. It wants to fold space into useful shapes."

He put the beginning of the crane down, and held out his hands, fingers spread. "And how do we fold a crane out of paper?" He wiggled his fingers. "Watch."

First he tried to fold the crane using only one finger. "This doesn't work." He tried it with a finger and a thumb, and then with one hand. Finally, shrugging and smiling, he said, "We don't need huge amounts of energy to make our crane. But we need two hands . . . many fingers . . . precise small amounts of energy applied from all sides to shape two dimensions into three." He creased, folded, tucked, and the square of paper became a serene white crane, wings spread. "And we must have the same many hands and many fingers, the same small precise amounts of energy applied to all sides of the three-dimensional universe to fold it into hyperspace.

"We have those hands. When I built my little, weak hyperspace engine, which I designed to apply pressure to one part of our universe, an infinite number of other Isas Yamamotos built their small engines. Each of us built a finger; together we built the hands; and with all of us working together from our own probabilities, we folded space and time into a shape we could use.

"Now we will have the stars," he said. "They're waiting for us. We'll touch them in my lifetime, and spread out into them in hers." He hugged his daughter.

The tears that had filled my eyes broke free and rolled down my cheeks. I stopped the interview; it was over and in the next part a scientist narrator told about Yamamoto's method for plotting the locations of the origami points—the thin places in the fabric of the universe where space and time could be most easily folded. Then it told of the first manned hyperspatial flight.

Isas Yamamoto had been right about humanity settling the stars in his daughter's lifetime. He'd been wrong about Old Earth's people reaching the stars in his own. He was a passenger aboard *Alice's Looking-Glass*, the first hyperspace ship.

The *Looking-Glass* successfully traversed hyperspace without requiring the predicted impossible amounts of energy. It followed the same short path Yamamoto's probes had taken, from one side of the moon to the other. The course was preprogrammed: go out, broadcast a prerecorded message, and come straight back. The ship slipped from one side of the moon to the other, sent its message, and returned, making Isas Yamamoto a hero whose name would live as long as men breathed.

But *Alice's Looking Glass* returned from her short journey incomprehensibly twisted and mangled. The four explorers inside lived long enough to babble about having been gods. Then they died, leaving hyperspace to long emptiness until we created a hull strong enough to withstand the enormous reshaping forces hyperspace applied.

I sat in the darkened holo-room, looking at the man I had chosen as my soul father. When I was ten, his story sang to me with the glories of invention and martyrdom. By the time I was fifteen, I yearned to follow in his footsteps. At eighteen, a terrible thing happened in my home, and my mother accused me and put a price on my head. I ran away, stealing some of my mother's money and taking Badger with me; my home city in my home planet still listed me as wanted for murder, kidnapping, extortion, thievery, and a swarm of lesser crimes. Death waited behind me for the woman I once was, but I reached my stars. And if hyperspace humbled me with the fact of my own insignificance, still I survived.

I was Isas Yamamoto's spiritual daughter, and I had followed my dream. I'd won the stars he desired. I had my own life, my own ship. If I was insignificant compared to my infinite, all-knowing meta-self, still this mortal iteration of me had not let the universe pound me into submission.

I sat up straighter. This job for Peter Crane was going to pay off my ship, and leave me accountable to no one but me.

"I thought I'd find you in here," Badger said, and the lights in the holo-room came up.

"I'm too predictable." I rose and turned.

We hugged, and in that hug there was the wistful tenderness of one-time lovers who cannot be lovers anymore. "You aren't predictable at all most of the time. But when it has been a bad crossing, I know where to come."

"I survived it." I tried to sound invincible when I said it, but I don't think my intended air of invincibility came off too well. After the humbling fist of hyperspace, I yearned for Badger and for his human touch with a hunger akin to pain. I did not let myself see the kindred hunger in his eyes. I loved Badger, but I carried too many scars on my soul to give myself to anyone. I tried once, and I made both Badger and myself miserable. So I smiled a bright, false smile. "And how about you?"

"I'm still myself," he said. "I keep hoping that one of these days it will get easier."

We laughed together. We both suspected it would get easier when we died. Not before.

We walked down the corridor into the galley, and Badger told the shipcom to begin his meal. By the time we reached the galley, the reconsta unit, an old Berliner Reconsta-Chef, was humming to itself. While it built his meal, he leaned against the unit and his voice dropped to just above a whisper. "I have some interesting news. I created a tiny little passive steady-level trace to keep an eye on that . . . um . . . patch on our hull . . ." The chime dinged softly and he retrieved his meal from the unit. He settled into a seat so he could watch me while I ordered up my own food. ". . . I just wanted to see what it was doing, you know. It obviously is designed to use energy but it has no internal source of energy and isn't hooked into a visible external one."

He paused, waiting, and I gave him an encouraging nod. My own meal—Steaklite and Potataline, CornJoys and a steaming cup of Tea Magic—finished cooking and the Chef called to me in a less-than-compelling voice. "So . . . what did you find out?"

When I sat, he leaned across the long table, his face so close to mine that I could feel the warmth of his skin. "My probe reports that when we hit hyperspace, the patch came to life; it drew an unholy amount of power from the dispersal fins and used it to gather data out of the shipcom, digging through all sorts of private places and taking I-don't-know-what-all. It didn't leave any tracks. If it had known about my watchdog and had avoided it, it would have been the perfect security breaker. And when we came out and the dispersal fins started draining off all the accumulated energy from the crossing, the spy sent off a huge burst of data."

"Where? To whom? Surely it didn't beam the information back to Cassamir Station. It would take a hundred years to get there."

Badger said, "This was a tight burst transmission, very narrow beam. And in-system. Someone is already here ahead of us, and now whoever that is knows we're here, too."

Chapter Seven

A Galatia Fairing Port Authority security controller met me at the debarkation gate, did my security scan, and punched my temporary clearance badge into the palm of my left hand. It stung for a second. The dermabadge would work for my entire stay at Galatia Fairing. When I left, the security system would burst a short self-destruct message into it, and it would reduce itself to biodegradable components and flush itself out of my system through my kidneys.

Galatia Fairing guards its data.

My doppler didn't set off alarms, though it was the first device I've ever tried to smuggle through the Port Authority that made the trip. I ran it constantly, leaving it hooked straight into shipcom via a mole Badger tricked into the Port Authority power grid. I didn't want to overrun the memory of the dopplerchip, and I didn't know how long I would have to search for what I needed.

Long, painful hours, as it turned out. I ate three erratically spaced meals over twenty-four hours in the PA Commissary, finding them even more tasteless than the reconsta my own Chef served up. Between meals, I took stims to keep myself going and ferreted through databases, trying to account for all twenty-seven Stardancer-class ships.

I eventually achieved a headcount for all of them, but

I lost six to convoluted routes and unmet destinations, and I had to wonder why the percentage of ships that wished to hide their destinations should comprise such a large part of the whole. This was precisely the scenario I'd hoped to uncover, but I was hoping to uncover it with only one ship, not six.

I set the downloader to flag arrivals of any Stardancer ships at any destinations, unrelated to point of departure, and with that done, went for my fourth dreadful meal.

While I was forcing down Fishims and High Carbohydrate Concentrate, a woman came to my table.

She looked at the reconsta-dreck, made a face, and said, "Mind if I join you?"

My doppler was running. I didn't mind a bit.

"I've seen you in here three times since yesterday; we're evidently set on the same station-cycles, but I'm sure I've never noticed you before. Were you transferred?"

"I'm not on station cycles. I'm a spacer; since I arrived yesterday, I've worked straight through."

Her eyes widened. Pretty, friendly eyes. "I don't think I could do that. I'm a slave to sleep; if I don't get my six, I basically shut down."

I found myself telling her, "I'm captain of my ship. I have to be awake when things need to be done, and those things rarely fall on ordered hours."

"I don't suppose they do." She laughed. "I'm honored to meet you. Ships' captains always eat in the VIP Lounge. They have real food there. A captain who eats reconsta . . . you're the rarest bird who's flown through here in a long time."

Between shoveling in mouthfuls of the station sludge, I said, "Perhaps I'm the poorest, too. Until I own my ship outright, every rucet I save goes to make my payments."

"You *own* your ship?" She seemed stunned, and very admiring. "Is it a real ship? I mean a working ship. I thought corporations owned everything but pleasure yachts."

"Most of everything, but a few independents are out there. I'm one of them." I was flattered that she was so intrigued by what I did, but I was wary, too. I held out a hand to her. "My name is Cadence Drake. And you are. . .?"

"Unforgivably rude." She laughed and took my hand and shook it. "Fedara Contei. I'm one of the poor wretches who collates data."

A gift from the gods, I thought. Here was someone who did for a living what I was doing clumsily and part-time. I wanted to spill my story to Fedara . . . and it was that desire that chilled like a block of ice in my gut and made me back off. Why did I like this woman so much? I never told anyone anything; currently I was being paid an exorbitant sum of money to keep my secrets, which certainly made not telling all that much more attractive. So what was it about her that made me feel I could trust her . . . that we could be such good friends?

I gulped the last bit of my reconsta and, bleary-eyed and muzzy-headed from lack of sleep, rose and smiled. "I wish we had more time to talk," I told her, and my voice sounded beautifully sincere. "I need to finish my search and get back to my ship, though. I owe my crew their pay by the week, and on the days when we're stuck in dock, they don't earn their pay."

Disappointment flickered in her eyes, but she hid it well. "If you have any time at all before you have to leave, here's my address. I'd love to have you stop by. Maybe I could even help you with your records search."

I took the datacard she handed me and was astounded to see that it was full-access. I could scan the card into the transport and it would deliver me to her door. Unless I missed my guess, I could scan it into her door and walk inside. I raised an eyebrow.

She smiled again. "Chemistry," she said, and her face, beautifully enigmatic, became beautifully seductive.

I swallowed hard and pocketed the card, but did not put it in my skinflap. If someone searched me, I didn't want the card to let out its "find-me" whistle. I was afraid I'd lose a leg that way—and one of my best secrets. "I doubt that I'll have time."

She pouted.

I don't click with women, and I still felt the pull of that pout.

"Just try."

"I'll try," I told her, lying like Hell's fiends and at the same time appalled that part of me wanted me to be telling the truth. As we parted company, she rested her hand on my shoulder and I fell into the deep, perfect pools of her eyes and didn't come up for air until I was entering my cubicle.

I stopped in the cubicle door, feeling lost. I didn't remember walking there. I didn't remember leaving Fedara. I looked at my com but I didn't know what time I'd gone to eat, so I didn't know how long I'd been . . . sleepwalking?

"This is ridiculous," I muttered. "I've got to get back to the *Reward*. I have to have some sleep. If I hadn't been so tired, I wouldn't have reacted so oddly to Fedara Contei."

I know I'm tired when I start talking to myself.

I put a seal on my work and on my cubicle and went straight home, annoyed with myself for reacting so oddly to a stranger who was obviously trying to pick me up.

Badger stood staring at me through the faceplate of the MEDix. And how the hell had that happened? I distinctly remembered going to my quarters when I got back to the ship. My quarters in no way resemble a MEDix. I mentally retraced my steps: the Galatia Fairing cubicle, the cafeteria, back to the cubicle, then to the *Hope's Reward*, and finally to my quarters. At no point in that itinerary did I detour through the medichamber.

I had a good memory, an excellent memory, and I resented the fact that it had suddenly quit on me. First details of the beating on Cassamir Station, none of which I could recall. The descriptions of my attackers, reduced to a giant and three pairs of compelling eyes. Then wandering from the cafeteria to the cubicle without remembering getting there. Now this. I shook my head, disgusted with myself.

"What happened?"

"I carried you up and plugged you in after I reviewed the doppler data in the shipcom." Badger looked like the ass end of a starship collision. I hadn't seen him so weary or so scared since we ran away from home. "I've been over every minute of that data," he told me. "I did stim and ran it at one-hundred speed so I could get through it. Cady . . . you stepped into something bad."

I waited.

He lifted the clamshell and helped me out of the MEDix. I was starving; I told the shipcom to make me something hot and filling, and when it said, "Your meal is ready," I pulled some very bad lasagna and a decent croti pie out of the med room's wall unit.

"Bring that with you." Badger was heading for the door. "We need to go to the holo room now."

"So what's the big mystery?" I hurried behind him. "It's the woman I met in the cafeteria, isn't it? Fedara Contei? She's a member of the third party."

"The third party?"

I realized I hadn't told Badger about my conclusions. I quickly described the assumptions I'd made about the three men and the fact that I felt whoever they were working for would have to try to contact me again.

When I finished he said, "It fits. The woman who is pretending to be Fedara Contei is another representative."

"Pretending?"

"Fedara Contei is what she called herself, but that isn't who she is."

"Who is she?"

His lips pressed into a thin, hard line. "I can't find that out anywhere. She's erased every record of her original self from every database I can find. She's as invisible as the three men."

"If her cover is perfect," I said, "then maybe she's Fedara Contei." I didn't trust her and I still wanted to like her. Dammit, that didn't make sense. I didn't know why I had found her so compelling, and I couldn't imagine what might have made me want to bare my soul to her, but I couldn't deny that I wanted to find out she wasn't lying to me. Maybe I was hungrier for a human relationship, for human touch, than I'd realized.

"No. You'll have to see the doppler holo. You'll have to see what she did to you." Badger stared into my eyes, his own more troubled than I had seen them since we fled our homeworld.

My stomach knotted and ice crystallized in my blood. "She did something to me?"

He didn't say anything.

We dropped through the grav-chute to Deck Two and took the first right off of the central corridor. Badger already had the dopplerchip set up, with action paused at the moment where Fedara Contei and I got ready to leave the Commissary. The holo-room projected a life-sized tableau: me and the woman who was perhaps not Fedara Contei posed amid dozens of non-players. In the glossy charcoal gray of the projected images, I didn't look so tired, and she didn't look so beautiful. I perched on the edge of my favorite chair and got ready to see myself turn and walk away.

That wasn't what my image did, though. It took a step forward and wrapped my arms around Fedara's waist, and Fedara dragged her fingers down the line of my spine and kissed me. I slammed my hand onto the chair console and the image froze. I stood and turned to face Badger. "That isn't what happened."

"Sit down, Cady," he told me, his voice soothing. "It happened, and it isn't the strangest or the worst or the most unlikely thing that did."

"No," I whispered. I probed and prodded at my memory, trying to bring the scene before me to mind. I might as well have been fishing in deep space; I wasn't going to get any bites.

"Sit, love."

I sat.

"Come home with me," Fedara said, and I watched

her fingers trailing tiny circles around the small of my back.

My image smiled at her, and nodded, and leaned forward to kiss her. "I can spend a little time with you," it said.

"I didn't do that," I told Badger. "Dammit, dammit, dammit! I went straight to the cubicle where I was working, and then, because I was so exhausted, I came home."

He shook his head, face grim. "Keep watching."

I kept watching. I watched myself follow the stranger home. I watched her sit me on a chair, as if I were an automaton, and then I watched a slender, graceful young man step out of another room. I sat in that chair, staring zombielike at nothing, and the man said to Fedara, "You got her."

And Fedara said, "I told you I would," in tones so bitter and angry I expected the man to recoil.

Instead, he smiled. His smile was sweet and innocent, as beautiful as any I had ever seen. "My beautiful love. You'll do anything for me, won't you?"

"Go to Hell."

"I am the Prince of Hell, my darling. I bring Hell with me."

"I brought her to you. Are you going to let me die now?" Fedara asked him.

He laughed. "Only when you're a good girl. You're going to do something else for me, and when you have done that, if you do it exactly the way I tell you to, I'll let you die." He leaned against a wall, ankles crossed, hands shoved into pockets, unshakable smile on his handsome face. "She's going to fall in love with you, and she's going to take you aboard her ship. You'll go with her wherever she goes, and you'll do whatever she wants you to do, and when she completes her task for Crane, you'll go back with her. You'll kill Crane, and then you'll kill her. And then I'll set you free."

"Why make her fall in love with me, Danniz? She doesn't go that way and neither do I. Why not find some man to do what you want? Or do it yourself?"

"This is much more amusing for me." He left the room and returned with a small syringe.

Fedara hissed. "That isn't—?"

"Of course not." He cut her off, his expression disgusted. "I don't need to compound my problems. This is simply a larger dose of the drug you gave her. It will make her suggestible for the next forty-eight hours. Within that length of time, you should be able to insinuate yourself aboard her ship." He leaned over me and injected the drug, and I sat there like one of the brain-dead. "You are going to fall in love with Fedara Contei," he told my double, and my image's head bobbed up and down in agreement. "You are going to bring her aboard your ship because she needs a job, and because you love her. You are going to keep her with you for the rest of your life." My head kept bobbing. Yes yes yes yes yes.

I stopped the holo. Now I knew why Badger looked so scared. "How did they drug me the first time?"

"Fedara either slipped the drug into your food or administered it through skin contact when she touched you. Perhaps it happened when you shook hands. I found traces of the drug in your bloodstream when I did a complete scan on you. I had the medichamber cycle your blood and I nanoscrubbed your tissues so none of it is left. You should be free of the compulsion he tried to implant in you."

"How would she have kept up the charade once the stuff wore off? Drugs like that don't effect permanent changes."

Badger gave me a disgusted look. "Think, Cadence. She would have been living with you. She would have been your lover. She would have kept you drugged, you idiot."

"Wouldn't you have said something about me being with another woman?"

"Of course I would have. That's why I suspect Fedara would have taken her first opportunity to kill me."

And I thought, yes. That's how it would have gone. Badger would have died, I would have spent the rest of my unnaturally short life as someone's malleable, unsuspecting slave, while I led her to the man who had hired me so that she could kill both of us. "He wanted her to kill me. And Crane. Badger, she's going to be waiting for me when I get back to my cubicle, and when I don't react the way she expected—"

"You aren't going back to your cubicle," he told me. "I explained to the woman who gave you your credentials that you were poisoned while eating in their commissary. I provided the original of your medichamber readout, which very clearly indicated poisoning, and then I showed her your pass record, which proved that you didn't leave the records compound until you returned here and collapsed in my arms. When I told her I intended to take the incident public, you would be amazed at how willing she was to get me the information you wanted, in spite of Galatia Fairing's unbreachable security precautions."

"You're a shit, Badg," I told him, grinning. I hugged him. "And I love you."

His eyes were sad. "I know. And I love you too, moron. And now we have all the information on Stardancer ships that we're going to get, so before Fedara Contei and her friend Danniz come looking for us, let's escape."

Chapter Eight

Badger and I spent two days analyzing the regions where the suspicious ships had appeared. From that list, I made up what we called the Short List: the subset of planets in the vicinity of any of the ships' appearances that did not belong to any sort of planetary alliance or government; that emphasized local autonomy and the rights of individuals rather than the rights and needs of government; or, that had a reputation for providing cover stories and false papers.

Our Short List wasn't all that short, but it was manageable. There were twenty-seven planets on it. That meant a lot of jumping through hyperspace; a lot of getting personal with parts of myself I didn't want to know. I figured it would take us two or three weeks to make the jumps, talk to people who would recognize a Stardancer-class ship, and determine which ones had been visited and which ones hadn't. From that point, tracking down the right ship would probably be tougher. But if I had a hot ship with brand-new fake papers, I would make sure to be a model citizen with that ship for a while, so that I didn't set off anyone's alarms. I figured at least I'd be able to revert to tracking by Spybee.

Badger and I went first to Contessa, an ugly terraformed planet in a marginal orbit around the star Gadmirion. Contessa didn't allow any physical contact between itself and the outside universe. It guarded its privacy with unreasoning violence, and though Spybees watched its origami points and tracked the ships that passed through its domain, it kept their information to itself. I had Badger, however. He used his worm program and extracted the log data from both Contessan Spybees. A Stardancer had been through but had been refused docking and sent on its way. With relief, for neither of us relished dealing with the virulently insane Contessans, we crossed their warped little planet off our list.

From Contessa, we went to Up Yours, a beautiful habitable planet which had been settled by Libertarians and which maintained its anarchistic way of life in spite of tenacious buyout attempts by the nearby Beatrix Corporate System, a repressive hell-in-space if ever there was one.

We were marginally luckier on Up Yours. A Stardancer had just been through, though it didn't match any of the registrations Crane had given me. The name it had given on entry was the *Mystic Dove*. Badger wormed its destination information out of the Spybee; then we docked, hopped a shuttle, and dropped into Up Yours's main spaceport town, Freeport. I wanted to see if I could track down anyone who might have done alteration work on the Stardancer. I was hoping to find anything that could link the *Dove* with *Corrigan's Blood*.

Badger and I went through Customs, which consisted of one cheerful man checking our baggage for plants or animals that might destroy local crops or herds, and giving us a quick briefing informing us that the government of Up Yours wouldn't extradite its citizens for acts committed against offworlders. We were advised to keep quiet if we didn't know what was going on, to avoid fights, to carry weapons, and to watch our manners. We'd been informed of the weapons requirement before, and so were both wearing heavy-duty stunners. The Customs official tested both weapons to be sure they worked, then gave them back to us.

"That's to be sure that you won't be able to say you weren't armed and warned when you came through Customs," he said. "Just in case anything happens to you."

And then we were through and carrying our bags, heading for one of the two hotels the customs official had said was both clean and cheap. Freeport was pretty, but archaic. The houses were primarily built of wood, or sometimes of sand-brick, or rarely of stone. Nothing was moleibonded. Steam cars crowded the narrow brick streets, growling and honking at each other. The walkways weren't moving walkways. They were made of brick, or sometimes concrete, or even packed earth. And I smelled wood smoke in the air, and saw it rising from chimneys in the houses and shops; and a man passed me, pulling a wagon full of wood cut into short lengths, shouting that he had dried wood for sale.

The men and women and children I saw were working, and most of them appeared to me to be working hard. Physical laborers toiled over the streets, the buildings, the vehicles, everything. I saw no bots. Few machines, and those simple.

The settlement worlds often opt to survive on their own resources rather than taking out loans from some of the larger planetary investors; this gives them unheard-of autonomy. But the people of these worlds often burn trees and walk on packed dirt.

Up Yours was a world where everything was available, and everything was legal. I would have said it was like my homeworld in that regard, but when I thought about it I realized it wasn't entirely true. Neither personal vehicles, nor private weapons, nor political information was available legally on Cantata. My home deals in leisure and entertainment, and in decadence. Up Yours dealt in something else, something that had an air of stoicism and integrity about it.

The people walked with a relaxed, confident gait that I had seen before only in spacers, people who could leave the petty rules of the worlds and stations behind. Most people wore some form of projectile weapon strapped to a hip. A few didn't, but I didn't assume they were unarmed; only that their weapons were of other, less obvious varieties. Still, though I saw plenty of weapons, I saw no action that made the need for weapons obvious.

I realized I'd been expecting rampant anarchy; mobs of people screaming through the streets; mass hysteria. I wasn't expecting the well-ordered traffic and overall sense of purpose and industry I found. The calm prosperity of the place clashed violently with everything I had been taught about the importance of relying on government intervention to maintain social order.

Following directions, Badger and I turned the corner at Wilkes Street and found the Espulin Hotel. It had obviously been a luxurious place at one time, but it looked like a woman who had worn the same lovely party dress for ten years; it was a very fine woman who had known better days.

We went in, bags slung over our shoulders, and asked for two rooms.

The desk clerk gave the two of us a little half-smile when we signed the register. "So how are things in the universe beyond?"

Badger laughed. I sighed. We were so obviously off-worlders. I said, "They're about the same as ever."

"Glad I'm here then," the man said, and chuckled. "If you got captain's registry or crew pass, you save ten percent."

I fished my registry chip out of my travel pack and Badger produced his crew pass. The clerk nodded and recorded our information. He gave us the rate, which was very reasonable, and took our money. "Off-worlders get more interesting-looking every day," he said as he handed us our door-cards. His Interworld Standard had a strong accent, but he was understandable.

"Bodyfashions change quickly," I agreed. I didn't see any point in taking offense. Maybe he didn't know about the Maryschildren. Maybe if he did the fact that I was one didn't matter to him. The more regressive settlement worlds don't do much with gengineering, so someone like me stands out worse than usual, but he didn't seem to be mocking either of us—only commenting. And while I was the way I was through no fault of my own, Badger's look was designed to be shocking in the heart of the fashion universe. In the settlements, he might as well have been an alien. He would have been disappointed if no one had noticed.

"Get many off-worlders here?" I asked.

The clerk shrugged. "The usual, I suppose. Traders, settlers, people looking for a place to hide. Freeport isn't a busy place. Grown a bit since I settled here. That was fourteen-fifteen terrayears ago, but it's still small enough to be likable. People know each other, watch out for each other." A little frown played across his face as if something bothered him about that last statement. He didn't add anything, though.

I slung my bag over my shoulder and fingered my door-card. "It's quieter than I expected."

"Was for me, too. Thought I'd see gunfights in the streets and have loose women throwing themselves on me the minute I set foot on the ground. Found out most people here just want to be left alone. Anyhow. What are you looking for while you're here?"

"Information on some people who left before we arrived," I told him.

"Depending on the type of information, I might be able to point you in the right direction."

"I'm trying to find out what a ship registered as the *Mystic Dove* was doing here."

"Sea or space?"

"What?"

"The ship. Sea or space?"

My blank expression made him laugh.

"I meant, was the *Mystic Dove* a sea ship or a space ship, but from the look of you, I'd say I probably already know the answer to that."

"Space," I told him. "I never considered ships in the seas." I grew up in a world without seas, a world claimed from the wastes of space, a world of tunnels hollowed out of rock and filled beneath the frozen, inhospitable surface with teeming, clawing life. Surface-based cities still felt alien to me, and the new idea of ships floating through vast stretches of open, uncontrolled water gave me the shivers.

"Space ships are easier," he said with a smile. "We have a huge seaport, and if you weren't lucky, you'd have to track down officials for half a dozen lines to find a sea ship. Space ships, you go to Space Registry. Corner of Bright Street and Fifth. You'll have to go there anyway to get your own departure clearance. When you go in, ask for Lucy. She can help you go through the records."

"Lucy," I repeated. I couldn't shake the picture of ships that sailed through water, threatened by gravity and storms, by reefs and winds, where the captain and crew worked out in the open, not separated from the elements that could claim them without warning. I promised myself that I would see a sea ship someday.

Evidently my distraction showed, for Badger stepped in. "Thank you," he told the clerk, and added. "We'll look up Lucy." He tucked his arm into the crook of mine and led me away.

Our rooms connected through a central door; 318 and 320 at the end of a long, narrow hall. We passed two older women pushing a cart in front of them; the cart was full of used linens and cleaning supplies. This hotel, too, used human workers instead of bots. I wondered if all of them did.

The human workers did a decent job, though. Our rooms were clean and pleasant; they smelled of fresh air and laundered sheets. Neither offered any amenities beyond a bed, a bathroom, and a locking door, but I didn't need any amenities. All I needed was some information and then I could get on my way.

I'd set my agenda for my own convenience; I put the

least developed worlds first, because they would be the most bother and I figured they wouldn't keep records as well as the more progressive worlds. Old trails were more likely to dry up and disappear altogether in such places. I hoped that after two or three more stops like this one, Badger and I would be able to do the rest of our investigating via shipcom from the comfort of the bridge.

Badger threw his bag in the closet in his room, then joined me in mine. "Still don't think there's any chance we'll find what we need today? I hate the idea of spending a night here."

"We'll be here the night," I said. I wasn't optimistic about getting the details on the *Mystic Dove* in just a few hours, but spending a day on Up Yours and in the small, quiet city of Freeport didn't bother me; I'm less dependent on entertainment than Badger. I'm always willing to brood if I don't have something better to do.

"I'd offer to stay here and break into the com system while you went out, but there's no com system to break into." He walked to the side of my bed and tapped a green box atop which rested a handset. The handset was attached to the box by a twisted cord. A round dial with ten holes in it and numbers beneath each of the holes completed the thing. "This," he said, "is the local excuse for a com system. No computers at all. If you pick up the handset, a *person* answers on the other end. It transmits sound by changing the vibrations of a diaphragm into electrical impulses."

I winced. I was willing to understand Up Yours's unswerving pursuit of independence, but I wished that pursuit didn't interfere with my convenience.

"We'll find out what we need to know," I said. "It might just take us a while to figure out how."

Chapter Nine

I'd expected a graying matron with thick ankles and a thicker skull. Lucy turned out to be in her very early twenties, bright, and energetic. She was short, slender and delicate-looking, with skin of a natural medium brown, long straight black hair, and surprisingly light brown eyes. I noticed Badger noticing her, and wasn't surprised. She wasn't the sort of woman I associated with him, but there was something compelling about her; it suggested she was deeper than her perky smile and her unremitting cheer.

We spent the half hour we needed on paperwork and got our return validations cleared so that when we were done on Up Yours we could go back to the *Reward*. Then I said, "The man at our hotel told us we ought to see you about a ship we're trying to locate."

"Where are you staying?"

I told her.

"That would be Mike, then. Isn't he nice?"

Badger and I both agreed that he was.

She smiled. "Well, Mike's right. I'm the person you need to talk to. Until a week ago I had a supervisor, but one day she just quit without notice; ran off and disappeared. She'd talked about some man she'd met—I guess she decided he was a better deal than this place." A shrug, that suggested she could sympathize with her ex-supervisor.

"I got an unofficial, unpaid promotion, which is to say I got all of the work but none of the rewards." Another perky smile, this one saying, *Aren't I bearing up well under all this responsibility?* "Since then, I've handled the records on every space ship that deals in Freeport."

I thought, That's more than I wanted to know about your life, Lucy. I wasn't overwhelmed by her suffering, either. The whole time we'd been in the office, the phone hadn't rung and no one else had come in. I'd worked harder in my sleep. Still I said, "That sounds difficult." Then I asked her, "Can you tell us about the *Mystic Dove*?"

I saw sudden curiosity in her eyes. "The *Mystic Dove*? I remember that name. The ship just left a few days ago."

"I knew we didn't miss it by much."

"Friends of yours?"

I considered lying, but claiming friends you don't really have can get you into serious trouble. "No. This is just business."

"Oh." She nodded, apparently satisfied, but I could tell she was still curious. She said, "Let me see what I can find." Her smile to me was polite, but the grin she flashed at Badger indicated more than simple manners. She tucked a few stray strands of hair behind her ears and walked to her file—a box filled with paper. Over her shoulder, she said, "That Melatint is a good look for you, Strebban. It's a little startling at first, but it emphasizes your perfect bone structure. Before I came to Up Yours, I used to love to be Melatinted." While she talked, she thumbed through stacks of paper cards. "My homeworld imported some of the best looks from Meileone and New Paris. Have you seen Starburst? I had that . . . metallic cobalt blue with these little light things the artist embeds in the skin. They flicker and sparkle. It was absolutely *rush*! The best look I ever got—I wore all my seethroughs with it and everybody was just stunned."

She shoved the drawer she'd been digging through closed and pulled the one beside it open. "I must have put the *Dove*'s file back in their first arrival date instead of moving it forward to its most recent visit. Give me just a second; I'm sure I can find it." She glanced at Badger again, then returned to her rummaging. "And your hair is terrific. Don't you shock yourself when you wash it, though?" She didn't seem to expect an answer. "L, L, L, *M*! Right. M-A . . . M-E . . . hmmm. M-U . . . M-Y . . . And here it is. *Mystic Dove*." She pulled several cards out of her file and looked at them. "Cargo of agricultural bioenhancers. Nanoinjections for local crops . . . genetic diversifiers for herds that have become too dependent on a limited number of bloodlines . . ." She looked up and said, "Nothing really interesting there. Is there anything else you needed to know?"

"Dates the *Dove* was here?"

She told me. The *Dove* had fit the parameters of my data search on Galatia Fairing because it had been to Up Yours within the time frame I'd specified, but it had also been there a month before the *Corrigan's Blood* was stolen. So it wasn't the ship we were looking for.

Badger and I could have left right then. We knew what we needed to know. But the *Dove* had taken pains to hide its route, and it was a light luxury cruiser with a listed cargo of agricultural supplies usually sold in bulk—and that bothered me. So instead of leaving I said, "Would you mind giving me the names of the captain and main crew . . . and the brands of the bioproducts they were selling if you have that information available."

"I can give you crew names. Those are a matter of record. Captain Janna Bell; crew is Kite Harrigan, Ti Demont, Paley Kotak." She wrote the names down and handed the slip to Badger. I didn't recognize any of them when she said them, but I would have been considerably more surprised if I had. When she finished, she said, "The brand names of the *Dove*'s bioproducts cargo you'd have to get from people who bought from them."

"Do you have any record of who those people might be? Or any idea how I could find them?"

"I could call a friend of mine from the Farm Bureau.

He'll know who farms. He might even know who bought from your people. Let me just phone him."

She made the call. "Kenjon Deel, please." She waited for a moment. "Ken. Hello. This is Lucy Zabada. . . . Oh, fine . . . no, she hasn't shown up yet . . . I hope so, too. Look, I have a favor to ask you. I have some folks over here who need to speak to you about the *Mystic Dove*. . . . Mmm-hmmmm. Business. They need to know something about the cargo. . . . The bio-stuff. . . . No. No. I don't think so. Seems pretty low-key." She laughed. "Yes, you can. So you can see them in an hour? Thanks, Ken. I owe you."

She hung up and beamed at both of us. "You're all set. Kenjon Deel, who is the head of the Farm Bureau, will see you in an hour." She wrote down the address for us on another sheet of paper, and handed that to Badger, too.

He glanced at the paper, then frowned. "What's this?" he asked, pointing to a number written along the bottom of the sheet of paper.

Lucy blushed. "My phone number," she told him. She met his eyes and her expression became intent. "I'd love to take you around and show you Freeport this evening. Call me if you get the time."

I was waiting for Badger to say, "I'm sorry, we're going to be working," but that isn't what he said. His eyes went round and his breath got faster and he began to nod. "Yes," he said. "Yes. I'll call you. I'd love to see Freeport with you."

He'd accepted? A date with *her*? I wanted to break his kneecaps. I contented myself with elbowing him hard in the ribs, which he didn't seem to notice. "We have a lot of work to do if you're going to keep your date," I said, and damned if Lucy didn't grin at me like she'd just gotten one over on me. There are, of course, women in the universe whose sole interest in men stems from getting one up on the women those men are with. I hadn't picked Lucy out as one of those. I decided I wasn't as perceptive as I needed to be.

Badger finally came to his senses and I dragged him out the door.

We flagged down a steam taxi and asked the driver to take us to the Farm Bureau. The midday traffic in the narrow streets was nose-to-tail, moving at a ridiculous crawling pace; it made me long for worlds where all transportation was public and regulated. The idea of unlimited numbers of private vehicles driven by people who weren't professionals bothered me almost as much as the idea of ships in the seas. But I couldn't allow myself to be bothered by traffic.

"Have you lost your mind?"

"What?" Badger said.

"Accepting a date with Lucy."

"What? I wasn't going to, but then . . ."

"But then your flagpole raised the flag and the rest of you stood at attention because your poor old brain couldn't think, right? God, Badg . . . we were going to work tonight."

"We found out what we needed to know. You're doing something unrelated to our investigation now."

"Maybe. But I think the *Mystic Dove's* behavior needs to be looked into. It isn't precisely our case, but it's a ship that is acting the way the ship we're trying to find would act. I just don't want to come here and not follow up on the things we're finding, and end up missing something we needed to know because we weren't thorough. You can never have too much information."

"I know all of that!" He snapped at me, then turned and looked out the window. "I knew all of that when I said I'd go out with her."

"Then why did you say it? It isn't like she's the woman of your dreams."

"I don't know why I agreed to go with her," he said. "I really don't. I can't even say it seemed like the right thing to do at the time; I knew I wanted to say no, but I said yes. She's pretty, but I can't remember the last time I heard someone talk so much."

"Fine. So you can cancel then."

And Badger turned on me, his face twisted with a fury I'd never seen in him before. "No!"

I sat for a moment staring at him, unable to think of a thing to say. "Are you feeling well?" I finally asked.

The fury drained from his face, replaced by an expression of bewilderment. "I don't think so. No. I'm not. Something's wrong with me."

I nodded, feeling like I was treading on land mines. "Do you want me to help you?"

He nodded.

"Do you want to go with Lucy tonight?"

Badger did the strangest thing. He shook his head, a vehement no, but he said, "Yes."

I started to get scared. I didn't know why. The whole incident seemed trivial. A man accepts a date with a woman; nothing to it. But my gut insisted that whatever was going on with Badger, it was something bad.

"I'm going to figure out a way to help you," I whispered.

He nodded, but didn't say anything.

The taxi driver was sliding his vehicle up against the curb. "Farm Bureau," he said.

"Thanks." I paid him, and the driver looked at me for a moment, worry evident in his eyes. "Watch your friend," he said. "What he's doing . . . he looks sick to me."

"Me, too."

The Farm Bureau was an ugly building on a street of ugly buildings. It was squat and square and built entirely of yellow brick. A few tall, narrow windows punctuated the otherwise smooth surface, their black glass sheets reflecting warped images of the two of us back at us.

I could see Badger staring at his reflection, while I trailed a few steps behind with one hand on the metal rail.

Five steps from the top, Badger stopped watching himself. He stopped on the stair and rested a hand on my shoulder, so that I stopped, too. "She's out to get me the way the way Fedara Contei was out to get you."

My hand tightened on the cold metal handrail. The statement hit hard as a gut punch, and my breath slammed out of me even as my stomach flipped with sudden nausea. We hadn't been careful enough, perhaps because I felt that when we eluded Fedara Contei, we eluded our problems and the "third party." I'd forgotten that we would be recognizable to anyone who wanted to find us on this world of plain-faced, plain-skinned people.

I thought of the pieces of paper Lucy had handed to him. What if one of those two slips of paper was merely the vehicle for the same contact drug that had changed me into Fedara's slave?

Had Lucy touched him? I couldn't recall a touch. That didn't mean it hadn't happened.

"I'm fine for this, anyway." He looked at me, a frown creasing his forehead. "We'll go back to the hotel when we're done. And then I'll . . . I'll figure out what I'm going to do."

We went into the Farm Bureau building and asked to speak to Kenjon Deel. The young man who took our message came back out and told he'd be with us in a moment.

Kenjon Deel turned out to be about my height but twice my weight, with all of it carried in dense muscle. He looked like a heavyworlder or a bodysculptor; he had a hard, mean face and cold eyes. "You're late," he said, and his tone of voice was neither welcoming nor polite.

I felt Badger stiffen beside me. I smiled, though, and held out my hand. "The traffic was terrible. I'm Cadence Drake." Deel didn't take my hand, and after an instant I let it drop.

Badger nodded. "Strebban Bede." He didn't offer his hand.

Deel said, "Tell me what you want." The rest of what he was thinking seemed to be, "then get out of my office." He didn't say it in words, but I swear I could almost hear him think it.

"We're looking for the brand names and lot numbers of some agri-bio products some of your farmers might have bought from a ship called the *Mystic Dove*." I added the request for lot numbers because a convenient and basically uncheckable lie was forming in the back of my mind.

"Why do you want the information?"

"The nanovirus designer who supplies agricultural nanoviruses for a number of agri-bio producers has reported a programming error in some of its products," I said. "These products received wide distribution but affect only a narrow band of any producer's supply. The designer, who wishes to remain anonymous, has sent out product warnings to its customers, but in order to limit its own liability, the company has also hired investigators to track down those shipments." I smiled.

Deel thought about that for a moment. "Oh," he said. "The *Mystic Dove* took on cargo at about the right time to have received contaminated shipments. However, we have been unable to reach that ship, which apparently has a new form of origami drive and which has proven nearly impossible to track. While we would prefer to deal directly with the traders, in this case we have contented ourselves with trying to locate the cargo before it can do any damage."

"And that's why you came here?"

"Yes."

Something went out of Deel's face—the edge of suspicion or hatred I had seen there, perhaps, or the fear of outsiders who might come in to make him look bad. I didn't know what, precisely, but he had changed his opinion of us. Now he was on our side.

"We maintain records on cargoes brought in from offworld for just this reason," he said. "If you'll wait a moment, I'll gather the records."

He was back fast, carrying a tan folder full of loose pages. "Our dealings with the *Mystic Dove*," he said, and started spreading out sheets on his desk. "These are the ones from its most recent visit." I glanced down the first cargo sheet. Purchase description, amount, lot number, identity of local buyer, and down at the bottom of the sheet, origin of the product and name of the producer.

Cassamir Station. Cassamir Biologicals.

I flipped through the next page, and the next, and the next.

Cassamir Biologicals.

Every single sheet listed the same origin, the same producer.

When I finished looking through the purchase records, I smiled and handed Deel his papers. "Well, this visit was a waste of our time," I told him, "but of course that's good news for you."

"Our purchases are safe?"

"Cassamir Biologicals isn't on our list," I said. "They didn't receive any of the contaminated nanovirus." I held out my hand again and this time Deel took it and shook it. We exchanged smiles. Badger shook his hand, too.

"Thank you for your time," I said.

And Deel spread his arms expansively. "Thank *you*. If there had been anything wrong with our purchases . . . well, out here, we would be the last people to know."

Badger and I left the office quickly after that. I had the feeling that Kenjon Deel had been hoping we would stay and chat, but something about him made my skin crawl.

Badger said, "Quite a coincidence, isn't it?"

"That the ship and the cargo are from the same place? That someone would use what is supposed to be an executive pleasure cruiser as a transport for agricultural goods? That most freelance traders carry a range of goods from different suppliers but this one had products from only one company?" I wrinkled my nose. "Or was there another coincidence that occurred to you?"

"That pretty well covers it."

I looked around for a taxi. The fresh air was making me nervous. I hate weather; I hate equally the feel of sun on the back of my neck and the feel of rain on my skin. I don't like the brush of the breeze, whether it is warm or cold. I don't like open sky above me or spreading vistas in front of me. Up Yours was full of weather, and vistas, and wild animals that ran down the streets and flew overhead. I was not used to animals, and they frightened me. I watched birds lighting on the Farm Bureau roof and taking off and I reminded myself that people had lived with such conditions for as long as there had been people. Reason didn't help. I was a creature of closed-in spaces, and I didn't want to change.

I finally saw a taxi and waved it down. When we were seated and the taxi was on its way back to the hotel, I said, "It strikes me as strange that this ship's registration doesn't check out, and that the *Mystic Dove* is going to a great deal of trouble to hide its trail, and that its cargo is something as mundane as agricultural products."

"Doesn't make sense."

"No. It doesn't."

"They're selling something else," Badger said after a long pause.

"I know. Something illegal."

"There isn't anything illegal on Up Yours."

"Then they're selling something that's worse than illegal. Something that's dangerous, or subversive, or . . ." I ran out of ideas.

"Something that isn't our problem," Badger said. "Our problem is the *Corrigan's Blood*, which hasn't been here. We found out that the *Mystic Dove* is up to something that doesn't make sense, but we don't have any reason to look into it any further. So just let it drop."

The traffic back to the hotel wasn't as bad as it had been. Late afternoon sunlight slanted off the low roofs and turned every wooden wall to gold. I admired the trees; unlike animals, trees never chase anyone, and they don't bite. And the scattered trees that adorned yards were tall and stately and verdant; sun-splashed, they looked like medieval monks had been at them with endless sheets of gold leaf.

Mike was in the lobby. "How did it go?" he asked us, smiling.

I wasn't sure how to answer. "Well . . . we found out that we wasted our time coming here." I shrugged and tried to look nonchalant, and at the same time studied him to see signs that he'd set us up. "The *Mystic Dove* wasn't the ship we were looking for."

"I'm sorry to hear that." I didn't see any sign of interest in his eyes.

"I'm starving," Badger said. "Are there any good, inexpensive restaurants nearby?"

"I thought we were going to get room service," I said, stepping on the arch of his foot and digging an elbow into his side again.

"The hotel's restaurant is good," Mike said. "If you want to eat in your rooms, I'm sure you'll be satisfied with the food. There are places outside that I can recommend if you'd like to try them, but there aren't any that are as good and as cheap."

"Room service sounds good." Badger pulled away from me and rubbed the arch of the foot I'd stepped on along the back of his other leg.

"I'm sure you'll enjoy it. Call down when you're ready to order. You'll find menus in the nightstands."

We went to my room and ordered an inordinate amount of real food that turned out to be better than the food at Ferlingetta. I decided I was going to hate going back to reconsta.

We sat at the table in my room and stuffed food in our faces, and I began to hope that the problem with Lucy had passed. But as the sun set behind the buildings to the east of our building, he pulled the paper she'd given him out of his pocket and began fingering it.

In the next room, the phone began to ring. Neither of us moved to get it. Badger played with the paper; I watched him.

"What are you doing?"

"I ought to call her," Badger said. He wouldn't meet my eyes.

"We're going to work. We can at least com in the names of the captain and crew to the *Reward* so that the shipcom can initiate a search on them."

"I ought to call her."

"You're going to tell her you can't make it tonight?"

He got a stubborn expression on his face and stared down at his hands.

"You're going to call off your date," I said again when he didn't answer me.

And he said, "I have to go." His eyes were haunted.

I'd spent some time thinking about what I was going to do if he insisted on going. I slid my hand over my stunner, strapped to my waist, and drew it on him. "You don't want to go."

The phone in Badger's room had stopped ringing, but it started again.

His head was shaking, no, no, no, but he was still standing. "I'm going." He drew his own stunner.

I shot him and he dropped to the floor, unconscious.

"Damn it." I stared at him, lying sprawled on the carpeted floor, eyes only partly closed so that I could see a line of white between the parted eyelids. I kept my stunner pointed at him and reached out with a toe to kick his stunner out of his reach. When it was directly beneath me, I squatted and retrieved it, never taking my eyes off of him.

Then I sat on the bed and tried to figure out what I ought to do next.

The phone beside me rang. I picked it up and figured out which end was for listening and which for speaking. "Yes?"

"This is Lucy Zabada. I'm trying to reach Strebban Bede. I called his room but he wasn't there, so I asked Mike to ring your room." She sounded so friendly, and so perky.

Dissemble, I thought. Dissemble. If she doesn't suspect that you're on to her, she won't be able to do anything to hurt Badger or you. And you can get out of here and back to the ship alive. I smiled and said, "He's going to be so sorry he missed your call. He was getting ready to go out, and realized he didn't have a few things he needed. He just left to look for a store. He'll be back soon; I'm sure he'll call you as soon as he gets back."

"He went out?" She sounded disbelieving.

"Yes?"

"You're certain?"

"Yes."

She was silent for a long, uncomfortable moment. "He shouldn't have been . . ." She cut off whatever she'd intended to say. She was silent again. "That's not pos—" Another, briefer silence. "I'll drive over," she said, and I could feel resolution in her voice. "I'll be there in half an hour. Less, if traffic goes my way."

Chapter Ten

He was lying on the floor, unconscious; I'd hit him hard, with the stunner set all the way on full, so he wasn't likely to come around any time soon. When he did move on his own, he was going to feel like hell.

Lucy Zabada was on her way to our hotel. She'd called both of our rooms; I couldn't assume that Mike had put her through to them without telling her which rooms they were, or, if he had kept that information to himself, that he would continue to do so once she arrived. Even though we would have had to find her eventually in order to get our return passes validated, he was the one who had recommended we speak to her about the *Mystic Dove*. Maybe he had ulterior motives for doing so.

So I couldn't go to him for help.

I couldn't hide in my room and wait for morning.

Unless I wanted to chance a fight with Lucy that would be on her home ground, with the rules leaning in favor of her because she was a local, and because she knew what the rules were, while I had no idea, I couldn't just stay put and face her down.

I had to run, taking Badger with me when I did. I had to figure out some way to keep our exit from looking suspicious. And I had to come up with something fast.

I re-stunned Badger and opened the connecting door

between our rooms. I grabbed his bag, which was not yet unpacked, then my own. Then I called down to the front desk.

A woman answered.

I said, "Is Mike there?"

"He left about an hour ago," she told me. "He works the day shift."

And I thought, Yes! One lucky break. "Could you please send a grav pad up to my room?"

"We don't have grav pads. However, if you'll tell me what you need, I'm sure I can find something that will work."

"I need to take my friend to a hospital. He acquired chronic gastrocomestosomnia on Brighton Five and he ate something at supper tonight that aggravated the condition."

"Acquired chronic gastro— Is he contagious?"

"No."

"Does he need medical attention immediately?"

"Yes."

"What did he eat? Do you know?"

"Something from the kitchen here."

"Oh, God! I'll call an ambulance for you."

"No. A taxi will be faster, and they won't be able to do anything for him in an ambulance that I can't do in the back seat of a taxi."

"All right, then. I'll bring a wheelchair up myself. You're in room 318?"

"Yes."

"I'll be right there."

She made excellent time, and the two of us dragged Badger into the wheelchair, a rickety-looking contraption that had none of the safety features of a grav pad. "Are you sure he'll survive the trip in a taxi?" she asked. She was young and nervous; I guessed she didn't have much experience with either hotels or emergencies.

"I'm sure. The disease is serious and he needs to have someone look at him as soon as we can get him to a hospital, but he won't stop breathing on the way."

"And it was something he ate from our kitchen?"

"That isn't the main issue right now. There are certain types of foods that set his disease off, and he avoids those foods, but evidently one was used as an ingredient in something else. It probably won't be a problem for your hotel." I didn't try to reassure her—she would ask fewer questions and remember fewer details about us and what we did if she were frightened.

"Oh, God," she said again.

The elevator ride and the trip through the lobby, with her carrying my bag and me carrying Badger's bag and pushing the wheelchair, was a nightmare. I kept expecting Lucy to pop up, take one look at Badger unconscious in the chair, and do something terrible.

And what did I think Lucy Zabada was going to do? Standing there hanging on to Badger in the wheelchair—Badger who was unconscious because I stunned him, no less—I found myself trying to see Lucy Zabada as a threat. She was six inches shorter than me, eight years younger, thirty pounds lighter. And the thirty pounds I had on her was all in muscle. What *was* she going to do? Attack us in the lobby? Pick Badger up and drag him away from me? Talk us to death?

As the hotel manager ran out to flag down a taxi, I almost convinced myself that I was being an idiot.

But if Lucy Zabada wasn't convincingly sinister as the villain of our drama, the events of the past few days made it impossible for me to ignore her as a threat. Badger had mentioned a possible connection between what Fedara Contei had tried to do to me and his reaction to Lucy, yet he had pulled his stunner on me because I tried to get him not to go out with her. Granted, I'd drawn first, but only because he was doing something I knew he didn't want to do, and he didn't seem able to stop himself.

And maybe there was no connection between Lucy Zabada and the woman, Fedara Contei, who had been hired to drug me, insert herself into my life, and then kill me. It didn't matter. If there wasn't any connection, I was willing to err on the side of caution.

The night manager waved to me; she'd caught the attention of a taxi driver.

She, the taxi driver, and I all lifted Badger into the back seat. I grabbed my bags and crawled in beside him.

"Saints Hospital is closest," the manager said.

The driver glanced at me. He was the same driver who had taken us from Lucy's office to the Farm Bureau.

I gave him a noncommittal nod.

He pulled out. "You don't look like you want to go to Saints," he said when we were moving.

"Spaceport," I said. "The manager was trying to be helpful, but you're right. I need to get him to our ship. We have what he needs to make him better onboard."

"Uh-huh," the driver said. "Doesn't look like much wrong with him to me, but whatever you say."

I wasn't in the mood to talk. I was trying to watch behind us without being too obvious. I hoped there would be a shuttle leaving soon; I hoped it would have seats; I hoped I would be able to get Badger into the MEDix and get whatever Lucy had done to him out of his system. Mostly I hoped I was overreacting and being an idiot and making a fool out of myself over something that was nothing.

The driver helped me carry Badger into the lobby of the spaceport and put him on a seat. "You look like someone in trouble to me," he said.

"Yes. Well." I started rummaging through my bag for cash. "I'm probably not. Everything is probably fine, and I'm being completely paranoid and ridiculous."

"Maybe not. There's been some trouble around here lately, and a lot of it has come to offworlders," he added. "Lot of offworlders found dead. A few accidents, some ugly murders, people going where they had no business being and ending up corpses because of it."

Ice crystallized in my gut. Those weren't the words I'd been longing to hear. I looked at him. I waited.

He shrugged. "I have reasons to look into this. I've uncovered some interesting facts."

"What kind of facts?"

"Twelve offworlders who registered at your hotel in the last ten months didn't survive to go home. None of them died at the hotel, and no one at the hotel appears to have been involved in any way. Causes of death have been various and frequently ruled accidental. A maid ended up cleaning the rooms of three of the people who died, three months in a row, and had to deal with offworlders each of the three times. It struck her as being strange. If she hadn't come to the police with it, I don't know that anyone would have suspected a problem. The police didn't link the hotel . . . The signs always pointed in other directions. We don't get very many offworlders here and they don't attract much notice . . . but to lose twelve of them is unheard of."

"Just my hotel?"

"No. One other, as well."

"So why is a taxi driver looking into something like this?"

He smiled and arched an eyebrow. "I'm not a taxi driver." He flashed some sort of ID badge at me. "Stephen deGuerres. Plainclothes officer, Freeport city police." He put his badge away. "I've been driving a taxi and hanging around the hotel, hoping to get lucky. Something tells me I just did. So. Get your tickets. The next shuttle won't leave for forty minutes or so. In the meantime, I'll stay with you. You can tell me what you're running from, and I can make sure whatever it is, it won't be a problem." He patted the weapon at his hip.

So I got the tickets. I watched him, I watched Badger, I watched the door. The man who sold me the tickets asked, "What's wrong with your friend?"

"Sleeping off too much fun," I said.

"Oh. Well, you seem awfully nervous."

"I had to take care of him while he was *having* too much fun. I'm tired and in a bad mood." My voice was sharp and cold. I was sick of people looking at me and seeing inside. Where was the Cadence Drake who never showed emotion, never lost her composure, never gave in to nerves? Wherever she was, I wanted her back.

I rejoined deGuerres.

"Any problem?"

"He was nosy. That seems to be my biggest problem today. Everyone is so damned nosy."

"I'm not going to break your streak. Who did you see while you were here?"

I told him. He took handwritten notes on paper. I thought the process looked slow and impractical, but I also know that some of the things I do aren't entirely efficient. And I found a certain pleasure in watching the even flow of bold black lines from his pen.

When I finished, he repeated the names back to me. "Mike, last name unknown, the assistant day manager of the Espulin Hotel. Lucy Zabada, the assistant director and, because of bizarre circumstances, director *pro tem* of the Freeport Department of Spaceship Registry. We found her manager's body yesterday, incidentally. A particularly brutal murder that someone went to a great deal of trouble to hide. We're investigating that now, but haven't made our discovery public yet. Kenjon Deel, the Offworld Acquisitions manager for the Farm Bureau. Anyone else you can think of?"

I shook my head.

"How did you choose the Espulin Hotel?"

"The man in Customs recommended it and one other when we asked him what was cheap and clean. It was the one within walking distance."

"Customs man," he said, writing that down. "We shouldn't have any trouble finding him. Any chance you remember the name of the other hotel?"

I thought hard, but came up empty. "No."

"Could it have been the Daydreamer Inn?"

It had been. I nodded.

DeGuerres pursed his lips. "That's the other one where we've been losing people. And you say every single one of these people passed you on to the next?"

"I didn't think of it that way at the time. They all seemed very helpful. But . . ." I nodded again, then told him about Lucy and the phone number, and Badger's response, and everything else I could think of, right up to the phone call from Lucy and the fact that she had been on her way to the hotel. I left out only my reason for being in Freeport.

When I was finished, deGuerres smiled slightly and shook his head. "Shot him to keep him from going."

"I just stunned him."

"Still a ballsy thing to do. Effective, too."

"But it leaves me without my backup, and with a hundred-plus kilos of dead weight to haul around. And I don't imagine Lucy is going to be fooled by the hospital story for very long."

"I don't suppose she'll be fooled for a minute. The question is, what is she going to do when she figures out you're on to her and you ran. As for your friend being backup, if he couldn't keep himself from running to her, he would be worse than dead weight. He'd be a liability."

DeGuerres looked at his chrono and said, "If she's fast and smart and lucky, she could be here at any time. You have another fifteen minutes before your shuttle boards." He frowned. "Let's get both of you out of sight."

I nodded.

DeGuerres commandeered another of those rickety wheelchairs and we strapped Badger into it. Then he led me out of the lobby, down a short corridor, and into a small, roped-off waiting room. "This is reserved for VIPs and private flights. We qualify as VIPs because I say so." He grinned at me.

Nerves and all, I managed to grin back.

I put Badger's and my bags down and dug through them. From mine, I pulled out a detachable watersilk hood. It was navy blue, and if I tucked the ends of my hair inside the back of my jumpsuit, pulled up the collar, and attached the hood, my hair would be impossible to see. Then I wouldn't be a dark-skinned, golden-haired woman, of which there seemed to be none in Freeport. I would simply be a dark-skinned woman, and there were plenty of those.

I found Badger's hood in his bag, attached it, and pulled it down so that it covered most of his face. I leaned him slightly forward so that no one would be able to see that he was vivid green, put his bag in his lap and tucked his hands beneath it, and hoped that the little wheelchair belt wouldn't break.

DeGuerres gave me an approving smile. "Good idea. You aren't so obviously offworlders now." He pulled out his weapon, opened the cylinder, checked to be sure it was full of projectiles, then snapped the cylinder shut again and slipped it into his holster. "This is merely precautionary. If the girl is smart, she won't come here after you . . . but I like to know I'm ready. What kind of armament are you carrying?"

I showed him Badger's and my stunners.

"Just stunners? Shit." He gave me a disgusted look. "I'm going to give you a little advice you didn't ask for and that you probably don't want. But one of these days it might save your life. People have shields for stunners. They have little turnarounds that will bounce the shock back on you—and if your own stunner takes you out, you're going to be in a hell of a fix. Get a real weapon." He tapped his own pistol. "Get something that will kill; something that will blow a hole in the person who is coming at you."

I made a face, and he sighed.

"You don't want to kill anybody, and that's fine. Nobody who is any sort of a human being does. But you don't want to die, either. So you get a deadly weapon, and you learn how to use it. And then you follow these three rules. One: never go for your weapon unless you or people around you are in deadly danger. Two: never draw except to shoot. Three: never shoot except to kill. Don't yell, 'Stop or I'll shoot.' Don't try to wound your attacker."

I rested my hand on top of his and said, "I appreciate your concern. But I've been in a dangerous line of work for close to seven years now, and I've never had to kill anyone, even though people have tried to kill me. That's important to me . . . that I can do what I do without taking human life."

"Then you've been lucky. And if you don't face reality, one of these days your luck is going to run out." He glanced down the corridor. It was clear. He looked back at me and said, "There's no sense in my giving you one of my weapons right now. Even if you were willing to use it, you haven't had any practice with it, and you couldn't shoot it with any accuracy. Keep your stunners ready. If we're lucky, you won't have to use them. And when you get home, get yourself something real."

I nodded. I was sure he believed what he was telling me, and was convinced that he was doing me a favor. I appreciated his concern. That didn't make him right.

"Shuttle Flight Eight is now boarding. Ticket holders, please report to the main gate. Shuttle Flight Eight is now boarding. Ticket holders, report with your boarding passes to the main gate."

The fifteen minutes had passed quickly. I smiled at deGuerres and shrugged. "So that's that. Either the terminal was too public, or she was never after us to begin with. This could all have been a lot of nerves and a lot of worry for nothing."

He smiled. "I didn't mind waiting with you—in fact, I enjoyed it. And maybe something good will come of it. Until you, the only leads I had were corpses. If any of the names you gave me are related to the murders, we're going to be way ahead in our investigation."

I slung Badger's and my bags over my shoulder again and started pushing the wheelchair down the corridor. DeGuerres walked beside me. "Thanks for helping us out," I said. "Not being alone made waiting here a lot easier."

"It's a shame you aren't staying . . . I've been hoping to meet a woman like you for a long time." He looked down at Badger and chuckled again. I liked the sound. "Stunned him for his own good. Ballsy."

We stepped out of the corridor into the main lobby. To my right, about forty people stood over by the main gate, forming a ragged queue. Flight assistants checked boarding passes. People chattered.

In the center of the lobby, families said good-bye. Hugged. Cried.

To my left, a few people walked toward the broad doors that led outside. I glanced at them, then away. Pushed Badger toward the main gate. And inside of me, something clicked.

"That was them," I whispered.

DeGuerres, who had been casually scanning the lobby, didn't flinch or show any external signs of having heard what I'd said. But so quietly that I almost couldn't hear him, he asked, "Where?"

"The door. Lucy, and Mike, and Deel."

"The three of them together? That would seem to indicate a conspiracy." He didn't seem to look anywhere but at the gate in front of us, yet he managed to identify them. "The blue dress, the red jacket, the long black coat?"

"That's all three of them."

"They stopped by the doors. Looking around. Keep a little in front of me; I'll shield you."

We walked at a steady pace. He dropped a step back and rested a hand on my shoulder. Not his gun hand, I realized.

I tried to imagine shooting through this crowd. Families . . . parents and grandparents and children. Lovers. Friends. It would be disaster. Complete horror. I didn't look back, but I discovered I could see the door behind me reflected in the long bank of windows in front of me. The same windows through which I could see the shuttle that was, I hoped, going to get me out of there. Lucy, Mike, and Deel still stood by the door. Watching. Looking from the crowd of people heading toward the gate, to the road up which latecomers would have to drive to reach the terminal.

All three of them. I wondered where the Customs official was, and wondered if he was in on this.

The three of them were in conference. Heads close

together, glancing around the lobby, out the door, around the lobby again. Deel pointed in our direction. Mike and Lucy nodded. Deel leaned against the door. Mike and Lucy split up and started working their way through the lobby, looking at people.

"The three of them are out here because you got close to something," deGuerres said. "They're taking risks; somehow you pose enough of a threat to them that they're willing to be seen together, and willing to come after you in a public place."

"I only asked them about that one ship and what it was carrying."

"I know. I know where to start looking now. I didn't before. But before I can start looking, I need to be sure you're safe." He frowned and slipped behind me a little farther, blocking me from the view of Lucy, who was working her way toward us.

The line moved forward. I shoved the wheelchair forward, bumped the calves of the woman ahead of me. It was just a light bump; I was nervous and not paying close enough attention to the wheelchair. She turned and glared at me and said, "Watch where you're going." No one offered to let me move forward with Badger. No one did anything that might help us.

Lucy was behind and to the right of us. Mike was behind and to the left—still looking the wrong way. The line was ragged, the families stood close, we moved steadily toward the door, they moved steadily toward discovering us.

Closer.

Closer.

DeGuerres shifted, gave my elbow a quick squeeze, and slipped away. I couldn't watch him directly without turning so Mike could get a good look at my face. Nice Mike. Right. So I watched deGuerres's reflection in the glass. He hurried to the main desk, where a bored attendant was busy selling a late ticket to an older woman who appeared to be in a big hurry. He pushed past the woman, flashing his badge. Said something to the attendant.

The line moved forward. Three people stood between me and the corridor to the shuttle.

Lucy disappeared down the side corridor that led to the VIP area where the three of us had waited. Mike kept coming toward us. He studied every face he passed. He was looking for Badger, looking for me. A woman stopped him, thought she knew him, and in the instant before he smiled and shrugged a genial smile I saw something hard and cold and evil in his eyes. For just that instant he was someone I had a reason to fear. I slouched to make myself shorter, tipped my head a little further forward so the hood draped over more of my face, and rested my hand on my stunner.

And I thought, This is the other part of why I carry a stunner. If I have to shoot him, I know no innocent bystander is going to end up dead from a stray bullet or the bounce from nerve disrupter fire.

I watched him in the glass. He was looking directly at the line. Not at me specifically, but at the line, and he wore an intent expression on his face.

"Attention, all visitors. Attention, all visitors." I jumped a little; I had been focusing so hard on getting to the gate that the sudden loud announcement startled me. "Anyone who does not have a boarding pass must leave the lobby immediately. I repeat—anyone who does not have a boarding pass must leave the lobby immediately. All passengers board quickly and quietly. All passengers board quickly and quietly! Clear the lobby. Clear the lobby." I caught sight of the attendant waving at the man who was checking boarding passes. It was a frantic wave, that said, "Get them onboard now!"

Suddenly we were being waved aboard, while behind me I heard the words, ". . . bomb in the building . . ."

And then we were on the shuttle and the shuttle doors were sliding closed behind us even as the shuttle engines whined and the shuttle pulled out and moved away from the terminal as fast as it could go.

The attendants helped me get Badger into his seat. The

moving shuttle threw us around a little, but no one got hurt. And I dropped into my own seat, sweating and relieved and scared all at once. That had been close. Too close, and potentially lethal—and I didn't know what it was about. If deGuerres hadn't come up with the bomb threat story, I might not have made it to the shuttle seat.

I stroked the rough red cloth of the seat and stared out the little window, at the receding terminal, wondering what I had gotten myself into.

Chapter Eleven

I had most of our next course entered into the shipcom when the MEDix released Badger and he returned to the bridge. My first sight of him took me back to the time when I was fifteen and he was nineteen. He'd been a poet then, quiet and withdrawn. He'd had a lot of talent, and I'd loved to listen to the poems he created, and I had loved the fact that we shared a deep understanding of the pain of being different.

He was as much of a freak as me; not a Maryschild, but a genetic misfit just the same. He was an albino—it was something the prenatal gene scans should have picked up but didn't. He wouldn't have been born if the technician had been a more careful, I suppose, and I was grateful for that single small error. Without Badger, my entire life would have been empty.

Standing beside me, his skin was so luminously white the bridge's lights made him seem to glow. His hair was white, too, and coarse. He squinted at me, pink irises raw-looking.

When the two of us were lovers, he left his skin natural. It was a sign of the way things were between us; we didn't have anything to hide. When I almost got him killed and realized that the reason I hadn't been sufficiently careful was because my attention had been on him instead of on the man we were dealing with, I broke off the romantic relationship. He tried to convince me for a long time that the incident hadn't been my fault. I knew it had been; he finally gave up trying to patch things up between us; and the next thing I knew he was Melatinted and Chromaglossed and eye-sheened, and beneath that colorful shell, the quiet, poetical boy I knew and loved was gone.

I liked the new Badger. He was fun and funny and flip. With his Melatinted armor, he could let himself be anyone, and he did. I think his heart became invulnerable.

But I loved the old Badger, and at that moment the old Badger was close enough to touch.

I didn't touch him, though I longed to. Instead I asked, "How did the tests turn out?"

"Clean as the day I was born. Cleaner, probably." He shook his head. "There wasn't a trace of any sort of drug anywhere in my system. I went over the MEDix readouts and checked for anything anomalous. I brought printouts for you to look at—sometimes I see things in hardcopy that I miss on a screen. But I haven't missed anything."

"Then what happened? What did she do to you?"

He shook his head. "I don't know. I still feel it a little—the compulsion to call her."

"We can quit this. We'll get another job, find another way to pay off the *Reward*."

"No we won't. We're going to keep this job. We are simply going to look for what we're supposed to be looking for from now on. No more peripheral investigations, no matter how interesting they might be." He leaned over my chair and rested his cheek against mine. It was the pose of lovers, not friends—but I didn't pull away from him. I still loved him, and no amount of rationality could change that. I loved him; I just couldn't let myself have him.

I said, "You're right, I guess. It wasn't looking for the *Corrigan's Blood* that got us into trouble that time."

He gave me a little squeeze. "Exactly. Cadence?" His

breath was warm on the side of my neck, and he smelled faintly of Field and Forest, which was the scent he kept in his MEDix.

"What?"

"Thanks for stopping me. I think you saved my life."

I leaned against him and sighed. "I'm glad you aren't angry with me."

I finished programming our course, and sent it to the station. When I got the go-ahead, I put the ship on auto with a ten-minute warning before the origami crossing.

"We're heading for Smithbright's World next," I told him. "If you'll take us through the point this time, I'll head down to my quarters. I haven't had any sleep since we left the ship."

He kissed the top of my head. "Get some rest. I'll come down and check on you when we're through."

"Fine. Keep an eye on that spy-patch on the hull, too, would you? I wish we could get somewhere to have it removed." I wanted to know if the device sent any more messages.

Badger muttered to the shipcom and a holo of the device began spinning above the shipcom display. "Done."

I heard the warning over the com as I was settling into my bunk—the countdown to the origami point. I braced myself, futile as that always is . . .

And then I was infinite. I touched all of time and space, and my problems and fears became nothing. Eternal and godlike, I was beyond the reach of my fleshself's pain. I saw my pasts and futures, my frail and feeble strugglings in myriad lives, and I, as my greater Self, was both sympathetic and slightly amused—to watch my hungry, desperate mortal selves strive so hard and achieve so little.

And the me who was Cadence Drake fought to swim in the powerful current of immortality, to keep my head up and to keep free of the seductive undertow of absorption into the Self. It was so beautiful to know that I would go on forever, and so terrible to know that the part of me that fought through the pain of existence as Cadence Drake would never be only Cadence Drake beyond the few brief, flickering instants that my fragile fleshself survived. I would be absorbed into the greater whole and would cease to exist.

While those truths seared and scarred me, the *Reward* broke through the origami point back into "real" space.

Badger came down from the bridge after a while and found me calm and in control of myself. He, too, had gotten rid of the residue of his fall from immortality. We greeted each other calmly. "I put her on auto," he said. "The bug didn't do anything this time. Maybe it was only designed for the one use, though I think we should still have it removed the next chance we get. And when I wormed the Spybees, one of them said a Stardancer called the *FireEater* had been here. Exactly the right time frame to be our ship."

I said, "Good. So we haven't wasted this trip."

"The *FireEater* may not be our ship, but it's one we have to check. Before we get to Smithbright's World, would you mind helping me do my tint? The last time I had to do it myself, it turned out hideous."

I remembered that time—after an emergency trip to the MEDix, Badger decided to do himself over in Wingun's Black Cherry Pearl. He came out looking like a cherry with a bad disease. I said, "I'll help."

Home Melatinting always turned out splotchy, but I did a better job of it than he did. I could reach all those hard-to-get-at places. He needed to have his eyes redone, but that wasn't something either of us could do. He was going to have to wear light-shield lenses for a while; they would protect his eyes, but they weren't a comfortable alternative to sheening.

In the rec room, he pulled his supplies out of one of the lockers, and started digging through tints. "Shimmer blue?" He held up one mela-inject unit for my inspection. "Or a high-refraction metallic gold?"

"Brown."

"Brown? But that's so . . . ordinary."

"Smithbright's World is a little more backward than Up Yours," I told him. "From what I've read, the culture is completely different. I scanned info from the shipcom, figuring that we were probably going to have to go to the surface. The world was founded by political and religious Luddites who followed a woman named Teresa Smithbright. She believed in the union of church and state and the elimination of personal freedom for the good of the masses. She was also, from the little I could find about her, a big believer in sin, and evil, and serious punishment for sinners." I thought about the articles I'd read—from her history, I had to believe that the woman had been a dangerous lunatic.

Before the bans on outside reporting, she'd ordered members of her society executed for a list of "crimes" that ranged from adultery to cheating on income taxes to practicing sorcery to being vampires to not having enough children. She had apparently gotten more paranoid and psychotic with every passing year, and just before Smithbright's World ejected all United Worlds observers and shut down communication with the rest of the universe, her own people had marched her out to the square she'd used for public executions, and had burned her at the stake. I didn't think Smithbright's World was the place where we wanted to look like outsiders.

"I hate looking drab," he said.

So I told him the details of what I'd read.

"I'll be drab. Maybe things have gotten better since they cooked Mother Smithbright, but why take chances?"

"My thoughts exactly."

"You don't look like a natural woman . . . So . . . you going to lighten up so your skin matches your eyes and hair, or are you going to do the eyes and hair to match the skin?"

"Eyes and hair. I don't want to get into anything complicated."

"Makes sense. Do me in . . . oh, CalaSkin's Nonreflecting Medium Almond Number 3, I suppose. That's about as boring as color gets. Hair in Kasai's Blended Dark Brown. What about my eyes?"

"Wear the hazel lenses. They won't stand out."

He sighed. "Promise me that when we finish this job, we'll go to the best bodyartist in the universe. I want something spectacular to make up for this."

I laughed. "I swear on my heart and soul. The very best. Who *is* the best, by the way?"

"Claudia Caldwell. Old Earth. She just won the IGABA's top award, the Derma. She's expensive, but worth every rucet."

"IGABA?"

"Inter-Galactic Association of Body Artists."

Badger would know a thing like that.

"I've been wanting to see Old Earth anyway," I told him.

I got to work; the process was long and complex enough that we were almost to our destination by the time I finished. Badger looked . . . well. If you knew what you were looking for, you could tell that he'd had a Melatint applied by an amateur. If you didn't know about Melatinting; if, for example, you lived in a culture that didn't go in for body art, Badger simply looked like a man with slightly blotchy skin. I'd seen a pale woman who'd been exposed to the rays of her planet's sun and who had received second-degree burns from the exposure who had looked much the same . . . although pieces of her skin had been peeling off. That had been disgusting.

Badger looked at himself in the holo, turning his image from front to back and side to side. He made faces but he didn't complain out loud. Since he was done and I wasn't, he handled the incoming requests for ship identity and the docking while I went down to my quarters and changed my hair. I gave myself deep brown eyes and glossy black hair to match my coffee-brown skin. I hated the feel of the lenses in my eyes. Still, I was doing this for the *Hope's Reward*. I kept reminding myself a little discomfort in the present would pay off with incredible freedom in the future.

Then I inserted a new chip in the doppler recorder beneath my fleshtab, packed my kit of weapons-that-didn't-look-like-weapons, because Smithbright's World didn't permit anyone not in the military to own weapons, and had the shipcom cut me a credit chit for a few thousand rucets.

Smithbright's World was still young and thinly settled. It had one country, five major cities, and only one spaceport. Kerrill Station supported that spaceport, but as stations go, it was nothing. It had a place to eat, a place to do paperwork, someone who was willing to take our money and exchange it for the utterly worthless local currency, and a few shops with shoddy goods and dreadful prices. We picked up local clothing that would be appropriate for our trip down to the capital city, Pincada. The fabrics were stiff and uncomfortable, the colors drab and muddy. The shirt I bought, a gray stretchy affair with long sleeves and a flocked inner surface, itched and made me sweat; but the saleswoman assured me that the weather in Pincada was cool and drizzly this time of year, and that I would appreciate the warmth. The pants she sold me were a dreary shade of blue; the material was so thick and unworkable that the makers had clamped bits of metal at the corners of the pockets and seams to hold them together. "Durable," she said of the pants. "They last forever."

I could believe it.

She completed my outfit with a heavy pair of boots made of animal leather and soled with hardened tree gum, and thick socks "to keep you from getting blisters on your feet until you break the boots in." I didn't take her up on her offer to outfit me in local-style underwear. I wasn't intending to become friendly enough with anyone on the surface to make the cut of my panties an issue.

Badger came out of his dressing room wearing clothes that were, if possible, uglier and coarser than mine. "You're sure people dress like this?" he asked. "It isn't a joke to make us look ridiculous when we arrive?" His mediocre skin job looked right with his ugly clothes. He wore what the saleswoman called a "sweat" and a "dungaree," and he looked miserable.

The saleswoman's smile was strained. "These are work clothes. You said you were going to work, and that you wanted to look like everyone else as soon as you arrived." We both nodded. "Then you'll be fine."

We didn't feel fine.

We boarded the shuttle to Pincada. On it I saw four obvious offworlders. Two sales reps from Huddle House Intergalactic, their hair done in matching silverflash and their matching executive uniforms holoprojecting the spinning claws of a spiral nebula overlaid with the HHI logo, whispered to each other and subvocalized into their compacs. They were selling quality dining to the universe but they were obviously representatives of a culture the people on Smithbright's World had willingly left behind; I wondered if they would have any luck.

Two young men in the primitive clothing of their religious sect—stiff white shirts, black pants with sharp creases, and bits of black cloth that dangled around their necks—looked out the shuttle windows, silent. I recognized them as Mormons, one of the sects that had spread as quickly as civilization itself when humankind went into space. Perhaps they would find a home on Smithbright's World.

The rest of the people were dressed much as we were dressed. I was relieved. We blended nicely. These people had the weary faces and tired walks of people returning home from long, hard journeys. One young couple settled into their seats, rested their heads against each other, and were asleep before we left the station. Two men, both big and brawny, tapped the infoscreens built into the seats in front of them, catching up on the events that had happened near their homes while they were away. I caught a few bits about a gory murder linked with a series of similar crimes, the scores of some team sport, and a political advertisement extolling the virtues of one candidate while brandishing the vices of another. The touch-screens were a bit more technologically progressive than I'd expected, but the contents on those screens fit the profile I'd begun to make of Smithbright's World.

These were the sort of people who depended on news. Up Yours had been a hotbed of news, and so was this backwater hole; personally, I thought news was despicable. It was publicly supported gossip, invasion into the lives and sufferings of strangers, and the love of it represented an unconscionable desire to destroy the privacy of people whose lives had been thrown into turmoil. Civilized worlds eliminated or downplayed news, replacing it with various forms of entertainment that didn't prey on the sufferings of the less fortunate.

I turned my attention to the last two passengers on the shuttle, a mother and a whining child who sat at the back. The woman bounced the boy on her knee and sang a song to him in a minor key, soft and plaintive and eerie. The words of the song were no doubt intended to quiet the boy, but in combination with the unsettling melody, they made my skin crawl.

"Hush, now, hush, for night is falling.
All outside is dark and queer,
Hush, child, listen, spirits calling
Beckon those whose words they hear.

"In the dark and in the silence
Come the ghosts who night roads roam,
Whispering, 'Come meet us, meet us,
Follow us, we'll take you home.'

"Hush, boy, hush, for if you're quiet,
Ghosts won't creep out of their tombs.
They don't steal the quiet children
From warm beds and from sweet rooms."

The boy was irritable and tired and that song didn't make any visible impression on him. Maybe he was too young; maybe he'd heard the song before so many times that he'd ceased hearing it at all. But I tried to imagine being a child and going to sleep thinking about ghosts that would come and steal me out of my bed if I made a noise.

God. I hadn't even reached Smithbright's World and already I wanted to leave. Badger, sitting in the seat beside me, gave me a look that said he'd pay to join me.

I wasn't any more impressed when, after a long, rough shuttle ride, I got my first look at Pincada. We had to step out of the shuttle directly into weather. The air smelled of ozone and sulfur and a dozen chemical smells I couldn't recognize, and of wet earth and animal waste and rot. Cold wind and drizzling rain ate through my "sweat" and my "dungaree" and straight into my bones. I wished instantly for even heavier, stiffer, uglier clothes if only they would keep me warm.

All of us walked across the paved landing pad to the Customs terminal, up slick wet metal steps that rang and creaked as we ascended them, and into a large gray-painted room lit poorly by an insufficient number of bare glass balls. Water dripped through the ceiling in the center of the single large room, forming a small, mud-tinged, oil-slicked lake in the center of the floor. There were no chairs in the room. There were four doors, two of them glass: the one we'd come in, and another that led out to a high wire fence topped with rolls of spiked wire. The other two doors were solid, and were on the side of the building that had no windows. On one door was painted the word "Office" in Standard and half a dozen other languages, on the other, "Interrogations."

I had the feeling this was not going to be the same sort of carefree pass-through I'd experienced on Up Yours.

A soldier in a black uniform stood glaring at us from behind a large, dirty table that was the only furniture in the main room. A second soldier, also in a black uniform, though without the decorations or black braid worn by the first, leaned against the wall in a position that let him watch all of us at the same time. He cradled a weapon—some form of energy cannon—in his arms. A line had formed on the opposite side of the table, curving to miss the lake and the dripping ceiling. Badger and I were at the back of the line.

The men who had been unloading the cargo from the shuttle when we'd disembarked now brought it in and dumped it on the floor beside the table. One of the two went into the office, but the other one stayed. He lifted the first bag in the pile onto the table. It was glossy and obviously expensive. I was betting on a Huddle House executive to claim it.

"Thanassa Tang," the decorated soldier said.

The female Huddle House rep stepped forward.

The soldier took her papers and went over them carefully. When he finished, he nodded and handed them back. "In order," he said. Then he opened the bag while she watched, and started spreading things out on the table. He didn't say anything else until he came to a portable holoplayer. He held it up to her. "What is this?"

"A holoplayer," she told him. Her back was to me, but I could hear the smile in her voice when she said it. She was being bright and perky, trying to project the image of Huddle House even in this festering backwater of civilization. "I use it for my presentations."

"Not here you don't," he said. He tossed the holoplayer to the man who'd brought in the baggage. That man turned without a word and started to carry the device toward the office.

"I see," the woman said. She took a breath. When she spoke again, her voice was still perky. "May I have a receipt for that, so that I can pick it up when I leave?"

"You forfeit contraband," he said. "You don't get it back."

My stomach started to twist.

"But," she said, and I wanted to stuff my fist in her mouth to keep her from saying anything else. The soldier against the wall had straightened up when her mouth opened again, and his attention had focused on her. She didn't see it. "You didn't have anything in your literature that said holographic equipment was contraband."

"In our literature? Since when are we required to explain ourselves to the universe? Did we ask you to come here?" the soldier asked softly.

Just say you're sorry and shut up, I thought at the woman. Or don't say you're sorry—but for God's sake, shut up.

"No," she said, oblivious to the tension in the room—oblivious to everything but her determination to make her stupid point, "but it seems that if you permit people to travel to your world, you should tell them—"

I saw the decorated soldier's eyes flick right, to the soldier who waited by the wall. I saw the soldier on the wall nod slightly and begin to step forward.

"—what they are and are not permitted to bring with—" Her voice cut off with shocking suddenness as the second soldier grabbed her by the shoulder, shoved the butt of his cannon into her ribs, and said, "Move."

He marched her toward the interrogation room while the rest of us watched. I saw her colleague shift his weight, and I heard him clear his throat, as if he were getting ready to protest. Behind me I heard the unmistakable click-scrape of a projectile round being cocked into the chamber of a weapon. I turned my head very slowly, and found that another soldier had taken up position behind us, and his weapon, primitive compared to the energy cannon but still lethal, now pointed at us.

The churning in my stomach worsened.

The woman said, "Wait! I'm not going to make an issue out of a piece of equip—" and the soldier slammed his fist into the side of her head. She dropped to the ground, blood trickling from the corner of her mouth, and he grabbed her by the hair and dragged her through the Interrogation door.

In the brief, awful silence that followed, one of the local men who had been reading news from a long sheet of paper turned in line to the other one. "Offworlders," he said, and his voice was full of scorn.

The soldier at the table said to all of us, "When you come to our world, it is your responsibility to know what you can and cannot bring with you. If you carry contraband, I will confiscate it. If you question my legal right to do my job, you will wish you hadn't."

The baggage handler threw all of Thanassa Tang's things back into her bag and carried the bag to the Interrogation room. When he opened the door to toss it in, screams poured out. "—oh, God, please don't! I'll give you anyth—" The door closed again. In the utter silence that followed the closing of the door, my heart could only hear the echoes of her screams.

The baggage handler returned and placed another bag on the table, this one plain and thin and threadbare. "Glory-With-Us Anders," the soldier said.

The woman with the child walked forward, the little boy trailing a few steps behind her. In her movements I saw no fear . . . no empathy for the woman in the interrogation room . . . no distress at the insanity of what the soldiers had done . . . at what they were doing. "Brother," she said, dipping her head.

He nodded. "Welcome home, sister." He said this without any trace of irony, and she accepted it in the same manner. He gave her papers a cursory once-over, then began going through her bag, carefully unpacking the clothing in it and laying each item neatly to one side. When he finished, he replaced things in the same manner. "Is someone waiting for you or will you need to call?"

"Family waiting," she said. The little boy tugged at one leg of her dungaree, and said, "Momma, I gotta pee."

The soldier smiled down at the boy, handed the woman her bag, and said, "Toilet is out the front door and first building to the left."

"Thank you." Mother and son strolled away as if nothing had happened. As if this were the way worlds ought to operate.

Badger's hand slid into mine and I laced my fingers through his and held on tightly. We'd brought nothing with us but a change of clothes each, a few light weapons disguised as personal items, and the compacs that we wore around our wrists that kept us in touch with the *Hope's Reward*. I hoped the sleeves of our "sweats" would keep those hidden, or that they looked enough like the timepieces I saw on the wrists of the local men that they wouldn't occasion any notice.

"Cadence Drake," the soldier said, and I walked forward, feeling my mouth go dry and my heart start to pound in the back of my throat.

He looked at my papers; he took his time with them. Then he looked at me. "Ship's captain?"

I nodded, not saying anything.

"You look sensible." He opened my day-bag and pulled out the toiletries and clothes I'd brought. "You aren't selling cargo?"

I shook my head. "Trying to trace cargo someone else sold."

He raised an eyebrow and waited.

"Agricultural goods. The manufacturer found that one lot was contaminated. The goods got out before they discovered the problem. The manufacturer hired me and a number of others to track down the bad lots."

He nodded. "What do you do when you find them?"

"Pay double to buy them back, offer the manufacturer's apology and an equal lot of replacement goods for free," I said.

He considered that for a minute. "That's more than fair. You do good by my people, so I'll do good by you." He stopped returning toiletries to the bag and my heart rose in my throat. A stunner and a nerve disrupter lay beneath his hand, disguised as a comb and a depilator, and I wondered if he'd discovered my duplicity. He didn't look at the weapons, though. His face grew both concerned and somehow kind, and he said, "You listen, now. This isn't your world. While you're here, keep to yourself. Don't try to be anybody's friend, especially if someone wants to be your friend. Don't go anywhere you don't have to be. And don't go out at night."

I nodded and took my bag, thinking about how this man had sent a woman to be tortured, had smiled at a child, had offered me advice that he seemed to feel would ensure my safety. I felt like Glory-whatever's kid. I had to pee, and if I thought about it too much more, I was going to have to throw up, too. I said, "Thank you," because I was too much of a coward not to, and I stood there and waited while the soldier checked Badger's bag and cleared him.

We walked together out into the stinking, frigid rain; I couldn't stop wondering what had happened to Thanassa Tang.

Chapter Twelve

We were assigned to a rooming house called The Traveler's Ease, which lay close to the spaceport. To say it was misnamed was to say that pathological liars sometimes stretched the truth. My boots stuck to the filthy floor and pulled away with little squelching sounds as I walked up to the desk. Smells of rancid food and wood rot and unwashed bodies and backed-up plumbing and mildew filled the lobby. The walls were covered with patterned paper, but years of layered dirt had obscured the patterns until they had become unidentifiable blotches no more becoming than the water stains that streaked the walls, in some places from ceiling to floor.

The woman who came out from the back room matched her surroundings; she was dirty and slatternly and scrawny and smelled like she didn't know a human body could survive the touch of soap and water without disintegrating. After years of bathlessness, perhaps her body wouldn't have.

There was nothing that would offer ease or comfort in the place, and the only traveling anyone would voluntarily do related to the place would be to travel away. We couldn't have gotten a better room in all of Pincada, though—not because such rooms didn't exist, for they did, but because we didn't have citizen cards, and were therefore eligible only for "Assigned Offworlder Housing." We would have had to sign a Statement of Intent to Settle before we could have gotten a room in someplace dry and clean and sweet-smelling. And in fact when the woman passed us the registration book, she passed us two grimy sets of settlement papers. I looked them over and said, "We aren't intending to stay."

"Your loss," she said, and pulled the papers back.

"I can see that." I watched her from the corner of my eye while I signed the book, but she didn't get it.

As we finished registering, the man from Huddle House walked in. Alone. He'd been crying.

I caught his attention and shrugged my shoulders slightly, tipping the palms of my hands upward. Something about The Traveler's Ease, about Pincada, about Smithbright's World, made me leery of asking a question out loud.

He knew what I wanted to know, though. He gave me the barest shake of his head. "He said they'll release her today," he said as we passed. His eyes said he didn't believe a word of it.

I didn't believe it, either. I'd heard the woman scream. I'd never forget that scream. I didn't know what they had done to her, but whatever it was, it wasn't something she was going to just walk away from in the same afternoon.

Badger's room was at one end of the hall on the second floor. Mine was halfway down the other end. My room matched the lobby in style and decor, and had the same ripe, lived-in smell. Furthermore, I heard sounds emanating from inside the walls that I suspected were biological in origin. The bed was flimsy, the mattress a single lumpy pad on top of bare metal slats. This room had neither bath nor toilet nor phone nor lock for the door.

I was initially glad I'd brought nothing of value with me; then I thought of the value of my life, and wondered if perhaps I should drag my mattress down to Badger's room to sleep on his floor. I wished we had been able to find out about the *FireEater* without ever setting foot on this ugly, miserable world.

Now, no matter how quickly we concluded our business, we would be here for two days. Our return trip paperwork, which we had filled out before we landed, would take that long to clear. I didn't even want to consider what would happen to us if someone decided not to grant the papers clearance. Such an idea had seemed inconceivable until I'd arrived here; but now my ship hung up above the clouds, beyond my reach without the cooperation of the Customs people. And they terrified me.

Badger and I said as little as possible walking back down the stairs to go outside and begin our search for information on the *FireEater*. I suppose I thought we'd talk once we were in private, out in the infernal cold wet stinking weather. However, a sallow, rat-faced man in a black coat stood from one of the chairs in a corner of the lobby and folded whatever he had been reading; he stuffed it into a pocket of his coat as we walked through the lobby and came out after us. He walked some distance behind us, casually, and he made a great deal of show out of not looking in our direction when he thought we might see him. He wasn't very good, though. I've been followed by people who make a good living at it. I have, over the years, become somewhat proficient at the art myself.

I didn't make any sort of sign to Badger. I knew he'd spotted the man, too.

Before we left the *Reward*, Badger had obtained a few names and organizations from the same databases I'd searched so ineffectively; they were places he thought might be able to tell us what the *FireEater*'s official excuse for coming to Smithbright's World had been. Most of those places were in Pincada. A few were in the distant city of Celerity, which was in a different county or state or hamlet. I didn't know how Smithbright's World had divided itself politically and I didn't care to stay around long enough to find out. If we were lucky, a brief stay in Pincada would give us what we needed. We set out for the first destination he'd marked.

Across the street from The Traveler's Ease, two black

cabs sat, drivers hunched in slickers to keep the rain off their backs. Draft beasts stood with bored expressions in their animal eyes. I wondered what sort of beasts they were, and whether they were dangerous.

They were a deep green-gray color, slick-skinned, split-hooved, long-faced. While we approached, one cocked its tail to one side and shit. Badger and I looked at each other, and without a word headed to the other cab.

The bulky vehicles I had considered so primitive in Up Yours looked luxurious compared to those two wooden monstrosities. Before walking through Smithbright's World to our rooming house, I'd never seen an animal-propelled vehicle. This place had nothing else. And it smelled like it.

Badger and I hired the man in the second cab to take us to the places on our list. We'd gone only half a block when the man in black reappeared, driving his own cab and following a few vehicles behind us. He kept out of sight pretty well. I only caught occasional glimpses of him, but we were never out of his sight. Except for the fact that I'd seen him follow us out of the lobby, I might not have realized he was there.

Half a day later, we crossed off the second of two places we could find that admitted to doing any sort of work on spacecraft. The first shop was hopeless. The second shop actually might have been able to handle the ID-switching procedure—it was advanced beyond anything else we'd seen on Smithbright's World. But the proprietor wasn't interested in gossiping about his work, and our attempt to get a look at his records resulted in our immediate ejection from the premises.

So we were on the move again . . . barely. Moving at draymus-and-cart speed, we weren't going to accomplish anything quickly. If the *Corrigan's Blood* had come here to get its work done, it had chosen its location well. It might take us months to find anything.

The next place on Badger's list, Offworld Merchandise,

seemed likely to have records of ships that came through. At that point, we just wanted to find some record of the *FireEater*—if we could find someone who would admit to dealing with the ship, we might also be able to determine whether it was the one we were looking for. According to Badger's sources, Offworld Merchandise was a sort of warehouse and store all in one, where cargo that had been cleared to enter the world could be sold.

The sorts of cargo that were clearable in Pincada seemed likely to be limited. I doubted that a ship could sell bio-enhanced agricultural supplies, for example. These people had limited their world to animal power and some steam-engine technology on purpose. They weren't doing genetic engineering. They were barely doing engineering. I doubted that anything beyond simple mechanicals would get beyond the unfriendly walls of spaceport Customs.

The cold, wet air permeated the cabin of the cab, rain drummed on the roof, and we heard the steady clop-clop of the beast's hooves on the wet brick road and listened to the crack of the driver's whip. In this manner, we traveled through streets laid out in straight, ugly grids, jammed with buggies and wagons; past sidewalks covered with people walking; between rows of tall, narrow wooden houses painted in graying white and sullen shades of yellow, green and brown; in and out of districts of brick and stone businesses and public buildings that turned blank, unwelcoming eyes to passersby. Leafless trees overhung the thoroughfares and wires strung on poles draped from building to building. In all my life I had never seen such a paean to ugliness as Pincada.

A broad expanse of mud-yellow brick pavement fronted Offworld Merchandise. A few buggies and cabs sat in rows, keeping themselves within lines laid out in black brick. Their draft beasts stood tied to poles, heads hanging. Our driver pulled into a space near the main doorway. "You want me to wait?"

"Yes," Badger said. "Please. We still have several other places we need to visit."

"So I wait."

We both nodded.

"Very good." He smiled at us. That smile stood out as much as a single ray of sunshine would have if it could have broken through the heavy clouds over the city.

We walked into the store and looked around, just to get an idea of what sort of offworld merchandise Pincada did permit. The place, a huge high-ceilinged open box with shelves that ran shoulder-high in long rows, seemed devoid of human life. A few shoppers wandered the aisles, but they were dwarfed by the scale of the place, and by the scarcity of their numbers. In the aisles nearest the entryway, luxuries sat piled next to things I wouldn't have considered buying under any circumstances. Lespumi furs and Mandinkan songstones rested beside boxes of unfinished wood planks and cartons of paper and dreadful religious artwork. Most of the merchandise was at least quaintly outdated; some of it was stunningly obscure. I recognized the uses of, at best, a third of the items on the shelves.

Nothing really shocked me, though, until I saw a whole block of archaic medicines. Among them were febrifuges, hypnotics, antiemetics, emetics, antidiarrheals, antipsychotics—an entire pharmacology of chemicals that had been eliminated from use by nano-technology. Who needed a medicine for a fever if the nano-machines in his bloodstream didn't permit the illness that would have caused a fever? I felt like I'd come across people trying to cure cancer by singing, chanting, and sticking pins in dolls.

Then I saw the antibiotics. My stomach knotted and I felt queasy. Sitting on the shelves in front of me, were drugs like gerancillin, septimycin, and considactan; broad-spectrum nightmares that had been late entries in the ever-escalating war between drugs and drug-resistant diseases back on Old Earth.

Antibiotics had gone from being a life-saving boon in the early twentieth century to being a contributing factor in the last great plague wave at the beginning of the twenty-first century. Antibiotic-resistant diseases had become fiercer and more resistant, uglier and more tenacious, almost cleverer in their approach, until at last all the conditions necessary for disaster—urban overcrowding, severe sanitation problems, a global transportation network, and a viciously resistant, highly contagious organism—came together in one place. New York City. The result was Fulminating Pneumocystic Plague, which before it ran its course wiped out eighty percent of Old Earth's population. No antibiotic was ever found that could stop it, though medical researchers wasted plenty of time looking for one. FPP was the disease that finally forced the evolution of the medical nanotechnology revolution.

I wondered what sort of fools would shun or forbid safe, effective nanoviruses in order to revert to a technology that by its very nature made diseases more dangerous and more resistant with every use.

Antibiotics. They sat in their generic boxes, labeled with contents, with expiration dates, and with not much else, in row upon row upon row. No manufacturer had claimed these products; public prejudice against anything linked to the FPP plague would have made it insanity to do so. Yet here on Smithbright's World, the antibiotic was, perhaps, the single pitiful piece of armor against devastating bacterial disease. It was another reason to hate the loathsome place.

Slow genocide by government decree, I thought. Voluntary stupidity at its worst. Typical of bureaucracy everywhere.

I started to turn away, but something caught my eye. Not all of the drugs had been unpacked. A hundred-box carton of generic strobocillin nestled in a packing case with a fifty-pack carton of Sevannight Sleeping Elixir. They looked like they had been shipped that way from the manufacturer.

And Sevannight wasn't generic. The manufacturer's logo

marked each package. Miltech Pharmaceuticals—Good Medicine for Good Health.

And down at the bottom of each box was a line of tiny print.

Distributed by Miltech Pharmaceuticals, a division of Cassamir Biologicals.

If the Sevannight was from Cassamir Biologicals, maybe the antibiotics were, too.

The hair on the back of my neck began to stand up. This isn't what we're looking for, I told myself. We're looking for people who stole a single ship, not for ships that are carrying weird Cassamir Biologicals products to marginal market worlds.

But what ship brought the drugs? Did the *Corrigan's Blood* carry them with it when it arrived? Did they arrive on the *FireEater*?

"It's not our problem," Badger said.

"It is if the *Corrigan's Blood* brought them."

"If the *Blood* was coming here to get an ID change, why would it carry drugs?"

"Let's find out." I picked up a bottle of the strobocillin and a bottle of the Sevannight, then reconsidered and put the strobocillin down. If the person I talked to knew how frantic people in the outside universe got about such drugs, he wouldn't give me any information on anything. Whereas I could ask questions about Sevannight all day long and not get near anything remotely uncomfortable .

Badger and I went looking for a manager.

We found one.

The manager's nametag said she was Kayda Ingram. She was stocky, short, bright-eyed. Her skin was halfway between Badger's Melatinting and my natural color, and she'd applied some sort of paint to her eyelids, cheeks, and lips. The paint had smeared and smudged, and some of it had rubbed off from her lips onto her front teeth; the paint did nothing favorable that I could see for her appearance. She said, "How can I help you?"

"I was wondering how you found Sevannight. I've been

trying to locate this for years, and I've looked everywhere, and," I tried a shrug and an ingenuous smile, "I found it here."

"You're an offworlder?"

I nodded.

"Why do you need it?"

"Nanotechnology isn't as wonderful as people might tell you."

She thought about that for a moment, then smiled a sly little smile while her eyes focused off into a middle distance, looking at nothing. "I always figured as much. Figured anything hyped that much had to be half lies and the other half shit." She refocused on me and said, "Ship brought it."

I tried to look delighted, but also tried not to overact. After all, we were talking about a sleeping elixir here, not the wealth of the ancients. "You've dealt with this ship before? You have a regular supplier? Someone I could maybe ask to place an ongoing order for me?"

Kayda Ingram looked up at me, eyes calculating. "You not planning on staying here?"

"I can't. My work takes me all over the universe."

"So no sense having me order it."

"That wouldn't work. I wish it would."

She pursed her lips. "I can get the name of the ship that brought it. It was a first run, but we set up a regular route with them. Don't see how that will help you, though."

"I can leave a broadcast message if I know who to leave it for. Until now, I simply haven't been able to find anyone to ask. I found this once on another world, and it was wonderful. I'd be grateful if you could help me find it again."

"Grateful?" Again that calculating stare. "I'll go find out who brought it. You think about how grateful you'll be, will you?"

She trudged off, the material of her pants making a shuss-shuss-shuss sound as her thighs rubbed together.

"Ship has never been here before."

"I heard that. Could be the *Blood*. How grateful should we be?" Badger asked.

"How much is twenty rucets locally? A bit over a thousand of the . . . the local money units? Quills?"

"Squabs or quabs or qualls . . . something like that. A thousand is about right. I don't remember the exact rate of exchange."

"You think twenty rucets would be grateful enough?"

"I'd think ten would be as grateful as anyone needs to be, but buy a lot of her drug. Make sure our story holds up."

Our course of action settled, we waited. Then we waited some more. Then, to spice up our lives, we stared at the junk on the shelves and pretended we wanted to so that we wouldn't feel like we were still waiting. She was taking too long getting back to us. I started getting anxious, wondering where she was and what she was doing.

"You think she decided now would be a good time to go to lunch?" Badger asked. So it wasn't just me who thought she was taking too long.

"Something's wrong," I said, though I didn't know what could be wrong.

And then I heard the shuss-shuss of her pants rubbing together, and the heavy tread of her feet on the concrete floor, and she came around the end of the shelves where she'd left us waiting and said, "I'm sorry. I can't help you. We don't have that information here," and she was lying and I could see the lie in her eyes; but worse, I could see fear there. She hadn't been afraid before. Greedy, calculating, looking out for herself, but not afraid of me, not afraid of Badger, not afraid of anything. And now she was afraid.

I walked forward, went to step around her to look down the aisle behind her, curious to see if I could discover what it was that had her so frightened; she moved to block me but I'm fast and strong; I brushed past her and caught sight of the tail end of a flapping black coat, a disappearing leg and dirty black shoe. The man who had followed us.

Someone didn't want us to know where the Sevannight came from. I hadn't even asked about the questionable drugs, the antibiotics. I hadn't asked for anything but the name of a ship that had brought a perfectly respectable, if mostly useless, sleep aid to an out-of-the-way planet. The man in black had decided this was dangerous information, and I had to assume that was because of the identity of the link, and not because of the cargo. The Sevannight was tied directly to Cassamir Station and Cassamir Biologicals, and maybe to the *Corrigan's Blood*. The agricultural bio-enhancers sold on Up Yours were linked in the same way. All the Stardancer-class ships came from Cassamir Station, as did Peter Crane.

Neither of the two ships was doing anything illegal that I could identify. I wanted to tell myself that what the ship back on Up Yours had been trading was not related to my search for the *Corrigan's Blood*. After all, that ship hadn't been stolen. It had been purchased from previous owners. Nothing tied it to the *Corrigan's Blood* except its point of origin and its sneaky behavior.

I'd been to three settled backwater worlds. All three had been visited by Stardancers acting in a highly suspicious manner. There weren't very many Stardancers in the universe yet. I thought it was beyond being simply unlikely to find three of them traveling to such unpalatable locations. And maybe I was jumping to conclusions, but I'd walked in blind, swinging a stick and trying to hit one particular rat, and instead I'd hit a couple of the wrong rats, and it was starting to occur to me that maybe they weren't the wrong rats that I was hitting. And I hadn't failed to notice, either, that the rats were doing their damnedest to hit back. People on Up Yours had wanted to kill us. Someone here was following us.

Maybe Cassamir Biologicals was making a fortune trading exotic biologicals and antibiotics to backwater worlds. Maybe if we'd taken more time and had looked harder, we would have found antibiotics on Up Yours, too. The cartons weren't too big. If the price was right, maybe antibiotic trading would justify the expense of some of the most expensive private luxury ships in the universe. And maybe it made stealing them irresistible.

Easy hypothesis to test. I walked past Kayda and back to the aisle where the drugs sat. She shuss-shussed behind me. I picked up one of the antibiotic packages and tossed it into the air, caught it clumsily, and turned to see that she hadn't blanched. Usually if you take something tremendously valuable to someone and treat it recklessly, the person to whom it belongs will react. Try it with someone's baby sometime if you doubt me. Or one of the universes five remaining Ming vases. And I got no reaction. "How much does this cost?"

"I can't sell you anything," she said.

I sighed. "I don't want to buy it. I just want to know how much it costs." Sitting out on the shelf. One of the most dreaded substances in the universe, rightly or not, just sitting on the shelf where anybody could walk by, pick up a box, slide it into a pocket, and make off with it. These people don't know how to run a market, I thought.

"If you can't buy it, why do you want to know?"

"I'm just curious."

"You don't need to be curious. You need to leave."

Badger stepped beside her and stood very close. He looked down at her and she realized for the first time how big he was, and how menacing.

"As soon as you tell me how much this costs, I'll leave."

She looked down at the drug in my hand. She looked up at Badger. She looked at me, and her face was tight. "Eighteen crullas and five," she said.

Which was essentially nothing. That translated to about five hundredths of a rucet. Nothing. These people might as well hand it out free on the streets. If they'd marked the product up any at all—and I had to believe they had, or else why were they in business?—then Cassamir Biologicals lost money producing it before they ever put it into boxes to ship it out.

"You're sure," I said. My voice squeaked a little when

I said it, and Kayda caught the surprise. For a moment her guard dropped.

"Yes. Well, we might have it marked down to eighteen since we have so much in the back, but I think eighteen-five . . ." She stopped and frowned, realizing that she'd cooperated with me, had given me information, and she wasn't supposed to do that. "You need to leave now," she said again, and glared at the two of us and started walking toward the door.

I put the antibiotic back on the shelf and Badger and I followed her, and meekly allowed ourselves to be sent on our way.

The rain had started falling harder while we were in Offworld Merchandise. Now it poured steadily, while a bitterly cold wind whipped it sideways and sent it slashing up under eaves and against windows. Any pretense of daylight was gone. The timepiece on my compac said the local time was still late afternoon, but the black streets insisted night had fallen.

And to make our situation even more pleasant, our cab driver, not yet paid and owed a lot of money, had nevertheless left without us.

Chapter Thirteen

We slogged through the gullies and rivulets and puddles of the parking lot toward the street. "No chance she might let us back in long enough to tell us how to find another cab," Badger said.

"None," I agreed.

"Hell of a night for walking," he said.

"Yes."

"Be a lot more comfortable to stand up under the eaves of the store and wait for some of this rain to let up." Badger's voice had taken on a false casualness that I recognized.

"Certainly would."

"Could probably just stay out of the way and watch the doors; see who went in and who came out . . . maybe figure out a way to go in and have a look later. Might be a nice night for walking by the time we'd finished."

"Might be." I looked back at the store and saw Kayda standing behind the glass door, watching us walk away. "Of course we might need to hike around the block once, first. Make us appreciate getting dry again when we finally do."

Badger nodded. We put our heads down and trudged across the parking lot and turned left onto the sidewalk, hiked along the street that was almost devoid of traffic, turned left at the intersection so that we didn't have to cross any streets, turned left at the next intersection, and then left again.

By the time we walked back up to the front of Offworld Merchandise, no one stood watching us. The parking lot had only one buggy in it. We waited around the side of the building, stood under the eaves where we were sheltered from the wind, and blew on our hands and shivered and cursed Kayda Ingram until finally she came out of the building, turned, hooked a simple padlock onto the door and clicked it shut, and walked across the parking lot with short, nervous little steps. She kept her head up and looked around constantly. Afraid of the darkness, or of being alone . . .

My skin crawled, remembering Customs. Remembering the soldier. What he had said to me. He'd said, *This isn't your world. While you're here, keep to yourself. Don't try to be anybody's friend, especially if someone wants to be your friend. Don't go anywhere you don't have to be. And don't go out at night.*

Don't go anywhere you don't have to be.

Anyone local and in authority would consider our reasons for waiting around Offworld Merchandise unnecessary. Unwelcome. Illegal. We couldn't make a case that we had to be there.

Darkness had overtaken us, and we were out, and not only were we out but we had a long, long way to go to get back to where we were supposed to be, and no real idea of how we were going to get there.

We weren't trying to be anybody's friend, but that was all we'd missed. Our first night on a planet where staying out of trouble might be our only chance for survival, and we were doing our best to get ourselves into trouble.

It sometimes amazed me what people would do for money.

Kayda untied her beast from its post, climbed onto the driver's seat, and eventually pulled out into the dark street and drove away, the tiny yellow beams of her headlights stabbing into the night only briefly before the rain swallowed them.

"Let's go," Badger said.

Finding things for people sometimes involves illegal activity. I've always justified this to myself by reminding myself that the people who took whatever was missing did so illegally. If they hadn't, I wouldn't have accepted the job of finding and returning it.

Peripherally, the missing ship *Corrigan's Blood* was related to breaking into Offworlder Merchandise. At least I'd convinced myself that it was. So I could let my conscience take the evening off.

It wouldn't, though. Any time I engaged in criminal behavior, justified or not, I got queasy. Badger delighted in thwarting the rules; I'd have been happier staying away from places that had them. We were very different that way.

We were both good at what we did, though. We could both break and enter, both pilot ships, both surf the comnet. This time, I stood watch while Badger picked the lock. He stood for a moment, working with a tumbler gun that looked like a hairbrush when it wasn't broken down for use. When he pulled the trigger, the tumbler clicked softly. He gave a tug at the base of the lock and it popped open.

Badger and I walked through the door and moved out of sight of the street as quickly as possible, trying to look as if we belonged where we were while we did it. Kayda had left about a third of the building's lights on, and we had been visible as silhouettes while we stood outside picking the lock. Once inside, in the light, we became easily identifiable people instead of anonymous black cutouts.

Badger waited until we'd moved behind the shelves to say, "Let's go through the whole place together before you check out the office. I want to make sure that we know about any other doors before you get distracted; I don't want any unpleasant surprises."

"You'll watch the front door while I go through the office."

He nodded. "But let's make sure we're secure to start with."

We went through the building cautiously. I carried my stunner and my nerve disrupter. Badger was similarly armed. We were in agreement; even in bad situations neither of us had ever killed anyone. That was always a point of pride with us. In spite what deGuerres and others like him said about self-protection, I considered my reverence for life a part of what defined me. Badger and I had discussed the issue at length. It wasn't that we didn't value our own lives—but what situation could possibly arise that the combined firepower of a stunner and a disrupter wouldn't solve?

The building was three times as big as it appeared from the front. The majority of the main floor was the display room; a small section at the back, with a single barred door leading out into the alley behind the store, acted as an unloading area. Storage was underground; two floors were stacked from floor to ceiling with crated merchandise. The long, jumbled rows meandered, lacking the regimentation imposed by the shelves upstairs. I couldn't see any sort of order in the arrangement of merchandise. I thought finding anything would be a miserable job.

Badger sighed when we finished our search of the second basement. "That took longer than I wanted. I'm glad to know we're alone in the place, though."

"We are if no one came through the front doors while we were down here looking around."

In the long shadows cast by the dangling lights overhead, his grin looked lunatic. "Charming thought," he said.

"The sooner we get out of here, the sooner we don't have to think such thoughts."

He started for the stairs. "By all means, let's get moving."

He left me at the office door, which was locked but which, again, proved to be no obstacle. He moved down the aisles to take up position where he could see the front door and any movement around it, but where no one would be able to see him.

The office light was out. I fumbled around until I found it; a toggle switch on the wall activated another of the dangling glass bulbs. Ugly illumination. Ugly office. A metal desk, a metal chair on rollers with a cloth seat and back, tall metal cabinets that lined one wall. Everything was gray, flat, square-cornered, slightly grimy. Nothing curved, nothing grew, nothing exhibited any signs of life or any appreciation of beauty.

I checked the desk first. Since I'd asked for the information, there was a chance that Kayda had pulled the file in which it had been kept, and had left it on the desk when the man in black interrupted her. Would save me time if she had.

But she hadn't. The papers in the folders were purchase orders from local companies. Not a word about Sevannight in any of them. No mention of any starships. I popped the lock on her file cabinet and started going through files. They weren't filed logically—at least, they weren't filed the way I would have filed them. I would have set up accounts by ship. Kayda, or whoever did the filing, had set up files by purchase item. There was a file for Lespumi furs and one for Braxmiller marble statue replicas; there were files for Cathnaral blackwood, for Sevannight, and finally, for strobocillin, though it took me a long time to find that.

The strobocillin file confirmed my suspicions but didn't answer my questions. The *FireEater* had supplied the antibiotics, but this had been its first run. So these records didn't eliminate the possibility that the ship was the *Corrigan's Blood*.

The person who brought them down, listed as second in command of the ship, was named Cal Basqueian. I couldn't shake the feeling that I was fumbling around in something bigger than a stolen ship.

I wrote down Basqueian's name. Then I put things back the way I'd found them, and left.

Badger hadn't moved. He turned when I slipped down the aisle behind him and said, "No problems. You find anything?"

"*FireEater* brought the drugs. This was its first trip; it might be our ship, or it might not. But it's bringing in something so bad that it's using antibiotic-trading as its cover, just as I think the *Mystic Dove* was doing the same thing, and that its cover was the high-tech agricultural supplies it was supplying to an essentially low-tech world. But what are they really smuggling?"

Badger frowned. "What could be so bad that they would use antibiotics as a *cover*?"

"Wrong question, but nothing that will ever bother you again," a voice said from above me. The man who had been following us dropped down from an opening he'd made in the ceiling by lifting a panel aside. He landed on the floor in front of us, on his feet, with impossible grace.

"Ceiling," I said aloud, to Badger or perhaps to myself. "We didn't check that."

"Bad oversight," the man said, smiling, and attacked.

The beams of Badger's and my stunners hit him simultaneously, chest and head. Two perfect shots. He should have dropped like a rock. He didn't even seem to notice the beams. He kept coming.

I shot him with my disrupter, thumbing the gain up to high.

Nothing. He kept coming.

There was one of him. There were two of us, and I had a couple of inches on him and probably a few pounds. Badger was both bigger and taller than me. The heavy gravity of our ship made Badger and me faster and stronger on worlds like Smithbright's World, where the gravity was a shade less than that of Old Earth. We were both trained fighters, and good ones. We should have cleaned the floor with the man.

Instead he threw me aside as if I didn't exist and lunged at Badger. I saw that he had a knife out. Badger dodged the knife . . . barely . . . and I got to my feet and charged from behind, leaping to land on his back. Except that in the split second it took for my feet to leave the ground in the leap, the bastard managed to move completely out of my range.

He wasn't where he should have been, and instead of landing on him, I sprawled on the floor on my face. I rolled, sensing movement or feeling pressure in the air, found that he had closed again, impossibly fast; his knife slammed into the concrete right where I had been and the blade broke off an inch below the guard. He'd missed, but not by much. And I couldn't recover quickly enough from the awkwardness of the roll to get out of his reach a second time. His fist slammed into my right kidney with agonizing force.

I screamed from the pain and he drew back to hit me again, but Badger grabbed him around the throat and pulled him off. I got to my feet, but I was hurt and I knew it. I was almost sure I was bleeding inside. My vision swam. I wobbled. The man had grabbed Badger's wrists and pulled Badger's hands off of his neck.

I wondered fuzzily how he had done that. Tremendous strength, impossible strength. He couldn't be as strong as he was. When you're fighting, weight and size matter. A short, thin, light man can't be as strong as a big, heavily muscled man. He can be faster, but he can't be as strong. But this bastard was stronger. And not afraid of anything.

He twisted around, hung on to Badger's wrists while he did it, and suddenly Badger was on the floor with his face in the concrete, screaming; the man crouched down next to Badger's face and twisted one arm so that it looked like it was going to pop out of its socket. He looked up at me and grinned, and I saw that he had filed his teeth to needle points, and that he'd had a bodyartist extend the canines to make them twice as long as they should have been.

He said, "You're dead, bitch, but he's first."

I looked around for a weapon that might do something to him, and found a stone carving of a leaping cat slightly longer than my hand that stood on a heavy square metal base. I picked it up by the cat, swung hard at the base of the attacker's skull, and felt a sickening crunch as the metal base sunk through bone and into brain tissue. Blood spattered. The man went limp and dropped on top of Badger. Neither he nor Badger moved.

"Badger?" I was afraid he had killed Badger somehow.

The statue fell from my hand to the floor, and the stone cat shattered. Shards of green stone sprayed across the floor. I wanted to throw up. The bastard was dead and I'd killed him. I had to, but he was dead. Dead. And I'd killed him.

"Badger? Talk to me." I rolled him off Badger, and Badger groaned and lifted his head. I felt a twitch in the dead man's arm as I dragged him away; muscles spasming but no visible movement—the feeling of life bleeding away from the corpse was horrible.

I grabbed Badger and pulled him to a sitting position. His face was bloody and he looked dazed.

"We have to get out of here," I said, and looked back at the dead man, who stared at me with unblinking eyes and a half-smile frozen on his face.

That was too much. My stomach lost everything in it. I leaned against the nearest aisle, retching. I saw blood in my vomit, and didn't want to think about where it came from. I was hurt, I was in trouble, and I had killed a man.

And Badger said, "Oh, shit," and I turned and saw the sallow-faced man, his grin broader, blink and start to get to his feet.

Impossible. Impossible. He was dead, had to be dead, I'd caved in the whole back of his head.

He wasn't dead. He said, "Good try. Not good enough."

Badger staggered to his feet and I reached for another stone statue, thinking as I did that it wouldn't do any good, that I had gotten lucky to get that one blow in and that I would never get a chance for another one like it; and the door to the parking lot opened and cold, wet air blasted into the store, and all three of us turned.

Fedara Contei stalked toward us. She looked at me and said, "You idiot. You've gotten into something you'll never get out of," and then she was past Badger and me and charging our attacker, and she had drawn a knife as long as her forearm.

"They're mine," the man said.

"I'm afraid not," she said, and stuck the knife into his throat.

Badger and I stood there, staring stupidly, unable to make sense of what we were seeing. She started hacking the man's head off with her knife, and he screamed and fought her while she did it. She snarled, "Take my buggy. Get back to your rooms and figure out some plausible lie for how you got hurt, damn you," without looking at us. The man's screams had become gurgles, wet and bubbling. Blood sprayed everywhere.

We hobbled out the front door and took the buggy. Neither of us knew anything about animals, but Badger was the less injured of us, so he sat up on the driver's seat and tried everything he could think of until the animal started forward. After some experimentation, he figured out how to make it stop. And we spent the next couple of hours finding our way back to our rooms.

Chapter Fourteen

I was awake again. I lay on the bed, pain-wracked, heart racing, panting and not getting enough air in, hoping I would be able to get back to the medichamber on the *Hope's Reward* before whatever the man in black had done to me killed me. I tried to tell myself that I'd lived through the night, that I was going to be fine. But my urine was blood-red and blood-thick and my tongue and nailbeds and the insides of my eyelids were dead-man pale. I was in trouble and I knew it.

Badger sat at the foot of the bed, watching me. Now that the muddy light of dawn trickled through the dirty windows, I could see the fear in his eyes. He'd managed to keep it out of his voice when he'd checked on me during the night. Had kept it out of his touch. But his eyes said I wasn't doing too well, and he was afraid.

When he spoke, though, it wasn't about how I was doing. "She followed us," he said. "And we didn't know."

I'd been thinking about that, too. Dreaming about it some when I wasn't dreaming about the bastard who wouldn't die. "She's used corollary origami points, come into each system from the other side or from a lot farther out. We've been using the closest and most convenient points."

"Maybe. Maybe there are other ways she could have

done it. But we didn't even suspect." He looked worried. "I've been watching our backs. I wide-wormed the information from the in-system Spybees when we arrived and right before we left, every time we jumped . . . after the incident with Contei, anyway. I should have seen the repetition of the ship registration one of those times. It was exactly what I was looking for. So why didn't I see it?"

I'd spent some of my time on deck looking behind us, too. I didn't want to believe we'd been careless. And I didn't want to believe someone could be so much better than we were that she could slip in right behind us, follow us down to planetary surfaces and around cities, and never give any indication that she was there. "Maybe she just now caught up with us. Maybe we didn't miss anything because there was nothing to miss."

"Maybe." Badger looked as doubtful as I felt. We were dealing with more than we'd been prepared to handle, and he knew it, and I knew it.

Footsteps sounded down the hall, and something hit our door with a crash. We heard other crashes along the hall. Both of us jumped and froze; then Badger picked up the board he'd pried loose from the floor to use as a weapon, and with it clutched in both hands, advanced on the door. The sound of footsteps receded.

Badger braced himself and opened the door. "No one there," he told me. "Just this roll of paper." He crouched, still watching the hall for signs of an enemy, and picked up the roll. He kicked the door shut and came back to the bed. "There's a note attached."

He held it up and read it out loud. "Newspapers are provided for all guests as a service of The Traveler's Ease. You will be billed five crullas a day for this service."

"News." I wrinkled my nose.

Badger was curious, though. He unwrapped the newspaper and studied the front page. "Oh, no," he whispered.

I sat up. "What is it?"

He handed me the paper, and I immediately saw what he'd seen.

A headline in bold black type said, **Offworld Woman, Unidentified Man "Bleeder" Victims.**

I read the article out loud.

> "Two bodies, badly mutilated and drained of blood, were found in the Westmarch District during the night. Both bodies fit the same pattern as twenty-three previous murders that have taken place in Westmarch in the last twelve months, all of which are considered the work of the so-called 'Westmarch Bleeder.'
>
> "The body of the first of the night's victims, offworlder Thanassa Tang, was found in a blocked drain on Blackwillow Street at 23:40 last night by city officers Brian Karpovtsev and Alex Leetch. The officers were called to the site by municipal workers who discovered the body while attempting to prevent a blocked drain from flooding nearby homes; when the workers attempted to clear the drain, Tang's body caught on their probes and was dragged to higher ground.
>
> "Identification was made by Tang's fellow traveler, whose name has been withheld. Tang was released on her own recognizance from the Customs Department of John Ardhal Memorial Spaceport following questioning at 15:30 hours, and was instructed to proceed to her assigned housing. Her colleague states that she never arrived."

"You know that isn't true," Badger said. "They didn't let her walk out of there. Those men killed her and dumped the body. And this Westmarch Bleeder made a convenient suspect, so they dumped the body there."

"I think you're probably right." I picked up where I'd left off.

> "At 04:10 this morning, Westmarch taxi driver Lee Fan found the second body in the back seat of his carriage. He said he had been in an all-night eatery taking his break, and when he came out he thought for a moment that a potential fare had climbed into the back seat to wait for him. It was only when he asked the fare for his destination and the man didn't respond that Fan turned and discovered that the body had no head. Police are still attempting to identify the man, whose fingerprints are not on record."

"No head?" I said. "How many murder victims do you think lost heads last night?"

"You think the second body was the man who attacked us, don't you?"

I lay back, feeling weak and sick. "Yes. I think so. Why look for a complicated answer when a simple one will serve?"

"No reason at all."

"At least we know he's dead."

Badger sighed. "For what little that's worth. We don't know why he was following us, we don't know how he almost killed both of us . . . and we don't know where Fedara Contei is or what she has to do with any of this. That, I think, bothers me as much as everything else together. Why did she kill the man who was trying to kill us?"

"I think I know the answer to that, anyway." I closed my eyes. The pain was getting worse. My abdomen was so tender I couldn't bear to rest my arms on it, and it was beginning to swell, too. I tried to imagine what would happen to me if I ended up in a Pincadan hospital receiving the quality of medical care that would be available to offworlders. I would probably die. They would probably kill me on purpose. At least I didn't have to worry about getting an infection. Three cheers for nanoviruses.

"Well?" Badger asked. I opened my eyes to find him staring at me.

"Well, what?"

"Why did Fedara kill our attacker?"

"Oh." I'd drifted and lost my focus, and I was having a hard time getting it back. Bad sign. "Because if we're dead, we can't lead her to the *Corrigan's Blood*, and we can't take it and her back to Peter Crane so that she can kill him."

"That's true." Badger made a face that made me laugh, and laughing hurt so much that tears welled up in my eyes. Someone knocked on the door. Badger stiffened. He picked up the board, but this time was less panicked about it. "I wonder what complimentary service the rooming house has decided to charge us with now," he said, and walked over and opened it. And immediately slammed it shut and leaned against it, legs braced. "Fedara Contei," he said.

Even though he leaned against it, the door began to open inward. "I'm coming in," Fedara said from the other side. "I'm not going to hurt either of you, but I'm coming in, and nothing you can do can stop me. It's important that no one see me here; it's important to you as well as to me if you want to leave this place alive."

"Let her in," I told Badger.

He tightened his grip on the board and backed up. Fedara entered, shut the door behind her, and walked over to the single filthy window and pulled the curtains closed.

"You need to get off Smithbright's World now," she said. "I've pulled a few strings at Customs; your papers are waiting for you. But if you don't leave immediately, friends of the man I killed last night will track you down. There are people who know who you are, and who know that the man I killed was following you. When they identify the body, and they will probably do that very soon, his friends are going to put all the pieces together, and if you are within their reach, they will utterly destroy you."

"What's going on?" I asked.

"You don't want to know. Find your ship. Don't ask any other questions, don't look under any other rocks. The only way you'll live through this is if you don't find the answers to your questions. You'll have a better chance of that if you stop asking."

I gave her a fierce stare. "You know what the Stardancer ships are smuggling out of Cassamir Station, don't you?"

Fedara's eyes widened slightly. She shook her head. The head shake was not, "No, I don't know," but "God, I wish you hadn't said that." "You probably already know too much for them to let you live. If you want to have any chance at all, though, go to the Customs office now, tell them that your friend Colin Hawke has his private shuttle waiting for you, and that he called ahead to clear your paperwork. They won't ask any questions about your appearances, they won't inspect your luggage, and they won't detain you for any other reason. Do you have that?"

"Our friend Colin Hawke," I repeated back to her. "Private shuttle. He called ahead."

"Colin Hawke," Badger said. "That's a stupid name."

"It isn't a name," I said. "It's a code. Right?"

Fedara rolled her eyes. "You aren't going to quit, and you are going to die." She didn't answer my question, but she might as well have. I knew I was right. She said, "Go now. There cannot possibly be anything here as important to you as your own survival."

I tried to get to my feet, nearly passed out from the pain, and toppled forward. Badger moved to catch me, but Fedara got there first. Fast. As fast as the man who had tried to kill us last night. Possibly faster, since he was dead, and she wasn't. She appeared to be genuinely concerned for me. Odd, since she was supposed to kill me pretty soon. Thoughts faded in and out of focus. She wanted to kill me, but I wasn't afraid of her. Why not? Oh, of course. "You want us to live so you can follow us back to Peter Crane and kill him, don't you."

In her eyes, fear flared and found tinder and burned. "You can't have heard me talking with . . ."

Even with my thoughts fuzzy, I remembered the name. "Danniz. I heard."

"Oh, God," she whispered, staring into my eyes. "Oh, God." She lifted me as if I didn't weigh anything, handed me over to Badger, and took off out the door.

The movement, being lifted and carried, pressed against my swollen, rigid belly. Blackness shuttered my open eyes, and everything seemed suddenly very far away.

From down a long tunnel, a voice I knew that I knew said, "I hope she was right about things being ready at Customs."

The pain got worse, became bouncing, jostling pain. The blackness got a greater hold on me. "Just hang on," the voice said, a world away. "Just hold on."

Chapter Fifteen

I told Badger, "I've been thinking about the news sheets on Up Yours and Smithbright's World. You know, I think I was wrong about news." He'd just come into the holo room where I had been watching Isas Yamamoto.

"You? Wrong? Tell me more."

I didn't laugh. "I think news is the way human prey tell themselves the predators are among them. Along with all their garbage, the news sheets announce murders and robberies and cons and deceits; I still think how they do it is exploitative and vile. But it has value."

"Civilized worlds have done away with news," Badger said. "The success of our civilization has proven that we don't need it."

I shook my head. "I have another, more sinister explanation for our civilized worlds. What if the places that don't have news are the ones where the predators are in control?"

Badger didn't have anything to say to that.

I didn't say anything, either. I was in a deep, despairing funk.

The bastard on Smithbright's World had ruptured my kidney, and I would have died if Fedara Contei hadn't pulled strings to get the two of us through customs and back to the *Reward*. The medichamber returned me to perfect physical health, but I was uncomfortably aware of my own mortality when I rejoined the world of the living. Uncomfortably aware that I had made a machine the sole link between me and death, and that I had let myself get too far from the machine. I didn't want to die, and now, if Fedara Contei was correct, I had people who were better than I was—stronger, faster, maybe even smarter—and they were violent and they were hunters and they wanted me dead.

And I didn't know why. Perhaps I was close to finding out the answer to that, but I didn't have it yet. I had another name—Cal Basqueian—but there was a good chance his name wouldn't give me anything more useful than I'd gotten from any of the other names. It was probably just another name.

I had a lot of questions, but I wasn't having much luck making sense of them, and I certainly wasn't finding any answers, no matter how close to the answers I might have been.

My biggest question, the one that wouldn't let go, was *Why was the man who followed us so much better than me?* Why was he so much better than Badger?

Restored to health, I was no longer whole. Every step I'd made since I was seventeen, I'd made based upon what I believed was the unassailable fact that I was capable of taking care of myself. I had done everything humanly possible to ensure that my self-confidence wasn't misplaced. All the training, all the fighting, all the heavy-gravity speed drills, all the meditation and education and focus on making myself ready for anything; what had it been for? Nothing. The pale man in the black coat dealt with me just as he would have if I'd been careless and sloppy and slow.

No, the voice in my head argued, *if you had been careless and sloppy and slow, he would have killed you right there. As it is, you're still alive.*

I was in no mood for inner rationality. I'd lost, and Badger, who trained as hard and long as I did, had lost, and we had been rescued by the enemy who was hired to kill us.

We were shamed and shamed again.

How? That was what I wanted to know. How?

Badger finally said, "I came in to tell you that we have some useful information. Cal Basqueian used his real name."

I switched off the holo and swiveled around to stare at him. "You're joking."

"His real name," Badger repeated. He handed me an infochip. I popped it into my compac and discovered that not only had Cal Basqueian used his real name, but that he'd made a mistake in doing so. He wasn't unknown, a model citizen, someone with no recorded past. Badger's query on him had yielded a list of sins that stretched from Tassamarkis to Old Earth.

Basqueian had been convicted of armed robbery, assault, and forgery; he'd been charged with both manslaughter and murder; he'd escaped from two prisons; and he had a list of known associates that read like a criminals' Who's Who. His whereabouts were listed as unknown. No surprise. We knew where he was, sort of. He wasn't a member of any known criminal organization. Most criminals aren't, so discovering that he wasn't shattered no hopes and gave no great disappointment.

He was, however, a member in good standing of the Universal Society of Antiquarian Gothicans, which I'd never heard of. According to the first report back from a query Badger ran, the membership was comprised entirely of people who liked to dress up in funny clothes and pretend they lived in early nineteenth-century London. London, according to the report, had been a dark, polluted city on Old Earth, known at that time for its foreboding atmosphere and for the suspenseful fictional stories set there.

That bit of information on Basqueian felt like finding out that in his spare time Attila the Hun grew pansies.

I reread the highlights of the report, then handed the

chip back to Badger. I laughed, for lack of a more appropriate response. "The Universal Society of Antiquarian Gothicans, for God's sake."

"That was my response, too. I'd never heard of them, but maybe they can help us. I'm running a query to locate other USAG members. Maybe, since he's still listed as a member in good standing, we can find out something about him from another member."

"I doubt that his criminal activities are going to have been a major topic of conversation at USAG meetings," I said. I tried to imagine what a major felon would get out of playing dress-up with people who had obviously lost touch with reality. "The members who know him will probably all say that he's a wonderful man, and so dedicated to his vision of the past, and that his costume is fabulous, and that everybody likes him. People have a real knack for overlooking the criminals in their midst."

Badger burrowed his hands down into his pockets, and with them there, shrugged. "You're probably right, but I figured we might find something interesting if we looked."

"Oh, certainly." I stood and brought up the lights in the holo room. "Whether it helps us or not."

We walked to the grav chute together. I felt solid aboard the *Hope's Reward*—solid and strong and real. Gravity tugged at me and I tugged back. I always felt slightly false in lower gravities, as if I had lost part of myself. The mass was still there, regardless of gravity, but I missed the pull of weight. In weight resides a power, a *presence* that reassures, that has nothing to do with mass or muscle but with the sheer joy of fighting gravity and winning.

I stepped into the grav chute, angled myself into the reversed stream, and floated upward to the first floor. Badger followed an instant behind me. *Hope's Reward* hung just above Maxwell's Station, a neutral location Badger had chosen that was well within the borders of the Verzing Community. I'd been unconscious and in the medichamber when he made the traverse through the origami point, and although I know I had to have been conscious at the time we went through the point—the nature of the omniscient overself makes that inevitable—I was unconscious both before and after the point, and therefore missed the usual angst associated with the crossing. He'd felt that we would be better off in known territory, in a place where we understood the rules even if we didn't like some of them, while we figured out what to do next.

Now that I was awake and healthy again, we were ready to do that figuring.

We settled into chairs and looked out through the long, curving ports at the station. Maxwell's was a gaudy little gem that hung among the stars, centered like the hub of a wheel between a circle of origami points, conveniently located within sub-light distance of an asteroid belt and two habitable and settled planets.

The station itself housed about five thousand full-time residents. It had rooms for twenty-five hundred visitors. Most of the time, there were very few rooms to be had. Maxwell's son ran a good station, as had his father. Kept it clean and honest and fair, made sure the people who worked there treated visitors well, insisted that the latest and best in entertainment was always available. The place made money for him faster than if he'd had his own mint.

We used it as an unofficial home base. We maintained rooms there, though we didn't list ourselves as permanent residents. We didn't have to pay a surcharge, because three years ago I found a secret little something of Maxwell the son's that went missing and I returned it intact. He liked the idea of giving us a place to stay better than paying fifteen percent of the item's worth, and we liked the idea too, so in a way we got a part-time home and a bit of family for ourselves that we wouldn't have had otherwise.

I wanted to go down to our rooms for a while. I wanted to forget about the *Corrigan's Blood*, and about unidentified people smuggling unknown items to backwater planets and thin, small, unkillable men who had almost killed me. I wanted to be pampered and fed good food and treated to entertainment.

I wanted, at least at that moment, to be unemployed.

I said, "We can drop this. It doesn't look like it's just a stolen ship. It looks like a conspiracy, and we have enough information on the killings on Smithbright's World and Up Yours that we can turn it over to VeCRA and be done with it. The links between the Stardancer-class ships and the murders are weak, but strong enough that I think we could interest VeCRA."

"We won't get paid."

"We won't get killed, either."

Badger's voice was soft. "Is that what you want to do—get out of this?"

"What I want to do . . ." I laid my head back against my seat and stared up at the ceiling. "What I want to do . . . I *want* to go find the *Corrigan's Blood* and turn it in and receive our reward. But you almost died down there and so did I. And I would have killed a man, except he didn't die when I tried. This isn't what I want from my life. This isn't the way I intended things to be." I closed my eyes. "Every day, I've thought, 'I'm doing what I'm good at, and I'm doing it without hurting anyone. I'm not like my mother. I'm not a killer like my mother.' But I've thought about what happened down there, and Badg, I'd do it again. If it came down to killing someone or letting him kill you, I'd kill him. I would take a human life."

He sighed.

I opened my eyes and looked over at him and said, "And that isn't the person I want to be."

"So then we'll get out." He gave me a gentle smile. "We're no killers—and this is something that is going to end up with people dead. Whatever the smugglers are hiding, they're more than willing to murder anyone who comes close to finding out."

"It's settled, then. I'll get a message drone ready to send to Peter Crane explaining that we got into a lot more than what we're willing to handle, and you make one last pass through the comnet to see what other information you can gather together to give to VeCRA. Let's substantiate our claims as best we can. We'll leave Crane's name out of it, and I'll return the money we didn't use." I was giving up my shot at twenty million rucets and freedom, and I felt better. That was how I knew I'd made the right decision.

I put a sincere apology into the drone along with an account of the things that had happened to us and why we were dropping out, and transferred the credit from my account into a secure chit that would transfer it on to Crane's account when the drone reached Cassamir Station. Once that was finished, I decided to go up to the bridge and see how Badger was coming with his information download. I decided I'd include that in the drone to Crane, so that when he hired someone else to get his ship back, that person could start where we'd left off.

When I reached the bridge, Badger said, "You haven't sent the drone yet, have you?"

"No."

"Good. Don't."

"I was going to include all the information you were getting here."

"See what I found first. You aren't going to like it."

He brought up the first part of the search on his data screen. "This is what our query regarding the three men who had tried to kill you on Cassamir station yielded."

That search had come up with identities for two of the three men. The giant was Gainer Holloway. Information about him was sketchy. He was from Coronado, and he was a licensed ship mechanic. He had no record and it was only because he held an interstellar license that the query had picked him up.

The other identified man was Ejus Gambidja. He was a transport security guard for United Package Interstellar. Had a clean record, had been bonded by UPI, and so had eventually been identified in our exhaustive query. That was all I had on him. I had nothing on the third man; he was probably someone who'd never done anything to anyone, had a perfect record and a job that didn't require him to have ID information in an interstellar database.

A bunch of sweet guys, my first batch of would-be killers.

"Now this is what I got on the name *Corrigan's Blood*. The query will probably still generate information for a few more days, but this is what we have now."

So far the search had generated thirty-two famous Corrigans, but only two that also met our second criteria, that of being associated with blood in some way. The first was a serial killer from Chezchizad named Paul Deine Corrigan who had died fifty-seven years ago. He had specialized in murdering small children, whom he had cooked and eaten after drinking their blood. The report indicated rituals that went along with this, and the psychotic conviction on the part of the killer that he was staving off the end of the universe with his actions.

The second blood-tied Corrigan was Dr. Haskell B. Corrigan, a brilliant researcher who had disappeared from his laboratory on Sprax while trying to develop a cure for old age. He'd been concentrating on altering the chemistry of human blood, and while no one felt that he was anywhere near a breakthrough—and though most people doubted that he was even looking in the right direction—his other contributions to medicine, most in the field of nanoviral design, had made his mysterious disappearance a tragedy and a loss.

"If it was either one of those two, let's hope it was the second," I said.

"Here's the last report—members of the Universal Society of Antiquarian Gothicans, the society Cal Basqueian belonged to. I cross-referenced the membership list with names that were already in the shipcom memory in any context, and with places we have been or were planning on going."

There were 38,478 names listed: Badger had evidently wormed directly into the organization's own membership database.

I glanced over his shoulder.

The computer had split up the results of its search into Places and People.

The Places list was a shock. Every backwater world we still intended to visit had a few USAG members on it. So did every one we'd been to. Every one. If there was a place with lousy communication, primitive living conditions, and backward social order, the members of USAG had found it and moved in. Cassamir Station had members, too. So did Old Earth. So did Cantata, my home world and one of the least primitive places in the universe. So did Galatia Fairing, the information world.

If the Places list was startling, the People list was worse. Much worse. I read down it and felt my pulse slam against the backs of my eyes and throb in my temples.

- *John Alder*, identity falsified, membership revoked
- *Janna Bell*, active member, Ten West
- *Cal Basqueian*, active member, Corollus Station
- *Fedara Contei*, active member, Galatia Fairing
- *Ti Demont*, active member, Searles' Planet
- *Kite Harrigan*, active member, Cassamir Station
- *Dr. Haskell Corrigan*, estate membership in trust
- *Kenjon Deel*, Planetary President, Up Yours
- *Lashanda Elenday*, Planetary Controller, Cantata
- *Ejus Gambidja*, active member, Cantata
- *Gainer Holloway*, active member, Cantata
- *Paley Kotak*, active member, Corollus Station
- *Danniz Oe*, Universal Over-President, no address given

I studied that list of names and started shaking. "That the same Danniz, you think?"

"Probably."

"Yeah. I think so, too."

I'd been handed the key to a door—a door that led to both *Corrigan's Blood* and the other mystery, the one that was tied to smuggling and attempted murder and perhaps the disappearance of a respected doctor.

And it tied in something else. My past.

My mother was Lashanda Elenday, and if she was a member of the Universal Society of Antiquarian Gothicans, then whatever they were doing had nothing to do with dressing up in funny clothes and reenacting dead history. The only thing that interested my mother, that had *ever* interested her, was power. How to get it, how to keep it, how to use it to make other people bend. She despised democracy and reason; she wanted to live in a universe in which her will was law. She would have only joined USAG because she knew it would forward her dream.

If my mother was a member of USAG, then USAG, or at least the part of it that she touched, was corrupt and dangerous and evil.

"We can't quit," I said.

And Badger nodded. "I know."

Chapter Sixteen

I said, "But the whole planet of Cantata has a death warrant on us." We sat in Badger's quarters surrounded by his ugly iridescent green furnishings and drank bad coffee from his wall unit while we tried to make some sense of what we had to do. The plan of action we kept coming back to— going to Cantata to spy on my mother—stank. But with my mother involved in this, whatever this was, I could no longer turn my back and walk away.

Badger put down the holo cube he'd been fingering and settled deeper into his chair. "You think I don't know that? You think I forgot how we left home? I promise you I did not wipe that whole ordeal from my memory."

The old guilt still stabbed at me whenever he said something about home. When Badger had helped me escape Cantata, he had thrown away his future, his name, his past, everything he owned, everything he was. Most of all, he had left behind parents and brothers and sisters who cared about him. He had run with me because he was my best friend, my only friend. And I had been young enough and scared enough to let him do it. That was the greatest shame I bore . . . that when I ran I didn't run alone.

"I still have nightmares that one of these days she's going to track me down and kill me," I said.

"So do I." He sighed. "But she hasn't done it yet."

She hadn't. I couldn't deny that. "So we're going to go back to the devil's lair. What fun." I stood and stretched, working the kinks out of the muscles in the back of my neck. They were tight—tension does that to me. "Don't set a course yet, Badg. I'll be in my quarters. The strain of the last couple of days is catching up with me. I need to rest."

I didn't need to rest. I did, however, need a dose of courage, of anger, and of moral outrage. I had those stored in my locker.

In my quarters, I opened my locker and shoved my clothing out of the way, feeling along the underside of the shelf until I found the hard silicon chip held there with tape. I pulled it down and peeled off the tape. Some bits of the sticky residue clung to the top of the chip; it wouldn't hurt the chip, but might gum up the reader.

I scraped it away with a fingernail and popped it in, and my mother appeared, looking at something off to my right. Her eyes were red and her cheeks were tear-stained. She was still beautiful. Her hair, tightly curly and rich ebony with blue-black highlights, was close-cropped, which accented her high, elegant cheekbones and strong jaw. Her eyes, huge and black, spoke eloquently of pain beyond measure or comprehension.

She held her head up and kept her spine rigidly straight, and even to me she looked like a woman holding herself back from collapse by will alone. Her upper lip, which traced the exact curve mine did, trembled slightly. Above and behind her, the soft golden glow of a Verilamp confirmed that she had told the truth about her name, her address, her other personal information.

A police officer sat off to one side of her. Occasionally I could see the line of his nose and part of his forehead and the top of his hair as he leaned forward. Once I saw him pat her shoulder, and with that human touch, fresh tears slipped from the inner corners of her eyes. She did not sob, though, and her voice was almost steady.

Willpower. You could see it in every line of her body, every slightest movement, every look. By the effort of my will, her body said, I will undo what has been done. I will right these wrongs.

The officer asked her, "Do you know who might have wanted to kill your family?"

She looked at him. Pain. Incredible pain, betrayal, grief. Those eloquent eyes, which had led so many so far. And she said, "Yes. I do."

I mouthed the words with her. I knew them by heart; I had seen her say them so many times—in my nightmares, in my waking dreams. I had heard her voice utter them over and over and over, always with that slight tremble, always with such conviction, such sorrow. This was the other half of my family; there was Isas Yamamoto, the father I desired, and then there was Lashanda Elenday, the mother I could not deny.

She said, "I had a fight with Tanasha just six days ago—"

I cringed at the sound of my old name, half-afraid, even in the privacy of my own cabin and the safety of my own ship, that someone, somewhere, would hear that name and connect the child I had been to the woman I was.

And the officer interrupted, "That would be Tanasha Elenday?"

"My daughter. My oldest child."

The officer nodded.

"We fought. Bitter, bitter words. She told me that I had betrayed her by marrying; that I had betrayed her by loving someone else. She's a Maryschild, you see. She always felt scarred by her differences, by the fact that she was special for a while and then the world moved on and didn't hold her up and see her as special anymore." Tears ran down her cheeks and her chin trembled. The globe above her head stayed warmly golden, insisting on the truth as she told it, promising that her version of events was the real version. She didn't seem to be lying at all, and in the interview I could see that the officers treated her with the compassion due a woman who had suffered greatly.

She stared down at the hands that lay, still and perfect, on her lap. She shook her head, paused, took a slow breath. I could hear, across the years and the empty reaches of space, how shaky that breath was. She looked up and her eyes met the officer's and they were guileless. "She wanted a father who was living and breathing, and I can't blame her for that."

One trembling finger reached up and wiped uselessly at the tear sliding down the cheek. "I made a mistake. I was wrong to create the Maryschildren . . . wrong to try to make the world better in that way." Steady gold light glowed, with never a flicker of red that would indicate that she was in the least ambivalent about what she said. My mother swallowed hard. Continued, still strong, still courageous. "And she blamed me when the man I married was not light-eyed or pale-haired; the children I had with him looked like us, but not like her. She blamed me for loving him and refused to believe that I could love her, too." The faintest flickering now . . . red, gold, red, gold, but such flickering doesn't indicate lying. It only indicates a strong emotional response. Guilt, grief, regret—all of these things showed on her fine face, and echoed in her clear contralto voice, and the flickering light above her head said nothing different. She was a good woman, and she had suffered much.

The officer was nodding. I could see the top of his hair—brown, brushed straight, cut short—moving up and down, up and down.

"I tried so hard to make sure she knew how I loved her." Red. Gold. My mother's head dropped, and her shoulders shook, and I heard the sniffle. With her head down, she said, "I failed her. If I had been a better mother, I would have found some way to reach her." Gold, red, gold.

And the officer said, "Some people are born bad, Mada Elenday. If she was born bad, nothing you could have done could have saved her."

My mother kept her head down and her voice grew softer. "She came home six days ago. I hadn't seen her in almost three months. She had been to the Sensos before she came home, and to the joy chambers. Her eyes were fever-bright and angry. She wanted credit. She said she'd used all the credits on her identicard and she wanted me to transfer some of mine." Red and gold, but mostly red. Anyone studying the recording would see what pain she was in and give her the benefit of the doubt. The officers made it clear that they felt for her, but no one could look at them and say they were unprofessional. No one else knew what I knew.

My mother was important in Meileone. She did so many public works. People liked her. People empathized with her—they always had. She always seemed so warm, so caring and compassionate, so devoted to her family, her causes, the common good. Strangers, on finding out I was her daughter, used to tell me how lucky I was, and how they envied me. And the people behind the scenes, the ones behind the camera and operating the Verilamp knew what people in Meileone thought of her. They could count on her halo effect to cover the flashes in the Verilamp. They could count on the viewers of the recording looking at my mother and saying, "Poor, brave woman. I don't know how she has managed to hold up under all of this."

My mother stopped speaking and leaned forward, a movement so boneless she seemed to topple, and her face dropped into her hands. She was silent, and her shoulders shook, and occasionally I could hear the muffled, tremulous intake of her breath.

The officer waited.

Waited.

Waited.

Said, "I know how hard this is. Take your time."

My mother took a long, shuddering breath and sat straight up again. "That's all right, officer. This is just so horrible. I lost all of them, and she's lost, too. My Tanasha is so lost."

He nodded. Waited.

"I told her I wanted her to come home. That I didn't like the friends she was with. Bangers, droppers, Senso-heads. I said I wouldn't give her money. I told my child to come home. That I loved her." And this was red and gold, mostly gold.

The officer was still now. Waiting.

"She said I was going to be sorry. That she would hurt me, take away everything I ever loved." A mother's convulsive sob, gushing tears, arms flung forward and down to grab tight to knees. "And I didn't say anything to anyone because I didn't believe she would do it. I didn't believe my daughter was capable of such atrocities. I let her walk away when I should have stopped her. I should have found her help. I should have told someone what she had said."

The officer rested a hand on her shoulder at last, and said, "You don't need to sit here any longer. You've been through enough. But I have one other question that I have to ask you before you go. I'm sorry I have to ask, but I wouldn't be doing my job if I didn't.

The guilt-wracked, wretched-voiced whisper. "Don't apologize, officer. You can ask me anything. Anything."

He took his hand away, and in the emotionless professional voice of a man who had to do unpleasant things every day, he said, "Did you kill your family?"

She looked up, doe-eyed and startled. "No, of course not," she said, and the light glowed golden as a sun.

"Did you have any part in their deaths—did you hire someone else to kill them, or solicit for their deaths?"

"No."

Gold.

"Did you know in advance that their lives were in danger and withhold information from any authorities?"

"No. Officer, I never believed that my Tanasha . . ." and here she began to weep.

Gold. Flawless unflickering glowing gold.

The questioning officer waited. Patient.

She caught her breath, lifted her head, looked into his

eyes and said, in a voice breaking from her grief, "I never believed that my Tanasha would be capable of hurting anyone. Never. And certainly not her own family, no matter how lost she has become. This was my fault. All my fault."

Gold. Gold. Only gold.

The officer said, "Thank you for your time. I apologize again for having to make you come down here, and for making you answer such terrible questions."

She wiped her eyes—my mother the martyr, brave and strong, with her shoulders once again back, and her spine straight, and her head held high.

She was perfect. Facing the hard questions, the Verilamp had glowed golden. It lied the way my mother lied.

With that final flawlessly staged bit of motherly anguish, when she had seemed to blame herself for doing what most caring mothers would have done, she had cleverly told the listening officer the absolute truth and had, in the same moment, condemned me with the lie of it.

Their deaths *were* her fault, but not because she didn't think I could kill them. She *had* killed them; rather, she had hired a friend of hers to do it, but the deaths were on her hands. You can't lie to a Verilamp—but if you own the man who operates it, he can make sure that you don't have to worry about lying. He can do what the police in that room did—he can give you a good interview, make you look sympathetic, and turn the damned thing off when the questions get dangerous.

With that one short, well-staged interview, my mother disposed of a man and two children who had begun to stand in the way of her ambition. She had cleared herself completely of any slight suspicion anyone might have harbored regarding her involvement in the deaths. She had shoved the guilt onto an embarrassing Maryschild daughter. She had made herself the good mother, the long-suffering martyr. And she had created the first plank in a platform that launched her again into the limelight and power, this time in the legitimate government of Meileone, in what would prove to be an unstoppable political career.

When the city police came for me and took me from my apartment to my old home to face the cooling bodies of my half-brother and half-sister and my stepfather, they pretended to disbelieve my shock. They charged me with the deaths, and in my interview with the Verilamp, they played the same tricks with the lamp that they'd played with her, only in reverse. When I said I wasn't guilty, that I would never have hurt my stepfather or my brother and sister, the Verilamp glowed red. When they asked me bluntly if I had killed them, I denied it, and the Verilamp bled like a martyred saint. Red and red and more red at every turn, and I screamed that something was wrong with the lamp, and that I was being framed, and that I was innocent, and the light mocked me. And the police mocked me. They knew I was innocent—they had great fun playing their game with me and watching me suffer through their harsh questioning.

When they were through with me, they locked me into a securicell to await my trial.

Badger heard about my arrest from a neighbor who had seen the removal of the bodies and who had been more than willing to share the gossip. Badger knew I hadn't killed my family—even if he had thought me capable of it, I'd been with him constantly during the time when the murders took place. He knew my mother, too, though, and knew that if she were involved, we had no hope for justice, only for escape. So he used his skill with compac and mind, found out where I was being kept, and by altering the records in the comnet and creating false identities and a clever series of misdirections, he got me out. We ran, and in a way I suppose we never stopped running.

The holo had flickered out, and I realized at last that I'd been staring at empty air.

I stood in the darkness of my quarters, a woman far different than the child I had been when I fled Cantata. I had found the first step toward adulthood when I stripped my last tightly held illusions away; when, at seventeen, I finally admitted that my mother harbored no secret fondness for me. That she was not hiding love deep down inside her heart. That she was exactly as cold and calculating and manipulative as she had always seemed. That the day when she would hold me in her arms and tell me that she was sorry and that she regretted all those lost years and painful memories would never come.

The first step to adulthood hurt like hell, and it kept hurting for years, holding me chained to it, unable to take the second step.

I broke the chains only when I earned my private craft license and won a third-captain's berth on a tramp cargo freighter. Badger signed on as crew, and the two of us, false identities established by legitimate work, traveled, learned, and began making plans for a future in which we would have our own ship and owe nothing to anyone. I found that even in a life bereft of illusions, hope existed. And without the illusions, hope was not constantly destroyed, because it was based on reality instead of fantasy.

Reasons for living existed. I took that second step when I embraced hope and made my own life.

I thought that was all there was to being an adult. Two hard steps, then a long plateau. Now the third step faced me, steep and deadly and promising the pain of old wounds reopened and the agony of new wounds. But the third step in adulthood was to take responsibility for my past. I had to find out what my mother was involved in. If I could, I had to stop her. This wasn't about the *Corrigan's Blood* anymore, except peripherally. It wasn't about the money. It wasn't about a job. It was about making my mother pay for the evil she had done, not just to me and to my family, but to everyone whose life she had touched and altered for the worse.

I paged Badger. "I'm ready now. We'll keep Crane's money and try to find the *Corrigan's Blood*; I think it's all related and even if it isn't, we're going to need the money we have to keep on this. I'll go revert the credit in the credit chit to our account. While I do that, work out the course to Cantata. We can stop first at Tegosshu to get makeovers and two deep identities from Storm Rat, and a switchable ID for the *Hope's Reward*. Then we'll go home."

Chapter Seventeen

Deep IDs belonged to someone once. All the numbers are real, all the facts are checkable, and only DNA stands between the purchaser and the reality of being the person who first wore the name.

While Badger oversaw work on the ship's ID switcher, Storm Rat tucked himself into his seat and squinted at me. "I chose two people for you who were traveling companions who owned their own ship."

"Good."

"Maybe." He shrugged and pulled his knees closer to his chest. "You're going to be Adana Gantrey. Pirates killed her and her lover and destroyed her ship out by the Terbian Nexus. The planet that noted her death doesn't maintain links with any of the nets, so the only place where she is officially dead is that world."

"Where's her home planet?"

"Dresden, but she doesn't have any family to speak of. When she was quite young, she married old money attached to an old man." Storm Rat grinned. "Her husband died in an unfortunate accident. Since marrying old men is a lousy way to make money ever since nanomedicine, I suspect she helped the accident along."

"She killed him?"

"Had him killed, I imagine. But she was smart; she was

never charged, and when she finally got her hands on his money, she parlayed his million-rucet fortune into multimillions by diversifying into some fields he wouldn't have touched." He sighed. "Officially, all she ever did was collect her husband's money and make science Sensos."

"Unofficially?"

"You aren't going to like this part. She produced shock-porn Sensos; bankrolled an underground nanotech lab that created some weird, weird drugs; involved herself in gambling and money laundering and bought herself a few politicians. She wasn't big, but she was bad."

"Lovely. Where am I most likely to run into the people who want to kill her? Me, I mean."

"Stay away from Dresden. For that matter, if I were you I'd avoid the entire Borland Quad. She doesn't seem to have developed any sort of a reputation beyond that—and she doesn't have any record universally, of course, or I wouldn't have bought the ID in the first place."

"That works. I won't be going anywhere near the Borland Quad. So who is Badger going to be?"

"Brian Darkman, her professionally unemployed traveling companion, who met her when he was starring in one of her productions—one from the second line, not the first."

"He's going to be a Senso star?" I rubbed my temples briefly. "Oh, he'll just love that."

"Really?"

"No."

"Oh. I hadn't thought he would."

But Storm Rat, knowing we wouldn't like the people we were to become, had made us those people anyway. Good IDs were hard to find, and these were people who could go where we needed to go and do what we needed to do.

"Thanks, Storm Rat. What kind of physical modifications are we going to have to do to be Adana and Brian?"

He tapped a key on his desk and a life-sized holo appeared in front of me. "This was her current holo at the time of her death."

I groaned. She was a fair-skinned, short redhead with big tits and freckles. Her face was nothing like mine. "I'm going to have to have my melanin lifted to be that pale, and have major osteosculpting to be that short. And our faces . . . lots of osteo there, too. And after I've done all of this, I'm not going to be able to go anywhere near reju."

Storm Rat looked concerned. "I don't have any other deep IDs that will work for you and Badger."

"Oh, I'll take her." I'm sure my smile was wan. "I just don't want to *be* her."

"I understand. If I had anyone more suitable, I'd offer." He sat up straight and put his feet on the floor. "Look. We can change the recorded body stats if you want to keep your height. You are highly unlikely to meet friends of hers where you're going. We'll alter her DNA records and ret scans and palmlock signature to conform to yours—you aren't trying to access her bank accounts or any other part of her life anyway. We could have you Melatinted instead of doing a melanin lift. Underneath you'd still be dark brown instead of pale, but who would know?" He tapped on his front teeth with a finger. "I still think you ought to have your face osteosculpted."

"I want the full treatment. Retinal cheaters, palm detailing, dental reshaping. I'll have my melanin lifted, too." I stared at the woman I was to become. "I might even have my tits enlarged a little—but not enough to throw off my balance. I'll keep my height. This is the height and weight I'm used to. I don't want to have to learn a whole new way of fighting and walking."

"That makes sense. I'll have Marait get to work on you, then." He flicked his finger over the button again, and Adana Gantrey dissolved. "If you see Badger, would you have him come up? I want to go over his ID with him."

I nodded and left.

I hadn't enjoyed the painful procedure of having my melanin lifted, and I'd hated the injection of the retinal cheaters, but except for my DNA, I was no longer connectable to the child from Cantata. And Adana's ID chip claimed my DNA as her own. As long as I stayed out of trouble with Cantata's law enforcement system, no one would have a reason to compare it against the back files. I could travel safely through Meileone and any other city on Cantata.

Badger and I wouldn't have recognized each other. He was beautiful. His hair was black and wavy, his eyes were amber, and his skin was rich honey brown. His face had adorned the most perfect of ancient Greek sculptures; his body belonged on the greatest of modern dancers.

I, with long, curly, intractable red hair and the face of a second-rate Botticelli, would have had reason to hate him—except that Badger and I learned the value of appearances long before we could change ours with the simple exchanging of credits.

"You'll like the switcher," he told me as we headed for the origami point that would take us out of the Tegosshu system. "When we stop to alter the external ID, it will take us just a second to change all the internal records."

"Except for changing the numbers embedded in the moleibond on the hull. That will take a while."

"Well, yes. But there isn't any fast way to do that. They made it as easy as they could. The *Merry Widow*'s number is now only two away from ours. We'll have to change an eight to a three and a one to a four. Anyway, once we're done on Cantata, another flip of the switch and we'll be the *Hope's Reward* again. Storm Rat's people did a brilliant job on the circuits. They scraped off that hull bug, too."

"I'm glad it's gone."

The layover on Storm Rat's planet had cost us two days and twenty thousand rucets, and even though it had been necessary, we felt the pressure of time passing. So we were doing what we could to get to Cantata without leaving a clear trail.

More than almost everything else, we worried that Fedara Contei was somewhere behind us, even though we couldn't find any sign of her. We'd chosen a convoluted route to the Tegosshu system, and we chose an equally convoluted route away from it, dropping out of hyperspace twice in each direction to file route plans in systems with multiple habitable planets and numerous busy stations, places we had no intention of visiting. We hoped that she would lose time searching for us in those systems, but we couldn't count on fooling her. However, we hoped to break our trail entirely when we switched IDs.

Two origami points from Cantata, we dropped out into an untenanted system—no habitable planets, no terraformed planets, no mining operations, no traffic except through traffic to other systems. We put ourselves into orbit around a miserable ball of rock and ice. From this location we intended to change the *Hope's Reward* into the *Merry Widow*.

"Do you want to work on the ship now?" Badger asked. He looked as tired as I felt.

The two times that we'd dropped out of hyperspace to lay a false trail had resulted in three trips through origami points. I'd had a rough, emotional time of it, and Badger had, too.

The external modifications on the ship meant deep space work. That was going to be tiring even when we were well-rested. "No. It's going to take us hours to do the numbers. Longer if we're tired and make mistakes. We both need to sleep."

We had not been able to change the ship's identity in the Tegosshu system. Storm Rat's security lay in the fact that the few ships that came to his planet appeared to leave in exactly the same condition as they had come in. No one mysteriously disappeared from the Tegosshu system. No one mysteriously appeared there. Storm Rat lived in a fortress, and ran a quasi-legitimate bar/trading post/repair station out of it to provide an acceptable excuse for the traffic to and from his world, and while the majority of his employees never went near the legit parts of the business, a few could double as bartenders, waiters, and traders if anyone who wanted to cause Storm Rat trouble showed up.

Anyone who trailed or backtrailed us would find that we vanished here, not there.

We shut down everything except the shields and the alarms and both of us went down to our quarters to sleep.

I had nightmares. I often did, but these nightmares were different. This was the resurrection of the unavenged dead. I hadn't dreamed of my half-brother or half-sister or stepfather in a long time. In this dream, they came back to life, hunting me through the city where they had died. Blaming me for their deaths. Even my mother's victims believed my mother; *everyone* believed my mother. And I ran through the endless underground maze of Meileone; through the glossy moleibonded tunnels with their embedded strellitas glittering like nearby stars; through the broad, tree-lined malls with the walkways crowded with happy people hurrying from place to place; and I was invisible, doomed, haunted, pursued by the vengeful dead.

Sleeping nightmare became waking nightmare in an instant; my sister's ruined, rotting face became a red light flashing, a klaxon blaring in my ear, the shudder of the ship as something slammed us broadside. I was out of bed, through the gravdrop and to the bridge before I was fully awake. I'd brought up the tactical holos while still trying to shake off the nightmare.

Beside me, Badger flung himself into the navigator's seat and began plotting our evasive maneuvers. His role was defensive; shields and flight. I was in charge of our offense.

Badger shut down the red lights and the goddamned klaxons. They'd served their purpose; during battle they would only distract us and make us edgier than we already were. In the blessed silence that followed their shutdown, he said, "I make two ships . . . both light cruisers, both of them sending Smithbright's World registration. Not warships . . . probably not pirates."

I was halfway through my weapons-engagement sequence when the relevance of that sank in. We weren't under attack for trespassing in somebody's space, we weren't about to be robbed by pirates . . . and we probably weren't in the middle of another encounter with Fedara Contei. She wasn't likely to pilot a ship registered to Smithbright's World.

Unless coincidence plagued us—and I didn't believe in coincidence—these ships were fallout from the trouble we had gotten ourselves into on Smithbright's World. These were the people who frightened Fedara Contei.

"Is everybody following us?" I snarled.

"Evidently." Badger was quiet for an instant, working on the nav console. Then he said, "The shields held against their first volley. Record says they're using lasers and big concussion missiles. They don't want to take us prisoner. They want us dead." He watched his holo. "They're both turning. Sloppy turns. Doesn't look like these people do this for a living."

"Lucky us," I muttered. I watched the pair of ships arc through their turn on my display and saw the sloppiness Badger had commented on. The lead ship held a tight turn. The second ship drifted out of the arc, overcorrected and came too far in, backed off to keep from ramming his leader, then tried to make up distance with a grav boost that lurched him forward like a drunk tripping over his dropped bottle.

Two-to-one odds scared me; I wasn't a fighter pilot. Nor was I a battle-hardened vet. I got my starcraft license commercially. Badger and I had been involved in one bout with a single pirate ship who backed off as soon as he realized we were armed with more than the factory-installed repellers. Something told me these attackers weren't going to back off. My mouth dried and an icy dribble of sweat slid under the neckband of my jumpsuit and rolled between my shoulder blades.

I tried to plan a battle strategy that would get us out of this alive and make sure they didn't keep coming after us. Nothing brilliant came to mind.

I had fifty pulse charges; twenty energy-seeking grav-flux charges; twenty sticky pies; four turreted sweep lasers forward and four aft. I had twenty slaveable phantom rounds that would broadcast a silhouette identical to the *Reward's* for ten minutes each. I had the best shields I'd been able to afford; they were a thousand times better than standard factory flight shields, which were intended to deflect nothing but microscopic space debris, but they were still far from top-of-the-line.

Those were all standard weapons. I didn't have any of the expensive, hard-to-obtain armaments like Anabond drillers or hull piercers. I did, however, have one untested piece of armament—not just untested by me, but entirely untested. Storm Rat had installed it for me for free, with the understanding that if I used it and survived, I would return to let him know how it worked.

My secret weapon, such as it was, was a gravity shear; according to Storm Rat it was a weapon of last resort, intended for use if the *Reward* became crippled and the enemy ship came within grappling range. It was supposed to use the enemy ship's own artificial gravity system to create narrow bands of opposing gravity; these bands would theoretically incapacitate the enemy by making movement impossible.

Storm Rat set it up to run through the gravdrop and into the enemy's gravdrop, on the theory that that was the only way they could reach us. He said that he didn't know how well the shear would work—laboratory test versions of it had caused some internal bleeding in lab animals, but he said he had no way to figure for the effects of vacuum, distance, hull shielding, engine power, or what he called the "oops" factor. He said he thought it might do a little something, but he couldn't guarantee it. There was an awful lot of "theory" in his description of the gravity shear, and while I'm not one to turn my nose up at free armaments, my confidence in Storm Rat's invention was not high.

"They're coming at us," Badger said. "I've plotted our evasive maneuver. Coordinates to you now."

They'd completed their turn and now came racing toward the *Reward*. My display showed us as a gold blip, them as red blips surrounded by a thin green line that indicated the presence and condition of their shields. The shield of the forward ship blanked for a fraction of a second and a thin row of white specks moved toward us. Their second volley.

I checked my weapons launch vectors and adjusted them to the evasive maneuvers Badger had set. As the ship bucked upward and accelerated painfully, I launched two phantoms, which each shot out in a course one hundred eighty degrees from ours and mirrored our evasive maneuvers precisely. "Phantoms deployed."

Now five ships showed on my holo, three of them gold. One ship latched on to us, one to one of the phantoms. Pulse charges began rocking us as their second volley caught up with us and tried to blow us apart. Badger accelerated, and when he did, the phantoms, linked to our shipcom until their systems died, accelerated too. I freed the phantom that hadn't attracted a ship from the slave navigation and sent it tearing toward the nearest origami point, as if it was the true ship and had fooled the attackers. The pulse charges stopped.

Our tail and the other attacking ship went into tight turns and hared off after it.

The shipcom said, "Damage in the TFN unit—TFN secondary rotor snapped. Repair units activated."

"Damn," Badger said.

"It can repair that."

"I know."

Badger took us in behind the second ship and I released a short barrage of pulse charges. He pulled us up as they both came around, realizing that they had been duped.

I launched four pulse charges out the back, and sent two targeted sticky pies after them. While Badger began a series of brutal twisting maneuvers, the pulse charges slammed against their shields.

We shot straight up, veered hard to starboard and

dropped away from the planet. I saw twin lines of return fire trace after us from the red blips. Badger yanked us to port and down relative to our previous position.

Not fast enough, not hard enough. Shock waves ripped through the *Reward* and the holo blinked off, then on again.

"Damn," Badger said.

"What did they get this time?"

The shipcom's voice said, "Serious damage to the forward number three engine, shattered filter in back-up air plant. Weakening in moleibonding of ventral dispersal fin."

On my tac holo, the second ship blossomed; the sticky pie had hit the shield, reversed its energy to attract itself so that it wouldn't be repulsed, and exploded. The concussion charge might weaken the hull, but more importantly it ought to send enough shock waves through the ship to do serious internal damage.

"Hit," I said.

"Good. Now just cover us for a while. I'm going to see if we can get far enough ahead of them that we can double around and get behind them." Badger pushed us to the limits of our engines, running flat out away from the planet, up from the system, toward deep space. I set up a laser pattern with the aft turrets to destroy incoming missiles before they hit us, and held my breath. I could hear the whine in the number three engine, a high-pitched squeal at odds with the deep, musical thrumming of the healthy engines.

Both ships came around again, though one limped through the turn. They moved after us, accelerating fast.

"Looks like I got a repulsor on the second one," I said. If I could screw up their navigation systems, they would be helpless.

"Let's hope."

I cut the lasers and dropped our aft shields long enough to launch a quad of the grav-flux charges. A blast rattled through the hull again and red lights flared on the systems board. I was flung against my restraining straps so hard I couldn't breathe. The bastards had been waiting for the lasers to cut out. They'd had a missile riding out where the lasers couldn't reach, something that masked itself, something smart enough to stay put and wait for an opening. Whatever they'd launched hurt us. I heard the stutter as one engine died, the change in the voice of a second as it rose to a tortured machine squeal.

The shipcom's voice broke in. "Main life support unit twenty percent damage. Backup life support destroyed. Breaks in water lines at junctures seven/twelve/thirty-four, one-twenty-eight/ten/thirty-four, fourteen/ten/thirty-four. Engine three irreparable. Engine one critical. Engine four damaged. TFN unit has sustained additional but reparable damage. Repairs initiated on all reparable units."

They had bigger, more deadly weapons than we had. They outnumbered us and outgunned us. And now, with us down to one fully functional engine and two badly damaged ones, they were closing fast.

"We can't win this," Badger said, echoing my thought.

"We have to. I'm not old enough to die."

Badger's chuckle was humorless. "I'll never be old enough to die."

I was scared to drop the lasers long enough to send anything back, but I wasn't going to go without making them pay. I prepared a massive salvo: twenty pulse charges, twenty grav-flux charges, ten sticky pies. If I could take out one or both of them this time, I would, but I was still going to play dead. I told Badger, "On my mark, hard starboard." He nodded.

"Three."

They launched a few pulse charges. I cut them up with the lasers.

"Two." My hands hovered over the aft laser button and the launch button.

"One."

Badger and I leaned forward, holding our breaths.

"Mark."

I hit both buttons and we tore into a starboard turn so

tight I thought we were going to meet ourselves. I hit the lasers again and we were covered. Nothing got through this time, and even better, we threw our pursuers; they kept going straight long enough to take the worst of our huge salvo. One ship glowed brilliant red on the holo for an instant and the green edge around the blip died. The killed ship tumbled away from us, falling upward. Its blip went black and cold. The other ship kept coming, though, and kept gaining.

A blinding white starburst erupted below us, and I felt rather than heard the fourth engine explode in its moleibond compartment. The ship bucked like an animal. My seat, with me strapped into it, ripped loose and flew backward into the manual nav console, and sparks spattered and hissed for an instant before the console went dead. The artificial gravity died. I rebounded into Badger, who wasn't able to get out of his straps fast enough to avoid me. A ragged edge of something tore the palm of his hand open, and fat red droplets of blood floated through the air. The shipcom was ticking off damage, but it didn't need to. We had partial use of one engine, and our TFN unit was dead. More than that I couldn't hear—nor did I want to.

We tumbled through space, not losing any speed but picking up a nightmare spin from the explosion. Without gravity to brake my inertia, the *Reward* slammed me around the cabin like a pebble in a rattle. I fought with the straps and got partly free, hit a wall and flopped against it. The seat snapped around and smashed my face between it and the wall. Red sheets of pain shuttered my eyes for a moment, replaced by white lights like shooting stars. The seat bounced off of something else and my head snapped back and hit that before we rebounded, sailing through the air, aimed at yet another obstacle. I was still bouncing, the ship was still spinning. It was going to spin and tumble like this forever and I wasn't going to get free of the straps and I was going to be beaten to death.

A hand grabbed me and hung on. I felt another belt

slip around my waist; all the while, the seat kept swinging, pulling at me, hitting me, slamming me from side to side. The pain screamed through me. Badger worked at the straps that still bound me to the seat and eventually unstuck the damaged locking mechanism and got me loose. He slid the seat into a locker and shut the locker. No more flying debris.

I waited while my vision cleared. I looked up into his face.

"Can you tell if we have any ship function left at all?" I asked.

"The main power plant is fine. We have twenty-percent function in one engine. Our life support system is almost dead and the auxiliary system is gone. Main bridge is dead, but the auxiliary bridge is still functional. The shipcom is still operational, though it has lost connections to most of its subsystems. Our weapons systems, excluding lasers, are intact, but we don't have much of anything left."

"What happened to the lasers?"

"They hit us with some sort of moleibonder, something I've never seen; it sealed the laser turrets over, made them integral with the hull. If we try to use them, we'll blow ourselves up."

"That's bad. We needed those lasers."

"It gets worse."

"How much worse can it get?"

He sighed. "The TFN unit is utterly destroyed. Irreparable."

"We're stuck here? Here? We're a hundred light years from *anything*! We picked this point because nobody came through here. And nobody we want to find us is looking for us. We could be here for years before someone comes through the point. Or forever."

Badger said, "Not a problem. We have a day's worth of drinkable water, a couple days' worth of breathable air, and if the life support system functions at its current level without repair, the two of us will be able to breathe normally for about three hours a day after that without the carbon dioxide buildup killing us. We're dead right now, Cady. We just haven't caught up with reality yet."

I wasn't ready to be dead. "Maybe the ship we killed has a working TFN unit. Maybe we could salvage that."

Badger shook his head. "We will probably be able to stop our spin, course-correct and hobble back to the origami point before we run out of air, but even if we could build up the speed to overtake the ship we destroyed, we don't have any way of knowing if their TFN is still operational . . . and by the time we found out, we'd be out of time."

"The shipcom can't repair life support or the remaining engine?"

"Self-repair is one of the functions shipcom lost."

"Oh."

I said, "What happened to the ship that we didn't kill?"

"If they're smart, they have figured out that we're crippled way beyond anything we can come back from, and they're on their way home right now. Or maybe they're setting out to retrieve their friends."

"We have to convince them that we aren't hurt as bad as we look. We have to make them think we're playing dead."

"Why?" Badger asked. "So they'll come in and finish killing us?"

"Yes. Exactly."

"Have you lost your mind?"

"No. They still have a working TFN unit. I want it."

"You have lost your mind. The blow to your head has rattled your brain. We're in a dead ship. They don't look like they're even hurt much. If we try to convince them that we're still a going concern, they are going to pound the hell out of us, grapple and board us and go through making sure nothing is alive in here. Better to let them think we're dead."

"No." I was determined not to give up. "Not better. If we can get them to grapple before boarding, we can try out Storm Rat's gravity shear. We can incapacitate them while we go through the airlock, take them prisoner, then cut their TFN out of its bay and replace ours. *Maybe* then we can find out what's going on."

"You're going to risk our lives on Storm Rat's untried gadget?"

"We're already dead, remember?" I unhooked myself from the wall belt, preparatory to crawling along the handholds toward the door out of the bridge. "We aren't risking anything we haven't already lost."

I started crawling. I hurt, and that surprised me. I would have thought pain would have started seeming routine; after all, in the last two weeks I'd been beaten almost to death twice. But every ache and stab and white-hot flare was fresh and new and startling.

"I suppose you're right," Badger said. His voice was thoughtful.

We worked our way aft, through the shambles of the medical unit, into the dead gravdrop, where we climbed cautiously down the handholds provided by the manufacturer for emergencies like this. We went past the opening for the second floor, which smelled faintly of smoke and chemicals, and down to the third floor, where the ship's power core, the auxiliary weapons and shields, and the auxiliary navigation deck were. When I bought the *Hope's Reward*, I'd had a couple of Storm Rat's talented shipwrights remove the luxurious captain's suite from the third floor. I'd wanted back-up systems much more than I'd wanted my own little galley and sitting room or the decadent bathing chamber or the bedroom that had been done up to suit the previous owner's tacky bordello fantasies.

My rare foresight was going to pay off. Maybe.

While Badger used what was left of our remaining engine to gradually slow us down and stop our wild tumbling, I created a message to send to the surface of the planet we'd been orbiting. It said:

> Survived. Engine damage, weapons gone. Proof of link between Corrigan, Cassamir Biologicals, USAG and multi-planet conspiracy on board.

We're playing dead. Don't reply.

Badger brought up the tac holo and sighed. "The second ship went after the one we killed. It's there and coupled—I guess it's rescuing survivors."

"So we'll have more prisoners we have to keep track of."

"Awfully optimistic of you. I was thinking they would have more hands to kill us with."

"Thanks, Badg. Always looking at the positive side of things—that's you." I set up the transmission pattern I wanted. Then I waited. Badger slowed the *Reward*'s roll further, just enough that I could get a fair fix on the surface of the planet. I didn't want a perfect shot. Then I'd have no excuse to miss. And missing was important. As soon as the roll slowed enough that I could manually direct the transmission, I sent the message in a tight-beam burst, simultaneously spraying a broad-beam of static that should alert our enemy that we weren't dead. I hoped the static would look like a leak in the shielding of my communications system that I didn't know I had. If my enemies were good, they'd still be watching us. They would catch the static. If they were very good, they'd intercept the transmission on the first time. I wasn't going to count on that, though. I was going to do two more quick bursts, acting like I wasn't sure whether the tight beam had gone to the right place the first time. Under the circumstances it would seem like a logical thing to do.

I waited until we'd rolled to face the planet again and sent the second transmission. I didn't need to send the third.

"They're uncoupling from the other ship now," he said. "Rapid breakaway . . . I wonder if they had time to get everyone off."

"Let's hope so. Be a nightmare to rescue them if they didn't."

"I'd like to let them rot in space," Badger said. "That's what they would have done to us."

"Not necessarily." I was watching the holo. The enemy

ship was closing fast. "They might have come back and killed us quickly. Start evasive maneuvers. Don't do anything that would keep them from catching us, though."

Our shields were up and we were putting most of the power from our core straight into them. We didn't intend to let fly with so much as a stinkbomb this time. They had to believe we were in defensive mode only, and they had to want to come aboard to get the information we had on them.

So we ran . . . rather, we limped. We weren't going as fast as we could. We weren't doing anything that would put real strain on our last engine. On the other hand, we managed to thrash around and look like we were trying like hell to elude them. We aimed ourselves for the closest origami point as if we'd jump anywhere just to get away. The chase ended with the thuds of their magnetic grapples connecting to the embedded metal in the moleibond hull.

I waited. Held my breath. Sound won't travel through space—I couldn't hear the rumble of their engines and wouldn't until both our shields were off, when their hull touched ours and transmitted the vibrations. I felt them reeling us in. They eliminated the last of our spin and hauled us to a standstill, killing our inertia. I cursed them. We were going to have a hellish time building any kind of speed again with only one engine. I waited for the little jolt that would precede that click, the jolt of their shield touching ours and the two ships repelling each other.

And there it was. The jolt. They caught us. They had us where we wanted them. They would be rolled back to back with us to permit them to extrude their coupler so that they could board us. They would have to turn off a portion of their ventral shield to do that.

I felt another tiny jolt, and heard the metallic scrape, thud, click of the coupler locking into place against our hull. Now they would come across the short distance, armed with moleibond cutters to tear open our airlock. They wouldn't worry about finding the right airlock code. When they left, the *Hope's Reward* would be left open to space;

our bodies, mangled by decompression, would probably be sucked out into space along with anything else that wasn't attached. The odds were good that no one would ever find us, and the only people who would even look were the investigators from Fidelity Mutual of Ganymede, to whom I still owed a lot of money . . . and perhaps Peter Crane, to whom I still owed the return of the *Corrigan's Blood*.

If my plan didn't work, I only had a few more minutes to live. I hoped it would work.

I heard footsteps echoing through the gravdrop. Here they came.

Now!

I switched off the shields and at the same moment turned on the gravity shear, feeding one hundred percent of the ship's power through it, blasting the shear straight up into the coupler and through that into the partially unshielded enemy ship. The roar the gravity shear made was indescribable.

From the gravdrop I heard screams; sharp and terrible and bewilderingly brief, as if I'd pressed a button to turn them on, then immediately pressed it again to turn them off.

Our lights went out. The roar of the gravity shear shut off with a clang I was sure indicated it had broken, and I smelled metallic smoke. The few remaining normal shipboard sounds that indicate things functioning properly ceased. Our ships clapped together like a pair of hands and I heard an ominous squeal of metal from the gravdrop. The gravdrop terminated ventrally in the airlock, and the airlock was edged with the coupler. The sudden shift of the two ships had damaged either their coupler or our airlock, and Badger and I wouldn't know which until we went to investigate.

"Shit," Badger said, "now they'll be through the door in a heartbeat and we're sitting here in a totally dead ship."

The absolute darkness, the silence, the feeling of being isolated and beyond the reach of help all scared me, but we weren't helpless yet. I unstrapped myself from the weapons seat and launched myself backward, toward the auxiliary weapons room. Badger and I had stun guns and a couple of laser rifles in there. I was taking a laser rifle this time, in case the people who were after us were as deadly as the man who'd tried to kill us on Smithbright's World.

Badger thought the way I did. We both floated to the gravdrop and tugged ourselves up. Weightless, we ascended through the silent darkness. I could hear myself breathing; the sound was too raspy and too fast, loud enough that I was sure the enemies on the other side of the airlock could hear me coming.

And I thought, maybe they found a way to open the airlock silently. Maybe they're already in here, in the dark, with us. Maybe they're waiting.

And I thought, don't be stupid. This is just darkness. That's all. You'll fix the engines and you'll get their TFN unit and you'll take them prisoner and everything will be fine. It will be fine. Don't panic yourself because you're in the dark.

In my first year in business and after I'd wrapped up my second case, the client, Jenfer Greeling, said she was surprised I had been able to spend so much time in the dark without going to pieces. I'd been locked in a drop tube in the bottom of her ex-consort's cruiser for two full days while he tried to make the time in his busy schedule to take the cruiser out for a pleasure run so that he could eject me into deep space. I was lucky that his client backlog got the better of him. That time I was lucky in a lot of ways. But Jenfer said that humans had a natural, instinctual fear of darkness because in the beginning they were prey. She said that even now they hide in the light, cluster in packs, make noise once the sun goes down, or if they are alone, they become quiet and still and watchful.

I told her that was nonsense. I'd been afraid because her ex had been trying to kill me. I hadn't gone to pieces because I had a plan for getting myself out of trouble, and my plan had worked. Darkness, I told her, was just the other half of daylight, and instinct was nonsense for the mortal appendages of the immortal spirits we all really were. We didn't need instinct.

But there in the darkness, floating up toward the airlock, the instincts I insisted I didn't have were screaming that I shouldn't go through that door, that hunters hid in the darkness and that they waited for me. And my instinct was to make myself very small and very still and to wait for the return of the light . . . which would have been forever because until I went into their ship and stole their TFN unit and then came back and fixed my ship, there wasn't going to be any light.

At the airlock, I pulled on my thin, flexible breather suit and waited while Badger donned his. When we were both ready, I grabbed one half of the manual handle for the airlock and started twisting. Badger grabbed the other half. When the seal separated, there was no hiss of air escaping into lower pressure. No indication that what we faced on the other side would be the vacuum of deep space. And as the airlock slipped into the groove that would let us push it to the left, light shone through into our darkness. Little fingers of it at first, beams that shot down the gravdrop and illuminated the rungs of the ladder we didn't need at the moment. The fingers grew fatter and then merged as the door opened wider. Light. It looked so warm and welcoming.

I started to move into the coupler corridor, looking for the enemy. Badger, right behind me, had his weapon ready.

I found our enemies waiting for me.

What was left of them, anyway.

Chapter Eighteen

If I looked carefully at the bloody smears on the white walls, at the embedded chips of bone, at the little gobbets of tissue that clung to the inside of the coupler, I could make out vaguely human outlines. The gravity shear had left almost nothing, but what it had left it had left in distinct regions, so that I could see that these stains and globs and tatters were part of one victim, and those bone shards and smears and blotches were part of another. Badger and I counted six distinct bloody stripes where someone had died. The splotch right against our airlock was the biggest, and the only one with any sign of human remains. Pulpy tissue lined with needle-like slivers of bone, a lot of hair in several colors, a couple of small white objects I realized at last were intact teeth. Twisted metal that had to have been weapons. Tatters and wads of material that had the color, if not the appearance, of breather-suit fabric. The scrambled mess seemed impossible. There wasn't enough flesh there to make up a ten-year old child, much less six adults.

Then Badger shook his head and his voice crackled over the speaker in my ear, "It was so strong it compacted them. When it ripped them to ribbons, it was also compressing the remains."

I considered the human puree smeared across the moleibond of our airlock and nodded. No other explanation fit. Still, how much energy had it taken to rip living human flesh into pulp between one beat of a heart and the next? To compact that mass as these people had been compacted? If we had scraped up the remains, they would have no doubt weighed the same as they had when they were living, but their total body volume had been reduced so much that we could have poured all six of them into one spacer's kit-bag. I was mute, horrified, comprehending the violence at the moment of their deaths only with difficulty, and unable to visualize the force that had destroyed them. Six of them.

Badger added, "I guess we can tell Storm Rat his thing worked better than we expected." Through his faceplate, he gave me a weak smile. Trying to make it easier.

It wasn't easier. I'd planned on taking these people prisoner. Getting them safely back to Cantata, or perhaps taking them someplace that would be less of a threat to me and what I was looking into. I intended to find out what they knew, certainly. To make sure they were safely out of circulation so they couldn't hurt me any more . . . of course. But, dammit, when I was done with them they were going to be alive. I told myself that was the difference between them and me. I understood the value of a human life. No. It was more than that; I more than understood. I *believed* in the value of a human life, even when it belonged to my enemy. Even when the people who were now nothing more than a blot on a wall would have killed me . . . when those people had tried to kill me.

I floated forward carefully, swim-kicking, trying not to brush against what was left of them. I was grateful to get inside their ship. The airlock was intact and partly open, the way they had left it; after all, nothing but a moleibond cutter or the catalyst Anabond will destroy moleibond. Not even, evidently, a gravity shear. And the gravdrop beneath the door showed no signs of damage. However, I saw another bloody mess spattered against the walls just about the entrance to the first floor, and another giant splotch two floors down.

That made eight. Probably eight. Maybe more.

When we drifted into the gravdrop, the current caught us and started floating us downward. I wanted to get out on the first floor; I righted myself and angled toward the periphery of the gravdrop, my speed slowing as I did. The inside of this ship seemed to be in working order. The lights were still on, gravity functioned, the ship made the normal noises ships make. I stepped out into the first floor and lifted the faceplate on my suit. The air hadn't leaked out; the ship's atmosphere was breathable. I took a deep breath. Badger joined me, lifted his faceplate too. I switched off my radio to conserve power in the suit and Badger did the same.

"We may not have much time before someone comes looking for these people," I said, "but let's go through all the floors and the holds before we get to work on the TFN. Maybe we'll find something useful."

"Maybe we'll find a survivor or two," Badger suggested.

I tried to imagine surviving the gravity shear, all or most of my body reduced to flesh puree, and I shuddered. "Probably not."

"If they weren't all going to board us, they weren't all in the way of the gravity shear." Badger was already walking forward, being cautious, rifle cradled in both arms, ready for a quick shot. "Still, you're probably right," he agreed. "I'd want every available fighter if I was getting ready to board a hostile ship."

We surveyed the ship anyway, checking every floor and every room. It was bigger than the *Hope's Reward*, but not by much. Five floors instead of four, berths for twenty instead of twelve, another dramatic captain's suite that had been decorated like a medieval Terran bordello. I wondered if everyone used the same decorator for captain's suites, or if bad taste was as much a requisite as money when buying a quasi-recreational cruiser.

On the third level, we almost tripped over a cleaning bot that was scrubbing the floor. I had mine set to run only when no one was around unless I had a major mess, but evidently these people hadn't found the machines annoying.

Then the bot scooted into the gravdrop, and I recalled the major mess that had triggered it into activity. I cringed.

The arms room had been ransacked; when they came for us, our enemies had not been neat. The rest of the ship was in good enough shape, though. I considered taking this one through the origami point with the *Hope's Reward* still attached. Briefly I thought that traveling to the nearest station that had a good docking and repair facility would make sense.

Then I considered that I wouldn't be able to maintain any sort of anonymity if I did that. This ship might have gravity and life support and a working TFN and working engines, but my cover story and my fake ID were for my ship. The cover story wouldn't stretch far enough to cover a ship I'd stolen . . . taken from defeated pirates . . . whatever. Nobody would connect the *Merry Widow* with anything, but somewhere, someone was watching for this ship. I was going to need to tell a bunch of lies as it was, to explain why I was limping into Cantata on part of one engine and almost no life support.

We didn't find any more spattered bodies, and we didn't find anything that would tell us about the people who had been after us. Their ship was the *Fortune Favors* and the one we'd killed was, ironically, the *Eternal Lover*. They'd had more weapons than they'd used; they had pursued us from Smithbright's World; they were following orders in attempting to kill us, but the orders came from someone unnamed. We found nothing else. Nothing useful. Our search completed fruitlessly, we decided it was time to remove the TFN unit, carry it to our ship, replace ours, get our power plant and engines moving, and get to Cantata. "Did you spot their TFN access?" I asked Badger.

"Third floor inside wall. I saw the seams in the bulkhead; they look like they've got a quick-access port already partly cut in."

"I hope their unit will fit in our housing," I told him.

He pursed his lips and nodded.

We spent the next couple of hours using the ship's moleibond cutters to remove the inner wall of the TFN housing. I've always wished someone would develop a TFN that could work in an atmosphere instead of only in vacuum—life would be easier if getting at the unit only required opening a compartment door instead of cutting through moleibonded hull. I got filthy and hot and tired, and my lower back started to burn like it was on fire. Badger seemed to be oblivious to the bone weariness I was experiencing, but when I stood to stretch and work some of the kinks out of my back, he said, "If you're up anyway, would you get me something to drink? I'm about to fall over."

"I could use something myself. Do you remember seeing a dispenser any closer than the galley on second?"

He shrugged. "There will be one in the med room. I don't know if there was anything closer than that."

"That was straight back and port on this floor, wasn't it?"

"Think so. Last room down that corridor."

"You want anything in particular?"

"Something cold. And maybe some food, too, if the med dispenser has anything palatable."

I nodded and hobbled down the main corridor, rubbing the knuckles of both fists into my lower back. Walking felt good.

I turned to my right where the corridor split off. The med room was at the end. Last door, but right or left? I didn't remember. Maybe one of the closer rooms had a dispenser? I was so tired it almost seemed to make sense to go digging around in the other rooms instead of going straight to the room where I *knew* drinks and probably food would be available, where they had to be available for people just getting out of medichamber recovery.

I considered that weariness. Perhaps I was simply shocky after the battle. I'd been wakened from sleep by the klaxons;

I didn't even know how much sleep I'd had. The stress of coming so close to dying had to be taking its toll. Knowing how much damage had been done to my ship, and how hard it was going to be to get it even marginally operational . . . yes. A lot to deal with all at once. A lot.

Right door? Or left?

I tried the right door first. I was correct. Telling myself that getting the correct door on the first try was a sign of superior memory, and not just dumb luck, I went through. I didn't know where the dispenser was; I only knew that it would be in there somewhere.

The med room was ugly, done in a style I'd never seen. Most shipboard med rooms are clean and sparse, with pale walls and shiny surfaces and the tech-heavy science-can-*fix*-this air that also permeates research labs. These walls were hung with maroon velvet, big heavy swaths of fabric that draped from ceiling to floor and crumpled in melodramatic folds in the corners. The medichambers were done entirely in black, with even the face area lacquered over so that it was impossible to see in. Probably impossible to see out, too. I shuddered, considering waking from an extended stay in one of those chambers, finding myself effectively blind. It was an unpleasant thought. The fittings in the room were brass, the walls dark wood, the floors black marbleite. The lighting overhead was subdued, and I couldn't find anything that would make it brighter.

I also couldn't find the dispenser. I started a methodical search around the room, lifting the velvet hangings away from the wall and sliding my hand along underneath, hoping to feel the familiar curves of a drink dispenser's face. Wondering at the same time why in hell anyone would go to such trouble to make a med room's necessities so damnably inconvenient.

I didn't find the drink dispenser. Instead my hand ran over a depression in the wall, and I heard the hiss of a door opening. I felt a blast of icy air, and smelled something I didn't like but couldn't immediately place. I lifted the hanging farther away from the wall, and stepped behind it and walked through the door.

The light inside was dimmer than the med room's light had been, and even though the air had been refrigerated, the smell became stronger as I moved in and the door hissed shut behind me. It was still faint, but foul as a cesspool, and sickeningly sweet, and corrupt. Frightening.

I felt along the inside wall for a dimmer, and this time found one. I brought the lights up. I wished I hadn't.

Corpses lay along the walls in the part of the room I could see, stacked in bundles. All of them were nude; their wrists were bound behind them with spot-grafted moleibond braid restraints, their legs sprawled, ankles scarred and bloody from futile struggle against other bonds now removed. Their eyes, mostly open, stared in milky white horror past me to the nightmares in which they had lived and died. The killers had shown no preference in gender, no preference in skin color, no preference in appearance; the only similarities I could find in those walls of dead was that they had all been young adults, and that they had all died horribly.

The women's breasts had been lacerated and punctured. Men's buttocks had suffered the same treatment. Many of the wounds looked to me like bite-marks, but certainly not all of them. The killers had ripped open stomachs, had slashed genitals, had torn through tendons and arteries and smeared blood everywhere. Every throat was a gaping hole. The murderers had not disfigured any of their victims' faces; they hadn't needed to. Their brutality had done that for them. Fear and desperation and anguish contorted every frozen face into a mirror of hell.

Shocked into immobility, I couldn't draw air into my lungs. I heard a noise in the room, a faint, frantic mewling. Someone alive in those piles, I thought, horrified, and then I realized the noise came from my own raw, hurting throat. "Oh, my God," I whispered.

And then I heard a noise that didn't come from me. A

thump, which sounded like it came from the part of the room I hadn't yet seen.

The room was, as far as I could tell, L-shaped. I could make out darkness beyond the space where the right wall ended, and no bodies were stacked along that corner. I assumed when I noticed it that the room formed an 'L.'

Another thump. Something . . . someone . . . was alive back there. It could be another of the victims. It could be one of the killers, finishing off a survivor.

Thump.

My heart hammered and my breath raced. I remembered my laser rifle now, lying on the floor next to the opening Badger and I were cutting for the TFN. My back had been hurting and I'd wanted to massage it. There had seemed no point in carrying the rifle.

I could go back, I thought. Get it. Return when I was armed.

If I did that, though, and the thumps came from a victim, perhaps he would be dead. Perhaps the few minutes that would serve to get him to a medichamber were all he had left. If it were one of the killers, the noise of my leaving could alert him that this place had been discovered. He could arm himself, go anywhere in the ship, come after us.

I took a step forward.

Thump, thump.

My heart was going to rattle my ribs loose if it beat any harder.

Get this over with fast, I thought, and ran around the corner and oh, God, oh God oh God . . .

A woman lay tied to a table, her wrists bound together and secured over her head by a hook, her legs spread and tied at the table corners. Her breasts had been ripped open, punctured, chewed; she'd been violated; her body was smeared with her own blood. Her throat was still smooth, though. Still intact. She stared up at the mirrored ceiling above her, then squeezed her eyes shut and thumped her head down on the table as hard as she could.

She looked like she was trying to kill herself before whoever had done this to her came back.

More men and women lined the walls . . . twelve, maybe fifteen. No time to count. They stared at me with terrified eyes, frozen into the silence of helpless prey. They were bound at the wrists like the corpses were, hands down behind their backs, their bodies held in place by straps that had been run under their armpits and up behind them and hung on hooks. Their toes touched the ground, but only barely. They were helpless.

"I'm a friend," I said. I ran to the woman on the table, undid the strap beneath her breasts that kept her from rolling off, and lifted her. "Medichambers are just outside this room," I told her. "I'll get you into one." She stared at me, uncomprehending, and wailed. Shrieked. I ran, holding her in my arms the way I would have held a child. She wasn't a large woman, not very strong; very near death.

"You're still alive," I told her. "You're going to make it. Just hold on."

I pressed the door switch and it slid open with a hiss. I carried her through, fumbling a little with the velvet hanging that blocked my way.

"Almost there." I was encouraging myself as much as I was encouraging her. She was slick with blood, half frozen and feverish at the same time, awkward to carry. Hang on, I told myself. Don't drop her. Don't let her fall.

I reached the bank of medichambers and ran between the two nearest. I laid her on the lid of the one to my left and, holding her in place with one hand, pressed the release switch on the lid of the second. I heard machine whines, hissings, clicks from inside; the sounds a medichamber makes when it is disengaging from a patient.

A patient?

I pressed the latch again, panicked. Someone was in there, and now that someone knew I was out here. Unless he was in dreadful shape, he would press the inside release latch, and I would have, at most, a minute to get away.

I lifted the woman off of the lid and prayed no one

would be in this first medichamber. This time the lid swung up immediately, lifting at the bottom on its clamshell hinges. Empty. I dumped her in without ceremony, pressed the lid closed, and ran. Behind me, I could hear the snicking and chittering of the machine as it began to diagnose her troubles and set them right.

I was only at the door to the corridor when I heard the pneumatic whine of the second lid raising. Too fast . . . much too fast. I flew down the corridor, my footsteps ringing like chimes on the moleibond floor. "Badger! Heads up!" I screamed as I ran. "We missed one!"

Behind me I heard an unearthly wail; an insane ululating shriek of rage and terror. I ran faster. "Oh shit oh shit oh shit oh shit!" I yelled, in time with the pounding of my feet. I heard footsteps in the corridor behind me. I turned the corner but I knew it wasn't going to be fast enough. My enemy had to have seen me.

Another shriek, more horrible than the first, chased after me, and I heard running footsteps behind mine. Uneven running; maybe, I thought, afraid to hope, maybe he's still hurt. Maybe he won't be as strong, as fast, as invincible as the man in the black coat had been.

Maybe Badger and I will be able to kill him.

I realized that I wanted him dead, and I wanted to be the one who killed him. The bodies stacked in that room, the living men and women still trapped in there waiting to be the next victims of torture and horror, the woman half-dead who had lain on the table; all of these had changed my mind. The monsters who had done this to them deserved death. They were not men and women like me. Not people on the other side of an issue, not wrong-thinking human beings arguing over a difference of opinion. Not even people following orders, doing what they believed was right. They were evil.

Badger was waiting for me, his rifle in one hand, my rifle in the other. He handed it to me and I turned, breathing hard not from the run but from fear. I gasped, "He's behind me. Sounds like he's limping a little." And then I said, "We've got to kill him, Badger. Don't try to take him prisoner. Just kill him."

The enemy came around the corridor, moving at a shambling half-run, half-stagger. The lights in the corridor were widely spaced and in the dark patches he was hard to make out. He looked wrong, but I couldn't decide why. I sighted the rifle on him and hooked my finger around the trigger as he moved into a bright spot and I got a good look at him.

My finger fell away from the trigger.

His head and the right side of his body were normal. The left was an animate version of the bone chips and bloody smears spattered on the walls of the coupler corridor. On that side he had no skin, no defined muscles. Ragged bone edges erupted from his leg and his arm.

Only part of him had been in the way of the gravity shear's blast. That part had been scrambled. I didn't know, couldn't even begin to imagine, how he'd gotten to the medichamber. How he'd collected the pieces of himself and dragged himself there. But he had. The pieces clung together now and I could see where the medichamber had begun to sort them, to knit them back into something man-shaped. Given enough time, I was willing to bet it would have brought him back to perfect health. Perhaps, if he healed like the man in the black coat, he needed the medichamber only to increase the speed of the process.

I got myself under control and pulled the trigger, and this time a searing pencil of light dotted his chest. The right side. His skin beneath the point began to bubble and smoke. He kept coming, moving to one side as he did. The laser sliced a line through his shoulder, then back as I returned it to his chest.

I held the trigger down, not firing the short bursts the weapon had been designed for, but one continuous blast that would drain the rifle in just over a minute—that already had it overheating in my hand. Laser-pierced; scored; burned; he still kept coming, the bastard. Kept half-running, half-dragging himself toward us, keening like a madman, moving from side to side so that I couldn't fix the laser on the same spot. He wouldn't fall. Badger pulled his trigger and held it, his aim fixed on one of our enemy's eyes. The eye exploded when the beam hit and our pursuer stopped for an instant, but he didn't fall, and after he'd stood still for only the shortest of intervals, he started toward us again, moving slower but still moving. I kept firing, even though he was getting closer, even though I was scared.

No one could be this tough, this unstoppable . . . but this man was. I moved my aim up to his head, pinned him in the other eye, and I held the beam in place. Prayed. The bubbling, burning skin began around the beams began to liquefy, while inside of his brain fluids turned to steam. Some of it vented from the holes the laser made, but not enough to save him. His skull couldn't vent the superheating gases expanding inside of him. It exploded, spattering burnt chunks of flesh and bone against the corridor and Badger and me.

Badger and I leaned against each other, wordless, shaken.

It took his death, finally, for me to know without doubt that I had uncovered their secret. I knew what the expensive ships were doing in the backwater worlds. I knew why they hid, and why they would do anything to keep their secret. "This is their secret, Badger," I told him. "This is what they're smuggling. An invulnerability nanovirus. Something that doesn't just fight disease—something that reforms and rebuilds tissues. This makes them almost unkillable."

Almost. The bastard in pieces on the floor in front of us was undeniably dead. The one Fedara Contei had killed hadn't come back either.

I didn't know how they had done it; in spite of nanotechnology and automedical cellular regeneration, hyperresilience was supposed to be impossible to achieve. The longest expected lifespans now range in the three hundreds—an enormous improvement from the time when lives were measured in decades. But this discovery of theirs was not about lives lived carefully and within reach of the medichamber. This was about near-invulnerability. Autoregeneration. Maybe even genuine immortality.

I didn't know how they did it, but by God, I knew who did it.

Dr. Haskell B. Corrigan. Namesake of the *Corrigan's Blood*.

Chapter Nineteen

We didn't have time to be afraid, I took Badger back to the med room, where we checked the medichambers for other deadly survivors. None remained. I led Badger to the room I had discovered behind the velvet hangings. We went in, released the survivors, cut away their bindings with moleibond cutters and applied Plaskin dressings to the points where we had to cut through skin, helped them find food and clothing and got them warm. They were in various stages of shock, most of them unable to speak. A few babbled incoherent things about legends. One woman, a few years older than the other eleven and the survivor of other ordeals, had a toughness the rest of the captives lacked. She told us her name was May DeChang, and that she had escaped from a reeducation camp in Peting City on Gamion.

"I saw things this bad there," she said. Her eyes didn't have the flatness or the dead look I saw in the eyes of the rest of the survivors. "I saw things this bad, and I got away. I figured maybe if I didn't panic, I could get away this time. But these," she shook her head and gestured with one hand to take in the whole of the *Fortune Favors*, "they weren't people. They looked like people and they talked like people, but they'd made themselves into something . . . else." She gave me a hard look, then turned her attention to Badger. "*You* know they aren't human anymore, don't you?"

We both nodded.

"Right. You killed them somehow—the only way you could have done that was if you knew." She shivered and rubbed her hands up and down on her thin arms. "They call themselves legends. They talk about legends, though in a way that doesn't make any sense. They say they are immortals, the new gods of the dark places, the old gods returned. They're almost unkillable. I saw them when they turned on one of their own. Brought her in, tied her to the table where they tied us . . . their food." She took a deep breath.

"They savaged her, the way they did us. Raped her, beat her, cut her, tore out her throat with their teeth. She wouldn't die. She was screaming, frantic, in pain and going mad, and she *couldn't* die. Before they tore out her throat, she begged them to kill her, to burn her or cut off her head. To throw her into the vacuum. To release her."

Badger and I looked at each other. "Did they?"

"No." That flat syllable, said without emotion, conveyed a horror as deep as everything I had yet seen. "They laughed. Then they put her in the quiet room."

"The quiet room?"

"The room behind the one where they kept us. The torture room. It's soundproofed."

My stomach began to twist, churning, knotting. I tasted bile and acid at the back of my throat. "She's still in there, isn't she?"

May DeChang nodded. "It's a good place for her. She'll never be able to get out. She'll eventually starve to death—even these monsters have to eat or they starve."

My first thought was, good. We'll leave and she'll die and there will be one less monster in the universe. But I wondered, could the enemy of my enemy be my friend? I had never thought so. I had always been sure that even enemies who shared a common cause would still be enemies. If I rescued her, though, might that give me some hold on her loyalty? Would the fact that I had saved her from a slow, agonizing death mean anything? Or would she also consider an enemy with a common cause still an enemy? Or worse, would she look at me as mere prey? Another meal.

"We need to go take a look," I said to Badger.

The thin veneer of May's self-control vanished instantly. "NO!" she screamed. "She'll kill you. Then she'll come after us. We're food to her—just food! She'll rip us apart." She grabbed the front of my suit with panic-strong hands and shook me.

I slapped her once, hard, across the cheek. "Stop that," I said, keeping my voice coldly neutral. I knew her fear viscerally; I felt it as deeply as I felt the necessity of breathing. Thinking about going in and facing another of those . . . things . . . I wanted to do what she had done; I wanted to scream and shake some sense into myself.

But I needed someone on the inside. This would probably be the only opportunity I ever got to recruit one of them to my side. If I let this go, I would be losing information I might never be able to get again.

May DeChang stared up at me. I turned to Badger. "Well take the plasma arcs and a full pack of recharges."

When he left to get the recharges, I returned my attention to DeChang. "You're going to keep everyone here out of the way. Find a room with a locking door, get all of them into it, and lock up. We'll come and get you when it's over."

"How will we know it's you?"

"I'll say 'The legends are dead,' " I told her.

She almost smiled at that. "I hope when you say it, it's true."

The survivors went to the captain's quarters and barricaded themselves behind the door. Badger and I, armed and scared, returned to the med room, let ourselves into the secret room, and tried to keep from looking at the piles of dead bodies stacked on the floor.

"They could have dumped them into space," Badger

said. "They didn't need to have them lying around like this."

"They liked having them lying around like this," I said. "It gave them a thrill, to think that they were going to live forever, that they could do whatever they wanted. They liked this."

"How could they?" he asked. "How could anyone?"

That I didn't know.

We walked past the blood-stained table, past the hooks where the living had been forced to watch what would become their fate at the hands of their future executioners. Behind the table there was a door. It had no switch panel, no handle. May DeChang said the killers would slide their hands along the underside of the table before dragging their next victim into the room beyond. So Badger and I crouched at the edge of the table and looked underneath. A small switch panel was there. We had no idea if there was any way the door could be opened from the inside; one of us was going to have to stay behind until we found out for sure.

"What now?" Badger asked, eyeing the switch.

I inhaled slowly, breathed out fast. Nibbled on the inside of my bottom lip. "How about opening the door and waiting on this side of it. If she's loose in there, she may come charging out."

"If she does, we'll have to kill her. We won't have a chance to find out what she knows; we won't be able to talk to her. It will be too dangerous to try."

"I know." I looked at the faint line in the moleibond that was the only evidence of a doorway. "If we're lucky she won't be loose in there."

Badger stood and aimed his plasma arc at the doorway. With mine ready at my side, I pressed the switch.

The door slid back and sideways, disappearing into the wall. Its soft hiss, and Badger's and my breathing, were the only sounds. We waited.

Nothing.

I knew she was in there. May DeChang said she had

been tied to the wall when they put the woman in, and no one had ever returned to take her out. She was in there. What was she doing? Crouching in a corner, keeping still, waiting to tear her torturers apart when they walked through, perhaps. Or maybe she was dead already, tortured and beheaded and burned.

Whatever she was doing, she wasn't coming out the door. We were going to have to go in.

Badger, a better shot than I am, went first. I covered him. He slammed around the corner, his weapon dropping into firing position; I rushed in behind him, turned, aimed . . .

They had hung her on the wall. Not the way they had hung the others. Her head was turned away from the door, hanging against her chest. Her hair, tangled and matted with blood, covered her face. They had driven spikes through her shoulders . . . and slashed her belly open so that they could pull her intestines out . . . so that they could . . . could . . . and her breasts . . . and . . .

I couldn't breathe. Couldn't see. What they had done to her was worse than anything I could have imagined. I turned away, sick; leaned against the wall feeling light-headed, while the floor of the room lifted toward me and my stomach heaved.

I heard Badger gasp. "No," he said. "No. No."

I looked up. The woman, impossibly still alive, raised her head and stared at us. Her throat was gone, and no sound came out of her mouth, though her lips formed the words "help me."

I knew her.

She was Fedara Contei.

Chapter Twenty

She terrified us. Knowing what she was, we took Fedara down off the wall hoping that she wouldn't kill us and eat us as soon as we did. She was gaunt, and I could not imagine how she had become so emaciated in the couple of days since I had last seen her. Nor could I imagine how she had survived the horrors they put her through, no matter what sort of nanovirus she'd injected into her bloodstream.

She didn't fight us, though. She made no move at all, other than to stare at us with a look of vague bewildered incomprehension.

We put her in my medichamber on the *Hope's Reward*, locked it so that she couldn't get out and the people who had every reason to hate her couldn't get in, attached the repair shield over it, and told the people we had rescued that she was dead. I didn't like lying to them, but as soon as we had the *Reward* functional again, we were going to take them to Bailey's Irish Station, which was one fold away and in the direction we needed to go, and then we were going to be gone from their lives. The fact that we had one of the monsters tucked away in our ship didn't need to concern them.

Within hours, we finished removing the TFN unit from the *Fortune Favors* and a day later we had it fitted into the bulkhead of the *Hope's Reward*. Then we switched the breakers on the power plant and that came back on. During the last few hours, when Badger was doing testing, I worked to get the shipcom's autorepair back up. I finished shortly before he did, and the shipcom, faster and more efficient at ship repair than I'll ever hope to be, improved our life support to sixty percent of optimal and got us partial use of a second engine. Finally, we changed the ship's internal and external ID's and call codes to match the ones Storm Rat had given us. When that was completed, we were ready to go.

I joined Badger on the bridge.

"The survivors are settling into the spare quarters," I told him. "I cleaned all the clothing I could find out of the *Fortune Favors*. Our guests all have families to go home to, and most of them have InterPlan accounts, so as soon as we get to a station, they'll have money. They're going to help each other get home; they've all been in this together long enough now that they seem to feel like family."

Badger looked up. "They've been together long?"

"I suppose it depends on how you define time. Some of them had only been in there four days, but the longest survivor had been hanging on the wall for a week. That, plus everything they went through together, was evidently enough to make them feel they have something in common."

"Wait a minute. Are you sure none of the survivors joined them when the *Fortune Favors* evacuated the *Eternal Lover*?"

"I'm positive. They were very clear about that. Four days . . ." I stared at him as the realization hit me. Both ships had carried the flesh-eating killers who had pursued us; it only stood to reason that both ships had carried victims for them to torture and feast on. Getting those victims off the ship when the *Fortune* discovered we weren't dead yet hadn't been a priority or they would have been confined with the other victims. "Oh, God, Badger. There are probably still people on the *Eternal Lover*!"

I knew time was running out for us. Neither the *Eternal Lover* nor the *Fortune Favors* had shown up back on Smithbright's Planet to report success. Someone was waiting for them, knew where they were going to be (or could easily follow where they went), and had either realized by now or would soon realize that their hired guns weren't coming home. When he or she realized that, other ships and other killers would probably come after us.

We needed to move, to get away so that we could disappear. Our hunters knew who they were after, but they didn't know who we had become. If we could hide these new identities, we could escape.

And now maybe there were survivors on the *Lover*. Terrified of another confrontation with people who wanted to kill us, watching the time race past us faster than the speed of light, we uncoupled the *Reward* from the *Fortune Favors* and limped away from the origami point we needed toward the dead *Lover*. Up close it looked undamaged; the moleibond hull had held against the worst we'd been able to do. Inside was another story. Our final attack had destroyed most of the systems, including the air filtering system, but not the temperature control. The atmosphere was bad, and the smell of death and putrefaction so overwhelmed us that after one breath we wore our faceplates down and breathed the recycled air in our suits.

Badger and I searched the ship's med room and found another nightmarish storage and torture chamber like the one on the *Fortune Favors*. The refrigeration unit had died, though, and the bodies stored along the walls were decaying quickly. I will never erase the sight from my memory. I averted my eyes and hurried to the back, but the image of those piles of bloated and rotting meat, which had once been men and women with hopes and dreams and futures, seared itself into my brain.

For most of the remaining victims, we arrived too late. Of the fifteen that had hung on the wall waiting to become meals, only five still breathed when we pulled them down.

The dead we left. The living we carried to the *Reward*. And the fact that even five survived created another problem for us, another delay.

I had four medichambers on the *Reward*. That was eight less than the number the ship would have carried if I ever took passengers, but because I'd never used the ten extra berths, it was two more than I had ever needed before. Two of my medichambers were in use—the first wounded victim and Fedara Contei filled them. All five of these latest rescuees had to be chambered; none of them would live without immediate attention. The two worst Badger and I loaded into our empty chambers. Our first rescuee wasn't healthy enough to give up her space yet, and I had no intention of letting Fedara Contei out of her prison until Badger and I were alone with her. If she got out of control, only he and I would suffer; I was determined on that point.

So Badger and I went into the *Lover* three more times, and salvaged three medichambers. We spent one heart-pounding minute while we made sure each medichamber was empty. Ten minutes each to unhook the supply lines and power, secure the cables, and unbolt the chambers. An hour each to fumble them from the *Lover*'s med room through corridors and the gravdrop and more corridors and into the *Reward*'s med room. Stumbling and swearing in the gravityless *Lover* as the mass of each unwieldy box threw us into walls and ceilings and smashed our fingers and bruised our bodies; a slightly better time in the reduced gravity we'd given ourselves aboard the *Reward*. Ten minutes each to reconnect the supply lines and the power.

The healthy survivors cycled the dying ones through the available chambers while we worked, giving each ten or fifteen minutes at a time, making sure no one died.

I could feel the next hunters coming. They were at my back, following my trail; they would reach me soon.

We dove into the origami point as the *Hope's Reward* used Storm Rat's ID switcher to change all our ID programming in hyperspace; we emerged after another hellish traverse of eternity as the *Merry Widow*, captained by Adana Gantrey and Brian Darkman, with a weary cargo of pleasure-passengers who wanted to book cruises home. I got the hail from the traffic controller at Bailey's Irish Station, welcoming us in.

No call sounded sweeter in my entire life.

We met with the survivors before they disembarked.

"You know you can't tell anyone what happened to you," I said.

They hadn't known.

I said, "There are more of them out there, maybe a lot more." I handed out lists of USAG members. "Some of these people are just like the ones who wanted to kill you. Maybe the rest of them aren't—maybe they're perfectly good people who wouldn't hurt anyone—but the ones we've met have been involved, and most of the ones we've met have been killers."

Badger said, "We've given you these lists so you can protect yourselves. But if any of these people suspect that you know anything, they'll come after you and kill you."

The survivors scanned the list. One of them said, "My God! This is the group my ex-wife belonged to!" Everyone looked up and stared at the man. "Yes," he added after a moment. "Here's her name. She was supposed to be on the Five-Systems cruise I was taking, but at the last minute she couldn't go. She sent . . ." He stared at us, horrified. "She sent me the ticket . . ."

The silence in the room took on a terrifying chill.

Into that silence, he said, "My daughter is with her now."

Eyes stared downward again.

Another soft voice. "I'm the other one who survived the Five-System cruise. My partner Jacquin is on this list. He bought me and my husband cruise tickets for our anniversary. Big celebration, he said. Big surprise for us." I could see rage seething in her. "My husband is dead because of him . . . and Jacquin knew, didn't he? He knew."

Two others discovered they had a direct connection

to a USAG member. The rest seemed to have been unlucky . . . but how could they be sure?

Badger and I realized our survivors were going to have to stay dead. They had to have new identities, and they couldn't touch the money that belonged to them because if they did, people looking for that sort of activity would know they had survived.

We couldn't go after the man's daughter. We couldn't avenge the wrongs the woman's partner had done to her. We couldn't save the world.

But, goddammit, Badger and I had the better part of two million rucets in our account, and we knew someone who could make every one of these people into someone new. A brand new man could charge to the rescue of his own kid. A woman with a new name and a new past could avenge her husband's murder. We could give them a chance and the element of surprise.

By the time we reached the dock, our plan was all worked out. Each of them could get a new identity from Storm Rat for a thousand rucets. That was seventeen thousand. It would take them roughly three hundred rucets apiece to book passage to Tegosshu. They couldn't go together; they would have to book separate passage and take different routes. So we rounded up to four hundred rucets for transportation. Another four hundred rucets apiece for transport to wherever they wanted to go afterwards. That was just over thirty thousand rucets. And two thousand apiece to buy clothes and food and to live on in the interim.

Fifty-three thousand two hundred rucets.

I had to get it in cash. When we docked, I called in a request for a balance transfer from my old account, as Cadence Drake, to my new account, as Adana Gantrey. Badger did the same for his half of the money. As Adana Gantrey, I made a quick trip to the station bank and made gushy noises to the human teller about some of the wonderful things I'd found in the specialty emporiums. I don't know what sort of story Badger gave when the banker asked him why he wanted so much cash, but we each removed twenty-six thousand six hundred rucets from our new accounts, returned to the ship, and gave the survivors cash and instructions on how to reach Storm Rat and what to say when they did.

Then we left them with our best wishes . . . and our worst fears.

"Now we have to deal with Fedara Contei," Badger said as we received clearance to enter the origami point.

Chapter Twenty-one

For a while, while we were working so hard to help the people we'd rescued, I managed to forget about the fact that Fedara Contei was waiting in the medichamber for us. It was not, unfortunately, the sort of thing I could forget any longer. We entered the origami point with me thinking about her, wondering if perhaps she would be our ally, but fearing that she would be our death.

We linkjumped through three points and came out of hyperspace in the Sertavo Folds, a stretch of space lumpy with dense matter following the supernova of its sun. It wasn't any prize destination; it was convenient, though. Because of the huge number of origami points in the region, we would be able to cruise through normal space from the point we'd exited to a point that would take us to Cantata without spending more than a few hours in the process. It was one more way we hoped to scramble our trail behind us.

While the ship moved along its programmed course between the two points, we decided to release Fedara Contei from the medichamber. There didn't seem to be any safer place.

We stood on either side of the clamshell lid, plasma arcs in hand and packets of recharges ready.

"I wish we knew what to expect," Badger said.

I nodded. "Maybe she'll be so grateful we rescued her and got her healthy again that she'll agree to work with us."

"Maybe she'll be so crazed from the torture they put her through that she'll jump out of the medichamber and rip our heads off before we can shoot."

"Certainly bears thinking about," I said.

Badger and I aimed our arcs at the head of the medichamber, and with my left hand I punched in the lock code, with a fifteen-second delay at the end. The lock chimed once and Badger and I stepped back. We watched the numbers on the release mechanism count backward from fifteen . . . then ten . . . then five . . .

I could hear the whine of the machinery disengaging. As it did, my knees grew weak. She hadn't killed us before, I told myself. She'd had chances to kill us, and a chance to let us be killed, and she didn't take advantage of any of them.

. . . Four . . .

My mind raced. What if she's a homicidal psychopath? What if nobody cares if I'm alive anymore . . . or whether or not I get to Peter Crane? What if the only reason I was alive was because the killers didn't want me dead yet, and now they don't care?

The muscles of my forearms ached, and my index finger tightened on the trigger.

. . . Three . . .

Maybe it would be better . . . smarter . . . to just kill her immediately. It probably was. It almost certainly was. Kill her before she could kill me.

The clamshell separated from the body of the medichamber, and the pressurized air inside hissed out.

I wanted to run. They'd tortured her in ways that would have broken a human . . . a dozen humans. They'd wanted to break her. If there had ever been a time when she could be reasoned with, that time had probably passed.

. . . Two . . .

Room air cycled through the medichamber, and the last tubes and support lines disengaged.

I couldn't just cold-bloodedly kill her. I had to give her a chance. Had to, even if it wasn't the smart thing to do. I needed what she knew, yes; but I needed to know that I hadn't become one of the killers.

. . . One . . .

Badger said, "God, I hope she's willing to be reasonable."

The clamshell opened.

The medichamber was empty.

"What?!" Badger ran to the side and looked in. I ran with him.

She'd peeled the protective coating off of the wiring, and had worked the wiring loose and twisted it together again so that it fed itself normal readouts. And she'd figured out some way to short out the lock. The medichamber had been cycling oxygen and fluids through its own tubing and treating itself as its patient. Of Fedara Contei there was no sign.

My mouth went dry. I looked at Badger, hoping he would have an idea of what had happened.

Badger's right eyelid developed a tic; it twitched steadily. "I want to know where she got out. At Bailey's? Is she at Bailey's right now, sitting in a bar beside her next victim listening to the Ulstersingers?"

I said, "Maybe one of the *Fortune* survivors found out we were hiding her in here, and found a way to sneak in, open the medichamber, and burn her. And they jimmied the wires to make it look like she escaped."

We stared at each other, considering possibilities. Neither one of us wanted to offer up the one that frightened us worst. She could, we knew, be on the ship with us. Waiting. Biding her time until we were alone. She was stronger and faster than the two of us combined, she was virtually unkillable, and now she was loose. Somewhere.

I closed my eyes for an instant, trying to find on the insides of my eyelids solutions not apparent to me while I stood staring at the med room. Truth, brilliance and an easy answer failed to resolve the problem, though, and with a sigh I looked at Badger again.

"Onto the bridge now," I said.

We ran into the next room. As soon as the door hissed shut behind me, I said, "Shipcom, go to Condition One protocol. Condition One protocol."

"Condition One protocol in effect," the shipcom said. It immediately shut down the auxiliary bridge, locked and sealed all rooms and bulkheads, and isolated the first floor. The doors to the gravdrop shut and sealed and both power and gravity to all portions of the ship except for the main bridge switched off. Life support was cycling air for each sealed area separately; considering that we didn't have full life support, that fact could cause problems in a short time, but I hoped we would have this problem resolved before oxygen became an issue.

I'd designed our Condition One protocol to solve problems I never had but worried about anyway. I have the sort of mind that envisions disasters, and I'd always wanted to be prepared. I'd considered poisonous gas flooding the ship; pirates boarding us intent on rape and pillage; some sort of dangerous cargo escaped from its cage; a miniature black hole piercing the moleibond hull. I hadn't envisioned Fedara Contei, but she was definitely within the scope of a Condition One disaster.

"Scan us for life-forms," I told Badger. "I'll try to talk her out."

If I was lucky, I caught her off guard when I cut off gravity to the rest of the ship. If I was lucky, she was floating in a corridor with no place to hide. Of course, I hadn't been too lucky lately.

I had the shipcom set the shipwide speakers in two-way mode, and I said, "Fedara Contei. This is Cadence Drake. I need to talk to you."

Silence.

Badger slowly scanned the first floor, taking his time and making sure he didn't miss anything.

I caught flashes of the areas he was looking at from

the corner of an eye, and the even green of the thermal scan overlay that indicated everything up here was of the expected temperature.

"Fedara. Listen, I want to make a deal with you. I need to know about USAG, and Danniz, and the nanovirus you have in your system, and what it all has to do with the *Corrigan's Blood*. In exchange for information, I'm willing to help you however I can. I've already proved that, Fedara. Badger and I got you down off that wall and into a medichamber. We helped you. We can still help you."

Badger was monitoring the second floor. The visual showed nothing out of the ordinary, but on the thermal overlay a human-shaped blip in the galley glowed dark red. He pointed it out to me and I nodded, feeling chills down my spine. I'd been in the galley not too long before Badger and I decided to go up to open the medichamber. She might have been in there when I was, hiding in one of the small pantries, listening to me moving around. Hiding close enough to touch me if a door hadn't been between us.

That was too close.

"Fedara, I know you're in the galley. I don't know what all happened to you, but I know it was bad. I'll help you if I can."

A scream that began as a thin wail and rose in volume and urgency to a shivering, nerve-end-tearing shriek tore through the bridge, reverberated off the walls, and echoed at long last down into silence. It was the scream of a hell-bound damned soul, the scream of a creature who was discovering its life only at the instant of its death. It was nothing less than the sound of the complete destruction of all hope.

Badger and I, stunned speechless, didn't respond for a moment.

Then I said, "Fedara? I can help you."

A soft sob. "Helf-f-f me? *Kill-l-l-l* me." The com's sound system is very good. I could pick up the nuances of despair, anguish, rage. Her voice wasn't clear. Her once-pleasant voice rasped and growled, and she sounded as if she were talking with something in her mouth. "Kill me quick."

The muscles across my shoulders tightened and for a moment breathing became difficult. "You don't have to die. We'll find a way to help you, whatever you need."

Badger moved the viewpoint of the monitor until he got us a good picture of Fedara. She was crouched near the floor, hanging onto the cabinet handles to keep from floating around the galley, with her face pressed against the cabinets. In spite of all the time she'd spent in the medichamber, she looked skeletal. Her hands were leathery talons clinging to the countertop. She lifted her head and stared upward, and her lips peeled back in an insane grin. Badger sucked in a breath. I gasped. Her four canines were long and white and sharp, and the rest of her teeth looked like she had filed them. They were teeth identical to those of the man in black who had tried to kill us on Smithbright's World.

And they hadn't been that way when we put her in the MEDix.

She laughed a harsh laugh, hysterical and madness-tinged, that rolled down into another wet sob. "Need?" She began to pound on the cabinets in front of her, rhythmically and with a lot of force. Metal rang and thudded, and the awful screeee of fingernails dragged down the elegant carbonaboard cabinets. She began babbling something, over and over so softly and quickly that I couldn't make out for a moment what she needed. "—bluh-bluh-blooh-blooh-BLUH-blooh-BLOOD-blood-blooh-bluh-BLOOD—"

Eerie. Creepy. Terrifying. "You . . . need blood?" Badger asked.

She was curled into a ball on the floor, tucked fetuslike with her knees against her chest, sucking her thumb. It took both of us a moment to realize she was sucking her own blood out of her thumb.

I shuddered. Badg and I stepped closer and he slid an arm around my shoulder. Comfort—I needed it right then, and he did too. I wrapped my own arm around his waist. Took a deep breath. "We can dummy up some plasma in the dispenser units." My dispensers were old technology; cranky and difficult and obsolete. They worked, but if you wanted something special, you had to sweat to get it. I said, "I can work with the dispensers. What part of the blood do you need? Some special nutrient, some difficult protein-to-carbohydrate ratio?"

Silence for just a moment. Then, "BLOOD. BLOOD! *BLOOD*!"

"I would guess that means plasma won't do," I said, and tried to give Badger a smile. It failed.

Raw blood. Lovely. There were exactly two sources of raw blood on the ship, and neither Badger nor I felt like having our throats ripped out to supply our guest with a meal.

Badger said, "We can use some tubing and one of the medichamber needles to draw out some of our own blood. Keep the galley locked but open up the corridors to it. Put the blood on one side of the bulwark door between the galley and the exercise room. Then we could come back to the bridge, lock the ship down tight again, and open only the galley door. She could get her blood, and we could see if she made any better sense after she had it."

"Or we could shoot her," I said. It wasn't funny and I knew it wasn't funny. I didn't mean it. But, God. What a situation. I thought about Badger's suggestion for a good long moment, but didn't come up with anything better to offer. I said, "Well. Let's get her some blood."

Drawing my own blood was painful, but I tried to look at the bigger picture—the way she would have gotten it on her own—and told myself a little pain wasn't such a terrible thing. And while Badger and I watched our twin red rivers simultaneously running into a single two-liter vacupac, I reminded myself why it was necessary to spare her life.

It wasn't only because the killers had tortured her as

they had tortured their victims; in sparing her life, I was exhibiting both compassion and hard-headed common sense. She was sure to be a database of information I needed. Sure to be. Anyone would do what I was doing.

Well, probably not, but she hadn't tried to kill me yet, and she had saved my life once by getting me off Smithbright's Station. So I weighted my empathy for her more heavily than the information she might or might not provide.

When the vacupac filled, Badger and I removed the needles, dressed our tiny wounds, and drank ReHydra, which is supposed to be wonderfully refreshing but which in fact tastes like strong morning piss smells.

Then Badger worked with the shipcom and temporarily returned gravity to the parts of the ship I'd be using. Meanwhile I walked through the corridors, emergency bulwarks opening in front of me and closing behind me as I went, carrying the still-hot blood back to the gravdrop, then down and forward again. In my own well-lit ship, my home, I was scared shitless.

I moved quietly, left the blood at the door, and backed away. The bulwark doors opened and closed for me again, this time carrying me away from my fears. I returned to the deck and gave Badger the nod. "Open the galley door."

He did. We heard the hiss of the door. Another hiss, this one from Fedara. Frantic scrabbling and a howl and the sound of the vacupac popping and then licking, licking, licking, licking.

And then silence.

We waited, but the licking sounds didn't resume.

"Fedara?" I said.

The silence continued a moment longer. Then, her voice still rough but now at least controlled, she said, "Thank you. I was starving."

"The medichamber should have kept you nourished."

"It couldn't. It's programmed to meet the needs of humans. I'm not a human anymore."

I said, "I know. I've seen. But what are you?"

"A monster. A killer."

Badger cleared his throat. "The survivors from the *Fortune Favors* mentioned legends."

"Yes. Many of Danniz's monsters call themselves that. Danniz calls me that—the bastard."

"If you wanted to be one of these things, why do you sound so bitter now?"

"I didn't volunteer. You could say I was volunteered. I met a charming, friendly young man in a bar, and the two of us liked each other a lot. I suppose in his own way he thought more of me than I did of him—after all, I only intended to spend every minute for the rest of my life with him. He, however, decided we should be together forever."

I frowned at Badger. She didn't seem to be making much sense.

He shrugged.

Fedara's voice developed an edge. "I spent the night we met with him. I was in love—or I believed myself to be in love, though later I found out he used his eyes on me. You wouldn't understand about that—never mind. I believed myself to be in love, and I had never been in love. And I thought, *finally*, and he was so wonderful, and I took him home with me."

She was silent for a moment. When she resumed speaking, I heard bitterness in her voice. "What I remember of the night was wonderful, too. What I remember. But I woke up the next morning feeling like death. Couldn't tolerate the sight or smell or taste of food, started throwing up constantly. The symptoms lasted for three days, and at the end of three days I was ravenous . . . but food didn't interest me. Danniz went with me to the market to see if I could find anything I wanted. On the way back, I did. Two thugs attacked me, and I hit one with my fist. I was wearing a ring, and the ring cut his cheek . . . and the scent of the blood drove me completely outside of myself.

"I came around to find both of them lying dead on the ground, their throats ripped open and their bodies drained of blood. I felt wonderful physically. Sated. Powerful. Orgasmic. Intellectually, I wanted to die.

"I was standing in this back street, horrified, covered with blood, trying to get him to explain what had happened, trying to understand how I could have done what I did. Trying to get him to help me. But he wasn't sickened by what I'd done. Instead, he praised my ferocity and told me that he loved me so much he had made me like him—that he'd been planning on killing me and drinking my blood the night we first got together, but that I had enchanted him. He said I was the woman with whom he wanted to spend eternity . . . and now I had an eternity to spend with him. I would never grow old, he said. I would never grow weak. I would never die."

She made a strangled noise. "Never."

Badger and I looked at each other. We had theorized something of this sort, but we hadn't guessed the details.

Fedara continued. "I tried to kill myself several times, but no matter what I did, I always got better. And no matter how hard I tried to keep from killing, eventually I became hungry enough that the blood-rage overtook me. I killed then, but horribly. I cannot die, and now I am a murderer. I learned later that if I drank a little blood at a time, I could control myself and I didn't kill my victims. But then I have to eat often. Two, three, sometimes four times a day. I'm a parasite and a blood-drinker and a killer and a monster, and I hate myself as much as I hate him."

Her voice grew even softer. "But you could kill me. He promised that if I did what he told me to do, he would kill me. He said he would release me, and I would never have to kill again. But he was lying."

Badger said, "We mentioned this before, when you were so . . . upset. I understand now why you were upset, but I think I have a solution for you. I think we could design a blood substitute for you."

"I was a medical researcher before this," she said. "I tried everything—even managed to duplicate the red blood cells in one solution. It was perfect. I added tracer to it and injected it into the bloodstream of a friend who didn't know why I wanted to develop artificial blood or what I intended to do with it. Her body accepted it without any question. My stomach didn't. I need raw, whole blood, human blood. *Living* blood. Not even blood from laboratory animals will work; I tried that too. I can eat food until my stomach bursts but my intestines won't absorb any of it. I would starve surrounded by food; except of course that my body won't let me starve. It will turn me into an insane, bloodthirsty monster before it will let me starve."

I said, "You say he made you this way. What did he do?"

"I don't know. I went to sleep with him and woke up the next morning with him beside me and I thought all I had done the night before was make love and sleep."

"Why would he do this?" I asked her. "What does he want?"

"It's a huge secret. I know he's in charge of some group, and I know he has important friends all over the universe. But I wouldn't be a happy blood-drinking killer for him, so he didn't let me in on his plans. Instead, he told me I had to stay with you until I could kill both you and Crane." She laughed. "He doesn't even know I wasn't with you when you left. He doesn't know you found a way to listen in on his conversation."

"He doesn't?"

"No. If you heard the conversation between the two of us, you know that he told me if I failed him again, he wouldn't let me die—that he would do terrible things to me?"

"I remember that."

"I believed him. When you left, I ran. He still thinks I'm working for him. He doesn't know I'm going to find a way to kill him."

"You weren't following us for him on Up Yours?" Badger asked.

"I was following you for my own sake. You are his enemy.

So I thought perhaps we could work together. Maybe it was a stupid idea, but for a while it seemed to make sense."

"I thought the same thing."

She said, "It wouldn't work."

"We could try."

"I can't trust myself. I can tell you what he wants, though. Maybe that will help you fight him. He wants to be the dark prince who rules the universe. His words, not mine. He wants to live forever, and he wants to live on blood and fear. And his friends worship him."

"He has friends?"

"Quite a few. When he still thought he might convert me to his cause, I met some of them. They were frightening. They dressed in dark colors and only came over at night, and they read vampire myths to each other."

"Vampire myths?"

"Stories about immortal blood-drinkers who could be killed by silver or by a stake through the heart or by sunlight. Monsters who were already dead, who hunted the living through the darkness. Who could shapechange, fly, mesmerize with their eyes; who were bound by magic so that they could not cross a threshold without an invitation, who could not cross running water. Who were stronger, faster, more ferocious than any living human; ethereally beautiful and terrible and terrifying. Who lived on blood and fear."

Badger cleared his throat. "Then Danniz and his friends have found a way to turn themselves into vampires."

"That's what they call themselves, but they didn't succeed completely. Not completely." Over the com, her sigh sounded weary. "At least not if I'm an example. I'm very much alive, not undead in any form. Sunlight bothers me, but doesn't hurt me. I have severe photosensitivity, but that seems to be connected to the general improvement of all my senses. I have incredible night vision, much better hearing than a human, much better senses of smell and taste and touch. Silver does nothing to me. The wooden stake through the heart didn't either—Danniz proved that to me when I tried to kill him that way. The cardiac muscle simply closes off around the wood and keeps pumping." She sighed. "I can't shapechange. I can cross doorways at will. I can't fly. As for having a hypnotic stare . . . that works quite well. I can die, but only if you rip off my head and take it away from my body, or if you burn me."

Badger and I ruminated.

"So you see," she said into the long, hollow silence, "You can't help me after all, unless you kill me. If you do it when I'm not starved, I won't defend myself."

I closed my eyes. "I'm not a killer—"

"But I am," she interrupted. "And if I don't have enough to eat, and often, I'll end up killing you even though I don't want to. Do yourselves a favor. Come down and destroy me now, while I can keep myself from fighting back."

"We'll find a way to help you. There has to be something that will counteract what he's done to you. The only way he can have done what he did to you was to inject you with some form of nanovirus. I haven't found a nanovirus yet that can't be reversed."

Silence. Then, "I have." A longer silence. "You don't need to spend your time worrying about me, anyway. You need to take care of yourselves. Danniz will be after you. So will more of your enemies from Smithbright's World. You didn't get out of this while you could; now you won't get out of it at all."

Cheerful words. I was surrounded by optimists.

"Would you like to go to a room and rest while we finish the trip to Cantata?" I asked. "Can I open up the ship for you?" I didn't want to hear any more about the people who wanted to kill me. I would deal with them when I had to, but not worry about them before.

"Leave me in here." She sounded miserable. "Leave everything locked down. I'm still too hungry to be loose. I can't guarantee your safety."

If she didn't trust herself, we couldn't trust her. I wished I could do something good for her. The best I could manage was a lame promise. I told her, "We'll figure out a way to feed you." I meant it. Badger and I would come up with something . . . but I couldn't imagine what.

None of us had anything else to say, and as we neared the origami point, I shut down the comlink so we could all have privacy after the jump. Neither Badger nor I had anything to say even after the link was closed, though. I know I was too lost in the details of her story to feel like speaking. Badger kept his thoughts to himself, too.

I hurt for Fedara Contei. I kept thinking about the young woman who met a man she thought she could love, and who had been destroyed by him. She should have been more careful, I told myself. She should have known him better. But she said he had used his eyes on her. What had that meant?

I wouldn't have made the mistakes she made, I reassured myself. She couldn't be me.

But I was lying to myself and I knew it. I'd done stupid things in my lifetime, and sometimes I paid for them. Sometimes I got lucky. And it didn't matter anyway, because no mistakes she had made, no fault of hers, could ever have justified what he had done to her.

Knowing what I knew, I couldn't kill her now even though I believed her when she said she wanted to die. I was glad I hadn't killed her already. Surely there was some way to restore her to normal health. The medical miracles of the age could not, must not, fail her. She deserved to become the woman she had once been. She deserved to find the love she'd wanted. And she deserved to have her revenge on Danniz Oe. I didn't know how I could help her accomplish those things, but I intended to help her try.

Chapter Twenty-two

We entered the origami point to Cantata with Fedara locked in the galley on the second level; Badger and I stayed together on the bridge because, I suspected, neither of us could face the idea of being alone.

One instant the two of us were listening to the countdown to hyperspace, and the next . . .

I was dying. Dying in a thousand ways, dying because I'd trusted the wrong people, taken the wrong risks. Dying. I watched my little mortal fleshselves burning out like the sparks from a fire. Glowing, growing dim, blanking into nothing but cold, dead, ash. The infinite me thought, Why didn't the stupid girl see that coming? It wondered, What will it take for her to learn? My omniscient overself didn't care that my fleshselves were dying all around me . . . the overself was immortal, and while it could learn from mortal pain and suffering, it didn't have to experience it if it didn't choose to. Instead, it was simply and dispassionately interested in how we would die in all the thousands of lives we lived, and why the fleshselves weren't smart enough to make themselves survive.

And then we were through, and I became only myself again, mortal and frightened and terribly alone. I was going to die. Soon. This was not the eventual mortality that I faced every day and managed to tolerate. This was not the little hollow spot in my gut that came from contemplating my eventual cessation. This was the dire knowledge that my death waited for me on Cantata, and that it would almost certainly find me.

But I couldn't turn back. I was haunted . . . by the savaged corpses stacked shoulder-high in the hidden coolers of two ships, because I knew that those two ships weren't the only ones captained by self-styled vampires. I was haunted by the father who discovered his daughter was in the hands of a killer. I was haunted by the woman screaming in the Customs Interrogation room on Smithbright's World.

Most of all I was haunted by my mother's involvement in this nightmare—my mother, who had sacrificed my family and pinned her crime on me; who had flourished in the wake of her sins; and who now either was one of the vampires, or sought to become one.

If I died, at least I would die doing something that mattered. I wouldn't die the way I'd lived before; running and hiding. I forced myself to let go of my knees, to pull my shoulders back and lift my head. I took a deep breath. I would find out what the vampires were doing and I would find a way to stop them. I would do everything I could to survive, short of running away yet again. I wouldn't disappear. I wouldn't let my fear control my actions or dictate the direction of my life.

Badger watched me dry the tears from my cheeks. He knelt down beside me on the floor and wrapped his arms around me. "You're going to be fine," he whispered. And then he said something he hadn't said since we decided to end our romantic relationship and satisfy ourselves with being partners and friends. He said, "I love you, Cady."

I thought about dying and leaving Badger behind. I thought, I don't want to die without telling him how I feel. So I said, "I love you, too." I rested my head against his chest, remembering what it had been like to sleep with him, to kiss him, to make love with him. I wasn't his lover anymore because I had listened to my fears when they told me to push him away. All of those days we'd spent apart, we could have spent together.

Stupid, stupid; to throw away love because of fear.

I pulled him closer and kissed him. "We've wasted too much time," I whispered, and buried my face against the smooth skin at the curve of his neck. "Oh, love, I'm so sorry I wasted our time."

He held me with one arm and braced himself with the other, and lowered both of us to the floor. The warmth of his body and his weight pressing down on me were comforting rather than erotic. He brushed his cheek against mine. I remembered how much I had always loved the slight scratchiness of his beard stubble, the surprising softness of his lips.

"I love you," he said. "I know you're afraid, but you deserve to be loved. And I love you. There has never been anyone for me but you, Cady. Never. You're the only person I've ever loved."

Badger was my one love, too. I didn't think I *could* love anyone else. I had let fear deprive me of so many things, but in whatever time I had left, I promised myself I would banish fear to a corner of my life where it had no power over me. I would love Badger. I would hunt down evil. I would become the person I should have been all along.

We didn't have the time to do more than kiss. The com began to chime, and then Meileone Station confirmed that it had received our autorequest for a routing and docking assignment. The holos lit up and information started coming in.

Badger sighed and pushed himself to his feet.

I took over the flight control while he ran worms on the Spybees, and then through various systems in Meileone. He kept muttering to himself, and several times I heard him swear and start hitting keys.

Two and a half hours into the trip, when I was only thirty minutes from docking us, he gasped. "Unbelievable! I had the worm going through ships in long-term dock and you won't believe what I just pulled out of the dock records." Badger grabbed me away from my work and pulled me to the display he'd brought up. "You have to see this!"

The hologram of a Stardancer-class ship floated in the center of his display. He keyed in the request for an ID overlay, and Peter Crane's missing ship appeared in the display beside it. To me he said, "Watch this. I'll run it for you again." To the shipcom, he said, "Mark points of similarity between the *Lazy Rider* and all Stardancer-class ships."

The holo flashed as green lights sparkled along the sweeping dispersal fins and the sleek body. They outlined the elegant arches of the viewports and the placement of the fuel doors and airlocks. All of those things varied from ship to ship according to the customer's specifications and very few ship exteriors were identical. From the information I got from Crane just before we left Cassamir station, we took the specs for every Stardancer his company had ever made. At first all of them showed on the holo, but I watched the numbers of possible matches decrease with every detail. We were down to five possible ships when the program finished running its external comparison.

It was when the holograms peeled off the surface and displayed the grid of metal plates embedded within the moleibond that I got excited. The placement of those plates was done by hand by the shipwrights, and was therefore fractionally different in every ship; it provided the only true "fingerprint" in identifying hyperspace ships that were otherwise mechanically extruded and identical. The plates in the ship docked in Meileone, the *Lazy Rider*, matched the *Corrigan's Blood* plates to the micrometer.

When the words POSITIVE ID: CORRIGAN'S BLOOD flashed beneath the holo of the *Lazy Rider*, Badger and I turned to each other. He was grinning like a madman.

"Who brought it in?"

"I'm trying to get the crew records now, but they have a high-priority security screen—it's going to take me a while to get through to them."

It was there. Two million rucets worth of reclamation fees, docked in a long-term high-security bay waiting for me to come get it. With two million rucets, I could pay off my ship and do a lot of other things I wanted to do.

"I found its cargo log," Badger said.

"What do they say they're carrying?"

"Robust Y. From Cassamir Station."

Of course. Another link to Cassamir Station, and the biological company. "Robust Y? That sounds vaguely familiar."

"Male chromosome enhancer," Badger said. "The Y chromosome in human males is vulnerable to breakage during meiosis and because, unlike the X chromosome, it doesn't have another X to make up for its defects, the damage stays. And over millennia, the Y chromosome has become less and less able to protect men from all sorts of genetic defects, diseases, and disorders."

"And Robust Y fixes chromosome damage."

Badger nodded. "It sounded good when I read about it. It doesn't do all that much for the man who takes it, but if he has sons, they're supposed to inherit complete, undamaged Y chromosomes."

"You sound like you know more about it than someone with just a casual interest would. You wanted to try Robust Y?"

"Only when I thought that I might like to have children. I didn't want them to inherit my albinism."

We looked at each other. I realized when he'd been thinking about having children, he'd been thinking about having them with me. I hadn't ever considered a family. I kept discovering whole huge facets of Badger that I'd overlooked.

I said, "Oh."

Badger flushed and shrugged. "Maybe someday."

I could only nod.

The shipcom broke the awkward silence by announcing, "I have established ownership of the *Lazy Rider*."

I was grateful for the interruption. "Who owns it?"

"Directly, Meileone Healthcorps. Indirectly, Meileone Healthcorps is a subsidiary of Meileone Brighthope Industries, which in turn is owned by the Bradomar Corporation; Bradomar is a holding company owned by two separate dummy corporations which in turn are owned exclusively by the partners Lashanda Elenday and Dagmar Teach."

My mother. And a partner.

"Can you locate a holo of Dagmar Teach?"

"Teach's dummy corporation, Dagmar Productions, has one on file." The shipcom took only an instant to find it and bring it up. Badger and I stood studying Dagmar Teach for a few moments. I recognized him. I just couldn't believe he hadn't been more careful in hiding his identity. "That's John Alder," I told Badger.

"I know."

"They're working together. They're both in this vampire thing, and stealing a ship from Peter Crane." I stared down at my feet for a moment, trying to untangle the threads of the conspiracy Badger and I had uncovered. "We're working for Crane. Danniz Oe's in this for himself. And my mother is the third party. We and Oe are both out to get her." I looked up again. "If she's lucky, we'll get to her first. She's in deep."

"But so are we."

I nodded. "We can't back out. The only way out is through."

Minutes after Badger's positive confirmation of the presence of the *Corrigan's Blood*, we docked at Meileone Station. We'd been assigned to Level Five; this was not a level for working ships and working crews, but a party-and-profligacy level that suited the falsified status of the *Merry Widow*, and that would add some verisimilitude to our act as Adana Gantrey and Brian Darkman. I hated party levels, though. I hated the noise and the chumminess and the instant, false camaraderie of nosy dock neighbors. I hated the busy-busy little shops full of touristy junk that always lined the inside of the dock corridors. I hated the way I knew real captains looked at pampered rich dilettantes who took their ships out for entertainment once or twice a year, and knew only enough about ship-piloting to keep from killing themselves . . . and sometimes not even that much. In all the time I'd been a captain, I had avoided the party docks.

And now, here we were.

I locked us into our berth, started the two-way communication between us and the station, then stared in disbelief as every alarm light on my console panel went from green to disaster-red.

I yelled, "Badger," but he couldn't jump in to assist me. The lights on his console had lit up, too. He was already talking to the shipcom as fast as he could, tracing alarms back one at a time to their sources. I started in on my own batch of alarms; every time I successfully traced one back, I found out the same thing. It had been jammed, but the system was fine.

"Nothing's wrong," I told Badger.

"I know, but keep checking anyway."

We worked faster. If someone had created all the false alarms to hide a real alarm, we might not have much time. I traced back system after system, and watched light after light go from red back to green as soon as I'd manually queried the circuit. All the while, sweat trickled down my neck as I imagined one of those circuits hiding a break that connected it to explosives, or poison gas, or something.

Green light, and green light, and green light.

Dammit. The shipcom wouldn't just clear them. I tried to override all the alarms at once, but nothing happened. I went back to clearing.

"Found something," Badger said.

"What."

"Airlock just went from red to green without me clearing it first."

"Get a visual."

Badger activated the monitors inside and outside the airlock. Two flatscreen pictures appeared on the holos.

The first was of the gravdrop. It was clear. We hadn't been invaded. The second was of the short connecting corridor outside the airlock, the one that led to the station. We got a good look at Fedara Contei's back as she ran down that short corridor and turned right.

Badger slammed his fist into the wall. "Dammit, she got away. We weren't fast enough." He stared at the monitor where we had seen her disappear. "How did she do that? First the medichamber, then the ship."

I got a sudden chill, thinking that if she was able to make the bulkheads raise for her, she probably could have done it at any time.

Including when she was starved. She could have come after us and killed us, in spite of my Condition One precautions.

"Should we go after her?"

"No." He glared at the monitor display of the empty corridor outside of our airlock. "No. She told us what she knew, and she told us she didn't want our help. She is not really a part of what we're investigating."

I thought about that for a moment. I wanted to get her back, but he was right. She didn't want our help, and we didn't have any real help to offer her. She found a way to countermand the orders I'd given to the shipcom; she tricked open the bulkheads that lead back to the gravdrop, she climbed out, and she ran. And as much as I wanted to be able to do something for her, maybe she was right to run. Her life would be less complicated if it weren't bound to mine and Badger's.

"We won't go after her," I agreed.

We needed to get seats on the shuttle down to Meileone, but not much else. I'd done some work with the worm to be sure I could use the program, and confirmed that *Lazy Rider*, the erstwhile *Corrigan's Blood*, was in from Asher's Star (another of the backwater worlds we would have eventually gotten to) and had already paid docking for the next two weeks. Our bags were packed, Badger had two shipwrights on the way to look into repairs on the

Reward, and then we could go. We intended to check on my mother, then go through the list of USAG members in Meileone and find out what we could about each of them.

Before we even commed out for our tickets to planetside, the station comlink chimed and Fedara's holo appeared. She was breathing hard and dark spots of color stood out like bruises on her pale cheeks. Dark circles under her eyes made them look huge. She glanced over her shoulder at something the holo didn't pick up, then looked back at us.

"He's here," she said.

I had a good idea who she was talking about, but I asked anyway. "Who?"

"Danniz."

That's who I'd guessed from her level of apparent fear and the tone of her voice. "Did he see you?"

"No. He and some of his flunkies were doing another sort of hunting at the time. I ran into a lavatory to hide. I, um, got a little something to eat while I was there—" She winced when she said it; I guessed I understood why. It sounded so normal. So much like running out to a restaurant for a quick bite. "Anyway, I washed up when I was done and waited until I was sure they were gone. Then I found a pay comlink."

"How did he find us? How did he pick up our trail? Do you know? We should have disappeared when I switched the ship's IDs. If he found us, maybe the next batch of hunters from Smithbright's World will, too."

She shook her head. "I don't know of any way outside of the usual ones by which he could have tracked you. Maybe one of his associates has come up with some new technology." She shrugged. "It doesn't matter how he did it. He's here."

Badger was already running his worm program through the station systems, looking for a newly arrived ship from Galatia Fairing. The shipcom's end-of-search bell chimed, and Badger said, "Right! Ship called the *Space Tempest*."

"That's Danniz's private ship," Fedara said.

"That's what this says." Badger hunched over the display, reading. "Registered to Danniz Oe, carrying a crew of three. No passengers. This is odd. They docked half an hour before we did, and Oe has purchased three tickets on the next shuttle to Meileone. Which is leaving in . . ." He looked at the chrono on his compac, ". . . sixteen minutes."

He muttered comments to the shipcom, and after an instant, it said, "That number is not available."

"I can't get Oe's ID number off of the ticket purchase. I was hoping we could track him through the city with it; maybe see where he was going."

Fedara looked at Badger. "He has a VIP high-security number. You won't get it."

"The number doesn't exist that someone can't get if he works at it long enough, and knows what he's doing." Badger stared at the console, thinking. "If Oe arrived before us, it could be because he found our destination and came straight here. We took the long way; it would have been easy to get ahead of us. Or it could be that he doesn't know we're here. Do you know what he might want here?"

"I know he has contacts in Meileone, but I don't know who they are." She turned, looked at something behind her, and said, "I have to go." Neither of us had a chance to wish her luck. Her image vanished from the holo. She was gone again, perhaps this time for good.

I checked my chrono and squeezed Badger's arm. "We know who the contacts might be, but there are so many possibilities that the only way we're going to be able to be sure is for one of us to go after him. We only have a few minutes until the shuttle he'll be on leaves. I can be on it if you'll get me a ticket. Is the flight full?"

For the first time in years, Badger balked. "You aren't going to follow Danniz Oe. He met you." Badger didn't even look for a shipcom report on the shuttle status.

"Not when I looked like this. And I am going. You're going to need access to more than a tourist com in a hotel if you're going to find his ID number, and we need to have that. Stay here until you find it, then follow me down."

"You stay. I'll go. You're competent with the worm and he doesn't know me." Badger touched my cheek with one finger. "This life without you in it wouldn't mean anything to me."

I shook my head. I understood his concern, but he wasn't thinking logically. "I can use the damned worm, but I'm not you. I'd take time that you wouldn't need and that we don't have. I'll follow him. That's one of the things I do best."

I took his hand. "There aren't any safe places. Not there . . ." I nodded toward the porthole and the white-and-black planet that hung over our heads. ". . . And not here. When we get some idea of what's going on, we'll meet up. I'll get a room for us; just get through here as fast as you can."

"He's going to kill you if he catches you."

"I know."

"If you get into trouble while I'm up here, there's no way that I'll be able to reach you in time to help."

I read the concern in his eyes. The friendship. The love. The fear. I said, "I know that, too. I'll have to make sure I stay out of trouble." I moved closer to him and rested both hands on his shoulders. "I have to do this, Badg. I ran away the first time and let my mother win. I let her get away with killing the rest of my family and blaming me. Maybe I couldn't have beaten her and her cronies then. But maybe I can now. I have to try." I smiled at him, doing my best to look confident. "So, are you going to get me a ticket or am I going to have to take care of that myself?"

He kissed my forehead and sighed. Then he turned to the shipcom console and directed subvocal commands to the unit, and after a moment said, "Your seat is waiting. Don't forget you're Adana now. Don't forget your new ID number." He kept his back to me. "And for God's sake, don't get hurt."

I took my newest false ID and ran for the shuttle, hoping that my breathless arrival wouldn't cause too much commotion. I didn't want to be memorable. I wanted to be just another self-indulgent too-rich weekend captain on my way to a shopping spree in the Oldcity sector of Meileone.

Chapter Twenty-three

I ended up sitting two seats in front of Oe. I recognized him from the doppler holo; he looked different in color than he had in that flat charcoal gray, but the lines and planes of his face were unmistakable. He was boyish, handsome, innocent; he was broad-shouldered and lean, but not heavily muscled. I permitted myself just one look at him when I got on the shuttle; then I turned away so that if he glanced up I wouldn't be staring. But he didn't look up. Didn't notice me at all. I was relieved. I would have been happier in a seat one or two rows behind him, but this shuttle trip was almost completely booked, and all of the seats toward the back were taken. I had a window, and spent the trip alternately dozing and staring out of it at the bleak ball of ice and rock that was Cantata. Going home.

Looking at the surface of the planet, there's very little indication that it's inhabited, and nothing to suggest that a billion people live beneath its grim and unwelcoming exterior. The lights of the shuttle landing field were on by the time we touched ground. They were the only lights visible in any direction. The cliffs to the north of the field had been carved by eons of wind and dust; in the twilight the resulting pillars and spires and arches looked like the ruins of an ancient, alien city.

Cantata had never been inhabited by anyone but humans, though, and none of them had ever lived on its surface. To the south, the icefields glowed purple and red in the last rays of the red sun's light. Cantata's surface is extraordinarily beautiful, but sere and unforgiving.

The planet got its name from the winds that sang through the stones in one formation not too far north of the Meileone landing field. Time and wind and serendipity had carved away at a series of igneous towers; bubbles and tubes, natural inclusions in the volcanic rock of these towers, had worn through over the eons, creating flutes of various sizes. The wind blew over these stone flutes almost constantly, eddying and gusting over first one surface and then another. The result was music of a sort; some of the flutes had the rich timbre and booming depth of the low notes of an ancient pipe organ, some soared with the vibrancy of a piccolo. Sometimes the listener could hear the reverberation of a contra clarinet and the wail of a saxophone sounding in counterpointed melodies.

But if it was music, it was music as played by a tone-deaf orchestra of thousands, each blowing away at a different song and none of them ever running out of breath. Stash Belview, who discovered the planet and the formation, chose to name the new world Cantata. I suspect old Stash was tone deaf. If I'd named the place, I would have called it Cacophony. Or maybe Caterwaul.

The shuttle taxied to the airlock. Cantata's air is too oxygen-poor to be breathable, so our shuttle would connect to the airlock and we would disembark directly into the shuttle terminal, then travel to the gravdrops that would carry us to the heart of Meileone. We would never step on the surface of the planet. Almost no one did anymore, unless they went to the Choirstones. The surface of Cantata was an easy place to die.

I retrieved my bag from the compartment beneath the seat in front of me and took my time getting to my feet when the light indicated that we could safely disembark. I wanted to let Oe get a few people ahead. It didn't work that way, though. I was still in my seat, rummaging through the bag pretending that I was looking for something, watching the people who went by out of the corner of my eye, when Oe took the seat beside mine.

"Hi," he said. "Lose something?" Feeling sick and scared, I looked up. His smile was broad and friendly, his face as open as sunshine. He looked to me like he was in his early twenties. Like me in my Adana guise, he was red-headed, pale-skinned and vigorously freckled. Where my eyes were blue, though, his were a warm and inviting brown. And they were enchanting. I looked down at my bag and smiled.

"Nothing important. I was just looking for my guidebook. It isn't in here, though, so I suppose I'll have to buy another." I stood, determined to get both of us on our way. I was certain that I didn't want to be alone with him even for an instant. "But thank you for asking."

He stood, too. "So you're a tourist. I'm from here—just getting back on business, actually."

Liar, I thought.

He said, "My name is Danniz Oe. If you have the time, I'd be delighted to show you around. There are parts of Meileone that are just stunning. Oldcity is wonderful, of course, but everybody sees Oldcity. They wander around Level Seven like they'd just discovered heaven, but you haven't seen anything until you've dropped to Level Twenty-three."

Twenty-three was one of the lower levels in the city, and I, who at one time knew the city with a native's cocky assurance, wouldn't have gone there if I'd been bet a million rucets to do it. There was nothing on Twenty-three a tourist would want to see. It was the home of Banger gangs and Joy-merchants and Sellers and Senso chambers; the place where unspeakable needs met unspeakable greed to do business. His attempt to pick me up was unnerving, but his suggestion that we go to Twenty-three suggested that he wasn't interested in anything more long-term than a meal. He was hunting, and I tasted bile in the back of my throat. My stomach knotted, and I hoped that I wouldn't throw up. Trying my best to look unperturbed, I nodded toward the last of the other passengers, who had just edged ahead of my seat. "Excuse me," I said.

Oe looked annoyed, but he took the hint and stepped into the aisle. However, he stepped back so that he could follow me. Damn.

"I'm afraid my agenda is quite rigid," I told him. "I'm researching Oldcity for a Senso that my company will be producing." Adana's history included the fact that she owned the wildly successful shock-porn Senso business, but also, surprisingly, a small moderately successful educational Senso studio. Going to Oldcity to do research for that seemed like a clever lie, and one that I could back up if for some reason he decided to double-check.

He snorted. "Another Senso set in Oldcity. How trite. A Senso about the lower levels would have some excitement to it. Some muscle and sinew and blood." His face held the faintest touch of a secret amusement when he said that.

There was nothing attractive about his manner—he was far too pushy to be someone who would have interested me under normal circumstances. And knowing what he was gave me every reason to be brusque and uninterested and cold. So why, then, did I feel drawn to him? Why did he seem so magnetic that I wanted to touch him even as every cell of my body was screaming for me to get away? What dark current sprang to life between us, making me think that if he were with me, it would be different? That I would be special to him? What madness was that?

I struggled to find my voice. When I managed to speak, I didn't like the tremor I heard there. "Perhaps the setting seems trite to you. But since it's about the life of Jadius Meklenbaum, who lived and died in Oldcity, I'm afraid I don't see much point in visiting the rest of the city."

We walked through the airlock into the passageway that connected the shuttle to the terminal. The passageway temperature was drastically lower than that of the shuttle.

And through the moleibond walls, I could hear the Choirstones singing—insane background music that swelled and crescendoed, played by the mad organist for the damned. Homecoming music for hell.

Oe didn't try to speak over the noise. He waited until we stepped out of the corridor into the terminal proper. The bustle of the place and the improved insulation silenced the distant Choirstones. Then he said, "Jadius Meklenbaum? Who the hell was he?"

"She." I was walking at a good clip, heading for a kiosk where I saw the glowing screen advertising guidebooks. Hundreds of people scurried past us in all directions, staring at chronos, muttering to their compacs, rushing into the arms of friends and lovers and families. Security agents stood around in their dull navy blue speedsuits, looking unflappable and alert, like nothing was going to happen to anyone while they were around. I didn't feel any safer for their presence. "She was a researcher in nanocosmetic alteration. She did the preliminary work on integumentary redesign; Melatinting was a direct result of techniques she initially developed. Jon Hardly expanded her research and brought Melatinting to the public, but I'm more interested in her."

And just to think, when I was struggling my way through my mandatory Juvenile Pre-Citizenship Broadening Experiences, I swore I'd never use anything I learned about Meileone history again. Ha!

"Oh," he said. "So did she live some sort of wild life that would make her an interesting subject for a Senso?"

I reached the kiosk, swiped my ID card through the slot, pressed the button identifying the guidebook disk that I wanted. In clipped tones I said, "Of course not! She was an ideal role model. If she'd been any other sort of person, we certainly wouldn't make a Senso of her life." I took a deep breath and risked giving him a scathing look. But I did not risk looking in his eyes. When I did that, I felt him touching inside of me. The pull he exerted by simple proximity was bad enough—as compelling as the gravitational pull of the sun on a stray planet. He wanted to draw me into his orbit, and I didn't want to go.

"My company makes *educational* Sensos. We won a number of awards last year for our full-sensory exploration of the meiotic division of cells, done from within the cells themselves." I elaborated. "The feeling of participating with the DNA as it split and doubled itself was exhilarating—"

He cut me off with a wave of his hand. "Very interesting for you, I'm sure," he said. He made no attempt to hide the fact that I'd bored him beyond his capacity to feign interest, and at the moment that he lost interest in me, the pull I'd felt vanished. Click—I was free. "You looked like you would be a lot more fun than you are. I hope you find everything you want in Oldcity," he said, and with a curt nod, turned and walked away.

I took the guidebook chip that popped out of the slot and slid it into the chip-reader in my compac and stood beside the kiosk, willing my heart to slow down. That had been too close—and closer even than I realized until he let me go. I hadn't realized how near I'd been to going with him.

I looked stupidly at the guide I'd purchased, for a moment unable to comprehend how it had come to be in my hand. But the effects of Danniz Oe wore off quickly, and after a few seconds I was able to press the chip-reader and activate the guide. I thought it would still be a good idea to play the part of a tourist, and it wouldn't kill me to consult the guide from time to time; after all, it had been years since I'd been home. Surely a few things had changed. I punched in a code at random and pretended to listen and watch the video.

All the while I watched Oe. He headed for the gravdrops. I slid my hand through my pocket, pressed my fleshtab, and changed out the dopplerchip that was in the recorder, replacing it with a fresh one. I pressed the used chip into the storage slot and sealed the fleshtab again.

"—open tours of the Branlara Hydrofarming and Air Treatment Cooperative from 0600 to 1400 Meileone Time every day but Tuesday. For a video of highlights of the tour, press Details now—"

I was still scared, but now I was angry too—the kind of angry that left me shaking and on the verge of tears. The bastard. He didn't know me, he didn't know he had any reason to want me dead, but he had decided he was going to kill me. He had been trying to set me up so he could torture and murder me, and it had been random. Just random. He'd liked the way I looked.

And the fact was that my escape only meant someone else would die. He was going to find somebody else to slaughter, and somebody else after that, and then even someone else. And they were going to die random deaths like the one he'd tried to lure me into, just because they'd had the misfortune to be in the wrong place at the wrong time. How could evil be like that? How could it be so capricious, and so casual?

I felt a flare of kinship to Fedara Contei. I wanted Oe dead.

I kept my head down as he met up with a tall, gaunt man and a slender brunette woman who had apparently been waiting for him . . . and perhaps for me as well. They all looked my way, and Oe shook his head, giving the impression that he was disgusted.

Double bastard. He'd intended to share me with his friends. I remembered those corpses in the cooler and barely suppressed a shudder.

I waited until all three of them stepped into the gravdrop. Then I strolled casually over, stepped in, and floated after them.

They started edging out of the fast-grav stream at around Level Eight. I kept them in view, maintaining a safe distance and being sure that I didn't look like I was watching them.

They didn't get off at Level Nine or Ten, which I'd expected from their lane change. Evidently they weren't used to the huge Meileone gravdrops, which have a maximum drop speed of over three hundred kilometers per hour and which have simultaneous up and down bands in the same tube. The bi-directional gravity bands are tricky, but extremely convenient if you miss your stop and want to go back without changing drops, like every other city makes you do. Gravdropping when traffic is light is one of the more interesting sports in Meileone, one I'd participated in regularly when I was younger.

I didn't bother to switch into the slowdown lanes when I saw them finally veer toward their exit. Instead, I stayed in the through-traffic lane until I saw them get off on Level Twelve.

My old home level. I wondered if my mother still lived there. I was past them and heading downward fast. I hadn't wanted to seem like I was paying them any attention, and traffic was light enough that I was afraid I'd be conspicuous if I slowed down at all. But with them out of the way, I needed to get back up to Twelve before I lost them.

I rolled myself into a tight ball and flipped across the slowdown lanes and shot into the reverse-direction lanes and careened into the high speed lane and then through that into the upward-flowing slowdown lanes, still tucked into cannonball position. I didn't uncurl until the tug on my midsection lessened and I felt myself gliding upward at an easy speed.

"Damned irresponsible kids," someone I'd cut off muttered.

I grinned briefly. It was nice to know that some things really didn't change. People had bitched and complained when I pulled that stunt at sixteen, too.

I stepped off at Twelve and saw Oe and his two companions hurrying onto the I-5 tramwalk, westbound. I took my time following after them, and when I did I made sure I didn't watch them. Instead I marveled at the changes the years had wrought.

The I-5 hadn't changed much. It had been one of the newer tramwalks when I lived on Twelve, all gleaming moleibond and colorful inlays and glowdots on the tracks to mark the paths and lanes. The center lane rolled faster than I remembered, and there were more exit ramps.

The real changes were in Level Twelve itself. Twelve had been a moderate-income neighborhood when I'd lived there. It had been nice . . . if you said the word "nice" with the muscles of your jaw tight and your teeth clenched. The homes, carved out of living rock and moleibonded, had always seemed plain to me. When I'd lived there, the harsh white glare of lightstrips drenched the main thoroughfares, while puddle lights provided inadequate illumination to the back streets.

Now everything I could see was done in strellitas—the tiny, expensive lights embedded in the moleibonded surfaces of the buildings and the overhead arch that cast a glow reminiscent of the last light from a perfect sunset. Looking up at them was like looking at the stars, but warmer and friendlier.

Sunlights gave extra illumination to the trees that now grew along both sides of the tramwalks. The trees—which never would have ground in the Twelve I knew— arched over the walks in places, lush and green and abundantly covered with sweet-scented flowers.

The buildings were the same. And yet they weren't. They still rose three stories, forming pillars that supported the stone arches overhead and the rest of the city that piled on top of them. They still had the same glossy surfaces, the same broad doors and tall, narrow windows. But they were undeniably different.

I finally figured out what had changed. Almost every residential building had added balconies, and on most of the balconies flowers and trees grew beneath private sunlights. The air, always stale before, now smelled naturally sweet.

The place was beautiful—as beautiful in its way as Oldcity.

The people on the tramwalk were different, too. Calmer. Happier-looking. More relaxed. For the most part, they had the air of people who weren't worried about money or taxes or work or anything else. Twelvers always used to have that slightly desperate air of people living a meter beyond their means. They'd always seemed to me to be on the hustle, looking for a way to make an extra rucet.

I was so intrigued by the subtle changes that I almost missed Danniz and his friends when they walked off the exit into a broad, busy plaza. I recognized the place by its location, but not by its appearance. Tadra Mall had benefited from the same prosperity that had touched the other parts of Twelve that I'd seen.

Danniz led his associates through the crowd to a new hotel, the Cantata Regalle. I waited outside, leaning against one of the windows. I could see the three of them registering at the com port. When I saw them get keys, I walked away. I had enough to go on for a while. I walked farther through the plaza, admiring the grass and flowers in the landscaped gardens, the huge trees, the central waterfall. If it weren't Cantata, I would have wanted to buy a place in Twelve, settle down, and only go into space for entertainment.

But it *was* Cantata, and no matter how delightful everything looked on the surface, something was very wrong deep inside.

I found another hotel in the plaza—the Forest Radisson. Radisson was a good intergalactic chain, and if it was a bit pricey, it was also worth the rucets. I went in, got myself a two-room suite, and let myself up to it.

I needed to call Badger, but I didn't want to use my compac. It would work, but the compac's transmission went from air to the local satellite transceiver. No matter how new my compac model was, I'd learned from experience that there were always people around who had the most current airwave decoders. What's worse, they listened to them. I remembered telling Badger once that I'd found a corpse in the sauna of the hotel where I was staying while he was doing background work in the *Reward*. I'd been joking—the trip had been entirely routine and we were both bored beyond words. However, within five minutes the local police showed up in the sauna, as did half a dozen gawkers. The police weren't amused . . . and neither was I. I never sent sensitive information over the compac again.

People could tap direct feeds to the satellite, but it was harder, and they had to know which line they wanted to tap, and when; all in all, the odds were better that someone would show up at my door wanting to know what the hell I was doing.

I used my room com to call.

"I just found Oe's ID number," Badger told me. "He used his ID card in an unsecured hotel terminal, and I had an open-ended search for all ID numbers used to secure rooms. Just for the record, you showed up, too. Since both of you are on Twelve, I take it you didn't lose him."

"I followed him to the Cantata Regalle. He's there with two associates." I debated telling him about the fact that Oe had tried to pick me up, and decided it would be smarter to let him know how dangerous things had gotten and then have him bitch at me than it would be to hide the information about what happened. So I told him, not sparing any of the details.

To my surprise, he didn't bitch. "Close call. Sounds like you handled it well, though." He took a deep breath and let it out slowly. I imagined that he was reminding himself that I'd had a lot of practice doing what I was doing, and that I was as safe in the Radisson as I would have been in the *Reward*. "I can create a backfile on your activities here," he said. "So that if Oe decides to find out who you are, he'll come up with information that supports your story. I can make it harder for him to find out about the shock-porn line, and easier to quickly verify the educational Senso story."

"I don't imagine he'll try to find me. I didn't even tell him my name. But go ahead and do it," I said. "I'd rather be able to sleep nights."

"Speaking of sleeping, I also think I ought to change the records on your registration. I'll book you into someplace expensive on Seven, and change the registration on the room you're in so that it belongs to someone from Branning." Branning was a city on the other side of Cantata.

"Fine. But how would he even find my name?"

"He'd download a shuttle passenger list, run a picture ID check on everyone listed, and eliminate everyone who wasn't you. If he was any good, it would take him about ten minutes. In fact—" Badger's voice got muffled—I could tell he'd turned away from the comlink. "—if you'll wait just a second, I can tell you whether there have been any queries for that sort of information. Just to give us a baseline."

For a moment, I heard nothing. Then Badger said, "Get out. Now! Not only have I found a shuttle list query, but someone has asked for and received your hotel and room number."

"Shit!"

I broke off the connection, grabbed my bag, and ran. I left my room and turned down the hall to the right. I tried to recall the layout of the hotel. It was a corner pillar, facing onto the plaza and two streets. I turned right again at the first intersecting hallway I came to, and walked quickly. If I didn't have my directions confused, I could get to the elevator at the far end of the hall, travel down three stories, and step out onto the street that paralleled the plaza. Behind me, I heard the soft *shussh* of the elevator and the subdued tingg that indicated it was stopping on my floor.

The elevator was in the corner. The people who got out would be able to see me no matter which hall I was in. If it was Danniz, I was in trouble.

A cleaning bot beeped and a door five doors ahead of me clicked open. I sprinted down the hall, shoved my hand in just in time to keep the door from closing, and ducked inside, breathing hard.

"Pardon me," the bot said in a gentle, neutral voice. "But this room is unoccupied."

"I know," I whispered.

"Pardon me, but this room is unoccupied." Still the same

gentle, neutral voice. If I didn't stop it, though, it was going to get louder.

I bent down, hit its emergency reset button, and before the bot could reset, popped the hinged back open and ripped loose all of the wires I could get my hand around. When I did that, I knew a light went on down in a central maintenance board, indicating that this bot had developed a malfunction. I probably only had a couple of minutes before someone showed up to find out what had gone wrong.

I pulled a nail file out of my bag and used it to pry the bot's central processing unit loose from its motherboard. The CPU was the size of my smallest fingernail—for what it was, relatively large and obsolete. That was a piece of luck. A smaller one would have been nightmarish to pry loose. I let the CPU drop down into the guts of the bot, and smiled a little at the thought of how tough it was going to be to get it back out. One of the advantages of working constantly with an older ship was that I'd learned a lot about machines and how they worked.

I reattached all of the wires, though probably not in the right places. Then I opened the baggage storage compartment door, slipped inside, and pulled the door shut behind me. Something in my bag poked me in the kidneys, and the air in the tiny compartment became stifling very quickly, but I didn't care. From down the hall and around the corner, I could hear someone pounding on a door. As best I could tell, the pounding came from the approximate location of the room that had been mine.

Had been. Paid for or not, I wouldn't be going back to it.

I could barely hear the elevator tingg again. The pounding stopped. A moment later, the door to the room I was hiding in opened, and a male voice said, "What the hell happened to you?"

The bot, of course, didn't respond. It was temporarily brain-dead. If I were lucky, it would be a bot that didn't have an emergency backup battery to ensure that it remembered what it had been doing when it so unfortunately lost power. I couldn't imagine why anyone would pay extra to have a cleaning bot remember its last words . . . but maybe managers knew there were people like me in the world. That would be a reason.

I heard the man pressing the reset button. Waiting. Pressing it again. He was obviously of the button-pushing school of maintenance and repair work—good news for me.

"Great," he muttered. "Now I have to drag you all the way down to Maintenance." I heard the whine of an antigrav pallet and the clunk-thud of the bot being lifted onto it by the machine arms. The sounds would be unmistakable to anyone who ever loaded or unloaded cargo. I'd done both. If this scenario followed itself to a logical conclusion, the man from Maintenance would now shove the pallet out into the hall and shut the door behind him.

I heard the hall door open.

Yes. Yes. Now close it and go away.

But someone stopped him before he could get out the door. "Excuse me, mado. There's a problem in room Three-Fourteen. My friend is in there, but I can't get her to open the door. I'm afraid something has happened to her." The voice belonged to Danniz Oe. Only the thin, primarily decorative storage compartment door separated the two of us.

That wasn't enough. How could I have been cocky enough to think that he would just walk away when I didn't go with him? And when he looked up my name, he found out that I'd chosen a hotel on Twelve, not Seven. That I was only three buildings away from him. That I'd checked into my hotel only minutes after he checked into his.

He would have wondered what I was doing . . . would have wondered at the coincidence of my ending up so close to him. And he would not have believed the coincidence. I wouldn't have. I never believe coincidences.

So he had come looking for me.

"How odd," Oe said. I heard him sniff. "I think I smell her . . . perfume. In there."

I wasn't wearing perfume. Could he smell me? I pulled myself into a tighter ball, resisting the urge to squeeze my eyes shut.

The maintenance man stepped out into the hall and closed the door behind him. I heard the reassuring chunk-click of the automatic security locks sliding into place. He said, "I can't just open any room, mado. You'll have to give me some proof that you have a right to be in there."

Oe said, "My friend's name is Adana Gantrey. She's a pretty girl—red hair, tall. She's a tourist who just arrived—her ship is the *Merry Widow*, registered at the Meileone station. She and I arrived together; you can check the shuttle manifest or the readouts from the security scopes on One for verification. I would hate to have to call the police to open the door, especially when you can do it without causing structural damage to the hotel," he said.

And the employee, who should still have refused to open the door for him, said, "I'll be happy to help you, mado. I wouldn't want you to have to call the police either."

I thought, That's completely against hotel procedure! And then I remembered Oe's eyes. I remembered how I'd been drawn to them. Perhaps the maintenance man wouldn't be able to resist Oe's stare.

"Thank you. My friends and I do appreciate that. We don't want anything bad to happen to Adana." He sounded so honestly concerned. Listening without knowing what was going on, I would have been convinced.

I crawled out of the storage compartment and pressed my ear to the door.

I heard the whine of the pallet floating down the hall. I heard Danniz speaking with a woman, the maintenance man, and another man whose high, nasal, unpleasantly reedy tenor I felt sure I would recognize if I ever heard it again.

The sounds grew fainter. Then I heard the maintenance man again. "Yes. Adana Gantrey is registered to this room."

A pause. "Let me see if she's returned here first." I heard a knock. "Mada Gantrey? Are you all right? Mada Gantrey?" Another pause. "Perhaps she's just out."

"No. Our meeting together was vital; she wouldn't have missed it."

The maintenance man again. "I'll just open it and peek in." I heard the door open. "Wait! I didn't mean for you to run in—"

Silence. Then Danniz shouted, his words understandable but muffled. I realized he was inside the room. "Mado! Please! Come help me! Something's wrong with her!"

And the sound of running feet, and the sound of a single shrill scream, and a thud, and then silence. I heard the door to what had been my room shut after a moment, heard the sound of the deadbolt sliding into place.

The room was registered to me. When the body was found there, it would be traced to me—unless Badger was thorough enough in erasing the signs of my presence from the system. If he wasn't, then the police were going to be looking for Adana Gantrey in connection with a murder. And I couldn't let them find me, because they wouldn't have to dig any further than my DNA to find out that I was wanted in connection with three other murders, all of which had taken place a number of years before but only a few streets over from here.

I did the only thing I could do right then. I fled.

Chapter Twenty-four

If luck ran against me, someone would find the maintenance man's body quickly. Then the Meileone police would go looking for Adana Gantrey to ask her what a corpse was doing in her room. The Adana Gantrey ID would appear throughout the comnet, waiting for me to trigger alerts with any use of the net. I had to assume that luck would run against me. Which meant I didn't have much time.

I went to the nearest financial center and requested the balance of my account transferred to two credit chits. The man doing the transfer balked when he saw the amount involved, but I insisted. He did a complete ID check, and I forced myself to remain calm while he ran my DNA verification—I knew it would match the Adana Gantrey ID. I was afraid, though, that somehow the Meileone system would correlate my DNA with Tanasha Elenday's, bringing me face to face with my past.

But he frowned at me when the Gen-ID scan cleared me, and put just under a million rucets into each of two cash-equal credit chits. It was a dreadful amount of money to carry without a security lock, but the security lock would defeat the purpose of taking it out in cash.

Of course when the police found the body, if the room were still in my name, the fact that I'd withdrawn such a huge amount of money was going to look suspicious. No more suspicious than a corpse in the room, I supposed. I'd have to hope that Badger was having luck transferring the room to someone else's account and creating new reservations for us elsewhere in Meileone.

I had plenty of cash. Now I needed a new look. I'd have the best chance of finding one at one of Meileone's universally renowned pavos.

I was fairly sure I remembered the locations of a few pavos on Twelve, but I wanted to put vertical distance between Danniz Oe and me. I wanted to minimize the chances of passing him on a tramwalk, or meeting up with him in a restaurant. In a level that housed more than a million people, my chances of avoiding him were good. But if I left the level, my chances were better.

I'd take better.

I ran from the financial center to a gravdrop cluster and dropped to Seventeen, for no reason except that it was someplace I'd never been. I'd missed something worth seeing.

My first impression of the place was of auditory hush and visual noise. In the section where I dropped, Seventeen's designers had favored garish colors, bright lights, sharp angles, sweeping arches, and minimalist architecture, all carefully baffled to keep the normal city noises to a hush. All of the moleibonded stone had been dyed first, primarily in blues and reds and purples. All the tramwalks had forward-swept white padded rails. The treeless plazas featured lighted fountains and holobirds soaring through the air and darting in and out of the water.

Most of the people matched the level. They didn't run; they didn't shout. But for all their quietness, they were impossible to overlook. A woman passed me wearing black-and-white Melatint. Her scoop-backed speedsuit showed off lean shoulders upon which a talented bodyartist had rendered a copy of the great ancient M. C. Escher's hands drawing each other. Two androgynes hurried away from me, one horizontally pinstriped in metallic pink on metallic cobalt blue, the other done in a scaled pattern of greens and blues that made it look like a giant carp. Copper people and gold people and green and orange and red all scurried to their separate destinations, looking like so many candies in a bowl. I got a few glances—on Seventeen I was the rarity, the woman who wore her skin bare.

That was going to change.

I stopped a woman with Chromaglossed hair done in gorgeous opalescent blues and lavenders and with her skin Melatinted in white mother-of-pearl and asked her who did her work.

She pointed over her shoulder. "Tangerine at Saint Everything's Pavo." She smiled, pleased to have been asked.

I nodded and thanked her, then followed the tramwalk signs to Saint Everything's. It was huge. I pushed my way past the usual crowd of Sellers hawking their bodies into the vaulted main dome of the pavo. Senso chambers and food stands vied for space with the glassteel walls of the paratenka courts, in the nearest of which a heated game had drawn a circle of gambling spectators. The two teams floated in face-off positions, the ball hanging in the center of the court. The whistle sounded and the two centers headdropped through the high-grav down columns and snap-rolled toward each other. Blue arrived first, red a millisecond behind, and the six other fielders exploded into action. The ball described an erratic course through the court, accelerating through the downdrops and updrops and careening off the glassteel walls. Both goalies crouched in their ends. Waiting.

I wanted so much to stop and watch—I loved paratenka. At sixteen, I'd been a ranked player in the Twelve Champion intramural league.

But I had no time.

I pulled myself away from the wonderful spectacle and hurried past the food dispensers and joy chambers and verity rooms, and finally found Tangerine's Dream.

It was a small studio, but busy. Three bodyartists chatted

to each other as they worked on clients; I had no trouble figuring out which of them was Tangerine. Blindingly orange from hair to eyes to skin, with a rich wet-look Melatint job that made him look like he'd just stepped, dripping, from a vat of metallic tangerine paint, he seemed to glow as he did the final touches on a young woman's Chromagloss job.

I waited until he looked my way, then waved him over. At first he said his schedule was too full, and that he could make an appointment for me Thursday after next. When I offered to triple his asking price, though, he grinned and called me *buski* and said wasn't it amazing that he'd just had a cancellation in his schedule. Then he commed his "cancellation" and told the man he'd had a sudden emergency, but would work late that night if the customer wanted. The customer wanted.

We agreed on an opalescent Chromagloss on my hair, plus straightening and a shoulder-length blunt cut that would show off the body work. I decided I wanted the hair done in cobalt blue, black, and emerald green. And we discussed skin patterns, coming up at last with a soft blue hue that he would shadow into darker blue to create the illusion of greater depth. I knew I didn't want a metallic, but had a hard time deciding between the mother-of-pearl finish and the wet look he wore.

I finally decided the mother-of-pearl would go better with most of my clothing, and Tangerine color-tested the Melatint on my skin. And that was when he gave me a bad scare.

"Whoever did you last was brilliant," he said. "May I ask who it was?"

"What?"

"The person who did your melanin lift. I would never have known. The freckles are perfect—no one would ever guess they weren't the . . . original equipment. Your birth color is quite dark, isn't it?"

I swallowed, imagining myself suddenly revealed as Tanasha Elenday. "How did you know?"

He laughed. "*Buski*, I work with skin all day. Natural redheads have the thinnest skin in the universe. Yours is thick and the texture is *completely* different."

"Oh."

Tangerine winked at me. "Don't worry, lovely *buskinatchka*. I won't tell." He ran his fingers through my hair and frowned. Before I could stop him, he pulled a single hair from my scalp and ran it through his fingers. "Texture is all wrong for red *or* black. Maybe brunette, but I don't think so. Wicked girl! You're a natural blonde, aren't you? Brown-black skin, blonde hair. How about the eyes?"

I looked up at him from my chair and sighed. "Blue."

He arched an eyebrow. "Maryschild, eh?"

"Yes."

His smile was enigmatic. "Me, too. What my mother *did* to *me* . . ." He rolled his eyes and waved a hand as if brushing away the thought.

I nodded. "Mine, too."

"Well, you'll like this, my fair Mary-sister. And seeing as we're kin of a sort, you can just pay me the regular price."

He liked my muscles—and more so once he found out I'd earned them. "I was a Banger for a while," he told me. "I reached Ninth Shada—went all the way to Flying Two-Hand in the Pits." I was impressed. He liked my ass. "It doesn't look like you just use it for sitting and shitting," he remarked. And he liked my tits. "I had a pair just like them once," he said. "My second female genderflip, I decided to go small. The little ones were so much more comfortable, and the boys still liked me just fine."

I'd heard of genderflipping, but as far as I knew, it hadn't spread beyond Cantata. It was a very high-tech procedure, involving programming a special medichamber to treat half of all X chromosomes as Ys, or conversely to treat all Y chromosomes as Xs.

"It was expensive, but delicious," he told me. "Having

all those men lusting after me." He laughed. "Of course they still do, but it's different men, you know."

I nodded and said I could imagine how that would be intriguing.

"You really ought to try it sometime," he said. "You'd love having a big dangling schkloppitter to swing around. It's such fun."

"I can only imagine," I said, and chuckled.

Tangerine made me laugh; by the time I was done with my bodyart, I felt lighter and happier than I had since I accepted Peter Crane's job. Better yet, when I walked out of Saint Everything's, I looked like an original piece of living art, and still managed to give the impression that I belonged in Meileone. I bought myself a set of loose, gauzy pants that bloused around my ankles and a sheer top that floated loosely and draped beautifully, and a simple flat black speedsuit that set off my new coloring. I wasn't being a creature of fashion; I needed to get rid of my jumpsuit that declared me to one and all a spacer. When I'd changed and dumped my old clothing in an incinerator, I traveled around Seventeen for a while, taking tramwalks and walking through pavilions, admiring the place and the people and being admired in turn. I found a place to eat and got some *sho* and some *dit-det*—both reconsta foods, but good ones, and things that I still remembered fondly from my childhood.

After about an hour of doing nothing while I waited, Badger commed me briefly. "I'm on Four, at our place," he said.

"I'll be there as fast as I can," I told him, and jumped the nearest gravdrop.

"Our place" lay at the back of a small series of natural caverns on Level Four, just past the point where severe irregularities in the earth's mantle—and the likelihood of earthquakes that those irregularities implied— had convinced Four's excavators to stop and expand in a different direction. The passages that led to the caverns were dark and cold and mostly blocked off.

The caverns themselves were unlit and for the most part,

ignored. Children explored them from time to time, but few did it with quite the determination Badger and I had shown. We'd found a passage at the back of a narrow crevice in the last cavern, a passage that had been far too small for even a child to fit through. We'd worked for months to enlarge the opening, and had been rewarded to discover a good-sized room beyond. We made that our place.

And when, a year or so after the initial discovery, we got our hands on a miniature moleibonding set, we fabricated a plug for the opening, and spent an enormous amount of time making our plug look like the rock that surrounded it. We hadn't done too bad a job, as I remembered. When we weren't there, we used our moleibonded plug to close the passage off so no one else would bother our things. We didn't have that many things, but what we kept there were our treasures. Badger rolled some of his poems into a waterproof tube and wedged them into a deep crevice. My Japanese *netsuke* of a wizened man folding a piece of paper I put on a flat rock, and placed candellas on either side to illuminate it, creating a small shrine. The *netsuke* was only a replica, and it had no monetary value, but it reminded me of Isas Yamamoto.

Soaring upward through the gravdrop, I had time to wonder whether anyone else had ever found our place. When Badger and I ran, we didn't have time to get our things. I thought I'd like to have that little carving back, and I imagined he would be pleased to recover his poems. They were childish things, but they were a part of our childhoods that hadn't been sullied by the events that followed.

I was pleased to discover that the route hadn't changed—and equally pleased that I remembered it. The hole we'd created was tighter than I recalled, and the secret room was smaller, but I still felt the pleasure I always had when I slipped through. Badger was waiting. To my surprise, so was Fedara Contei.

"My God, you're blue," Badger said.

"Do you like it?"

His eyes were round. I'd never been Melatinted. "Yes. Decided you didn't want Oe to have too easy a time recognizing you?"

"I thought this would help."

He said, "We'll need all the help we can get."

I nodded at Fedara. "Are you in with us?"

"We're still trying to figure out what to do," she said. "But when we decide how we're going to attack Danniz and his friends, yes . . . I'm in."

Badger said, "All the loose ends are starting to come together. I found out the identities of the three crew members on Danniz's ship. They were trying to backtrail the *Hope's Reward*; because I had the worm monitoring the comnet for anything related to us, I caught their query and traced it back to them. Guess who they are."

I shrugged.

"How about Gainer Holloway, Ejus Gambidja, and the previously unnamed third person, who turns out to be Sonny Dorsey?"

"The three men who beat me up on Cassamir Station?"

"Yes. They work for Oe."

Fedara nodded. "They hunt for him. He hired them to kill you and take the infochip they were sure Peter Crane would give you, but Crane was smart enough not to give you a chip. So they didn't kill you. When you filed your flight plan to go to Galatia Fairing, they tagged your ship with a hyperspace bug, expecting that when you came through on the other end, the bug would have pulled out all of Crane's information from your shipcom. Except that Crane's information wasn't in your shipcom."

"That was when Oe decided to stick you with me?" I asked.

"Yes. He felt you would lead him to the people who stole the *Corrigan's Blood*, and he wanted me to take care of you and Badger and Peter Crane once you did."

My fleshtab and my decision not to enter Peter Crane's data into the shipcom's general database had saved my life. I looked at Badger, who, crouched on the cave floor with a tiny light globe clutched in one hand, looked as spooked as I felt.

"And then we left early, and you ran after us."

"Yes."

Something about what she said bothered me. It took me a moment to identify what it was, and once I did, I wasn't sure if I should ask her about it—allies, after all, being something we didn't have enough of. But I decided knowing was always better than not knowing. "You said before that you didn't know anything about what Oe was doing."

"No. I don't know many details—but I was there when he hired the killers."

I nodded. "Why did you decide you could work with us after all?"

Fedara smiled. I noticed that her teeth had returned to normal and I tried not to stare. She said, "I want to see Oe dead. If I can take him with me when I go, it will make my death worthwhile. And while I was following him, I realized that if I work with you, we have the makings for a perfect double-cross. Remember, he doesn't know that you left Galatia Fairing without me. He still thinks I'm working for him. Because of that, I can get close to him. I can find out what he plans to do, and I can let you know. The three of us will be able to figure out a way to destroy him."

"I can't focus only on Danniz Oe," I told her. "I want to make sure he can't hurt anyone else, but I have other things I need to look into while I'm here."

"Badger told me about your mother. He said you found her name on the membership list you discovered—the list of people who belong to Oe's group."

"Yes. From the listing, she appears to be someone of importance within the organization."

"If she's important," Fedara said, "he'll meet with her while he's here."

I considered that. "If we had a weapon that was effective against vampires, and if we could attend that meeting, we could resolve most of our problems right there."

Chapter Twenty-five

Badger had transferred our reservations to a suite in a Solar Lodge on Level Five. Even though the room in the Radisson ended up registered to a citizen of Branning just as we'd planned, and the police had no reason to look for us, Oe would still be watching. I felt it. He wouldn't be satisfied to let me get away from him, even though as Adana Gantrey I was a stranger to him. He was a hunter and he had chosen me as his quarry; now I suspected he felt it would be a slap in his face to let me go and admit defeat.

So we paid for the room with cash, and gave false names and used no IDs.

Our room wasn't much to look at—certainly not anything to compare with the Radisson—but the hotel's management was willing to accept cash without first asking embarrassing questions, and even better, the room's net lines were poorly shielded. Badger was able to do a bit of wall surgery with a moleibonder and a microcircuit patch, and when he was done, we had a free, untraceable, direct line into the Meileone comnet. He set loose a copy of his worm program, and working with his compac as our illegal connection to the shipcom, he starting reeling in information.

The first thing we did was look for my mother.

She'd gotten rich and powerful in the years since I last saw her. She was a First Councillor of Oldcity; she held one of the highest offices in Meileone. Badger managed to find out details of how she got her office—he came up with a series of people several offices above her who had died suddenly, making way for the people immediately above her, and indirectly making way for her. He discovered scandals she'd engineered, and blackmail, and bribery; if Meileone had permitted news, some reporter would have laid her open in front of the world.

But the only people who had any idea how dangerous she was were a few of those she destroyed—and even most of the people who lost everything because of her never knew who it was who had ruined them.

"How can we get in to see her?" I asked.

Badger was sitting on the floor next to the bed, muttering into his compac. He looked up when I asked and said, "I think your Senso connections would be the best way. Not the porn ones—the educational ones. If you were to suggest to her that you wanted to do a documentary of her life, and if you adopted a properly fawning tone, she might be willing to see you."

"Possibly. And what if, when she sees me, she reacts as Danniz Oe did?"

"She wants to kill you, you mean?"

"That was my concern."

"You're going to do a biography of her life, complete with all of its triumphs and tragedies. And her heroism in the face of tribulation. Emphasize her heroism. Who could resist a line like that?"

I thought about it for a moment. "Certainly not my mother. I'm afraid I'll throw up on her shoes when I tell her about this Senso I'm proposing."

"You can do it. But are you absolutely certain that you need to see her in person?"

"Yes. I have to know if she's already one of the vampires."

"And how will you know that? Fedara Contei doesn't seem any different to me than a normal person. Would you have suspected Danniz Oe was a vampire if you hadn't already known?"

I nibbled the skin on the inside of my lower lip. "I don't think so—but she's my mother. If she is already one of them, I think I'll know."

Badger said, "Do you want me to go with you?"

"No. If somehow she figures out who I am, she'll kill me. I want one of us to be able to get our revenge."

I held out a hand to shake hers. "Adana Gantrey," I said.

She smiled at me. She was still a beautiful woman—still as young as the day I'd left. Reju had been good to her. "Lashanda Elenday."

"It's a pleasure to meet you at last." I smiled when I said it, and while I smiled, I felt around inside my heart for the hatred that was there until the moment I walked through the door of her office. I couldn't feel it.

Seeing her brought back, instead, all my wistful childhood wishes for her love. I wanted to hear her say, "Tanasha, I was wrong. I've missed you so much, and I'm sorry for all the pain I caused you." Perhaps beauty went only skin deep, I decided, but stupidity went clear to the bone.

She pointed me to a comfortable chair across from her desk, and when I settled into it, she took her own chair, leaned her elbows on her desk, templed her fingers, and said, "You heard about me and you want to do a biography of my life?"

"I think, from everything I've heard, that you would be an exemplary subject for a biography. You have overcome so much tragedy, and you have accomplished so many things in such a short time." When I planned that speech, I'd expected to get queasy when I said it. But my stomach was made of stronger stuff than I'd anticipated.

She smiled. "My life has been hard, but I believe tribulations come along to make us stronger. They've had that effect on me."

I nodded, thinking, "Me too."

She said, "Before we discuss the biography, I have a few questions for you. When your secretary contacted me, he told me what you were hoping to do, and of course I was flattered, but I wanted to be sure that if someone did a biography of my life, the biographer would do a good job of it." She leaned back and crossed her legs. "I think that requires a certain amount of empathy, don't you?"

"Absolutely. If we are to do this, and do it well, you and I need to get along."

She studied me, her bottomless black eyes showing no expression I could read. "Why do you do pornographic movies?" she asked.

Startled, my first reaction was to laugh.

I saw the slightest quirk of a grin start at the corner of her mouth. "I looked very deeply into your background."

"I'm sure you did," I said. "I do pornographic movies because I enjoy them."

"And the side benefits of them, too—or at least so I hear."

"Brian? My lover?"

She nodded slowly. "I had an aide locate his movies for me." She paused, watching me for a reaction. "I can certainly see his appeal."

And I thought, Shit, I'm glad I didn't let Badger come along. I have no idea whether his voice matches Brian Darkman's and I know his face isn't a perfect match, and what about his physical type? I knew I hadn't done everything I could to make myself look like Adana Gantrey—just enough to look convincing when compared against ID holos.

But I didn't let any of that show on my face. "A lot of women can see his appeal." I smiled, trying to add just a touch of smarminess to my expression.

And my mother laughed. "Very good. You don't embarrass, you don't apologize. Oh, excellent." She leaned forward again. "You made your way in spite of some serious obstacles, too, didn't you?"

I said, "My life has been nothing but obstacles. I succeeded anyway." She was sure to think I was speaking of Adana's murdered husband, and the other people Adana had trampled on her way to success. I was thinking only of her. Still, my voice held a ring of conviction that she evidently liked.

"Yes. You'll do. We shall get along wonderfully; we are certainly kindred spirits." She smiled. "Did you want to discuss this project of ours. Will you require bankrolling? When do you wish to start?"

I smiled but shook my head. "All I needed today was for us to get a sense of each other, to find out if we could work together. We can discuss the details at a later date, when you've had a chance to put together the facts of your life as you want them portrayed and I have had a chance to scout locations and interview actors who might be able to play you and the main people in your life. For now, I've found out what I needed to know."

She stood, and so did I.

I wanted so much to say to her, "Look at me. Don't you recognize me? I'm your daughter." I wanted to touch her. My mother. The woman who gave me my life. What woman doesn't need to know that her mother loves her? I did.

"I'll be looking forward to seeing you again soon," she said.

I reached out and took her hand, and shook it again. "I'll call you within a week so that we can set up our next meeting."

And I walked out of her office. In the gravdrop my confidence wore off, and on the tramwalk back to the hotel, I started trembling. When Badger opened the door, he instantly knew something was wrong.

He put an arm around me. "Was it bad? Do we need to get out of here?" he asked. "What happened?"

I answered only his last question. "Nothing happened. We talked briefly . . . just . . . just chatted. It was a very simple meeting. But I found out that she's already one of them." It hurt to say it. Saying the words, I wanted to cry.

"You're sure?"

"Yes."

"How did you know?"

I pressed my face into his chest, and let his warmth soothe me. "Because she can manipulate emotions, just as Oe can. Maybe as Fedara can. She manipulated mine."

"Did she try to intimidate you? Try to make you do something that you didn't want to do?"

I pulled back and looked at him. "She didn't try. She succeeded."

He paled. "How?"

"She made me like her."

Chapter Twenty-six

Fedara joined us in our rooms. "It went beautifully," she said. She was so happy she glowed. "Better than beautifully. It went perfectly." She took a chair next to the holoscreen that showed a real-time representation of the streets of Oldcity. "I found Danniz. He was surprised to see me, but pleased that I was here with you—well, he thinks you're here as yourselves, and I didn't disabuse him of that notion. He wanted me to tell him where you were staying, but I reminded him that you were here working and that when you finished your work, we would be heading back to Cassamir Station and Peter Crane."

She looked down at her hands for a moment. "He hates Crane so much . . . it's like every time he says Crane's name, I can feel the flames burning inside of him."

"I'm surprised he doesn't want to kill him himself."

Fedara looked up at me, surprised. "I wondered the same thing. But he wants me to do it."

Badger had settled against the wall again, next to his link with the comnet. He was listening to what we were saying, but his eyes were on the data screen at his wrist. He asked, "Did you find out why he's here?"

"Yes. Someone who knew someone told him that the people who stole the *Corrigan's Blood* were USAG members from Meileone. He came here to find out who they were."

"He told you this?"

Her smile was sly. "I had a change of heart," she said. I heard the hint of a chuckle in her voice. "I decided I was grateful to him for what he'd done for me. I was ready to live forever, and ready to spend eternity with him." She rolled her eyes. "He told me everything."

"What else did he tell you?"

"There's a schism in USAG. The founding members, of which Danniz is one, want to maintain their vision of what vampires are and should be. They want to direct vampires to the low-tech worlds like Up Yours, where communication is poor and where someone who lives forever will be able to quickly take control of the social structure. Danniz and his cronies want to make these worlds over into this image they have—foggy, narrow streets; twisting alleyways; nights in which humans huddle in their homes in fear, trembling at every thump and creak and cry. He loves terror, and he wants to create worlds in which terror is the dominant emotion."

"And the people who have broken off from his group?"

"They're all staying in the civilized worlds. They aren't dressing up in dark clothes and creeping around in alleys and instilling fear. They're hiding their presence completely—the people here on Cantata have no idea they have monsters in their midst."

"They don't kill their victims?" I asked. "They don't torture them?"

Fedara laughed, and the sound was harsh and bitter. "Of course they do. They just don't leave most of the bodies around to scare the rest of the herd. And that is part of what infuriates Danniz. The Meileone vampires aren't playing the game."

She turned to watch the view of Oldcity on the holoscreen. People moved along the tramwalks, wandered in the strellita-lit plaza, and touched and smiled and talked beneath the arching boughs of great, ancient trees. For a long moment she was silent, watching them. She looked so sad. Then she seemed to shake herself out of her reverie. "That's why he's called a meeting. He's pretending not to know about the schism. He's announcing, instead, that his researchers have developed a breakthrough in the nanovirus that created the vampires—the serum he calls Legend. He told me he's going to tell them that Corrigan had finally succeeded, and that Legend II is done."

"Legend II?"

"The improved nanoviral serum. Corrigan has been working on it since he finished testing Legend."

"I thought Corrigan was dead."

"Apparently not. Danniz says he's in hiding. In any case, the rest of the vampires have been waiting for this since the development of the original Legend—Legend II is planned to permit shapechanging at will. The nanovirus will respond to the mind's cues and give its users complete control of their bodies. He's calling the Cantata vampires together to see a demonstration of the serum."

I tried to imagine what these monsters would become if they were able to restructure their bodies. They would become the ultimate chameleons, more terrible than they already were. Theoretically, I knew a nanovirus could be made to reshape bone and tissue constantly, though problems with the process had prohibited any commercial applications of the technology so far. I suspected that it was this reshaping mechanism that had changed Fedara's teeth when she was blood-starved. Still, I could not imagine how such nanomachines could be controlled by the will.

"Does he have this serum?"

"No. Not yet, anyway."

I felt a slight wash of relief, but not much. Corrigan, after all, was still out there. "Then what does he intend to show them when they come to the meeting?"

She said, "He intends to kill them. He has a serum, all right, but it causes the Legend nanovirus to bloom—the serum switches on all the viral instructions to reproduce and destroys the viral code that could stop reproduction. Within fifteen seconds of injection, the blood in the coronary arteries develops clots, causing coronary infarctions; within thirty seconds, the blood thickens to the point were it will not flow through even the major arteries. Within one minute, the majority of the body's cells have ruptured, including those in the brain and spinal cord. The body swells and explodes. Death is unstoppable and irreversible. Medichambers cannot do anything quickly enough to prevent it."

"He told you all of this?"

"He was delighted that he had at last won me over. I think at that moment he would have done anything for me." She frowned and stared down at her long, tapering fingers. "I think he loves me. At least I believe he thinks he does."

I nodded, then turned my attention to Danniz's plan. I came up with an objection almost immediately. "There are so many vampires on Meileone. How can he hope to inject them all before they turn on him and destroy him?"

"He has chosen a moleibonded chamber with vault locks on the doors where he can shoot the injections down on them from an upper chamber. They won't be able to escape, and he and his colleagues will keep shooting the drug darts until the last Meileone vampire has fallen. His plan will succeed."

I sat, thinking and trying to sort out my feelings. This was cold-blooded killing on a large scale; I tried to feel pain at the thought of Oe's intended destruction of human life. But in the vampires I had not met humans, nor had I found any indication of humanity. I'd found evil. Evil is real—as real as good, and I could no more deny the existence of one than of the other.

Fedara Contei was an exception, but she had not become a vampire by choice. She hadn't sought the life of a destroyer; she did not relish fear, or glory in the pain of others. She didn't indulge in the fantasies of power and darkness. She was, as far as her nature would permit, humane. She didn't kill or maim. She was the innocent exception to a terrible rule.

So one of their own was going to destroy the vampires. I remembered the dead, and found that I was glad.

I said, "This will be the end of my mother. However, Danniz will still go free."

Fedara shook her head. "No. He won't. Neither he nor his friends will walk away from the killing room." She leaned forward and rested her hands on her lap. She looked from Badger to me, her expression intent. "This is where we come in."

"We?" Badger asked.

"I have already asked to be permitted to join in the kill. Danniz was amused, but also pleased. He agreed to let me help him. He showed me his boxes of the anti-viral serum, and told me how he keeps a few humans captive in his ship, growing the serum in their bloodstreams so that all he has to do is draw off their blood and spin it out to have a ready supply of the drug." Her mouth tightened into a grim smile. "Apparently he has discovered other vampires whom he does not feel are fit to live."

"The serum grows in the human bloodstream?" I asked.

"Yes. He said it did nothing to the subjects."

"What would happen if one of the vampires drank this blood?" I asked, thinking that the anti-virus would be as good as a vaccine.

"He didn't say. I assumed it would be neutralized by stomach acid . . . though I cannot say for certain that the anatomy of a vampire stomach is the same as that of a human. At the very least, it would be a slower, much more ineffective method of delivering the poison." She sat for a moment, her face thoughtful. Then she shrugged. "No matter. I stole two of the darts. We can inject them into the two of you, and you can grow enough of the poison that we can draw off a little of your blood, spin it out, and make our own darts. Then I will find a way to hide you in the upper chamber. When the last of the Meileone vampires is dead, you can shoot the darts into Danniz and his friends."

She pulled two capped darts out of her pocket—tiny fletched things that shone golden in the light. When she held them in her hand, she said, "I swear, I died a hundred times carrying these through the gravdrops and the streets. They could kill me a thousand times over. I know I want to die, but I'm not ready just yet. I'm not going without Danniz."

She handed one to Badger and the other to me.

I held mine up to the light. Inside the glass cartridge, the minuscule amount of amber liquid looked like nothing so much as a single drop of pale ale. "How do the cartridges work?" I asked her.

"If you pinch up the skin of your thigh between two fingers, then press the tip of the needle quickly through the skin, the pressure on the needle with release the anti-virus within. I imagine the needle will hurt, and I would not be surprised if the serum burned, too."

I held the cartridge. I glanced from it to Badger to Fedara.

She must have read the look in my eyes, for she shook her head slowly. "It won't hurt you. If I wanted to kill you, I could do it easily enough. Both of you together aren't strong enough to fight me off." She smiled. "I don't want you dead. Trust me. I want you to help me destroy Danniz and his friends, and if we're going to succeed, we're going to have to have enough of the serum to do it. You can't count on hitting every shot, and neither can I."

I wore the gauzy pants with the wrap ankles. I untied the left ankle, slid the pant leg up above my thigh, and stared at my blue skin. I slid the cap off of the needle tip and held my breath. Then I pinched my skin between the thumb and index finger of my left hand, and before I could talk myself out of such madness, plunged the needle into my flesh .

It didn't hurt as much as I'd expected. When I looked

up, Badger was withdrawing the needle from his thigh. "We'll take our chances together," he said.

We waited for symptoms—horrible pain, swelling, bleeding, sudden death. But nothing happened.

Fedara smiled. "You see? Now we let the anti-virus multiply in your blood. We'll draw some off each day, dilute it a little to make it go farther, and by the time Danniz is ready for his killing spree, the three of us will be armed with something none of them can fight."

Chapter Twenty-seven

We spent four days in and around the hotel room. I took care of obtaining the supplies for the darts and dartpistols we would have to make, while Badger spent most of his time monitoring the comnet—keeping track of the *Corrigan's Blood/Lazy Rider* and our ship as well as the movements of my mother and Danniz Oe and the other USAG members.

We discovered some interesting, if terrifying, facts about the members of USAG on Cantata. They were people in charge—heads of corporations; chiefs of police; the administrator of public education; the chairman of one entertainment network and three of the vice-presidents of the other; the head of medical research; two cardinals and a number of priests—and because they were strategically placed, every avenue by which we could have sought aid was cut off. We discussed trying to find a way to go public with the information that we had, until we realized there was no one to whom we could take it. In every case, when we followed the hierarchy upward, we found a vampire sitting at or near the top—and the instances where our enemies were not in complete control, they blocked all access to the person who was.

So Badger kept up with the movements of the vampires as best he could. By doing so, he was able to correlate suspicious deaths to their activities—he only counted those murders that were brutal and unprovoked and that left a blood-drained corpse for someone else to find—and we figured that for every death we could confidently count, at least a couple of bodies would end up in incinerators or someplace where they wouldn't be discovered for days or weeks. Or years. Our conservative estimate was that a hundred people were dying in Meileone every day to vampire attacks. We doubted that the vampires were as conservative as we were.

Sometimes while we sat and I worked on our weapons—first building the dart guns, then making the darts—Badger would look away from the comnet long enough to scribble with pen on paper. He wouldn't show me what he was writing, and when I asked, he just shrugged and said, "Notes."

But then he found something on the comnet that made him put down his paper and begin issuing commands to the compac at a frantic rate. His voice got louder as it got faster. He was staring at the tiny comnet screen, muttering, "Cut C-five. Cut C-four. Cut C-Three. No. Cut all C and B connections." His eyes never moved from the screen. "No, dammit. No. Cut all A connections. Cut numeric connections from ten to five. Get past that, you bastard." His shoulders stiffened. "Shit. He did it. Cut all connections. Cut all connections and destroy all records now. Now!"

He looked up at me with his face gray and sweat glistening on his upper lip. "That's it. We have to get out of here. Oe found us." He stood. "I've been watching for anything that connected Adana Gantrey's name with this address. I just got an alert that the connection had been made—from Danniz Oe's hotel room." Badger started throwing his belongings into his bag.

I'd been living out of mine, so the only things I had to pack were the cartridges I was working on, the centrifuge, the blood-drawing kits, and the cartridge launchers I'd built. "How did he find us?"

"Apparently he managed to track the information flow from the *Hope's Reward* back to us."

"How the hell did he do that? You didn't make any direct connections."

"If you're patient enough, you don't have to have direct connections. I'd say he was patient enough. And he had a really good, really quick worm program." Badger slung his bag over his shoulder. "Are you ready?"

I shoved the last of the glass tubes on top of my clothes and zipped the bag shut. "Ready."

We did a quick double-check of the suite to be sure we hadn't left anything that could connect Adana and Brian with us, and then we ran. We'd paid cash for three additional days, but I was willing to lose the money.

We were out the door of the main lobby and getting onto the B-14 tramwalk when I spotted Danniz Oe moving toward us on the oncoming walk. I slid an arm around Badger's waist and leaned my head against his shoulder. Keeping my voice low, I said, "There he is—the redhead in the copper speedsuit."

"I see him." Badger didn't give any indication that he'd looked where I'd indicated, but when we were past Oe, he said, "I'll recognize the bastard if I ever see him again."

Tramwalk traffic was heavy. We stayed on the fast lane and let it take us clear to the other side of the level; then we dropped. "Ten?" I asked as we were falling.

"No."

"Fourteen?"

"No."

"What level, then?"

"Thirty."

That was fine with me. I can't say I noticed much about the level. It was busy, it was well-lit, it was crowded, but neither the architecture nor the people caught my attention. Perhaps the level was simply bland, or perhaps I was too scared to see details.

Danniz Oe had missed me by minutes on two occasions. I was afraid the third time would be the time my luck ran out. It was then that I realized what we'd forgotten about our room.

"Oh, no!"

Badger looked at me sharply. "What?"

"Fedara Contei . . . she can't go back to the room."

He saw the danger immediately. Oe would certainly give himself some way of watching our suite. If Fedara showed up there, he might make the connection between us and our Adana and Brian personas. Worse, if he did make the connection, he could follow Fedara to us.

Badger was on the compac, using Fedara's private code. "Listen, don't go to our rooms. Meet us at our place." He waited. "That's right. We'll be there in half an hour."

So we turned around and went back to the caves and told Fedara what had happened. And then the three of us dropped back down to Thirty, got another suite, and settled in. We'd beaten Oe, and we'd escaped with our lives, but we'd lost our convenient access to the Meileone comnet. If he'd traced us before, he could do it again, and the next time his tracks might not be obvious enough to spot.

And we were cut off from the *Reward* and the shipcom and all of our data and the majority of our surveillance capabilities; wrist compacs didn't have enough power to do more than touch the surface of the information we'd been handling.

We wouldn't be sitting blind for much longer, though. Fedara returned to our new room on Thirty long enough to tell us she'd finally gotten the date and time of the meeting from Danniz. The meeting would be the next day at 22:00.

We spent the next few hours drawing and centrifuging our own blood, mixing the resulting plasma with a nutrient solution, and running samples on the serum and comparing it with normal serum just to be sure that when we found ourselves face to face with Oe, we wouldn't discover the anti-virus was a product of Fedara's imagination. Both of us showed the presence of high concentrations of a non-lethal nanomachined viral agent in our bloodstreams, where none had ever been before. Since we had no way of doing a field test of the serum, we told each other we were going to have to look to faith for this. We spent a couple of hours after that, injecting drops of the straw-colored serum into the cylinders, loading the cylinders into speed-loaders I'd developed for the dart guns, and finally loading the dart guns.

Then we told each other we needed to be sure we were well-rested, and we went to our separate beds.

And I spent the night lost in nightmares, in which Danniz Oe was tapping on the door of my hotel room, and calling my name.

Chapter Twenty-eight

Fedara Contei met us at our room early in the afternoon. "We'll have to go now. I've already scouted the location and found the place where the two of you can hide; you should be safe enough there, though you'll have to come out of hiding to shoot." She frowned, thinking about that. "I couldn't figure out any way that you could stay safe while you shot them. I'm sorry."

"It doesn't matter. Once this is over, we'll be safe."

She said, "There's another problem I've identified. I will be shooting the vampires below us with the weapon and ammunition Danniz will provide. And I'll be standing right in the line of fire; if you accidentally hit me, I'll die right there." She brushed her hair back from her face and looked from me to Badger. "That isn't the way I want to go. I've rented a room. When this is over, I want to take one of the cartridges and go back to it and inject myself. When I die, I want to do it privately. So when the last of the vampires below us is dead, I'll leave—that will be your signal that it's time to shoot."

That worried me. I had figured that three of us would be doing the shooting, and even then, I expected to be outnumbered. With just Badger and me, our odds of surviving seemed slim.

Fedara was watching me. "You don't like that, do you?"

"No. I don't. Badger and I were counting on you to be in on this with us. With just two of us, I don't know that we'll be able to get all of them before they get us."

Fedara nodded. "I understand, and I thought of that, but I'm not sure how else I can handle this. Maybe once we get there and you see the location, you'll have a better idea than mine."

The location was the Grand Celebrity Theater, which had an upper balcony serviced by a separate entrance and a large stage where at the moment live actors were performing a mediocre rendition of *The Taming of the Shrew* updated for the Meileone audience. They played to a nearly full house, but in a city as large as Meileone, anything that wasn't dreadful could play to a full house.

The balcony wasn't occupied, though; the management had locked the doors that led up to it. Fedara had a key—she said Danniz had rented the theater on the condition that no one else use the balcony the full day before his "presentation."

She showed us where Danniz and his associates planned to stand for the shooting, and where she intended to be. The balcony didn't have any fixed seating—a few folding chairs stood stacked against the wall, but the area was evidently intended to serve more than one purpose. There were four doors on the back wall, two that led to stairs and two that opened into restrooms. Both restrooms were locked. That wouldn't have been a problem had we decided we wanted to hide in there, but the restrooms wouldn't have offered a very good view of the front of the balcony, where Danniz and the other vampires were going to wait.

Along the back wall, perhaps a meter and a half off of the ground, one large air duct terminated in a moleibonded grill.

Fedara showed us the grate. "This is big enough for you to wait in, and it won't be someplace anyone should think of looking."

It was going to be an uncomfortable wait, but not an impossible one. She had already broken out the grate with a moleibond cutter, then set it on cobbled-together side hinges. One of us would be able to shoot from the inside of the duct, but the other would have to move onto the balcony—and there was no cover on the balcony. In our favor, there wouldn't be any cover for the vampires, either.

Fedara said, "There's a moleibond wall that drops down in front of the stage when it isn't in use. Its purpose is to keep out people who might be tempted to go through the props and costumes they store back there, but it also seals off one of the five possible exits. The other four are typical public-building doors; they have vault locks that set into the floor, the lintel, and both sides of the door. The wall will be down and three of the four doors will be locked when people start arriving. The fourth will be locked when the last member arrives. No one will be able to get out of them."

"How does Danniz intend to verify that everyone is here?" Badger asked.

"None of them will miss their only chance to get their copy of the Legend II virus. They'll all come. Nevertheless, Danniz is going to place an assistant outside the door. Each USAG member will have to identify himself before he's permitted in—the rationale they'll all get for this is that Danniz doesn't want Legend II getting into the hands of any but USAG members."

That statement bothered me. "Are there vampires on Cantata who aren't USAG members?"

Fedara laughed. "Almost certainly. You don't have to have the nanovirus injection to become a vampire. All you have to do is drink a vampire's blood."

I made a gagging noise and said, "That doesn't seem very likely. Normal humans aren't running around drinking blood, and even if they were, they'd have a hard time catching a vamp—"

"You've missed the point," Fedara said. "The fact that vampires can create others of their kind is part of the legend. Part of the mystique. And even more appealing, from the vampire's point of view, is that the vampires one creates by sharing one's blood become subservient to their creator." She glanced at me, a tiny smile playing at the corners of her mouth. "Considering the sorts of people who have sought this out, you can see that the idea of creating subservient vampires will be almost irresistible. Vampires offer their blood to those they desire, or love."

"Danniz suspects that they've done this?"

"He knows they have. But he'll be satisfied—at least for now—to kill the masters."

I closed my eyes. I had been thinking that Cantata would be purged of its vampires after that night, but I'd been wrong. My homeworld was only going to be purged of the vampires we could identify and track—the other, secret ones would certainly go into hiding, becoming even harder to root out.

I turned to Badger. "This isn't going to get rid of all of them. Should we still go through with it?"

He held my hand tightly and looked into my eyes. "Yes. We'll kill Danniz Oe. Your mother will die. And some of the people they're killing will go on living."

I'd wanted the plague to end, but it wasn't going to be that simple. Still, this was better than hiding and pretending we were blind to the evil in our midst. This was something. "We'll stay."

Fedara looked relieved. "Do you have any idea how I can help you kill Danniz and the rest who will be up here without getting into the line of fire?"

I said, "Yes. First, stop firing early, while you still have ammunition. Act like you're reloading, but don't." I pointed to a place along the wall just back of the duct. "Then, when they are almost finished with everyone below, step back to there. When we see you step back, we'll move out and start shooting. You do the same."

Below us, the audience began to applaud, and the actors lined up along the front of the stage to bow.

"It's time," Fedara said. "You have everything you need, don't you?"

"We would have been a little stupid to have come without

everything, wouldn't we?" Badger asked. He sounded annoyed.

Fedara raised an eyebrow but didn't comment. Instead, she said, "I'll be back as soon as I can. But Danniz or some of his people may get here early. Once you get into place, don't leave for anything." She smiled.

"We'll be here," I said.

Badger still looked annoyed, but he refrained from adding to his earlier remark.

Fedara left. We climbed into the duct. Badger insisted I get in first. I didn't want to be to the back, but I agreed. I slid in feet first and crawled backward, not stopping until I had enough room to lie down on my stomach while leaving enough space in front of me for Badger to do the same. He slid in when I said I was in position.

He slid backward carefully, but still managed to shove his feet in my face. I'd made enough room for someone of my own height, and had miscalculated his. I scooted deeper into the duct, and finally he was able to pull the door closed.

I couldn't see through the duct very well; Badger's silhouette blocked out the lower half of the mesh-covered square, and a leftward curve in the duct about half a meter in front of me made it impossible for me to see the place where Fedara was going to move when the shooting started. Still, I had a clear view of the edge of the balcony where Danniz and the others would stand.

We waited, our weapons in our hands, our ammunition ready. No one was in the balcony yet. I said, "Badger, are you certain there isn't someone we've overlooked? Someone we could go to who could help us?"

He sighed, but he didn't say anything.

I answered my own question. "There isn't anyone. I know. If this is going to be done, we're going to have to do it, but I don't want to. I don't want to declare myself judge and executioner."

"Neither do I." Badger's voice sounded hollow in the confines of the air duct. "I want to be able to believe everyone can become a decent human being under the right circumstances, but I know it isn't true." He lifted his head and twisted slightly so that he could look back at me. In the darkness, I couldn't see his face, but from the tone of his voice, I could imagine how he looked. Serious. Concerned. He asked me, "Are you having second thoughts? Do you want out?"

I considered that. "These are people who have chosen to give up their humanity. They have chosen to live on the deaths of others—on their blood and pain and fear." I ran my fingers over the spring gun in my hand. "They have chosen to be evil, and I've seen the results of their evil. And because I know what they are and have seen what they do, and because there is no one else who can fight them, I have to do this. If I don't, I won't be able to live with myself." I felt tears beginning to well up in my eyes, and I fought them back. "This is contrary to everything I ever wanted to be, Badg. Doing this goes against everything I've believed about myself all of my life. But if I knew what they were and what they had done, and I did nothing . . ." The tears began sliding down my face, hot and angry. I was glad Badger couldn't see them. "I wouldn't be the person I thought I was then, either."

I wiped the tears from my face and willed them to stop. "I can't do the right thing, because there isn't any right thing. So if I have to be wrong, I'll be wrong through action, not inaction. I'll stand and fight."

I think subconsciously I'd considered those things, but putting them into words gave them shape and form, and gave me courage.

Badger's voice, soft and gentle in the darkness, said, "And I will stand beside you."

I reached out and touched his leg.

And we waited.

Chapter Twenty-nine

They came softly when they came—half a dozen beautiful monsters that glided silently into the balcony and carefully laid out their weapons and ammunition with exquisite economy of motion and terrible, lovely grace.

I watched them, awed. In a crowd of a thousand, they would have stood out. They radiated health and beauty and power, confidence and pleasure, even joy. I looked for external signs of the internal ugliness that characterized them. I looked for some mark of evil. None existed. I wanted to feel repulsed by them, and I did not. They were more perfect than any human beings I had ever seen, and the perfection was not a simple matter of regularity of features or sleekness of physiques. Their faces were mostly ordinary, their bodies no better than any other bodies subjected to regular reju. Fedara was the only one who would have been a great beauty in any crowd.

But they were more than us. They had stripped off mortality like butterflies shaking free of their caterpillar selves, and immortal, had discovered they could fly. They wore eternity well.

Watching them when they were not hunting, when they were with each other and unaware that they were being watched, I found myself unable to hate them. It would have been so much easier to contemplate killing them if

I could have held on to my white-hot loathing. But part of me hungered to have what they had: that supreme confidence. That beauty.

I squeezed Badger's leg and wished I dared shift position. My lower back hurt from lying on my stomach for so long, and my nose itched, and I needed to pee. But Fedara had mentioned the vampires' improved senses. As it was, I was afraid they would hear me breathing; I didn't dare do anything that might make more noise than that.

They finished arranging their weapons. Then all of them settled onto the floor to wait. They were as quiet as we were—I found myself wishing they'd talk just long enough that I could rub my back and scratch my nose.

Then one of them said, "Do you smell that?"

Heads lifted, and a couple of the vampires looked around.

"People."

Danniz said, "More than just people; I know that smell. I recognize it."

Fedara looked at him. "Really?"

"It's the scent of a woman I met when I arrived. Adana Gantrey. I've been stalking her. I should have had her twice, but she's managed to elude me."

Fedara laughed. "Found an irresistible snack, did you?"

"I wanted to hear her scream," he said, smiling. Then his smile died away, replaced by a thoughtful expression. "But it was more than that. Something about her resonated. Her scent reminded me of a scent I'd caught just briefly somewhere before. And I haven't been able to recall the place, but I'm certain it was important. Vitally important. More than anything else, I wanted to make her tell me why she smelled so familiar." Then he frowned. "And I smell that same scent now. Dammit, that's frustrating."

I felt a gnawing horror in my gut—when I changed my appearance and my ID markers and everything else about myself but my DNA, it never occurred to me to alter my scent. Frankly, I didn't even know if such a thing was possible.

And now that tiny oversight might betray me. He sensed my presence, yet I didn't dare move—I'd make too much noise going through the air duct, and I wouldn't be able to back away fast enough to permit Badger to get to safety. I couldn't turn around in the duct, and even had I been able to, so what? We needed to stay.

We needed to finish what we'd started.

Danniz sniffed the air and said, "Oh. Oh, hell. I just recognized the scent." He gave Fedara a long, measuring look. "Adana Gantrey smells exactly like Cadence Drake."

Fedara laughed. "What a bizarre coincidence."

"It isn't a coincidence." His eyes narrowed. "Drake is on this planet and so is Gantrey, and I think it's because they are the same person. Where is Cadence Drake right now?"

Fedara raised an eyebrow. "How should I know? I'm here with you, enjoying your company for a while before I have to return to Cassamir Station. Drake is still trying to figure out where whoever stole it hid Peter Crane's missing ship."

"Is she? Then why do I smell her now?"

"Assuming that it is her that you smell, perhaps because I've been sipping at her from time to time. She's very tasty. You might smell her on me. That's a big assumption, though, Danniz. You probably smell someone very similar . . . time and distance could have dimmed your scent memory so that you're convinced a similar smell is an identical one."

"No." He looked around the balcony and toward the doors at the back, all the while sniffing at the air. "I am not mistaken."

He started to stand, but one of the other vampires put a finger to his lips and pulled Oe back to the floor. He pointed to the balcony, and when I listened closely, I could hear the sound of voices drifting up from below. So far I could only hear a few, and they spoke softly. If the vampire sense of hearing was as acute as the sense of smell, though, I understood why the killers in the balcony had become utterly still.

How long, I wondered, would it take Danniz to suspect Fedara of enlisting us in her cause? And from that point, how long would it take for him to decide that we were nearby—that he didn't smell me on her at all; that he smelled me because I was somewhere within reach.

If he decided to look in the duct, the two of us, lying trapped in the darkness, would have no choice but to kill him immediately instead of waiting. We would destroy our element of surprise. Worse, we would probably lose to the vampires.

I hoped for a diversion.

None came. The noise level below us began to rise, which gave Oe an opportunity to get up and move around without being heard. He walked to the back doors, and out of my line of sight. I heard metal snap, and realized he'd broken the locks on one of the two restroom doors. After a minute or two that felt more like hours, I heard the second lock snap. I didn't hear any more sounds that I could attribute specifically to him. I assumed he'd searched the first restroom and was searching the second. I didn't know how much Badger could see of his actions or position, but all I could do was wait and hope that he wasn't getting ready to come for us.

I started to sweat. And I thought, Great—sweating will give him something else to smell.

The noise level down in the main part of the theater became a low roar. That was when I heard feet thumping on stairs, a door opening, and a voice saying, "All accounted for."

After an instant, Danniz walked back into my line of sight, but now he wasn't looking around. His shoulders were back, his head was up, and he was smiling. He reached the balcony and leaned slightly over it, and called down into the crowd, "Children of darkness, heed me!"

I thought that sounded silly and contrived, but the noise below stopped as if he had switched it off.

He stood up on the solid balcony rail, looking to me like he was getting ready to jump. "I bring you Legend II," he said.

Below him, crouched down and waiting, his cohorts cradled their weapons.

And Danniz said, "Behold." He ripped off the speedsuit and stood naked above the crowd. He raised his arms and stood still, but even though he wasn't moving, he gave the appearance of movement. His body seemed to melt. His face stretched forward, his arms elongated and attenuated and a flap of membranous skin began to stretch between his ribs and thighs. His legs got shorter and thinner. Pale red hair sprouted on his back and the backs of his legs. His ears became enormous.

Legend II was real. It existed.

I looked at Fedara and saw emotions warring across her face. Rage and hunger and lust. Disgust. Envy.

I looked back to Oe. He had become a huge winged creature; ugly, terrible, nightmarish. I wondered if such a creature had ever lived or if this was the product of his own imagination. He'd maintained his mass in the conversion; I was certain he would never be able to fly. The hall was, I thought, too small to permit flight anyway. And there would be no winds for him to soar on. It was a breathtaking demonstration anyway, but I thought it would have been more awe-inspiring if he had flown.

Evidently he thought the same thing. He launched himself off the balcony and disappeared. I heard applause from the people below. I had to assume he had succeeded.

I heard the leathery flap of his wings, and the shrill squeaks he emitted as he flew. Then he reappeared on the balcony, lighting gracefully on the rail. He was uglier from the front than he had been from the back. He tucked in his wings, turned himself around, and the melting process reversed itself. Then he was a man again, standing above them, pulling his speedsuit back on while balancing on the rail.

When the speedsuit was back in place, he said, "I promised you when you joined me, when you partook of the first Legend, that there would be Legends to come. Do you remember?"

"Yes," voices shouted from below. And, "We remember!"

"I chose you to become Legends with me, to live forever, to bring myth and magic back to the universe. Do you remember?"

This time there was less eagerness in the voices that shouted, "Yes, we remember."

"You promised me that you would, from your positions of authority, move your world backward, destroying the mechanical feel of it, taking it away from comfort and security, bringing on a dark age of fear and magic and superstition. Do you remember?"

This time no one shouted, "Yes." No one said, "We remember." No one said anything at all.

"Can you have forgotten?" Danniz stared down at them, still as death. For a long, long moment he was silent. Then he answered his own question. "I don't think so. I kept my end of the promise. I brought you Legend II. But you lied to me. All of you. There is no fear in Meileone. There is no whisper of the supernatural. You have taken my first gift and you have desecrated it.

"You are not fit to live among the immortals," he said. His voice, which had been booming and rich and melodious, became with that last statement flat and cold. He had passed his sentence. His vampires rose from their hiding places and began firing down into the crowd.

The screaming started. I heard someone yell, "They're all locked?" I heard pounding on the walls, and running feet, and the human-sounding voices of unfathomable monsters begging for their lives over the sounds of the screams.

With that level of noise to cover our movements, Badger and I both moved from lying on our stomachs to crouching. With my chin shoved down against my chest, my body tucked with my shoulder blades pressed against the top of the duct, I waited for Fedara's signal and tried not to hear the anguish below me.

None of the screams lasted long. The shooting didn't last long, either. Not really. There were forty or so USAG members in all of Cantata. All of them had been in the room below. None of them made any sounds any longer. When the vampires stepped away from the balcony, I had to believe that all of them were dead. My mother was dead. I tried to feel something, but I was empty. My reactions would come later, no doubt; they would come when I was alone. For the moment, I had no time to grieve what might have been.

I watched Fedara.

She was grinning, her face alive and excited, her cheeks flushed. She smiled at Danniz. "You were right. It becomes easier," she told him. "Death becomes easier, and it becomes more entertaining."

"I'm right about a lot of things," he said. I couldn't see his face; his back was to me. But I didn't like the note of barely controlled anger I sensed in his voice. I tensed. She needed to move out of the way, but she wasn't moving.

"Give me a taste of your blood, Master," she said. Her eyes shone. She licked her lips.

The vampires were gathering their weapons together, putting them into the carrying bags they'd brought them in.

Get out of the way, Fedara, I thought.

Danniz wasn't moving. He stood with his back to me, looking at her. He didn't make a sound, but the smile vanished from her face and her eyes lost their shine.

She started backing toward the place we had agreed upon, but he followed her.

"What's wrong?" she asked.

He took another step. "Your sudden change of heart was too sudden."

"It wasn't. I came to my senses. I want immortality."

"I don't believe you."

"You should. I'm telling you the truth. And if you'll let me have a taste of your blood, I'll tell you where Cadence Drake and her friend are," Fedara said.

"Will you?" Danniz asked.

"I will." The smile was back on her lips when she moved out of my line of sight.

"But I suspect I already know where they are," he said, and took another step toward her.

That was all the signal we needed. Badger and I burst out of the duct, and all seven of the vampires' heads came up and they stared at us.

"It seems I don't need for you to tell me," Danniz said. He wore a smile as the words came out of his mouth, and even when he saw the weapons in our hands, the smile didn't go away.

Badger had fired half a dozen darts. I had, too. Some of them hadn't hit their targets—the ones that had, though, were doing terrible things. The vampires gasped, and broke out into gray-faced sweats, clutching at their chests and their heads. They started to fall, one by one.

Neither Badger nor I had shot Oe because he was too close to Fedara. He turned on her and grabbed her around the throat with one hand and said, "You betrayed us to the mortals." He was no longer smiling.

She screamed, "Help me," and Badger fired at Oe. The dart slammed into his back and stuck, and he let go of her, trying to pull it free. She backed all the way to the door and stood staring, wide-eyed and breathing hard, while he went to his knees, clawing at his chest and gasping.

She stared from him to us, back to him, back to us. The terror on her face melted away. She smiled at us. She started to laugh. Then she turned and vanished out one of the doors that led down. She hadn't fired a shot against any of them.

Danniz thrashed on the floor. The other vampires, hideously swollen and still expanding, lay unmoving where they had fallen. They were dead—unmistakably and irretrievably dead. But Danniz was melting. Changing forms again, shifting, screaming, trying to become something that the anti-virus couldn't touch. Or perhaps his partial immunity came from the Legend II. Perhaps the nanovirus that permitted him to alter his external form permitted him to make internal changes, too. In any case, he wasn't dying as quickly as the others had.

"He looks like he's getting stronger," I said.

Badger shot him again. The next dart lodged in his skin, but it didn't seem to do anything. The darts weren't going to work. He was mutating, flowing from man into beast—this time he was becoming a huge four-legged furry thing that lay on the floor wheezing and paddling its legs. It was vaguely dog-like, but bigger, with cold yellow eyes that glared at us and a toothy grin that seemed to promise our imminent destruction.

I had the moleibond cutter with me, the one I'd used to spot-weld our dart-guns. I pulled it out, jumped on him, and slashed across his throat with the narrow beam. He whipped around, still weak for what he was, but stronger than me. His blunt claws ripped into my right arm, the one that held the moleibond-cutter. Badger dove and grabbed the paws, and I continued hacking at his neck while he thrashed and snapped and bled. My blood dripped down my hand and into his wounds, and each drop that touched him sizzled as the anti-virus met the nanovirus and the nanovirus began to reproduce.

Oe grew weaker. I was through most of the skin and arteries, cursing the fact that he healed only slightly less quickly than I cut. Badger let go of Oe's paws and gripped his head, and I, sitting on the monster's chest, finished hacking off his head.

Badger grabbed it and threw it over the balcony.

The body stopped twitching and lay still.

I stood, splattered with Oe's blood and with my own dripping down my arms, and felt the room dip and spin around me. I was weary, I was heartsick, and I wanted to go home.

"I'll get the rest of our things," Badger said. He went back to the air duct, crawled in, and pulled out both of our bags. He handed me mine, nodded toward the restroom, and said, "Let's go wash up."

Chapter Thirty

We made it out of Meileone without attracting undue attention. Neither of us talked about what we had been through. I ignored the discomfort in my right arm, which burned and throbbed. We sat in the shuttle staring down at the icy ball that had been but never again could be our home.

"Should we pick up the *Corrigan's Blood* when we get back to the station?" Badger asked.

"No. We can file the papers with the station authority and hope they don't make a connection between us and all the people we left behind back there, or we can just steal the thing back, but whichever we do, I'd rather go to the *Reward* and spend some time in the MEDix first."

So we didn't do anything more with the *Corrigan's Blood* than make sure that it was still docked. When we'd confirmed that, we walked back to our own dock.

I was always happy to get home after a job, but this was the worst job I'd ever done. I was eager to feel the sweet tug of my own gravity, smell the oxygen-rich air, listen to familiar, soothing sounds. The *Reward* was the only real home I'd had since my childhood died an ugly death, and I was hellishly homesick.

I pressed my palm against the palmlock and said, "Open," and the shipcom said, "Welcome back," as it always did when I'd been away more than a day. I'd programmed it to do that, and I knew it was just a machine, but I liked the effect.

The airlock slid open and Badger and I stepped into the gravdrop holding hands. We reoriented ourselves to ship down, which was at a ninety-degree angle from station down, and dropped to the first level. "Medichamber for you, too?" I asked as I stepped out.

"In a minute." He caught me from behind and pulled me against his chest. He wrapped both arms around me and pressed his face into the back of my hair. "I love you, Cady," he said softly. "I will always love you."

"I love you, too," I told him. I'd spent some of my time while I was lying awake the last few nights figuring out what I wanted to do with the rest of my life if I survived, and everything I wanted to do had changing careers as a first step and spending the rest of my days with Badger as a second. I remembered with pain the question that he had asked me three times. I remembered my answer as well, which was "no" twice and "no, and please never ask me again" the third time. Stupidity might go clear to the bone, but sometimes and in some circumstances, even those of us who have been bone-deep stupid can find intelligence and redemption. So it was with me. Since he was a man of honor, and would never ask me his question again, I turned to him and said, "This is old-fashioned and corny and I don't care. Will you marry me, Badger? Will you have children with me and grow old with me?"

His arms tightened and he pressed his cheek against mine. I felt tears there, but he made no sound. "If we get out of this alive, that will be the first thing I do," he said.

I twisted in his embrace until I was facing him. "Badg—we're out of it. It's all over but taking back the *Blood*. Well, maybe not with the vampires from Smithbright's World, but we can become other people. We can stay other people."

"And what of Fedara Contei?"

"What of her?" I asked. In truth, I had spared very little thought for her on our return to the *Hope's Reward*.

"Have you considered why she asked Danniz Oe for a taste of his blood?"

I glanced at him. "I hadn't," I said. "Or I suppose I simply thought she was trying to win back his confidence in her long enough to move clear of him . . . so that we could destroy him."

Badger's voice was even and careful. "I thought at the time that was what she was doing." He began walking toward our med room. "I don't think so now, though. Think back to the look on her face as she watched Danniz transform into that flying monstrosity. Could you see her when she did that?"

"I could," I said. And as I paced beside him, I saw again the naked hunger, the sheer lust on her face as she watched the transformation and realized that Legend II was not a fantasy Oe had used to call together his victims, but a reality. Something that she could have.

"I think," Badger said, "that she told us the truth about wanting Danniz dead. But I don't think she told us the truth about wanting to die with him."

I considered what he said, and thought about what it meant to us. I thought about how she'd run from us after the slaughter—how she had vanished down the stairs. I recalled the sound of her laughter. "You're right," I said. "She used us to get rid of enemies. Do you think that, having used us, she'll be content to go her way and let us go ours?"

Badger's soft laugh utterly lacked humor. "With all we know? No, I don't think she'll be done with us until we're dead. We've served her purpose. We've destroyed her creator. Now she needs to be free of us and the harm we could do her. When we're out of the way, she can do whatever she chooses."

I stopped walking and leaned against the corridor wall, running my fingers over the cool, stone-smooth surface. I shook my head and gave my beautiful Badger a wry smile.

"This is so much conjecture to pile on the shoulders of a few actions taken by a woman caught in the midst of carnage and horror. Think about what Fedara has been through. Think about how much she has suffered, and what she has had to see, and to do. Think about how we found her in the *Fortune Favors*. We saved her from a horrible, lingering death. We stood beside her. Why would she turn on us?"

"Why would a mother destroy her family and frame her daughter for her actions? Why would people choose to become blood-drinking monsters or seek torture and murder innocents?" Badger took my hands in his and said, "All the good will in the world will not change the fact that power is a drug that demands greater and greater doses, and cares less and less for the cost of each dose. Gifted with immortality, tempted by the almost god-like power that Legend II could give her, how will Fedara destroy herself? At first, she'll tell herself that she doesn't need to kill in order to live." Badger sighed. "She'll tell herself a lot of things, I imagine, and convince herself that what she does she does for good reason. She'll turn herself into a hero in her own mind; she'll see herself as someone who suffered unfairly, who deserves to be repaid for her pain."

I could see Fedara through his eyes, and I could see the things he described happening. I didn't want to see them, and I didn't want to believe that they were possible. If I did, then I had to think that perhaps we should have shot her with the serum when we shot Danniz and his cronies.

I thought hard, looking for the hole in his argument, desperately needing to find one. After a moment, I thought I had it. "You're saying that because of *what* she is, she'll be pulled away from *who* she is. You're saying that because she has become a vampire, she will not be able to hold onto her hatred of killing. That she will become a monster whether she chooses that path or not. But I cannot believe that's true. Some people choose evil while others choose good. Some never choose at all, but are blown one way or the other as circumstances dictate. But she has chosen a path away from evil. Why shouldn't she be able to follow that path?"

Badger said, "These are ancient words, but their age doesn't make them any less true. Power corrupts. Absolute power corrupts absolutely. I'm not saying that she will consciously choose to become evil—that she will suddenly turn into one of those murdering monsters we left in the *Fortune Favors*. But she is no longer human, and the realities of being human will slip further from her memory every day. Her choices, even if they are choices made with the best of intentions, will begin to reflect that fact. She will realize, either sooner or later, that she no longer shares a common bond with the creatures she must consider her prey if she is to survive. And sooner or later, she will realize that what is good for her and what is good for her prey are worlds apart. And because she has enormous power, she will use that power to help her survive."

I could not deny his logic. "And sooner or later she will come to see us as a threat to her survival, and whether or not we saved her life will be incidental when weighed against the fact that we know how to destroy her."

Badger nodded, saying nothing.

"When do we start to watch our back then? How long until she decides we have to die in order for her to live?"

"We start watching our back now," Badger said. "And we never stop. Not ever."

"Well reasoned," a rich contralto said. "Poorly timed, my dear, but very well reasoned."

Badger and I jerked around to face down the corridor toward the bridge.

My mother stood there, smiling, a laser rifle in her hands.

My mind threw a thousand questions at me, and I don't doubt that most of them flashed across my face, for my mother started to laugh.

"I know you didn't expect to see me again, Tanasha,"

she said. "Dear daughter, you cannot imagine how it hurts me to see in your eyes such a plain wish that I was dead. I would think you'd rejoice to see me alive; after all, I'm the only family you have left." Her laughter grew richer and merrier.

I carried my kit bag over my right shoulder, which was still turned slightly away from her. In my kit bag lay the dart gun, and with it a handful of anti-virus darts already loaded into one of my makeshift speed-loaders. Right on top. In easy reach. I'd have to load the first dart with just the one hand, and without letting her know what I was doing. I said, "I have to admit I'm surprised to see you. I thought for sure Danniz Oe had killed you."

"He would have. If your friend Fedara hadn't told me to be sure to avoid his little gathering, he would have succeeded. I wanted Legend II, and I certainly didn't realize he knew we'd split off from his group. I was far too trusting. But of course I got good information in time to save my life. Instead if murdering me, Oe killed off an unimportant flunky of mine who had the misfortune to look somewhat like me. She was as loyal as one immortal gets to another, but I don't think I'll have any trouble replacing her. I'm not loyal, you see. Except to myself." Mother smiled, and I could see the beginnings of points forming on her teeth. "My poor associate wasn't the first item of importance on my day's agenda, however. You were."

I was still assimilating unthinkable betrayal. "Fedara told you about Danniz?"

I got my hand on the darts, and struggled to slip the first into the chamber of the gun without making any noise or alerting her. It wasn't easy. I hadn't designed my weapon for single-handed operation.

"She did. She said she wanted to see Danniz dead, but after that was taken care of, she didn't see why the two of us couldn't split all of Meileone between us. Not that I believed her for even an instant, of course. Why share between two something that can be kept to oneself, after all? I fully suspect she intended to destroy me when I'd done her dirty work for her—just to clean up all her loose ends, you know. But she won't get the chance to do that. I made sure a mishap was waiting for her as soon as she left the theater."

"Then she's dead?" Badger asked.

"By now?" My mother considered the question for just an instant. "By now I should think so, though perhaps not for another ten or fifteen minutes. I don't want her death to be public, and private deaths in Meileone take a bit more time to arrange."

"She told you where to find me, too, didn't she?"

"Oh, yes. How you had saved her life, but how you knew far too much about us. How she didn't have the heart to kill you, but how she knew it had to be done. She told me that if the two of us let you live, you would in time find some way to destroy us. She has found, finally, as I have found, that the long habit of living becomes unbreakable to an immortal. She sends her apologies, which I give you, for what they're worth."

My mother smiled, then nodded her head at Badger. "Dante Beddekkar. I always thought you had too much sense to stick with my Tanasha. She's trouble. I've known all along that one day she'd be the death of you."

Mother's finger had never slipped from the trigger of the laser rifle, and for all her amused chatter, her aim had never wavered. If I attempted to shoot her, she was going to kill me before the dart even reached her. I kept hoping for some sort of opening, some sort of diversion—but I didn't get one.

She said, "We've stood here long enough. My people should be in position now. "So you're going to leave your ship, both of you. You're going to walk for a while with some friends of mine, until you're well away from your ship. And then the two of you will have an accident, too."

"Why not just kill us here?" Badger said.

"Because that would leave bodies, and bodies can be hard to explain, and can raise some unpleasant questions.

And we don't want that." Her voice got colder and harder. "So turn around, both of you. Walk back the way you came. Slowly. Remember that if I have no other choice, I will kill you here. Bodies or no bodies."

"Now," Badger shouted, and he dove and rolled and threw his bag into the air at her as he did. He landed in a firing position. From the corner of my eye I could see that he had no gun, and even as I brought up the dart gun and aimed it, I wondered what he hoped to accomplish.

My mother fired on the tumbling bag first, and as it burst into flames I got off a shot. I thought it hit, then realized it had caught in her sleeve. I fired again as her aim dropped to Badger.

I screamed at her and fired again, and heard Badger scream, too. Mother swung the laser rifle toward me.

Badger still screamed. I fired again. I didn't know if any of the darts had hit—I was too scared to aim well or to focus the way I needed to, and the sound of Badger in agony drove me into a blind, helpless rage, so that I pulled the trigger again. And again. My mother swung the rifle back toward me, leading it a bit slowly.

I dropped and rolled, trying to get as far from Badger as I could, so that in trying to hit me she wouldn't hit him again. I could see then that a dart had wedged itself into her abdomen just below the rib cage—and then her laser rifle caught me and I felt fire lance through my left leg. Hers wasn't a lethal shot, though it felt like a bad one.

Two gravities, I thought. Thank God I have the ship at two gravities. She isn't used to it. If she'd been at one gravity, her reflexes would have been better than they were, and she would have had me.

I finished my roll, flinging myself to my good leg and realizing as I fell to the ground, unable to balance, that she'd taken off my left leg below the knee. The laser rifle had cauterized the wound as it made it. I wasn't bleeding, and I wasn't in shock. Yet.

I dove for her rifle before she could shoot either me

or Badg again, but there was no need. She'd dropped, her lips and the insides of her eyelids and her nailbeds had all gone a pale blue, and she'd started sweating. She grabbed her chest.

My mother.

I stared at her.

My mother.

I stared down at the place where my left foot should have been. She would have killed me, but I had killed her. My own mother.

"Why couldn't you have loved me!" I screamed.

Her face showed no change of expression. Blood began to trickle from the side of her mouth, and she started to swell. I'd finally asked the question I'd wanted an answer for all of my life, but I wasn't ever going to get an answer.

I waited an instant to be sure she wasn't going to get up again. I didn't want the sort of surprise Oe had given me. When her skin began to burst, I said, "She's dead, Badg. I got her. But she got me. You're going to have to help me get both of us to the medichambers."

He didn't say anything.

I hop-turned, and got my first look at Badger since he dove. He wasn't moving. His eyes were both open. He was not blinking. Not breathing. He stopped screaming, I thought. When did he stop screaming? He was ash gray dead white not moving not breathing and somehow I was at his side and dragging pulling crawling dragging crying. Me with one leg. Him with a massive hole in his skull that burned in the front and out the back. Head shot. Head shot. MEDix could fix a head shot. One-legged I crawled down the hall, dragging him, not letting myself look at him or feel his pulse or do anything at all that would waste a second of the time I needed to get him into the medichamber. As long as there was anything left—anything—pulse, heartbeat, a few brain waves, as long as he wasn't just flat-out dead the MEDix could put him back together. I crawled, getting light-headed, weak, feeling the chills starting. I pushed them back. I was getting him to the MEDix screaming, "Live, goddammit, live god damn you don't you die on me now."

I opened the clamshell and somehow, though he outweighed me by forty kilos at one gravity and was a limp unresponsive weight and I had only one leg and no strength, I maneuvered him up into the unit. Screaming all the time, "Live, goddamn you, I love you. Live for me. Don't you dare die on me."

Knowing that he'd made the first move to draw her fire. Knowing that he'd decided to sacrifice himself to give me the chance to live.

He was going to live, damn him. I was going to have my Badger back.

And the MEDix cycled.

I watched.

It cycled.

I waited. The numbers on the front said there was no one in the box anymore. Nothing to save. Nothing left. It said the important part of Badger was all gone.

I clung to the top of the MEDix, pounded on the readouts, begged God and medicine and magic to give him back to me to give him back give him back give him back.

Some things are final. Death, even now, is final. From the place where Badger went, there was no coming back.

Chapter Thirty-one

When I got myself and my reattached leg out of my own MEDix, I wandered around the ship for a while. The bots had cleaned up my mother's remains. There was no sign of her. I suppose that, like the other vampires, she had swelled until she exploded, and each cell had ruptured, and she had mostly liquefied. I wanted to feel that she had gotten what she deserved, but some small childish part of me still cried out for the mother I wanted and wished I had had.

Badger lay in his MEDix. It had returned him to his original albino form, so that when I looked at him I saw, one final time, the true form of the man I loved. I opened the clamshell half a dozen times, praying that a miracle would have happened, that the MEDix would have gone further, that it would have found something of mind and soul and spirit to save. I wanted to discover that all those years I'd wasted were not the only years I would ever have. I didn't get what I wanted. He was dead, and he stayed dead.

I did the chores I had to do. I put a "Stolen Property—Claim by Gen-ID" lock on the *Corrigan's Blood*. Without Badger to sail it home, I wasn't going to be able to physically return the ship. I would just tell Crane where he could find it and he could send one of his employees to pick it up.

And I would get my money, and pay off my ship, and I would own the *Hope's Reward*.

My ship's name mocked me.

This was, perhaps, another stage of adulthood. It was the moment where hope died and vacuum replaced it, where the future became bleak and empty and meaningless. I knew that my life was over, but I hadn't quit breathing. And so I went on.

There were things to do, so I did them. I'd made a promise to Badger, and I intended to keep it. I took his body to Old Earth, and found Claudia Caldwell, and impressed upon her the importance of doing the best bodyart she'd ever done. I could have remembered him as he had been when I had been his childhood friend and his adult lover, but he had loved the shocking beauty of bodyart. It was the last gift but one that I could give him.

I found a place in deep space, far from ship routes, planets, origami points. The stars there blazed with fiery intensity. No nearby sun challenged their glory. Black velvet eternity waited.

I went through all of Badger's things, looking for something that was special to him. I wanted to send it with him. I found a small book of Shakespeare's sonnets. He had loved them—many of them he'd known by heart, especially the dark sonnets. I wrapped the Shakespeare into the vacuum shroud.

In his travel bag, still sitting next to the gravdrop where it had fallen, I found a poem that he'd evidently written while we were in Meileone. It was, I think, what he was working on when he kept saying he was only making notes. The poem was either to me or about me, and if it was the first, it was the best thing I've ever been given, and if it was about me, he credited me with a greatness of spirit that I had only seen in him and never in myself.

When I could find no more excuses to postpone our last good-bye, I stood beside his body, looking at his face for one final time. He was golden. Firebirds flew across his cheeks and cold flames burned in his hair, and on his chest a phoenix rose from the ashes, promising the eternity and the change that awaited him beyond this meager mortality and this cold fleshself.

I kissed him good-bye.

And then I read to him the poem that he had written. He'd called it *Cadence*.

"My eyes still filled with unshed tears,
I face the path where darkness crept
Before me, taking everything
I once held dear and stripping from
Me joy's frail wings.

Death stalks after. Stillness follows
All of Life's unceasing chatter;
If I win still I shall lose.
Life's failures are but little deaths
That slink before.

Where once I flew now I must walk
And stumble over stones and roots;
Taste dust and ashes on my tongue
And bleed as failure's weight
Drives me to ground.

Wait. Knowing that I too must die
And fall at last beyond the reach
Of light and love and laughter I
Become unburdened: I become
Life's renegade.

I who have nothing left to lose
Must now have everything to gain
And driven down must now burst free,
And take from Life what Life won't give:
I own my soul.

Life's a miser; death's a thief that
Steals Life's bread when darkness falls.
I'll shame the thief; I will not weep
But, head high, stand and fight and bleed.
I will not call death friend; I will
Not ask for softness; I will not
Embrace the empty, silent night—
And when I lose, as I must lose—

With neck unbowed and back unbent,
I'll run the path where darkness creeps
And scream and shout and pound the walls
And death will cringe to hear me come—
And Life, well-lived,

Will weep.

"Goodbye, Badger," I said. "I'll see you on the other side."

I stepped back from the airlock, closed the inner door, and opened the outer door.

And he was gone.

Chapter Thirty-two

"I've spent a lot of time thinking about this," I told Peter Crane. "I had a lot of time to spend." We sat in his office in his home. The office was luxurious; done in dark natural woods and soft fabrics, with lush plants growing from the floor in several places. The walls were lined with books, and all of them looked like they were there to be read. The room smelled of leather and musk; it was a place both overtly proper and covertly seductive. I thought it personified Crane.

"I've scanned your report. It was very thorough." He rested a hand on my forearm. "I'm very sorry about your friend."

I nodded, but kept going. I didn't want his condolences for my loss of Badger. That was a part of my life I wanted touched by no one—not even someone who meant well, or who only intended kindness. I told him, "I'll find a way to get through that. This concerns you, though. I think you're in danger. Danniz Oe tried to force Fedara Contei to kill you, but even though he's dead now, and she is, too, I don't think the danger has passed. I've been all over this. Cassamir Biologicals was producing Legend to ship to other worlds, and now is producing Legend II. It has to be. If you'll look at the list I've given you, you'll see that there are vampires scattered throughout their organization. I think one of the employees is Corrigan—I think he's changed his name and his ID, but if someone could do a Gen-ID scan of every person in the organization, I think he would surface."

"I find it hard to imagine any of this. I'm friends with some of the people at Cassamir Biologicals."

"That may be why they don't need to have someone working in your organization."

"None of these vampires of yours works for me?"

"I can't be that definite. If they do, they aren't members of USAG. I would guess that they don't, though. If they did, they would have found a way to get to you."

He nodded. "That make sense."

"I suspect that you've unknowingly given information about Monoceros Starcraft to these friends of yours at Cassamir Biologicals, and they've used that little bit of information to track down your customers. Then they acquire the ships you sold; but they've been very careful not to permit a direct connection between Cassamir Biologicals and Monoceros Starcraft."

"Why not?"

"Because you're the only one in the universe who can sell the ships they need, but if they buy them from you directly, there's a clear connection between the cargo and the ship and the station. Someone who is investigating would follow them right back here."

Crane's smile was wry. "Which you did."

I shrugged and smiled back. "Well, yes. They didn't diversify their products in the two places I looked. I probably wouldn't have made a connection even then, except that the ships were from here, too."

"So coincidence undid them. And carelessness."

I sighed and leaned forward. "Peter, don't think they've been undone. You know what's going on now, and so do I, but you cannot imagine how dangerous they are. How ruthless." I thought of my mother. "How very ruthless. I'm just telling you this so that you can find a way to protect yourself."

"And what way might that be?"

I handed him a cylinder of the anti-virus. "Danniz Oe manufactured this to kill the vampires. I didn't include the information on it in the report that I gave you. I didn't want anything in writing—this may sound terribly paranoid to you, but I didn't want it falling into the wrong hands."

He stared at the cylinder. "It's lethal."

"Almost instantaneous. You can have one of your people study it. Or . . . you might think my paranoia is excessive, but I'd recommend that you do the research yourself."

"I think that would be best," he said. "Do you have any more of these? This isn't a very large sample."

"I don't have any more with me. I have several in my bag on my ship. I could send them over to you."

"If you would. This cylinder is worth more to humanity than a sea of unexplored galaxies, from what you tell me. I'll make sure it gets to people I can trust, who can manufacture it." He stood and smiled. "You have done extraordinarily well, Cady. So now we come to the matter of your payment."

I nodded.

"It's a great deal of money. I imagine you've spent some time thinking about how you'll spend it? A lovely young woman like you must have so many dreams."

"I'm going to pay off my ship. After that—" I shrugged. I didn't even try a smile. "I had some plans, but they died with Badger."

He held out a hand to me and said, "Perhaps I can offer you a new direction."

We walked down the main hall of his home together; the place was tastefully luxurious, beautiful without being ostentatious. His windows looked out on the origami point, where ships flickered in and out of existence in a steady stream. I slowed to look and he stopped and stood beside me.

"It's beautiful, isn't it?"

I nodded.

"But I find its beauty pales next to yours, Cadence. You

are lovely and intelligent and tough. You are courageous. You are tenacious." I turned to look at him and he smiled more broadly. "All the qualities I've looked for in a woman, I've found in you."

I saw desire in his eyes. I thought of Badger and I thought of my loss and I still found myself wanting to respond. He was so kind. So gentle. I didn't want to hurt him.

He tugged on my hand. "Come."

We went into a gracious room with three walls of creamy white and the fourth, a floor-to-ceiling curve of glassteel that looked out onto the diamond-studded blackness of space. A grand piano sat next to the window; across from it, a real wood fire burned in a fireplace. He noticed the direction of my gaze and said, "I play the piano daily. The fireplace I use only on special occasions."

"This is a special occasion?"

"Lovely woman, it is indeed." We walked to the fireplace and suddenly I realized we weren't alone. A man stood on the other side of the piano, staring out into the eternal night. The raised lid had hidden him from view.

The man turned as we walked toward the fireplace.

"Hass," Peter said, "this is Cadence, perhaps the most remarkable young woman I've ever met. Cadence, my oldest and most trusted friend, Hass."

I held out a hand, and Peter's friend took it. Instead of shaking it, though, he bowed and lifted it to his lips.

He released my hand, stood, and smiled at me. He was slender, dark-haired, green-eyed. His lean features and exquisite hands did a lot to offset a slight unpleasantness that I found in the coolness of his eyes and the downward turn of his mouth.

Peter asked Hass, "Have you heard?"

The other man nodded. "Everything."

"Extraordinary, isn't it?"

"Quite. I wouldn't have thought anyone could make the right connections on this and then follow them back to the right conclusions."

I was puzzled, but I felt I was interrupting a conversation they'd engaged in before I arrived, and that they were just picking up. I might have frowned a little, but I didn't say anything.

Still, Peter noticed the look on my face.

"Forgive us. In a quiet house like this, you would be amazed how the sound carries. Hass was listening in on what you told me. I wanted to have him here."

Something twisted in my gut.

"But before I arrived, I told you it was vital that the two of us meet alone, where you could be absolutely certain that no one else overheard us."

"I know. But I made an exception for Haskell. After all, he is my oldest and most trusted friend."

Haskell. Haskell. Haskell. I knew that name.

Realization dawned, and I said, "You're Haskell *Corrigan.*"

Both men laughed, and Corrigan dipped his head slightly in acknowledgment. "You were very clever," Peter said. "But the reason I was so cautious about who bought my ships was because if something went wrong, I didn't want anyone coming back and looking at me. As it turns out, this was a very smart move on my part. Otherwise, you would have come at me with your deadly little dart all ready. Haskell and I are the first vampires—we had no need for the silly organizations or the mysterious fantasies some of our . . . children . . . indulged in. Immortality and power were enough for us. And we were willing to share with like-minded others. Danniz Oe, for example—though as events have proven, he was a faithless friend."

Crane shook his head sadly. "Wiser men than I have said that power corrupts, and absolute power corrupts absolutely." I'd heard those exact words from Badger just before he died. The eerie coincidence made my skin crawl. "Well, you saw that with the vampire you rescued . . . Fedara. No doubt she hated what she had become at first. Immortality, though, has a way of convincing one that things aren't really so bad." He turned back to Corrigan. "You need to find out what idiot has been stocking the ships with Cassamir Biologicals products. Then kill him."

He turned back to me.

"You really would be perfect for me," he said softly. "I can't help thinking that you are the woman I've waited my entire life to meet. But even if I changed you, and even if you eventually came to see things my way, I have no wish to end up like Danniz Oe, who died because he found the woman of his dreams. I see no way that I can save you; but the fact that I'm going to have to kill you now absolutely breaks my heart."

I shouted, kicked, slammed a fist into his face and a knee into his groin, and ran. I caught him off guard, but it didn't matter. I made it no more than two steps before Haskell Corrigan caught me.

He smiled at me, and his smile stretched. His teeth grew longer. The points gleamed. The nanovirus reshaped the canines, forcing them out.

Behind me, Peter said, "Wait for me. And let's take our time, shall we? I'd hate to gulp the finest wine I ever uncorked."

I struggled, but Corrigan looked into my eyes, and a stronger version of the same hypnotic pull I'd felt before from Oe and Fedara and even from my mother overwhelmed me. Suddenly I didn't want to struggle anymore. I wanted to give in. I wanted Corrigan's touch. I wanted Crane's. I fell willingly into the dark and warm and seductive pull of their eyes and embraced my death.

The pain of the bite in my neck was an ecstasy. My heart pounded, and I felt myself merging with Corrigan. And then Crane bit my wrist, and the thrill deepened. The bite, the sharing of my blood with them, was power and sex and submission and lust and a blood-red driving need all at once, and I welcomed it and fell into it and begged it never to stop.

The surging tide of my blood swept me into the maelstrom, into the vortex of a whirlpool that led to annihilation, that led to rest and silence and peace. I felt the thundering of my blood in my veins, the hammering of my heart in my chest, and every beat was foreplay and climax and release, the sweet song of Kali.

But then it stopped.

First Corrigan, then Crane, backed away from me. I stood stupidly, still lost in the spell of their bloodlust and bereft at the loss of their touch.

I saw Corrigan go down on his knees, his hands clawing at his chest. "No," he whispered. Crane buckled, rocking back and forth with his head on the carpet. Then he was still. Then he began to swell.

My slow, sensation-dulled brain struggled to understand, but finally the answer came to me. My blood, I thought. They drank my blood and it killed them.

I stood and put a hand to my neck, to the place that hurt so much now that Corrigan wasn't touching it, and my hand came away red and hot and sticky. I felt my blood squirt out beneath my fingertips to the rhythm of my heart. Some tiny spark of my survival instinct came back to life then, and I pressed my right hand to my neck. I looked at my left wrist. Bleeding, too. Arterial blood, pumping hard. I shoved the wrist against my hipbone, and, finally more alert and truly frightened, I ran through Crane's house looking for his medichamber.

I lived, in spite of them, in spite of myself, in spite of my despair.

I lived.

I went back to Meileone Station in Cantata long enough to reclaim the *Corrigan's Blood*. Only I knew where it was, and since I didn't get paid the rest of the money owed me for the work I'd done, I took the ship in trade.

I towed the *Hope's Reward* near a busy space lane, where I blew out the airlock and ripped out everything of value. Someone found it not too long after that, and reported the ship hit by pirates. The shipcom's log confirmed that story; its record showed an attack by two ships, followed by the quick and brutal deaths of Strebban "Badger" Bede and Cadence Drake.

I stopped in to see Storm Rat long enough to have him install a gravity shear on my new ship, as well as to give both me and the *Corrigan's Blood* a new ID.

When times are hardest, I recite the part of Badger's last poem over and over—these words have become my mantra.

Life's a miser; death's a thief that
Steals Life's bread when darkness falls.
I'll shame the thief; I will not weep
But, head high, stand and fight and bleed.
I will not call death friend; I will
Not ask for softness; I will not
Embrace the empty, silent night—
And when I lose, as I must lose—

With neck unbowed and back unbent,
I'll run the path where darkness creeps
And scream and shout and pound the walls
And death will cringe to hear me come—
And Life, well-lived,

Will weep.

The softness of hope and of love that once filled me are gone. Fedara Contei's and my mother's murder of Badger burned them out of me, and replaced them with a cold, ferocious determination to live. I am not the same woman I was when Peter Crane asked me to find his ship for him. I am, I think, less than that woman was, for who can eliminate both love and hope and remain whole? Yet I am as much as I need to be. I am enough for my own purposes.

I stalk the predators now. My weapon is my own blood, and the darts I shoot are judge and jury and executioner—the innocent never die and the guilty never live. I could lie to myself. I could say that the killers killed themselves by the act of becoming vampires, but I don't lie to myself. I hunt them down. I take their lives.

If I could give my self-appointed task over to the rightful authorities, I would—but the authorities were the first to embrace the vampire kiss of immortality.

I've looked for the vampire victims Badger and I rescued, hoping to find allies, but Storm Rat hid them well enough that I have not yet found them. Some day perhaps I will. Maybe I won't always fight alone.

In the meantime, though, I have become the thing I hated; a hunter and a killer. I stalk nightmares and legends through the corridors of space. I don't try to fool myself into thinking I can win; this new evil breeds faster than I can overtake it. I am only one, and one could never be enough. For every monster I kill, ten rise up. But if I turned and walked away, knowing the evil, I would be accepting that evil. By choosing to do nothing, knowing what I know, I would be as guilty of evil as the ones who live on blood and pain and death.

There is no way that I can turn my back. I cannot hope to win; I know eventually I must lose. But I will never quit, and when I lose, I will lose on my terms. If I can find neither peace nor love nor hope, still I have found purpose.

For now, purpose is enough.